C J Parsons was born in Britain and grew up in Canada. She graduated from Montreal's McGill University with a degree in psychology and went on to earn a graduate degree in journalism.

She worked as a newspaper reporter at Canada's *Globe* and *Mail* before moving to Hong Kong, where she became a columnist at the *South China Morning Post*.

She also spent two years covering crime, seeing first-hand the disturbing forces that drive people to kill, something that has informed her writing to this day.

After returning to Britain, she moved into television news, working as a broadcast journalist for both the BBC and CNN International. She is now a senior producer at CGTN and lives in north London with her daughter.

THE GOOD SAMARITAN

C J PARSONS

HEADLINE

First published as an eBook in 2020 by
HEADLINE PUBLISHING GROUP

First published in paperback in 2020 by
HEADLINE PUBLISHING GROUP

1

Cataloguing in Publication Data is available from the British Library

ISBN 978 1 4722 7651 3

Typeset in Bembo by CC Book Production
Printed and bound in Great Britain by Clays Ltd, Elcograf S.p.A.

Headline's policy is to use papers that are natural, renewable and
recyclable products and made from wood grown in well-managed forests
and other controlled sources. The logging and manufacturing processes
are expected to conform to the environmental regulations
of the country of origin.

HEADLINE PUBLISHING GROUP
An Hachette UK Company
Carmelite House
50 Victoria Embankment
London
EC4Y 0DZ

www.headline.co.uk
www.hachette.co.uk

For my daughter Caitlin, who has shown me
all the wonders – and terrors – of motherhood

One

Sofia wanted to go all the way to the top of the rocket ship, just like Tommy Marks. Tommy said you had to be six years old to do it, but five-and-three-quarters was almost the same thing and, anyway, she'd beaten him at arm wrestling, so it wasn't like he was so strong. Tommy was probably just making it up, that six rule, to keep her from going up, so he could act like he was the best at everything. But she would show him.

Unless Mummy made her stop.

Sofia turned and looked at her mother, who was watching from just inside the playground gates. There were swings between them, and a boy with orange hair swung up and blocked Mummy's face for a second. Then he went down and Mummy saw her looking and waved. Sofia gave her a big smile. Mummy didn't smile back, but that was OK. She hardly ever smiled, on account of her assburger's. That sounded like a rude word, but Mummy had explained it was a condition, like Johnny B's lazy eye was a condition, and some of the kids at school seeing letters flipped around the wrong way inside their heads was a condition. It just meant that Mummy's feelings

1

didn't always show on the outside the same way as other people's, even though her feelings were the same on the inside. And another thing was: she couldn't tell if other people were mad or sad or confused just by looking at them. That part was called *facial espression blindness*. Sofia had overheard people talking about Mummy, saying she was weird or rude, but that was only because she didn't understand what they were saying with their faces. She could understand Sofia, though. She said her espressions were nice and clear and easy. Sofia thought it was too bad other people couldn't see how lovely Mummy was under the not-smiling-very-often face, so they didn't want to be friends with her. One time Sofia had asked Mummy if she was lonely and Mummy had said how could she be lonely when she had the best daughter in the whole wide world? But something in her voice made Sofia feel like Mummy was sad underneath. It would be nice for her to have a friend. Even a friend like Tommy, who sometimes pinched and said annoying things, like about five-year-olds not being allowed at the top of the rocket.

She looked up the curved climbing frame, arching into the sky, the bars painted blue and red, with flakes missing so metal showed through. There was a little boy with a Spider Man T-shirt hanging on one of the sticky-out bits at the bottom (Mummy said those parts were called 'fins', like on a fish). But otherwise, Sofia had the whole rocket to herself.

Tommy couldn't tell *her* what to do. She was brave, with strong arms, and she was going to climb all the way to the top and look down at the playground and get that dizzy but exciting feeling of being so high up.

Sofia glanced back towards the playground entrance, where

her mother was still watching. Then a lucky thing happened: Mummy started talking on her mobile, which meant she stopped looking over, and this was Sofia's chance.

She grabbed the rung above her head and began to climb, up and up, as fast as a monkey. The rungs got narrower the higher she went, so by the time she got to the pointy bit of the rocket, there was only just enough room for two feet right next to each other. There was a big piece of metal bent into the shape of a star at the top and she held on to it as she looked down with triumph swooping around inside her chest, imagining she was a queen and this was her kingdom, made of swings and playhouses and a curly slide. She could see Mummy, still on the phone, with one hand covering up her ear. The boy with orange hair jumped off the swing and ran towards the queue for the zip-wire, which was zooming children along next to the fence, with the woods on the other side.

Sofia frowned. Something was weird. There was a broken part in the fence that wasn't there last time: a rip in the metal big enough to fit through, like a shortcut. Her gaze moved across the branches crowded together on the other side.

Then Sofia's eyes went big with surprise. Something was leaning against one of the bushes: a huge toy penguin with a red bow around its neck, like a present. She climbed quickly back down the rocket, shoes bonging on the metal, eyes fixed on the penguin. She stepped off the bottom rung and ran towards the gap in the fence. But she stopped short when she reached it; Mummy would be cross if she went outside the playground all by herself. Sofia looked over her shoulder. Her mother was bending down to pick up something on the ground, the phone still stuck on her ear. If Sofia ran super-fast, she could go look at the penguin and be back before Mummy noticed she was gone. The thought gave her the acidy feeling in her tummy that came from doing something naughty.

She stared through the fence at the penguin. What was it doing there? Curiosity was pulling at her, playing tug of war with her conscience. She kicked the broken fence, making the metal vibrate. Looked at Mummy again (still on the phone).

Made a decision.

Sofia slipped through the gap with her heart kicking.

The penguin was leaning against the bush with its back against the leaves, the bow shiny in the sun. She looked around for the owner. Why would someone leave it there? She crouched down and stroked the fluffy tummy. Maybe the owner didn't want it any more. Maybe the penguin was like an orphan waiting to be adopted. The thought made Sofia's heart reach out and she grabbed the toy, hugging it against her face. But it had a weird smell, like something sweet mixed together with the stuff Mummy used to clean the oven. It went up Sofia's nose and inside her head and made her feel dizzy. She lost her balance and tipped sideways into the bush, still holding the penguin, the branches scratching her all the way to the ground. Sharp pebbles were digging into her shoulder, but for some reason she couldn't get up. She tried to push the penguin away to escape from the chemically sweet smell, but suddenly it seemed to be hugging her back, as though its flippers were wrapped all the way around her body, squeezing tight, not letting go. Everything started going around and around, like a carousel. Sofia and the penguin were spinning together, whirling faster and faster, until finally they spun right out of the park and into darkness.

4

Two

Sofia was standing at the base of the rocket ship when Carrie's mobile rang. She looked at the screen and the warm sense of wellbeing that came from watching her daughter play evaporated, replaced by a hard knot of dread.

'Simon.' She closed her eyes and the playground view was hidden behind a curtain of red: sunlight passing through her eyelids. 'What is it?'

Silence. Well, not quite silence, because she could hear faint background noise: distant shouts. Then he cleared his throat.

'It's happened again,' he said, and Carrie's stomach-knot tightened. 'Just a brief flash, maybe nothing, a one-off. But I went to see Samji anyway, to check whether the new stuff he gave me is working. And he said I should go back to Clearbrook, just as a precaution. I don't *have* to; there's been no sign of trouble since. But I think it's the right call. I'm on my way there now and I ... I wanted to let you know.' A pause. 'How is she?'

Carrie glanced over at Sofia, who had begun climbing the rocket.

'She's fine.'

'I miss her.' A long silence followed this statement. Had Simon said everything he'd called to say? Was it time for them to say goodbye and hang up? She hoped so. She used to love the sound of his voice, the baritone richness of it. And the posh accent, so different from her Canadian one, lifting away the r's that she sharpened. But that was *before*. He sighed down the phone. 'This is where you're supposed to say she misses me too.'

'Oh.' Carrie considered this. 'She does talk about you.' It was true. In spite of everything, Sofia had begun asking when she was going to see Daddy again. Carrie couldn't understand it. Wasn't she frightened? 'But after last time ...'

'I know. God, I know. And believe me, all I want in this world is to make it up to her.' Another silence. Was she supposed to fill this one too? Because that wasn't going to happen. A distant shout travelled through the receiver. Then a dog barking. Where exactly was he? Carrie was about to ask when he said: 'I'd like to make it up to both of you. If you'll let me.'

Carrie's eyes moved instinctively to the climbing frame. Sofia was right at the top, looking down at the children's woods. She was very high up. What if she fell? Carrie pushed the thought away. She had to learn to let go, give her daughter some freedom.

'I'm not ready for that, Simon. I made a mistake last time. A terrible mistake.' Guilt pressed down on her like a weight. 'I failed my daughter.'

'*Our* daughter.' He amended. 'And you didn't fail her. I did. But at some point, we all need to try and put what happened behind us and ... move on. Get back to where we used to be.'

She stared down at her feet. There was a crack in the tarmac and a dandelion was growing through it, wrapped in a dense orbit of seeds. She bent to pick it. Sofia would make a wish and blow, watching the seeds float away on their tiny parachutes.

'Was there anything else you wanted to tell me, Simon?'

A long pause. 'No, that's it.'

What was the appropriate thing to say? This scenario hadn't been covered in any of her books or sessions. So she settled on: 'It's good that you informed me about Clearbrook.' Thought a bit longer, then added: 'I hope your visit there is . . . successful.'

'Thank you.' Another sigh, louder this time. 'Goodbye, Carrie.'

Her eyes returned to the climbing frame, but Sofia wasn't there any more. She must have grown bored and moved on.

'Goodbye, Simon.'

She slipped the mobile back into her denim jacket as she strode across the playground, holding the dandelion carefully, to protect the wish-seeds. The rectangular space was packed with children: jumping, spinning, climbing, running. Their shouts filled the air like a cloud, shot through with parental commands ('Share with your brother!', 'Ten-minute warning!', 'Hurry up, or we'll be late!'). Her eyes darted from the spiral slide, past the roundabout to the queue for the zip wire. Sofia should have been easy enough to spot, in her pink polka-dot skirt and rainbow trainers, the silver top with a sequinned heart across the front. But there was no sign of her and Carrie felt a small kick of adrenalin. Irrational, of course. It happened every time her daughter stepped out of view, and she always reappeared. She was probably in the birdcage.

Carrie scaled the ladder leading up to it. Children were packed into the circular space like tiny inmates in an over-crowded prison. But Sofia wasn't among them. She pushed to the front and looked out between the bars. From up here, she could see the whole playground. Her eyes swept the rocket, the roundabout, the swings, the slide. Still no sign. She must be inside the playhouse. Carrie scrambled back down the ladder, dropping to the ground before she reached the bottom, landing hard and jarring her knees. She dashed to the playhouse, with its walls painted in primary colours, and thrust her head through the square gap representing a window. A small blond boy with a runny nose and a plastic shovel blinked up at her. But no Sofia. The dandelion dropped to the ground as she spun away, zigzagging across the playground.

'Sofia! Come here.' Her head whipped from side to side, ears straining for the familiar voice rising from some undiscovered hiding place. She'd had nightmares like this ever since her daughter was born – dreams that Sofia was lost and she was searching. And, just for a moment, she wondered whether this was one of them, whether she was actually at home, asleep in bed. 'I'll buy you an ice cream if you come out *right now*.'

But she didn't come out. And Carrie had been all around the playground, checked every piece of equipment and her daughter was *not there*. Not hiding in the space under the playhouse or in the shadow under the slide or behind one of the trees just beyond the zip wire, screening the chainmail fence that kept the children in ... That was *supposed* to keep them in. She stared hard at the metal barrier, noticing something for the first time. A section of the fence had been sliced through and bent back, creating a gap big enough to admit even an adult. Her daughter must have gone out that way. Carrie had been standing right in front of the entry gate when Simon's call came, so Sofia couldn't have slipped past unnoticed. She hauled in a breath, feeling some of the tension leave her as she released it. Mystery solved.

The 'children's woods' was a small slice of forest bisected by a trail. Sofia loved playing there, loved clambering over the fallen trees that interrupted the path, using the steps cut into their trunks, courtesy of the park keepers. So that was where she must be. It was the only possible explanation. Or at least, the only one Carrie's mind was prepared to accept.

She dashed through the break in the fence, stopping on the other side to scan the woods: a little slice of countryside for London's inner-city children. Sunlight angled through the trees, sending golden shafts across the trail. A boy was dragging a broken branch along it: material for a fort under construction at the base of an oak. Two little girls were building a lean-to against the back of the hut where the park keepers stored their equipment. But no sequinned heart. No flash of pink polka dots between the leaves.

She has to be here somewhere.

Carrie fended off the thought that she could hardly remember the last time Sofia had run off without saying anything. That it hadn't happened since she was a toddler. She would see her in a moment. Any moment. Any moment now. She jogged along the trail, *not* seeing her, dread expanding inside her until it squeezed out everything else.

She broke into a run, shouting her daughter's name, the calls growing louder as she neared the end of the trail. Her voice cut through the woods like an alarm siren, turning heads and drawing women – other mothers – her way. Five of them formed a rough circle around her as she reached the end of the path and stopped, breath coming in ragged gasps.

'Are you all right?' The speaker was younger than Carrie: late twenties or early thirties. Dark, wavy hair. Jeans and a running top.

'No. I can't find my daughter.'

Saying the words out loud set off a flash of white-hot panic. Carrie bent at the waist, palms braced against her knees, riding it out. The woman bent over too so that their faces were level.

'It's OK, love. I'll help you find your daughter.'

Carrie straightened and nodded, flooded by gratitude.

'What's your name?'

'Carrie.'

'Mine's Tara. This is a big park and there are loads of places for a child to hide. So how about we get some help?'

'Help. Yes, of course. Should we call the police?'

Tara smiled. Her eyes were blue-green, like a holiday sea.

'I think we can get help right here. It'll be faster.' She turned towards the other four women: a redhead, face swarming with freckles; a plump, dark-skinned woman in an orange headscarf; a pair of trim older mums, their matching blonde hair tied in loose knots, both sensibly dressed in jeans and T-shirts. They had similar features: sisters, presumably. Tara raised a hand in greeting. 'Hello, ladies. As you've just heard, Carrie here can't find her daughter. Which means that, somewhere in this park, there's a little girl who has lost her mum and is probably starting to get scared.' She looked slowly from face to face, before asking: 'Any volunteers to help find her?'

The woman in the headscarf responded first, with 'count me in.' Then the redhead nodded and the two blondes said 'absolutely' in perfect unison.

Carrie focused on her breathing, telling herself that everything was going to be fine, just fine. These women would be her search party. They would find Sofia.

'OK.' Tara clapped her hands together, like a teacher addressing a class. 'First off: someone needs to stay here and watch all the children while the rest of us are off searching.'

The redhead raised her hand. 'I'll do that.'

'Great. And your name is . . .'

'Emily.'

'Thanks, Emily. Everyone: before you go anywhere, introduce your children to Emily and tell them to stay within sight of her. I've just dropped my son off at the fishpond with his dad, so that's one less to keep an eye on.' She placed a hand on Carrie's shoulder. As a rule, Carrie disliked being touched by strangers. But right now, she found it oddly comforting. 'Can you describe your daughter, tell us what's she's wearing?'

'Five years old, almost six. Dark, curly hair. A pink polka-dot skirt and rainbow trainers. There's a heart on her top. In sequins.'

'I heard you calling her name. Sophie?'

'Sofia.'

'Where did you last see her?'

'On the climbing frame. She's not in the playground any more, though, so she must have gotten out through that hole.' Carrie waved in the direction of the cut fence.

Tara patted her arm, then gestured towards the blonde sisters. 'Can one of you search all through the children's woods, see if she's hiding behind a bush or a tree? The other one can check the tennis courts and the bronze turtle statues by the main entrance.' She turned to the woman in the headscarf. 'Why don't you take the Japanese pond and the section of trees right beside it? Carrie and I will give the playground

11

one last check. I think that covers everything. We can meet back here in twenty minutes.'

And before Carrie knew what was happening, Tara was towing her back along the path through the woods, pausing just long enough to ask a passing park keeper whether he'd seen a lost girl (he hadn't) before ducking through the gap in the fence.

'She's not in the playground,' Carrie objected. 'I searched it already.'

'Worth another try,' Tara insisted. 'My boy once squeezed into a space under the playhouse that I'd never noticed before. Hid there for ten minutes and frightened the life out of me.'

'I know the space you mean. I checked it.'

'Somewhere else, then. The cage with the ladder.'

'No, I looked, I . . .' But Tara was making Carrie doubt herself, the quality of her search, and they scoured the playground together, checking every inch. They finished up by the main entrance, where Tara stopped for one last scan before glancing at her watch.

'OK, let's head back to the woods. The others should have returned by now. I'm sure one of them will have found her.

Carrie didn't understand how she could be *sure*. She was about to ask, then stopped herself. It must be one of those things people only said to make you feel better. Words without facts behind them. Meaningless.

Two members of the search party were already waiting on the other side of the gate to the woods: the blondes. Sofia wasn't with them. Carrie felt her stomach twist, like cold hands wringing her insides.

'Any luck?' one of the sisters asked. Carrie didn't respond, because it was blindingly obvious they hadn't had any luck or she would be clasping a curly-haired child against her chest right now, smiling one of her rare, genuine smiles.

She shifted her attention beyond the wooden gate, to the path leading to the Japanese pond. All her hopes were now pinned on the one remaining searcher. She told herself that it was a good sign the woman hadn't come back yet; it meant Sofia was with her, slowing her down by stopping to look at a squirrel or pick a buttercup or complain that there was something sharp in her shoe that needed to be taken out *right now*. Carrie pictured them together, moving closer, as she stared at the empty path.

Tara followed her gaze. 'She probably went to look at the fish. That's what my son did.'

Carrie nodded, because that was what you were supposed to do. But a question was gnawing at her, eating away at the hopeful image of her daughter skipping alongside the woman in the orange headscarf. What could possibly have induced Sofia to wander so far away without saying anything? It didn't make sense. Perhaps she'd met a bossy older child who'd insisted on taking her there? But even that didn't ring true. Sofia knew her own mind, set her own boundaries. Carrie had overheard her angrily scolding friends for playing on their iPads, saying they shouldn't be giving all their attention to fake people when there were real ones standing right there.

Oh my little love, come back to me.

Her eyes locked onto the curving pathway to the pond. A magpie landed on it and pecked at the gravel. What was that saying about them? *One for sorrow, two for joy.* Carrie's eyes darted to the surrounding trees, suddenly superstitious, hoping to see a second bird. But the magpie was alone. Her gaze returned to the curving path, willing it to bring two figures into view: one tall and one small.

Two for joy.

Tara looked at her watch. 'It's been half an hour,' she said. 'Perhaps we should go to the pond and see if they're there.'

Carrie opened her mouth to answer, to say yes, anything was better than standing here waiting, with fear tearing around her body in trapped circles, biting at her insides.

And then she saw her: a plump figure in an orange headscarf, moving into view. The last member of the search party, slowly returning.

Alone.

Everything suddenly became hyper real, as though outlines had been razored around the leaves, the branches, the creases that had suddenly appeared on Tara's forehead. One of the sisters was saying something, but panic had short-circuited Carrie's brain, so it was like listening to a foreign language. She was dimly aware of voices calling out names. The other mums, summoning their children. And instinctively, she knew why. Until now, they had assumed that the monster Carrie feared existed only in a mother's love-addled imagination. But the failed search was making them think again. And she felt a flash of resentment towards these other children, these lesser children, these children who *were not Sofia*. Who didn't crawl into her bed in the middle of the night, saying 'Mummy, can I have a cuddle?' Or blow goodbye kisses at the school gate. Who didn't act out stories as Carrie read them, arms flapping furiously as a bird took flight. These children who were here, safe and accounted for, while her special girl, her beam of light, was missing.

Missing.

Then Tara took out her mobile and said: 'I'm sure it's nothing, but we might as well call for back up.' And her thumb touched the same spot three times: 999. The number of disasters, of emergencies. Of lives blown apart. And as she watched Tara ask for the police, the spark of hope Carrie had been sheltering inside herself was snuffed out. The police were coming because her daughter had disappeared. This wasn't a dream from which she would surface with a gasp, throwing back her duvet and padding down the hall to find Sofia asleep with Penguin Pete clutched against her chest. This was a nightmare from which there would be no waking. She tried to calm herself with deep breaths, but the air didn't seem to contain enough oxygen. She was suffocating. The trees wheeled drunkenly around her before suddenly receding, as though she were falling down a well. She was aware of grabbing fingers. An echoey shout.

Then nothing.

Three

DCI Juliet Campbell trusted her instincts. They had, after all, been proven right time and again, turning around cases that had hit a dead end, leading them down pathways no one else could see. In fact, it was probably fair to say that her hunches had acquired near legendary status around the station, referred to variously as 'Juliet's super hunches', 'intuition on steroids' and 'DCI Campbell's Caribbean voodoo' (that last one from DI Greer, a racist tosser of the first order).

Years ago, Juliet had dated a psychologist who'd informed her that these flashes of insight were simply her unconscious picking up on something her conscious mind had overlooked. They'd had a huge row after he'd shared this theory, during which Juliet had accused him, first of treating her like a patient instead of a girlfriend, then of taking her apart like a car mechanic hunting for defects. But if she was being honest, what had really upset her was the way he'd reduced her gift to something mundane: not a finely-honed ability to tune into frequencies no one else could hear, but simply one part of her mind failing to communicate properly with the other. The relationship hadn't lasted long after that.

Yes, Juliet Campbell trusted her instincts. And, right now, they were telling her that the missing girl's mother was hiding something.

Juliet shifted against the curved chair-back as she considered the woman on the other side of the dining table, with her pale skin and unwashed hair, a mug of coffee trembling in her hand. Had she even gone to bed? Juliet was pretty sure that was the same blue T-shirt as yesterday.

She took out her pocket notebook and flipped it open.

'How would you characterise Sofia's father's condition?'

'Her father's condition,' she echoed, the r's amplified by her Canadian accent. Juliet had established that Carrie Haversen came from a small town in Northern Alberta and had moved to Britain eight years ago, after being offered a job at a top London architecture firm. 'I don't understand the question.' The grey eyes fluttered through a series of blinks. She took a sip of coffee. 'Sorry.'

Juliet gritted her teeth in frustration.

'Well, would you say Simon's case is serious? Would a stranger be able to tell that he is ... unwell?'

Carrie's gaze pulled away, landing on the bronze-rimmed clock beside the kitchen fridge, now counting down the last few minutes before 11 a.m. Juliet could hear its ticks stacking up in the pause that followed and knew they had waded into another pool of silence. Her fingers tightened around her notebook as she fought against the impulse to shout at this woman to pick up the pace, for the sake of her child. But she knew that wouldn't achieve anything; Sofia's mother had been shocked into slow mo.

17

Tick-tick-tick. The house darkened then lit as a cloud passed across the sun. Then, just as she was about to give up and repeat the question, Carrie spoke.

'If you want information about Simon's condition, why don't you ask his doctors?'

The coffee cup made another juddering upward journey. Juliet examined the shadows beneath the woman's eyes, dark as bruises. It didn't look as if she'd gotten any sleep. Perhaps Juliet should speak to the family liaison officer about getting a doctor to prescribe some sedatives? Carrie had checked herself out of hospital against medical advice less than two hours after regaining consciousness and insisted on spending the night at home, despite having no family support system. (Her only living relative was a father in an 'assisted living centre' back in Alberta. Juliet had overheard Carrie talking to him on the phone. She'd had to remind him three times that she lived in London now. And twice: who Sofia was.)

'We did try to speak to his doctors, Carrie. But Clearbrook takes confidentiality very seriously. They refused to let my officers enter the premises or provide any information without a warrant. They won't even confirm that he's there.'

'Oh.' Another series of rapid blinks. Juliet had worked out that Carrie's eyelids fluttered like that whenever her mind was processing something. 'Confidentiality. I hadn't thought about that.' The pale features barely moved, but Juliet thought she detected the ghost of a frown. 'You shouldn't waste time on Simon. He has nothing to do with Sofia's disappearance. As I've already told you, he was on the phone with me when she went missing, on his way to Clearbrook.'

Or so he claimed, Juliet thought.

But there was no point trying to force the issue. Alistair would be arriving at Clearbrook with a warrant any minute now, so they could get hold of Ryder's history that way.

Juliet removed a sheet of A4 paper from her leather satchel and slid it across the table's teak surface. Carrie glanced down at the three handwritten rows of names and said: 'Oh fuck, not this again.' It was strange, the way her pitch never varied, even when she swore. 'I already went over these lists once at the hospital and again at the police station.'

'I know.' Juliet flipped to a fresh page in her notebook. 'And I'm sorry to make you keep answering the same questions. But the doctors say you could have suffered temporary memory loss when you fainted – your head hit that log pretty hard – so something you weren't able to recall yesterday could suddenly come back to you today. Which is why I'd like to go through these names again, from the beginning. Are you happy to do that?'

Carrie opened her mouth as though about to object. Stopped. Took a deep breath.

'Yes. I'm happy to do that.' She plucked at the inside of her wrist with a thumb and forefinger, as though pinching herself. Then she looked down at the piece of paper in front of her and placed a hand (clipped nails, no polish) on the first row.

'This is a list of all the people from the school I've ever spoken with: Sofia's teacher, her teaching assistant and the school head, plus four mothers who have invited Sofia over for play-dates or birthday parties.' She picked up the coffee mug again, raising it to her lips.

'And you're sure you haven't overlooked anyone? Another parent or teacher you got chatting to about Sofia one day?'

Carrie swallowed coffee. 'I'm positive. That's ev—'

The sound of breaking glass severed the word, making Juliet jump to her feet, pulse spiking. Carrie and her daughter lived in a terrace house on a small, oak-lined cul-de-sac just south of Barnes. On the outside, it looked the same as its orange-bricked, Victorian neighbours. But on the inside, it was bright, modern and spacious. The dining table was near the back, beside the kitchen: a slice of black-and-white tiles bordered by a counter that stuck out from the wall like a peninsula, leaving a gap just wide enough to admit one person. The open-plan layout allowed Juliet to see right through to the bay-windowed living area at the front, with its burgundy Chesterfield and Japanese coffee table, the brushed-metal bookcase and the African statue of a woman's torso struggling to escape from a block of unhewn rock. DS Ravi Hiranand was standing in front of the bookcase looking mortified. Juliet had instructed him to examine the photo collage pinned to a bulletin board on the wall, searching the most recent images for anyone who appeared in the background more than once, anything odd or out of place.

'I'm so sorry,' he said to Carrie, holding up a shard of turquoise porcelain. 'I broke your vase.'

Juliet managed not to roll her eyes, but it was difficult. *One thing*, she thought, running a palm across the surface of her tightly pulled hair. The movement dislodged a hairclip, letting an Afro curl escape. *I ask him to do one simple thing ... and this is the result*. She clipped the curl back in place with an aggressive motion.

'Don't worry about it.' Carrie closed her eyes for a moment then opened them again. Her voice never strayed outside its narrow band. 'The vase doesn't matter.'

Juliet shot the DS a warning look to let him know he wasn't off the hook as far as she was concerned. What if the vase had been a family heirloom? Or, worse yet, a birthday gift from Sofia?

'It was an accident,' Ravi said defensively. 'I slipped on this.' He retrieved something from the floor and held it up: a tiny, plastic wagon, its purple wheels still spinning.

Ah. Juliet released a sigh. 'OK. But please be careful where you step from now on.'

Sofia's toys still lay where they'd been dropped, making it feel as though she'd only just stepped out of the room and might return at any moment. A naked Barbie sat on the hardwood floor in front of the bookshelf, alongside a half-finished puzzle of a cartoon pig in a red dress. Lego blocks were scattered across the coffee table and a colony of plastic penguins huddled beneath the tripod floor lamp. Juliet wondered how long the girl would have to be missing before her mother finally put the toys away. She hoped she wouldn't have to find out. But as she returned her attention to the lists of contacts, she was painfully aware that every passing hour drained away some hope of ever finding the girl alive.

She gave Carrie a brief smile of apology for the vase before returning her attention to the names. 'So . . .' She pointed to the second column. 'Tell me about these people.'

'Those are just co-workers. There aren't many because I don't know the names of anyone outside my team, aside from the receptionist. And I don't see any of them socially.'

Juliet nodded. She'd already sent a DI to Wescott Architects to interview Carrie's colleagues. They'd all spoken about her designs in glowing terms but seemed to know virtually nothing about her personal life.

'Do you ever bring Sofia into the office when you're having issues with childcare? To wait and draw while you finish an urgent project or ...?'

'No.'

'Has Sofia's father ever handed her across to you at the office?'

'No.'

'Never swung by and dropped her off because he felt suddenly ill or unable to cope?'

'No.'

So much for the colleagues. She shifted her attention to the next row. Or rather, the place where the next row ought to have been.

'Are you still unable to provide a list of your friends?'

'It's not that I'm unable.' Carrie pushed her hands up the sides of her skull, stopping when both palms covered her ears. The pose reminded Juliet of that Munch painting: *The Scream*. 'It's that I don't have any friends to list.'

Juliet frowned down at the sheet of paper, with its missing row. She had spent much of her career on the force digging through society's scrapheap, interviewing druggies and misfits and losers. And she'd found that even the lowest of the low were usually able to count at least one friend to their name: a fellow traveller to share the downwardly spiralling journey. So how had a successful, talented, working mother like Carrie Haversen ended up completely isolated?

'Just to be clear, these don't have to be *close* friends. Perhaps a colleague or ex-colleague you've met for a drink once or twice?'

'No.'

'One of these mothers on your school list ...'

'None of them wish to spend time with me. I attempted to

22

form social relationships with them when school first started but ... I was not successful.'

'OK, then perhaps an old ex you stayed friends with after ...'

Carrie spoke slowly, isolating each word. 'I do not have any friends.' She took a final gulp of coffee before putting down the mug, pushing it to one side. 'The way I am makes people uncomfortable. So they choose not to interact with me.' The words were delivered without emotion: a simple statement of fact.

'I see. Thank you for explaining.' As Juliet jotted on her notepad, she tried to imagine a life without girlie chats, pub quizzes or post-work pints. And found that she couldn't. She had grown up with four siblings and a constant flow of visiting Jamaican relatives, her childhood played out against a backdrop of noise and chaos, her adult years an endless tug of war between her career and her social life. If she had been asked to list all her friends and acquaintances, she would have needed more paper.

'OK then, moving along ...' She flipped to the next page of her notepad. 'Has anyone shown special interest in Sofia recently? A delivery person or passer-by while you were out walking?'

'No.'

'And as far as you're aware, nobody new has moved into your neighbourhood?'

'No.'

Juliet bit back a sigh. They were just circling old ground, going nowhere. She needed to open up a new line of enquiry. She cast around for a fresh question.

'Have you noticed anyone looking at you or Sofia strangely?'

'I would be unable to judge that. I have social-emotional agnosia.'

Juliet's pen paused above her notebook. 'Sorry?'

'Facial expression blindness. I can't read emotions in people's faces. Well … Unless the expression is very clear and simple, not mixed together with other emotions.'

'Facial expression blindness,' Juliet repeated slowly. 'I don't think I've ever met anyone with that.'

'Yes, you must have, since it affects one in ten people to some degree. You probably just wrote them off as thick-skinned or insensitive or weird. That's what usually happens.'

'I see.' The answer made Juliet feel oddly defensive, as though she'd been accused of something.

'What is the cause of your condition?'

'That question has yet to be answered definitively. I was originally suspected of having damage to the amygdala: a part of the brain. But scans showed that not to be the case. I was later diagnosed with Alexythemia. And more recently, with Asperger's, although that term is no longer used; these days it's "on the spectrum". But I was reassessed early this year and told that I don't really fit into that category either, although I do have autistic traits.'

Juliet noticed that the rapid blinking had stopped. This was clearly old conversational territory: no information-processing required. She thought of Carrie's flat speech and long silences. She had assumed they were a temporary biproduct of shock. Maybe not.

'Does this condition also affect the way you …' She hesitated. 'The way you *express* your feelings?'

'Yes. What makes my case unusual is that my internal emotional responses fall within the normal range. I simply don't display them in the same way as others.' She tilted her head.

24

'Well, I do occasionally, when my feelings are particularly intense. But not often.'

Juliet flipped her pen between her fingers, viewing Carrie through the prism of new understanding. Imagine, going through life unable to gauge other people's reactions or communicate your own. It went a long way towards explaining her difficulty making friends.

She returned her attention to the sheet of paper: Carrie's meagre social life boiled down into three columns. She pointed to the last and longest list: sixteen names, all male.

'So these are your ex-boyfriends?'

'Yes.' Carrie plucked at the inside of her wrist again. 'Actually, no, that's not true. It's everyone I've had sex with since moving to London eight years ago. Men I met in bars.'

'And you are unable to provide their surnames?'

'Correct. I didn't ask and they didn't offer.'

'With one obvious exception.' Juliet's fingertip underlined the name at the top. 'Simon Ryder.'

Carrie retrieved the now empty mug, peering inside. Juliet hoped she wasn't going to stop the interview to make more coffee. Things were moving slowly enough as it was. But Carrie pushed the cup aside again.

'Simon and I had a proper relationship. The others were just sex.'

Juliet jotted on her notepad as she considered this statement. How had he managed to navigate Carrie's condition? It wouldn't have been easy for him, building a connection with someone who could neither receive his emotional signals nor transmit her own.

Unless … Juliet frowned. What if he'd never wanted to

navigate it? What if he'd *liked* having a girlfriend who couldn't read him?

'Let's go back over Simon's relationship with your daughter. You describe it as "close". Has Sofia ever witnessed his ... symptoms?' Juliet tried to force eye contact, but Carrie's eyes were locked on the clock.

'No,' she responded, then pinched her wrist.

And that's when it happened. Somewhere deep inside Juliet, a flash went off: a hot flare that rose through her consciousness like a bonfire spark, straightening her back and lifting her chin into what Alistair called her 'predator-catching-a-scent' pose.

That gesture means something.

Juliet was careful to keep her eyes aimed at Carrie's face even as she shifted her focus downward, to the pale fingers interlocked on the table.

'Yesterday you described Simon's parental visits as "uneventful". Do you stand by that?'

'Yes.'

The linked fingers broke apart. The left hand turned, so that its back was against the table, exposing the inner wrist.

Pinch.

Bingo. Juliet flipped back through her notebook, returning to the start of their conversation before moving forwards again, skimming through her notes as she replayed the interview in her memory.

'I'd like to go over these lists again – from the beginning. Are you happy to do that for me?'

'Yes. I'm happy to do that.'

Then, right then, was when Carrie had plucked at her wrist for the first time.

26

Juliet's eyes raced along the shorthand scribbles.

'These are your ex-boyfriends?'

'Yes.'

There! That was the next time, just before Carrie had said: *'Well no, that's not really true. It's everyone I've had sex with since moving to London eight years ago.'*

So what was it about those exchanges that had triggered—

Then she almost laughed out loud. Because, of course, the answer was right there in front of her, spelled out in black and white.

'No, that's not really true.'

The gesture was a tell. Carrie Haversen pinched her left wrist every time she told a lie.

Juliet sat back against the chair, triumph swelling inside her as she examined the woman across from her. Carrie stared back, her face an impregnable wall.

Juliet tapped a knuckle against her chin as she chose her next question.

'Has Simon ever harmed Sofia?'

'No.'

Juliet could hear the clock ticking in the gap that followed. Once. Twice. Three times. On the fourth tick, Carrie's fingers drifted to the soft skin of her wrist.

Pinch.

Shit. So that meant he *had* hurt her. But why would a loving mother withhold that kind of information? Was Carrie protecting Simon ... or was she afraid of him? Juliet turned the two theories over in her mind. Despite Carrie's lack of emotional expression, Juliet was in no doubt that she loved her child more than life itself. So, no, she wouldn't place her ex-partner's interests ahead of Sofia's. And as for fear . . . She'd seen no sign of that either. But what other motive could there be? Unless . . . Did Carrie feel that whatever had happened was *her* fault somehow?

Juliet leaned across the table on her forearms, reducing the distance between them. Knowing instinctively that it would make Carrie uncomfortable, doing it anyway to throw her off balance.

'Listen to me,' she said urgently. 'My only goal in asking these questions is to locate Sofia and bring her safely home. So it is absolutely crucial that—'

The ring of her mobile phone interrupted the sentence. She glanced at the screen. Alistair. He must be calling from Clearbrook.

'Excuse me,' she said, getting up from the table. 'I'm afraid this is urgent. I'll be back in a moment.'

Juliet dashed through the house, waiting until Carrie's front door had closed behind her before answering the call.

'Alistair. What's up?' Hopefully he had made contact with Ryder by now. Perhaps even interviewed him. She walked down the three steps between the door and the small front garden, with its stone slabs and flower tubs, their blossoms drooping. A heatwave had arrived in the night like a bad omen, thickening the air and baking the concrete, smothering the city in smog the colour of a nicotine stain. Juliet unbuttoned the collar of her shirt, flapping the material to ventilate it.

The familiar Irish brogue travelled down the phone.

'I had a nightmare getting past the reception desk, even *with* a warrant. I've been to maximum security prisons with a more *laissez faire* attitude. You want to know what I told them?'

Juliet sucked in her lips. She was fond of DI Larkin, but at this moment she found herself wishing he didn't always have to be quite so ... Irish. Alistair was a man who lived up to his country's 'gift of the gab' stereotype. He loved a good story and she could feel one building now.

'Not at this moment. Why don't you tell me later?'

'Oh. OK.' Wounded silence down the phone.

'We're racing against the clock here, Alistair. I just need to know what condition Simon Ryder was in, and whether he could be interviewed.'

'We couldn't interview him. The thing is he—'

'Damn,' she interrupted, heading off another anecdote. 'It's essential that we speak to him. We've gotten nothing from the CCTV footage, the witnesses in the park or the interviews with local sex offenders. So right now we are running out of leads, and I'm fairly sure the girl's mother is hiding something about Ryder's history with Sofia.' Juliet tilted back her head, frowning up at the sky. A white crescent moon was burned against the blue like a photo negative. A cloud rode across it, casting a shadow that didn't budge the heat. 'I need you to go back into that clinic and convince those doctors to give Ryder something to sort him out just long enough to answer a few questions. Can you do that?'

'No, I can't. That's what I've been trying to tell you. I couldn't interview him because he's not here. He was supposed to check in right around the time Sofia went missing. But he never arrived.'

Four

'That's impossible,' Carrie told the policewoman. She hadn't realised her hands were fisted until she felt fingernails digging into her palms. 'He called me on his way there. Sofia disappeared while I was speaking to him.'

The DCI turned to a fresh page in her little notebook and ran a hand down it, as though smoothing an unseen crease.

'The call you received was from a mobile phone, so he could have been anywhere. For all we know, he called you expressly to draw your attention from Sofia, then waved her over and was leading her away as the two of you spoke. His phone is now switched off, but one of my colleagues is working on finding out where the call was made. So we should know soon.'

Carrie stared across the dining table, nausea squirming in her stomach. Snatches of her conversation with Simon tumbled through her head like clothes in a drier, tossed together with freeze-frame images from the park.

Sofia, smiling at her across the playground.

It's happened again.

Sofia, placing a rainbow trainer on the bottom rung of the climbing frame.

I miss her.

What if he'd been watching the whole time, crouching in the bushes on the other side of the fence – the fence he'd sliced open with a knife?

A knife.

A memory was threatening to bubble to the surface and she pushed it back down. She couldn't think about that right now. It would only flood her with panic, making it harder to focus. And anyway, wasn't this good news? It meant that Sofia hadn't been snatched by some shadowy stranger driven by monstrous appetites. She was with her father. A father who loved her.

The knife. Dark blood on pale skin.

She closed her eyes and banged a fist against the table, trying to beat back the image.

'Are you OK? Would you like a glass of water?'

Carrie opened her eyes to find the policewoman looking across at her, eyebrows dipped together, nose wrinkled at the top. Carrie noticed, in a vague, uninterested sort of way, that she was pretty: almond-shaped eyes set in almond-coloured skin. Hair that wanted to burst into an Afro cloud, tamed flat by gel and a fleet of hair clips.

'Yes, a glass of water would be good.' She started to get up, but the officer held out a hand to stop her.

'I'll get it.' The chair scraped backward as the policewoman rose, still speaking. 'Sofia isn't at Simon's flat, so I need you to think about where else he might have taken her. Was there a place they liked to go together?'

Carrie closed her eyes as she considered the question. Heard

31

the squeak of the kitchen tap, then the swish of water against glass. She focused inward, tuning into memories of Sofia's bright voice chattering about her day out with Daddy.

Daddy pretended to be a shark and grabbed my ankle and I swallowed some water, but I spat it at him like a whale . . .

A girl got stuck in the rope tunnel and Daddy had to go and get her because she was crying and her mummy was too fat to fit in there.

I went on the pirate ship all the way up to the crow's nest but there was no crows and no nest . . .

The memories battered her heart, leaving fresh bruises.

When she reopened her eyes, the policewoman was back in her seat and there was a glass of water on the table between them. Carrie sipped from it gratefully, wetting her parched throat. 'The Kensington Leisure Centre pool. It's a five-minute walk from his flat.' Another sip. 'Bundy's: an indoor play centre in Hammersmith. But only when the weather's bad.' A longer gulp. 'The Princess Diana Playground.' She stared emptily over the rim of her glass, blinking fast. 'Oh. And sometimes the zoo. Sofia and I are members.'

The DCI nodded as she jotted this onto her notepad. Then she put down the pen and leaned across the table, making Carrie recoil automatically.

'Now, I'm going to repeat a question I asked you earlier. And this time I want you to think very carefully about your answer. Because it will help determine whether this case justifies the current level of police involvement.'

Carrie crossed her arms over her stomach and turned her gaze towards the living area. A couple of reporters had shown up a few minutes ago, so someone had drawn the curtains to keep their cameras out. It made the house feel smaller, like a cave. The kilim rug had been rucked up against the wood by all the investigators who had been and gone, distorting the geometric pattern. Carrie was suddenly conscious of her breathing – growing faster – and of the charged bursts of adrenalin now overlaying the nausea that had hung in the background since Sofia's disappearance. Because she didn't need to be able to read the officer's face to guess which question was coming back.

'Has Simon ever harmed your daughter?'

And just like that, she was trapped. Because if she lied, the police would think Sofia was safe and scale back their efforts to find her. And if she told the truth, they would know that Carrie was an unfit mother. She picked up the water glass again, just for something to hold on to.

A knife. Blood falling like dark tears.

The images boiled back up. And this time, she didn't push them away.

Her fault, all of it had been her fault. If Carrie had been whole, had been normal, it would never have happened. In fact, the entire relationship with Simon would probably never have happened. Because she had believed him when they'd met for the first time, in the waiting room of the Riverside Psychiatry and Psychology Practice. *Just here for a spot of depression. Nothing serious. Gone now, but thought I should speak to the doctor about it.* That's what he'd told her and she hadn't thought to question it. Because she couldn't read the lie in his face. And it had lowered her guard, meeting him that way. Because in that room, no one was a freak or an outcast. They were all adrift in the same boat: just a bunch of lost souls in search of a map. So she had told him straight away about her trouble understanding people and making herself understood. He had responded with a smile – a big, easy-to-read one – and suggested they go for a pint together after their appointments.

They had spent the afternoon on a breezy pub terrace by the river, drinking beer and eating mussels and fat chips. For Carrie, it had been a novel experience. Normally, she responded to the tug of sexual cravings by putting on her short black dress and going to a club – one with loud music, so she wasn't expected to speak. Lots of alcohol, so when she got things wrong, the men put it down to that.

But there was no music on the terrace and their conversation had lasted for hours. It was Simon who had kept the words flowing, with his easy banter and an endless supply of questions. And she remembered thinking that anyone watching would have believed they were just another couple, chatting over beer. She'd never felt so normal.

That evening, on her doorstep, he'd kissed her goodnight, tasting of lager and smelling of soap. Of clean, new things.

And it had been good. Great, even. For months, she had felt like she belonged in the world, as if somebody finally understood her – maybe even loved her, though he'd never actually said that. Carrie hadn't realised how dim and shadowy her life had been until Simon shone his light into it.

And then, on the day she'd found out she was pregnant, it had happened for the first time.

She had asked him to meet her at the Black Sheep. Christmas was only two weeks away, so the pub was decked out for the holidays. Tinsel snaked up the Edwardian pillars and a fake tree sparkled in the corner. A bartender in a Santa hat was ladling mulled wine from a plug-in cauldron. The smell of cloves drifted over, sending Carrie's stomach into a queasy roll. The pub was busy: couples and groups were crowded into booths and perched on stools, taking a break before the next assault on the shops, their purchases bagged at their feet. Carrie had been lucky to land a window table. Rain squiggled down the pane, warping the faces of the pedestrians hustling past, their shoulders hunched against the downpour.

Looking back, she remembered noticing the beads of sweat on Simon's forehead. Should she have read something into that? Or into his refusal to take off his woollen coat, despite the pub's stuffy heat? Perhaps. But, to be fair, she'd been distracted. Nearly two hours had passed since she'd taken the test, but the shock of it was still spinning inside her, making her feel sick. The world seemed tilted off its axis, her mind wheeling around the moment of realisation. How had this happened? Everything she'd thought she was, everything she had assumed her life would become, had been upended in less than two minutes.

She watched Simon pick up a cardboard coaster (an advert for London Pride) and spin it on its end, the disc blurring with motion before losing momentum and stuttering to a halt. It occurred to her that she was standing on the border between 'before' and 'after'. In a moment she would tell him and everything between them would change. How would he react? Would he get angry and stalk off? Or clasp her hands and say that it was all going to be OK – that she should let it happen? Carrie cradled her mug of tea. Was that really an option? It seemed impossible. Unimaginable. She wasn't the right sort of person.

Simon's shoulders jerked up and down: a fast-forwards shrug.

Then his eyes narrowed, as though trying to bring something distant into focus.

Carrie took a sip of tea. Her throat was dry and she could feel her heart surging.

'Simon, there's something I need to tell you.'

He stared wordlessly across the table, gnawing on a lip. Usually he was a talker, filling the gaps she seemed to create. But not this time. In the pause that followed, she could hear Mariah Carey singing 'All I Want For Christmas Is You'. A pair of women at the bar began swaying with the beat, high-heeled boots hooked over the struts of their stools.

She put down the cup. 'I took a test this morning. Because of what happened last month after we went to see that play? And—'

A muscle jumped in his cheek. She'd never seen it do that before.

'What are all these people *doing* here?' His volume rose with each word, drawing eyes their way. Heads turned. Carrie looked around, puzzled, scanning the pub's patrons, trying to work out who he was talking about.

'They're drinking and chatting.'

'No, they're *staring* at me, can't you see that?'

She glanced around again before shrugging.

'Maybe a few of them are now. But only because you raised your voice.'

He ignored her, twisting in his seat to address a couple standing beside the bar: a skinny man and an auburn-haired woman holding a Hamleys bag with an enormous stuffed giraffe poking out of the top.

'What the fuck are you looking at?' he shouted. 'Is there a problem?'

Mariah Carey's voice became clearer as the babble it had been competing against suddenly dropped away. The woman took a step backward, mouth opening. Her companion held up a palm and said: 'Whoa, easy mate, we were just looking out the window to see if it's still raining.'

'Raining?' Simon squinted, as though trying to see something hidden behind the word.

Then the woman picked up the Hamleys bag and touched her companion's shoulder, leading him away, towards the other end of the bar. A moment later the buzz of conversation rose again, swamping the music.

The muscles of Simon's face were squirming under his skin. Carrie put a hand on his and felt a tremor there, like a current passing through his body.

'What's happening, Simon? Is something—'

He snatched his fingers away.

'*Wrong?* That's what you're about to say isn't it? You think there's something wrong with me. I thought you were different, but you're just like all the others. Trying to get rid of me.'

Carrie withdrew her hand, letting it drop into her lap, where it clutched at the navy hem of her jumper as she tried to work out what he meant. Her gaze moved instinctively to the ceiling, taking comfort in the solidity of it, the physical logic. She understood perfectly the balance of brick and beam. The way a vaulted ceiling displaced its burden and the interlocking puzzle of the roof tiles beyond. Form, function, aesthetics. These were things she knew and was able to translate – into wood and stone, glass and concrete. But the crease of an eye, the pull of a lip, the tilt of a head. She couldn't translate those.

When her gaze returned to Simon, he was staring across

the table, teeth clamped together, breath loud and fast. Where was the patient lover who baked his own bread and brought her toast and coffee in bed? A stranger seemed to have taken his place. Had there been clues along the way? Signals that everyone around her had read in his face?

'I'm not saying there's anything wrong with you, Simon. I was simply asking . . .'

He banged a fist against the table, making her jump.

'Bitch!' A fleck of spittle flew across the space between them, hitting her on the cheek. 'I see what you're up to, but I'm not going to let you get away with it.' Then his voice dropped. 'You don't know who you're dealing with, do you? You're blind, so you can't see who I really am.'

He leaned closer, until she could smell the beer on his breath, and a sour smell underneath, as if he'd forgotten to brush his teeth. She sat perfectly still, paralysed by shock and confusion.

'Poor little Carrie. You have no idea what I'm capable of.' His lips curved into a smile-shape. 'But don't worry; you'll find out. You just wait.'

Five

The first thing Sofia noticed when she woke up was the pain. It felt as if a tiny person was inside her head, kicking the same spot over and over again.

Bang-bang-bang.

She squeezed her eyes tighter shut. Zion, who sat behind her at school, sometimes kicked the back of her chair over and over until she got so mad she shouted at him and then the teacher got mad at Sofia for shouting in class, which wasn't fair. But this was a million times worse, because that chair-kicking was just annoying, and this also hurt. And another thing was: her mouth felt sticky and dry. She needed a glass of water. She would ask Mummy to get her one.

Sofia opened her eyes.

And let out a shout of surprise. Because instead of the mobile of a seagull with wings that flapped when you pulled the string, there was a dirty ceiling made of planks of old wood. And lots of old spiders' webs that the spiders didn't want any more, which were called cobwebs. Sofia sat up, making everything swirl around her. The headache kicked harder and a school of white spots flickered in front of her eyes like burning fish.

Where am I?

Her heart banged against her rib cage as if it was trying to get out of there. Her eyes flew around the tiny room. She was on a blow-up mattress with a thin blanket that had fallen down onto her lap when she sat up. The penguin from the park was lying on the floor at the foot of the mattress. The only other things in the room were a broom and a rake with rust on it leaning in the corner. Then she saw something good on the floor beside her: a big glass of water and a plate with a cheese sandwich. Relief coursed through her. Mummy must have come in and left that there, which meant she was somewhere nearby. Sofia's panic ebbed, and she remembered that she was thirsty. She drank the water until she had to stop to catch her breath. Then looked around again. What was this place? How did she get here? She remembered going all the way to the top of the rocket. Seeing the penguin, going to give it a hug. And then ... She searched inside her head but there was nothing else. Maybe she'd played a game of hide-and-seek afterwards and this was her hiding spot, but then she fell asleep and forgot about it?

The kicking in her head wasn't so bad now that she'd had the water, and her thoughts were going in more of a line and less of a tangle. But now that her thoughts were clearer they were starting to get scary again. If Mummy had been here with the sandwich, why did she go away and leave Sofia all by herself? She stood up and the room swung around her. Except she could see now that it wasn't really a room. More like a tiny wood house with a door painted green. It must be a shed, like the one at the end of their garden, except with

40

no piles of boxes and no Mummy's bicycle. There were two windows with bars on. She could see the sky through them: cloudy and starting to get dark. The scared feeling was getting bigger, wriggling around inside her stomach. She went to the door and grabbed the handle, which was shiny and new, even though the rest of the door looked old. Tried to open it. But the handle wouldn't turn. She pushed and pulled and twisted and then she kicked the bottom of the door until she hurt her big toe. But it wouldn't move.

'Mummy?' she called through the green wood, then waited for the familiar footsteps. But there was nothing. Just a big, empty silence. She could feel the fear getting bigger now, expanding like a balloon until it filled up her insides, pressing against the walls of her chest. She beat against the door with both fists, screaming.

'*Mummy!*'

The house suddenly seemed quieter. Carrie could hear the clock above the fridge. *Tick-tick-tick*. The sound of time crawling and crawling, going nowhere. She spread her fingers against the kitchen table, pressing her palms against it. The policewoman's question seemed to spread, like a noxious gas, until it filled the house.

Has Simon ever harmed Sofia?

How long had it been since the officer had said those words? It felt like a long time, but she was still waiting silently, so perhaps it had only been a few moments. Time had been doing strange things since Sofia's disappearance. Stretching and sprinting and stopping altogether. Even moving backward, flowing into the past. She drew in a long breath. Clenched her toes against the wood floor.

'Yes, Simon has harmed Sofia.' It surprised even her, how flat her speech sounded. As though all the fear and confusion had been gated back somewhere along the synaptic pathway between thought and speech, refused permission to complete the journey.

The policewoman nodded. 'When?'

'Six weeks ago. May fourteenth.'

The officer's lips rubbed sideways, back and forth against each other.

'I'll need you to talk me through exactly what happened. From the beginning.'

'OK,' Carrie said. And in a way, it was easy. Because the memory was right there on the surface, just waiting to be let out.

Anyone can see he's not right in the head.

That's what the old woman had said. But it wasn't true, was it? Because Carrie couldn't see. Carrie was blind.

Still, she couldn't put *all* of the blame on her condition. The truth was, she had let her guard down. Because everything had been fine up until that day. There had been no repeat of the scene in the pub – not in the three years they'd been a couple, or the two years since the split. The heightened emotions of breakup had flattened into civilised routine. The childcare hand-overs had been uneventful, the conversations cordial. Simon was always friendly, punctual, respectful. So somewhere along the way, she had stopped searching his face, analysing his words, running through the memorised checklist of warning signs from his doctor. And, of course, Sofia loved seeing him. Daddy, with his booming laugh, animated speech and easy affection. Daddy, tossing her into the air and catching her, making jokes only the two of them could understand, setting off overlapping waves of laughter. There was no point denying it: Carrie had been jealous. Jealous of their closeness and their giggling and the way their faces and bodies moved when they were together. She'd certainly been jealous that afternoon, as she watched her daughter waiting at the living room window, hopping from foot to foot, as though her body wasn't big enough to house the excitement of waiting for her father to appear. The zoo, he'd said. Then dinner. Swimming the next morning. He would bring her back on Sunday at 6 p.m., as usual.

Carrie had noticed the sheen of sweat on Simon's forehead when she'd opened the door, but it was unseasonably warm that day, so she'd assumed that was the reason. And, yes, she remembered thinking his eyes were open a bit wider than usual, but she'd been taught that widening of the eyes was associated with excitement, so she'd put it down to anticipation of a weekend with his daughter.

Carrie had stood watching from the front window as the two of them headed off down the pavement, her daughter skipping at Simon's side, wearing her smile-emoji backpack. But as Carrie turned to face the silent house, she saw Penguin Pete lying on the floor by the sofa. Pete was Sofia's favourite stuffed animal: the one she cuddled in bed at night. A weekend without him was unthinkable. Scooping up the toy, Carrie slammed out of the house and ran down the pavement, chasing their retreating backs, catching them in front of the second-to-last house on the street: number seventy-eight. An elderly woman

43

was outside, pruning her hedge. She watched them over the top as she clipped.

'Petie!' Sofia flung her arms around the stuffed penguin, hugging it against her face. 'I'm so sorry, Petie! How could I forget you?'

'How indeed?' Simon said. 'It's almost as though he was kept behind on purpose.'

Carrie blinked as she tried and failed to interpret this remark.

'I don't understand what you mean by that. Explain to me?'

He was usually good about spelling things out for her. But today his only response was a headshake and a closed-lip smile. She didn't know what that meant either, but something about him seemed ... different.

'Are you OK, Simon?'

At least her instincts had got her that far. That far ... but no further. She looked at his face carefully, trying to latch on to something she could make sense of, a pattern she recognised from their time together. But his features were arranged in a way she'd never seen before.

'Oh yes.' A broad grin split his face, uncovering teeth tinged yellow by coffee and cigarettes. 'In fact, I am better than OK. I am *fantastique*.' And he laughed, throwing out his arms.

Had it set off alarm bells: his reaction, the width of his smile? Some flicker of doubt? She would ask herself that later, but, in truth, the answer was no. Other people's emotional displays always seemed so exaggerated, and Simon's even more so when he was around Sofia. So she had accepted his claim that he was fine, that he was *fantastique*. And she'd let the two of them go. Had watched them walk off down the pavement and disappear around the corner in the direction of the bus stop.

Carrie hadn't registered the rhythmic scissoring of the hedge clippers until the sound suddenly stopped. She turned to see the grey-haired woman stab the tool into the ground at her feet, the handles jutting from the soil. She took off her straw sunhat and used it to fan herself, squinting at Carrie.

'Are you sure that was wise?'

Carrie looked back at her across the plane of severed leaves.

'I don't understand what you mean. Was *what* wise?'

'Letting your daughter go off with a man like that?'

Carrie had been about to tell the old biddy that the 'man like that' was Sofia's father, thank you very much. But something stopped the words. She felt a cold clutch of dread, a creeping certainty that she'd missed something.

'Why . . . why would you say that?'

The woman's lips puckered, making the skin around them appear cracked.

'Well, anyone can see he's not right in the head. That smile . . .' Her shoulders made a shuddering movement. 'I know the polite term these days is "mentally ill" but I believe in calling a spade a spade. And that man is just plain crazy.' She returned the sunhat to her head. 'Of course, it's none of my business. But I wouldn't let someone *I* love be alone with a man who smiled like that.'

There was a beat of time, a brief pause before the weight of the woman's words hit Carrie like an avalanche, knocking the breath from her.

That man is just plain crazy.

Oh no, oh please, God, *no*.

She wheeled away and raced down the pavement after them, arms pumping, feet hammering concrete, lungs snatching air, two thoughts slamming back and forth inside her skull like a

45

battering ram: *Simon is psychotic. Simon is with Sofia. Simon is psychotic. Simon is with Sofia.* She had to get her daughter back, to catch them before the bus arrived and carried them out of reach. Every cell in her body strained forwards, towards Sofia. Her lungs were scorching as she rounded the corner.

And saw that it was too late; the bus was already pulling free of the curb. She chased after it, waving her arms over her head, shouting.

'Stop! Stop the bus!'

A man walking his dog up ahead shot a glance her way before quickly crossing the street. The bus picked up speed, belching exhaust as it heaved around a curve in the road and out of sight.

They were supposed to be going to the zoo, so that was where Carrie went first. Sofia liked to present her membership card at the entry gate because it made her feel grown up, so their arrival should have been logged in the London Zoo's computer system. Should have been ... but wasn't. Carrie had pushed past the queue at the entry gate, shown them her own card, on the same family account as Sofia's, and said she needed to locate her daughter right away; it was an emergency. The zoo staff checked and re-checked their computer records, but the answer was the same both times: if Sofia was inside the zoo, she hadn't used her card to get there. Carrie was already tapping at her mobile, ordering an Uber, as she ran back out onto the curved road that arched around the zoo. Panic was tearing at her, sinking its claws into her chest. How had this happened? Why hadn't Simon taken his meds? She knew why he *used* to skip them; his episodes were so infrequent, the drugs so strong, the side effects so severe, that it hadn't seemed worth it. At least, that's what he'd told her, after that first time in the pub. He'd said polluting his body with powerful, mind-dulling chemicals when he was absolutely fine, and might remain absolutely fine for months to come seemed (*to call a spade a spade*) crazy. But he'd changed his tune after Sofia was born. The stakes were higher now, he'd said. So he would take his pills every day without fail. For her sake.

But now he'd broken that promise and he was psychotic and Carrie couldn't find him. He loved Sofia, there was no doubt about that, but would it be enough to protect her from his demons?

The lift in Simon's block of flats was broken again, so she ran up the four flights of stairs through the trapped heat. By the time she reached the third floor her back was slick with sweat. She was halfway up the final flight when she heard the scream.

'Daddy, no!'

Carrie's heart spasmed in her chest. She reached Simon's door and hurled herself against it, beating the wood, shouting: 'Simon! Let me in!'

He answered in a voice she barely recognised, uneven and high-pitched.

'I can't open it! They're trying to kidnap her!'

Carrie stopped banging. She stood motionless in front of the door, toes clenched inside her trainers, blinking fast. Took a long pull of air. And as she released it, everything inside her suddenly went still. The gale of panic that had been flinging her thoughts in frantic circles dropped away. She was in the eye of an emotional storm. And in that silence, she was able to think, to recall what Simon's doctors had told her about the way his mind worked during these times – and the strategies for dealing with it.

She took a few more breaths, focusing herself. Logic. Calm. These were her allies. She marshalled them now.

Carrie put her mouth close to the door so that she could speak without raising her voice.

'Simon, I need you to think carefully about what I'm about to say. Can you do that?' Silence. She forged ahead. 'I love Sofia. You know that, don't you? I love her and I only ever want what's best for her.'

Another pause. Then: 'Yes. I ... I know that. But I love her too! And bad people are trying to steal her, to—'

She interrupted the building hysteria. 'I would die before I'd let anyone hurt her. You know that too, don't you?'

A faint rustling sound. What was he doing? Why couldn't she hear Sofia?

'Yes. I know.' He wasn't shouting any more. Which was a good sign, surely?

'Now tell me this, Simon. Accepting both those statements to be true, would I ask you to open this door if doing so would place Sofia in jeopardy?' Was it her imagination, or could she actually hear him breathing? 'I need to come in there so I can' – she swallowed – 'help protect her.'

She leaned her forehead against the door, ears and thoughts straining across the wooden barrier.

Please, Simon, let me in. Please-please-please.

There was a thud of footsteps and a scrape of metal: the bolt being pulled back. Then footsteps retreating.

'OK. You can enter.'

Carrie turned the knob and eased the door back slowly, so as not to startle him. Then froze on the threshold, as she digested the tableau before her. Simon's front door opened on to the main living space: a kitchen-diner with windows along the far wall. The shutters were closed, but lines of daylight leaked in through the slats, to fall like prison bars across the Ikea sofa, the small kitchen table, the yukka tree struggling in its pot. They striped the wall to her right, slashing across the poster-sized photo of a laughing Sofia and the 'Ryder Place' street sign he had stolen one drunken night at university.

Simon was crouched in front of the coat closet just inside the door, his eyes fixed on a point beyond Carrie's shoulder, as though expecting to see a crowd of enemies behind her. His right hand was raised, held level with his cheek. When she saw what was in it the breath locked in her throat.

Simon was holding a knife.

She recognised it from their time together; his favourite chopping knife, the one for slicing vegetables. His knuckles were white around the handle. As Carrie's eyes adjusted to the gloom, she saw something on the blade and a vacuum opened up inside her, sucking away every particle of oxygen.

Blood. The tip of the knife looked as though it had been dipped in it. As she stared, a single drop fell, leaving a red comma shape on the wood-laminate flooring.

What has he done to Sofia?

She stepped inside the flat, closing the door behind her. For once, she was glad that her emotions didn't show in her voice.

'Where is our daughter?'

But Sofia answered the question for him, voice clogged by tears and muffled by wood. 'Mummy!'

The closet.

Carrie's eyes stayed on the blade as she answered. 'I'm right here, sweetheart. Are you OK?'

The sound of sobbing ripped at Carrie's heart.

'I want to come out, but Daddy won't let me!'

Simon's face scrunched, his eyes screwing shut. 'You need to stay in there a bit longer, poppet! For your own good.' When he opened his eyes again, a bar of sunlight caught them, making them glitter. 'They're coming,' he whispered, moving towards Carrie, raising the knife above his ear, poised to strike. 'They'll be here any minute.'

'If that's true, then Sofia needs to leave right away. Stand aside so I can take her to safety.' He started grinding his teeth. Sofia had gone silent again, so Carrie could actually hear the sound of bone scraping against bone. *Krrr-krrr-krrr.* 'No one's here *yet*, Simon. So why don't I bring her down the fire stairs and leave you to ... to hold them back? You can buy us the time we need to escape.'

He was blinking fast, jaw still working. Side to side, as though his teeth were fighting each other. *Krrrr-krrr.* He closed his eyes and muttered something to himself. Drew in a deep breath and released it forcefully, inflating his cheeks.

Then slowly – agonisingly slowly – he lowered the knife.

Carrie stepped past him and opened the closet door. Sofia was curled up on her side with her eyes closed, the fan of lashes lying against her pale skin. She didn't move and, for a moment, Carrie felt a blast of fear so powerful it turned her bones to liquid. Then the fan fluttered.

'Mummy!'

'Come, darling. Time to go.'

Sofia's arms looped around Carrie's neck as she was lifted

from the floor. She turned her head, revealing the other side of her face. Carrie's heart lurched. Blood was trickling out from beneath the curly fringe, flowing down her cheek like dark tears.

Carrie turned to Simon with Sofia clutched tight against her chest.

'What did you do to her?'

His mouth opened and closed as he stared at the red trail.

'Nothing, I swear!' Then his eyebrows drew together, creating a crease between them. 'There was something on her head, a spider. I had to get it off her; it might have been venomous, so I killed it with the knife.'

'There wasn't a spider!' Sofia was crying again, her arms tightening around Carrie's neck, making it difficult to breathe. 'He said there was a spider and he was going to get it but it was just maginary and he cut my head and it really, really hurts!'

Simon held the knife in front of his eyes and stared at it, as though he had only just discovered it in his hand. His mouth kept opening and closing, but Carrie didn't stay to find out whether any words came out. She carried Sofia past him, out the door and down the stairs to the hospital, where she told the doctor her daughter had got a hold of a kitchen knife and cut herself accidentally. She had lied, not to protect Simon, but to protect herself. Because the truth might have cost her Sofia. Doctors had to report parents who placed their children in harm's way. And she had left her daughter with a man who was dangerously psychotic. So social services would have stepped in and handed Sofia over to someone better equipped to protect her – someone who could see danger when it was staring them right in the face.

Anyone can see he's not right in the head.

Anyone can see.

Anyone.

Carrie didn't tell the officer about lying to the hospital. She couldn't see how it was relevant, so she ended at the point when she'd carried Sofia out of the flat.

The policewoman put down her pen. In the pause that followed, Carrie had time to register that more journalists had arrived, their mingled conversations filtering through the closed windows. A TV reporter was talking in that voice they used when they were on air. The soundproofing wasn't up to much in this house. Normally it wasn't a problem; this was a quiet cul-de-sac.

'It wasn't your fault.'

Carrie blinked, trying to work out where the comment had come from. She hadn't said anything about her feelings of guilt and failure. Of shame.

'I didn't say that it was. I simply recounted the chain of events as accurately and objectively as I could.'

'Yes. But you blame yourself. I can tell.'

Carrie stared at the woman across the table, really seeing her for the first time: the liquid brown eyes and golden-brown skin, the wild hair pinned into submission.

'Can you? How?'

Dark eyes narrowed beneath a forehead that was crinkling slightly.

'I don't know. I just ... sense it.'

Carrie took a sip of water as she absorbed this statement. A guess. That's all it was. The policewoman must be imagining how a mother in her position was likely to feel. Because aside from Sofia, no one could read Carrie. Sometimes she tried to make it easier for people, pulling her face into the right positions, manufacturing smiles and frowns to match her emotions, attempting to look normal. But it never quite worked.

'What's your name?'

As soon as the question left her lips, Carrie realised the policewoman would have introduced herself when they'd first met, the information bouncing off the surface of her shock-numbed mind.

She expected the woman to briskly re-identify herself as DCI something-or-other. Officer somebody.

But, instead, she said simply: 'I'm Juliet.'

A ringing sound startled her: the officer's mobile. Carrie's pulse jumped. Was it news about Sofia? Had she and Simon been found? Maybe her daughter was in the back of a police car right now, wrapped in a blanket, on her way home. Carrie leaned forwards to eavesdrop, but, infuriatingly, the policewoman rose and said: 'Please excuse me for a moment.' She began walking towards the front of the house as she answered it, identifying herself as 'DCI Campbell'. It looked as though she was heading towards the door, intending to take the call outside. But then she must have remembered the reporters now lying in wait, because she stopped halfway there – on the edge of hearing range. Carrie strained to catch the words.

'What?' Pause. 'Where?' Another pause. 'You're sure?' The DCI turned and glanced back at Carrie, lips pressed together, one eyebrow dipping below the other. Damn it, what did that mean? 'And you've searched the entire area?' A longer pause.

Then she ended the call and walked briskly back to the table. Sat down. Placed her fingertips against each other. 'I have news.' She inhaled through her nostrils, letting the air escape through her mouth in an audible puff. 'Simon has been located, in a pub not far from Clearbrook. He was creating a disturbance so the pub owner called the police.'

Carrie felt as though something was stuck in her throat, like a cork in a bottle swirling with volatile chemicals.

'Sofia?'

The DCI shook her head. 'I'm sorry, but she wasn't with him. The train ticket in his pocket shows he had already arrived at the station nearest Clearbrook around the time she went missing. Of course we'll check the CCTV footage and phone records to be sure, but'– she took Carrie's hand, clasping it firmly – 'it looks as if it wasn't Simon after all. Someone else took Sofia.'

Six

Sofia's throat was starting to hurt from all the shouting. She kicked the door again and again, but it wouldn't move.

'*Mummy!*'

Where had she gone? Mummy never went far away. She was like a helicopter, that's what she'd told Sofia once. People called her a 'helicopter parent' because she was always floating around watching. Sofia had thought that was a funny idea, picturing Mummy circling around up there like a giant bee or maybe a hummingbird. But she wasn't being a helicopter now.

Sofia began to cry. Just the snuffling kind at first, but after a while she started making a wailing noise that scared her because it sounded loud in her own ears. Big and serious. Snot was flowing down her face, mixing with the tears trickling towards her chin. She was stuck inside this hot place and it was starting to get dark and she wanted to go home. She threw herself down on the blow-up mattress and lay there sobbing, wishing with all her might that she was in her own house right now, playing with Penguin Pete and listening to Mummy moving around in the kitchen making something for dinner. Pasta maybe. Spaghetti bolognese. She screwed her eyes tight shut. Maybe if she wished hard enough, pictured it hard enough, her house would actually be there when she opened her eyes again.

But it didn't work. When she peered out between her lashes, she could still see the stupid old shed, with its dusty tools and empty spider webs. She pressed her hands against her eyes, feeling a new wave of tears building. But before they could come out, she heard something.

Footsteps. Moving closer. Moving right up to the door of the shed. Then a scraping noise. Sofia jumped to her feet. The handle shook. Someone was coming!

'Hello!' Sofia shouted. 'Mummy? Let me out!'

There was a clang of metal so loud it made her jump, like a hammer hitting something. Then the door flew open really fast so that the handle banged into the wall, making the whole door wobble.

A man was standing there. Taller than Daddy, with rectangle-shaped glasses. Sofia didn't recognise him, which meant he was a stranger. She wasn't supposed to talk to strangers. But this man had opened the door, so he was helping her, so that must mean he was nice and wasn't going to make any 'stranger danger'.

Sofia looked at the man and the man looked at Sofia.

It wasn't Simon.

The words kept wailing in Carrie's head like a siren as she sat on her sofa, falling quiet for a moment only to scream back out again. Like an alarm she couldn't switch off.

It wasn't Simon.

56

A few hours ago, the thought of Sofia being held captive by her psychotic father had seemed like a nightmare made real. But she could see now that, from the moment Sofia went missing, it had been the best-case scenario. And this was the worst. A stranger had stolen her baby. A predator who might be doing something unspeakable to her at this very moment. While Carrie sat uselessly in front of the television, totally helpless.

It wasn't Simon.

Who, then? Who had taken her daughter and where was she now?

Carrie stared dully at the screen, which was showing BBC footage of the investigation: a line of police officers moving slowly across the grass on their hands and knees, gloved fingers spread, combing the ground for clues. The sun that had felt so warm and inviting when she'd headed out to the park two days ago glared down malevolently, bathing the searchers in pitiless light. Carrie had seen enough of these scenes on the news to know how they played out. First there was the search, then the police re-enactment. The officers vowing to leave no stone unturned. And somewhere along the way, the bewildered parents, seated behind a spikey nest of microphones, tearfully begging for their child's safe return. But none of it ever seemed to do any good. It was all just a ritual that changed nothing. It couldn't alter the bone-cold fact that a child had been taken, stolen away to some hideous fate. Leaving the parents to their nightmares, in which a young voice screamed for a mother who never came. And to their days, marooned on the sofa through all the bloated hours of waiting.

Waiting, waiting.

Until the body showed up.

Please, not my baby. Not my little girl.

The policeman who had broken the vase was now standing in front of her bookshelf, scanning the spines (*Modern Architecture, Frank Lloyd Wright: A Retrospective, A Parent's Guide to the Early Years, Raising Girls*). She saw him pull out a book and scan the back. She could tell which one by the cover: *How to Read Faces.*

Her eyes returned to the television, which administered a small jolt of pain as Sofia's image appeared there: the photo Carrie had taken on their day trip to Brighton, the wind whipping up her hair. Why had the police chosen that picture, she wondered, with her curls all blown out of place? It wasn't as though they'd lacked options. Sofia's image was everywhere, framed on walls and angled on shelves: baby Sofia smiling on a blanket; toddler Sofia in the bath squeezing a rubber duck; schoolgirl Sofia on her first day of reception, proud in her uniform. Carrie was an avid photographer where her daughter was concerned, phone-camera forever poised to catch the next fragment of childhood. But now she saw these images for what they really were – just coloured bits of paper: a futile attempt to dip a net into the rush of time, when all you could really do was watch helplessly from the shore as it swept past, carrying away everything you held dear.

Carrie stared at her daughter's TV-smile, gripping one of the dry tissues the family liaison officer had thrust at her. The woman had put boxes of them all around the house, clearly anticipating an emotional deluge. If only that were possible. What a relief it would be, to transform all this grief and horror into liquid and let it flow out of her body. But Carrie hadn't cried since she was three years old. A psychologist had once told her that all those unshed tears were still inside her somewhere, behind a dam buried deep in her subconscious, a lifetime of sorrow trapped behind it.

The presenter's voice droned sombrely as Sofia's face was replaced by a shot of Carrie's house, zooming in on the blue door before panning along the postage stamp of a garden, where the carnations Carrie and Sofia had planted in tubs were already starting to wilt.

What was happening to her daughter right now? Was she screaming? Was she even alive? The questions had been torturing Carrie for two days. She would fling them away in horror, only to have them come slithering back. The not knowing was driving her mad, making her want to tear at her own skin. She felt a powerful desire to *do* something. To run through the streets calling and searching. But the police had told her that, for now, the best thing she could do was sit here and wait.

'You should go to bed.' The family liaison officer – pony-tailed, petite, soft-voiced – appeared in front of her. She always seemed to be popping up unexpectedly, full of advice about coping strategies and staying healthy 'for your daughter's sake'. Carrie had to keep reminding herself that the officer was only trying to help, because for reasons she couldn't pin-point, the woman really set her teeth on edge. Right now, she was blocking the television screen: inner eyebrows curving upward, lips puckered slightly. Carrie had no idea what that expression meant and found she didn't much care. 'You haven't slept. You should go to bed. I'll wake you if there's a development.'

'No. I'm not tired.' Pause. 'Thank you.'

The truth was, Carrie didn't feel she was *allowed* to go to sleep. She needed to remain vigilant for as long as Sofia was out there. Alert and waiting.

But the mention of bed must have tripped a switch inside her, because she could feel her blinks growing longer. Carrie's thoughts turned blurry and began to swirl. She was being carried off on a warm, dark tide. She tried to pull herself free, but the current was too strong. She managed to force her lids up once. Twice. But after that they wouldn't open and she slid down into blackness.

Carrie dreamed she was with Sofia at the fun fair, the one that sprouted up on their local green twice a year. She could feel the tug of her daughter's small hand, towing her towards the trampolines, where harnessed children were bouncing to impossible heights, propelled upward by elasticated bonds.

'No, you're too little,' Carrie told her. 'You don't weigh enough for that one.'

But Sofia kept pulling, watching the older children doing mid-air summersaults in slow-mo, as though they were underwater.

'Please, Mummy, just one go?'

Her face glowed with anticipation. Carrie loved the way Sofia's life force hummed through her body like an electrical current, making her jump up and down with the sheer excitement of what might happen next, so that Carrie half expected to see rays of light escaping through the seams of her eyes. Love swelled inside her and she knew that her daughter had won, that she would give in. She gave in far too often, the parenting books warned about that; she was in danger of spoiling her. The day suddenly grew darker and she looked up, a hand shielding her eyes. Was there a storm coming? The sky had been perfectly blue a second ago. When she looked down again, she discovered that Sofia was already on the trampoline, strapped into the harness, waving cheerily. But there was something about the fairground worker Carrie didn't like. His face was round as a pumpkin with a few greasy strands of hair painted across the forehead. He grinned, exposing a row of sharp, yellow teeth. Fear clutched at her and she tried to shout 'stop'. But the word came out as a whisper. Then Sofia started to jump, bouncing higher and higher, a bright smile covering her face.

And now Carrie saw that the fairground worker was yanking her harness downward, sending her crashing into the trampoline so that she ricocheted higher and higher. Impossibly high. She was flying up into the stormy sky, her summer coat a pink splash against the grey.

And then the chords snapped. Carrie ran towards her, screaming silently. Up she flew, higher and higher. Until finally gravity reasserted itself, pulling Sofia back. Except she wasn't above the trampoline any more, she was plummeting towards cold, hard concrete, so Carrie ran, arms held out to catch her. But suddenly there was nothing above her but dark, empty sky.

When she woke up, something was happening. She could sense it – that same feeling she got when she woke before her alarm, knowing it was time to resurface into the world, that she was needed in it. She was lying on her own bed; one of the officers must have carried her here. The one from the bookcase, probably: the vase smasher. She threw back the duvet. Light no longer rimmed the curtains, so the sun must have set. She stood beside her bed, blinking, trying to decide what to do next. Then, quite suddenly, the noise of the reporters changed. The mutterings and chatter were replaced by a surge of sound. A roar went up, shouts Carrie couldn't make out. Excitement.

What's going on?

She ran downstairs to find the family liaison officer peering out through a gap in the curtains: eyes wide, mouth open.

'What is it?' Carrie's voice made the woman jump and turn. She looked from Carrie, to the window, and back again. The doorbell rang. The officer held up a palm, signalling for her to stop. Why? What had she seen?

'Who is that? What's happening?'

The woman tried to block her path to the door, but now she could hear the press roaring like a wild beast, see camera flashes stuttering against the darkened curtains and she was overwhelmed by the feeling that she had to take control of this situation. That whatever was coming, she must meet it head on. She pushed past the liaison officer, knocking her off stride. Threw open the door.

A man was standing on the doorstep. He was about Carrie's age, tall with dark hair, eyes framed by rectangular glasses. He looked familiar: perhaps one of the plainclothes officers who'd passed through earlier. She was dimly aware that he was saying something, but the words seemed to take a long time to reach her, like the pause between lightning's flash and the slow plod of thunder. Because, right now, all she could take in was the child in his arms. The grubby back of a silver top. The spotty pink skirt propped on a supporting forearm. The curly head against his shoulder, turning slowly. Then those dark eyes found hers, and there was a lightning storm of cameras flashing all at once. Carrie's arms opened even as her legs unhinged, dropping her to her knees.

And then the man's words finally arrived, like a low boom from a great distance.

Is this your daughter?

But by then Sofia was already in her arms, pressed against her chest, filling her face with those wonderful curls. Clinging to her neck and saying 'Mummy!' Then: 'Not so tight! You're hurting!' And she sounded so fine, so uncorruptedly herself, that Carrie actually laughed, right out loud, so that her whole body shook. The tremor passed right through her, down through all the dark, walled-off places, until finally it must have reached that buried dam, because she felt something inside her give. A wave surged outward, rising through her chest and up her throat, flowing out through her eyes. It poured down her cheeks to land in Sofia's curls.

So Carrie laughed and cried as the cameras whirred and the shutters clicked and the sun-baked concrete bit into her knees. And through it all, the dark-haired man stood over her, watching, his words still rolling in her head like a miracle.

Is this your daughter?

Yes, it's her. Yes, she's mine. Yes-yes-yes.

Seven

Sofia banged her head against the wall behind her hospital bed in frustration. Why wouldn't everyone stop bothering her and let her go home? They'd already done a million tests and asked a million questions and there was nothing wrong with her. She looked at Mummy, sitting next to the bed on a purple chair (almost everything in the room was purple, even the wall mural of a mummy elephant showering a baby elephant with her trunk).

There were two other people in the room, besides Sofia and Mummy. One was a police lady with kind eyes and lots of hair clips shaped like diamonds. Sofia had heard someone call her 'D-C-I', even though those letters didn't make a proper word. She was holding a pen and a little notebook, waiting for Sofia to say something good enough to write down. The other police person was short with freckles and her special job was talking to children. Except she called talking 'interviewing', which was the same as talking except mostly questions. She had a sing-songy voice, like a storyteller. It sounded nice. But her questions were annoying.

'You're sure you didn't see anything, even the toe of a shoe in the bushes, or the finger of a hand?'

'No, I already *told* you a million times. I didn't see anybody.'

Mummy gave her fingers a gentle squeeze. She had been holding on to her hand for a long time, as if Sofia was a balloon that might float away if she let go.

'Detective Sergeant Dutoit is just trying to work out how you ended up in that shed. She has to double check to make absolutely sure you aren't forgetting anything. That's her job.'

'Well, I'm *not* forgetting.' Sofia could feel her lower lip sticking out, but that was just too bad. Everyone kept asking the same things over and over, and it was stupid and boring. 'I didn't see anyone when I picked up the penguin and I didn't see anyone in the shed.'

'What about a smell?' the special detective asked. 'Cigarette smoke or a food smell or aftershave. Aftershave is kind of like perfume but for men.'

That question was new, so Sofia thought about it for a moment. But then she shook her head.

'No, the smell of the stuff that made me sleepy was really strong. I couldn't smell any other smells. And the shed just smelled of being old.'

The special detective gave her one of those smiles that meant she wasn't really happy but was trying to be nice.

'What about the man who came and let you out of the shed?'

'His name is Josh.'

'Was there anything ... familiar about him? Had you ever seen him anywhere before?'

'No.'

The other police lady undid one of her hairclips and then

65

did it back up again. Sofia noticed a few springy tufts sticking out here and there, like the hair didn't like being stuck in those clips and wanted to get out. Sofia knew how it felt.

'Can you tell us exactly what he said?'

'He asked me if I was OK, and what I was doing inside the shed, and I told him I got locked in there and I wanted to go home. He asked me if I knew my own address and I do, so I told him 14 Croyhurst Avenue, and then he carried me to a taxi because my legs felt wobbly and he brought me home. And that's *it*.'

The D-C-I police lady crinkled up her face in a way that meant she was thinking a lot about what Sofia had said, even though Sofia had said all those things before.

'Do you know your mother's mobile number?'

'Yes, it's 079001—'

'That's fine.' She interrupted Sofia in the middle, which was rude. 'Did Mr Skelter ... did *Josh* ask if you knew your mummy's number?'

'No. He just asked about my address.'

'But surely it would have made more sense to call your parents or the police, so an officer could be dispatched to collect you?'

She was using a different voice when she said that, as if she was talking to herself instead of Sofia. But Sofia answered anyway, because she didn't want the police lady to think bad thoughts about Josh.

'I didn't tell him I wanted to *call* my Mummy. I told him I wanted to *go home*. So he got a taxi and took me home right away. He was nice.'

That must have been a good answer, because the creases went out of the police lady's face.

'Yes, of course. I'm just trying to understand exactly why Josh did what he did.'

'If you want to know *that,* why are you asking *me*? Why don't you ask *him*?'

'Oh, believe me, I will.' She said that part in a funny, soft voice.

Usually Sofia was pretty good at working out what people's voices meant. But not this time.

'So you just hailed a black cab and brought her home?'

'Yes.'

Juliet looked across the table of the interview room. Josh Skelter was handsome in a bland, unmemorable sort of way: broad-shoulders and a square jaw, medium-brown hair framing medium-brown eyes. He was wearing a freshly laundered shirt and a necklace – or, rather, a ring on a chain. He had taken off his glasses and was polishing them with the tail of his shirt, staring at her with an unwavering gaze. Eye movement was what gave most suspects away. It was a simple fact of neurology that people tended to look right when accessing memory, up-and-left when thinking on their feet: one simple, tiny movement that could separate memories from lies. But his eyes stayed locked front and centre.

She had, of course, run a background check ahead of the interview; Josh Skelter was the only child of a single mother, a well-known architect who had died in a house fire when he was seventeen. A *Guardian* news brief had provided a bare-bones account of how young Josh had risked his life trying to rescue her from the flames.

Which made him ... what? A natural-born hero? A serial rescuer?

Alistair leaned forwards in the seat next to hers, parking his forearms on the table.

'It never occurred to you to call Sofia's mother?' he asked. 'Or 999, for that matter?'

Skelter settled back against the metal chair (bolted to the floor, so it couldn't be used as a weapon). His long legs were stretched out under the table, crossed at the ankles. He looked very relaxed for someone facing two police officers, a one-way mirror and a barrage of questions. But then, why *shouldn't* he look relaxed? He was, after all, the white knight in this little story: the good Samaritan who had ridden to the rescue and saved the girl. Who was even now helping police with their enquiries.

Except there was a problem: Juliet couldn't read him. Not at all. She had spent the last hour probing and pushing, attempting to find some foothold on the chinks and contours of his character. But it was like trying to scale a smooth wall.

He put his glasses back on and gave the two of them a small smile.

'The point of my walks is to unplug from work for an hour. Bringing my mobile phone along would completely defeat that purpose. Which is why I always leave it behind, on my desk.' His eyes moved from Alistair to Juliet and back again. 'Look, a frightened little girl asked me to take her home. So I flagged a taxi and did just that. It really is that simple.'

Juliet opened the file she was holding, taking out half a dozen newspaper clippings: front page stories dominated by photos of Sofia. She spread them across the table.

'And you didn't recognise her from the news? Didn't realise that she was the subject of a massive, high-profile search?'

'I run an architecture magazine and Tuesday was our monthly deadline.' He toyed with the chain around his neck, running the ring back and forth along it (a woman's ring, Juliet noted, the silver shaped into a zigzag on one side. She wondered fleetingly who it had belonged to). 'The days leading up to it are long: late nights, dawn starts. Barely a moment to breathe, let alone read the news or watch TV.'

'You run an architecture magazine. And Carrie Haversen is a respected architect. Had you met before yesterday?'

'We will, of course, have crossed paths at industry events: award ceremonies and so on. And I am aware of her work. But I don't know her personally.'

'Let's go back to your walk for a second,' Alistair interjected, leaning back from the table and crossing his arms behind his head. 'You say you were on deadline, not a second to spare, yet you decided to go for an evening stroll through an isolated corner of Perivale?'

'Yes, I go for a walk most days, to clear my head. I like that path because it's quiet.'

Leaving the newspaper cuttings on the table, Juliet returned her attention to the case file, allowing silence to build as she read one of the pages inside. Then she lifted her eyes to Skelter's.

'So, to recap your statement: you heard a child's voice screaming and crying from a shed at the end of a private garden, scaled the back fence to access the property and then attacked the lock with a shovel you found in the garden before kicking open the door to free her.'

'That is correct.'

She lifted her gaze from the document.

'It didn't occur to you to try knocking on the door of the house to see if anyone was home, to ask if the child who lived there might have become trapped in the garden shed while playing? Or even just to ask for the key?'

'No one's living there now. It's empty.' He gave her a slow smile. 'But I'm guessing you know that already.'

She tossed down the file and crossed her legs.

'This isn't about what I know. This is about us trying to understand the thinking behind your actions. Because, to be perfectly honest, some of it doesn't make sense to me.'

He tilted his head. 'Then allow me to clarify. I knew for a fact that nobody lived there because the entire row of houses had to be evacuated four months ago after the ground they're built on was found to be unstable – too many monster basements dug too close together. There's a legal battle grinding through the courts even as we speak. Meanwhile, everyone in the affected area has been ordered to move out or risk being swallowed by a sinkhole.' He waved a manicured hand in the air. 'And before you ask how I happen to know this, it's because we did a big piece on it in the magazine: a cautionary tale. Anyway, the path itself is on stable ground and the absence of anyone living along it makes for a quiet, peaceful walk.'

'A peaceful stroll through sinkhole territory,' Alistair said dryly. 'How idyllic. But just to dot my "i"s and cross my "t"s . . . can you tell me where you were on June 28th at 4.20 p. m.?'

'That's easy. Holed up in my office.'

'And there are people who can confirm this?'

'Of course. My secretary for one. Gabby Wells. Her desk is right outside my door.'

Juliet folded her arms across her chest as she searched Skelter's face for clues, some subtle signal or emotional vibration: a flicker in his gaze or a hitch in his breath. But there was nothing, just an infuriating blankness. Was this how it was for Carrie Haversen all the time? she wondered. How could she stand it?

Alistair looked at Juliet, transmitting silent messages: a sour mouth-twist of frustration (*I am out of ideas*) then a subtle lift of the eyebrows (*You got anything?*). She answered with a small head-shake. The interview was over.

She returned the clippings to the case file and they both stood up.

'Thank you for coming in.' She held out her hand for Skelter to shake, wanting to see whether his palms were sweaty. 'We appreciate your cooperation.'

The handshake was neither damp nor dry, loose nor firm.

'Any time. Happy to help.'

London Architects' Monthly was located on the top floor of a converted Edwardian fire station fronted by brick arches through which fire trucks had once raced in a hot blare of sirens. Now the arches were sealed with cool glass, allowing passers-by to glimpse the stylish interior: the curved sweep of the reception desk and the frosted glass staircase rising behind it with no visible means of support, so it appeared to float against the orange brick.

Josh Skelter had a corner office at the back of the top floor: a high-ceilinged space containing an art-deco desk covered in papers (neatly stacked), a leather swivel chair and a bookcase lined with reference books and back issues of the magazine.

There were two windows covered by linen blinds and a thriving ficus in a ceramic pot.

'Was there something in particular you were looking for?' Gabby Wells asked, hovering in the doorway as Juliet flipped through the papers on the desk (invoices, copies of articles, architects' drawings).

Skelter's secretary was a pudding-faced woman in a bright floral muumuu with an eager-to-please expression.

'No, I'm just having a look around.' She gave the secretary a smile. 'You're lucky to work in such a lovely building.'

Gabby Wells beamed. 'Isn't it beautiful? The *Observer* did a whole spread on it in their design supplement. But not until we'd already done one, obviously; it wouldn't do to get scooped by the competition on our own building!' She laughed louder and longer than the joke deserved.

Juliet forced a chortle before taking out her notebook and flipping it open.

'Just to go back over your statement: are you absolutely certain that Mr Skelter was in his office between 4 and 5 p.m. on Sunday?'

The secretary nodded firmly, making her surplus chins quiver.

'Oh yes. As you can see, my desk is right outside his door. We were coming up to the monthly deadline, our busy time. Mr Skelter popped out for a takeaway at lunch, but after that he had to write the Editor's Introduction and go through the proofs, so he asked not to be disturbed. Usually he gets those things done a lot earlier, but there were some issues with the cover story so I guess he fell behind. I stuck my head in to say goodbye before I left at seven and he was still working away. It wouldn't surprise me if he was there till midnight.'

Juliet observed Gabby Wells closely – the angle of her gaze, the set of her limbs, the cadence of her voice – for signs that she might be lying or holding something back. But there were none. Which meant that he had been inside this room at the exact time Sofia was taken. She would of course dot the 'i's and cross the 't's by checking the CCTV footage from the lobby and the street, but for now it seemed that Josh Skelter was exactly what he appeared to be: a good Samaritan who had happened to be in the right place at the right time.

'Is there anything I can do for you?' Gabby Wells asked.

'No. You've already been a great help. Thank you.'

The humidity seemed to have thickened while Juliet was inside. It wrapped itself around her in a clammy layer, pasting her shirt to her back as she walked along the street, scanning the shop fronts for private CCTV cameras. Station House was in the middle of Newman Road, flanked by a Greek restaurant and a faded pharmacy with a two-for-one deal on pregnancy tests. She stopped outside a news agent with a camera aimed conspicuously at the magazine rack outside the front door. But it turned out to be a dummy, to deter would-be shop lifters. A jewellery shop further down had a more promising camera and she was about to go inside when her mobile rang.

Carrie Haversen's flat voice travelled through it.

'Can you update me on the progress of the investigation?' A two-second pause, then: 'Please.'

'Hello, Carrie. I will contact you if there are any major developments. But as things now stand—'

'Sky is reporting that the man who returned Sofia is being questioned.'

'Yes, Josh Skelter has been assisting us with our enquiries.'

'Sky implied that he might be a suspect.'

'That's completely untrue,' Juliet said crossly. Bloody reporters. 'Quite the opposite, in fact; I've just confirmed that Josh Skelter was working in his office at the time Sofia was taken.'

'I see. So you have made no progress whatsoever towards catching my daughter's abductor?'

Juliet pulled a hand across her eyes. Was that an accusation? An expression of disappointment? Or a simple statement of fact? The featureless voice made it impossible to tell.

'We *are* making progress; we have ruled out all the people on your list and are now focusing our efforts on the park, canvassing for witnesses and interviewing staff. I will contact you if there are any breakthroughs. OK?'

'I just feel ... Not knowing is very ...' There was a pause during which Juliet could hear Sofia's voice singing in the background. 'Here Comes the Sun'. She smiled at the sound. Carrie exhaled into the phone. 'Very well. I will wait for you to call with an update. Goodbye.'

And the line went dead.

Eight

Carrie woke up and screamed. She'd been dreaming that Sofia was buried somewhere along an endless grey beach and she was clawing with her bare hands, trying to dig her out. But every time she threw a scoop of sand aside more spilled down into the hole, rising up its sides, like a grave being filled.

She sat up in bed, gasping like a caught fish, heart kicking as she waited for the nightmare to dissolve under the daylight leaking through her curtains. She pressed both palms against her eyes as her body downshifted out of panic mode, slowly resuming its normal rhythm. She rolled her shoulders to free the tension lodged there. Then she glanced at the bedside clock and did a double take. 8.42. She hadn't slept this late in years; Sofia always woke her well before eight. Throwing aside the duvet, Carrie walked quickly down the hallway to her daughter's room, with its wooden 'Sofia's Place' sign, the lower curve of the 'S' tucked beneath the cartoon figure of a cat. As usual, the door had been left ajar. Carrie eased it all the way open and stepped inside.

Sofia was lying under her duvet with her eyes closed, one

arm flung above her head, the other wrapped around Penguin Pete. Her 'Starry Sky' nightlight was still on, the projected stars now barely visible against the mint-green walls, overpowered by the morning sun. Carrie bent to kiss her daughter's forehead, listening to the gentle push–pull of her breathing. A slow surge of love rode through her. Normally Sofia would be bursting with new-day energy at this hour, filling the house with chatter and racing footsteps, snatches of songs and requests for Cheerios or Nutella on toast. But the stress of the last few days had clearly wiped her out.

Best let her sleep.

Carrie went downstairs and put a tin of defrosted bread dough into the oven (Simon had taught her how to make it), setting the timer before heading back up to her room to get dressed. She was pulling a T-shirt over her head when the doorbell buzzed. Must be the office courier.

Osman, her boss, had told Carrie to take as much time off as she needed. But she was keen to get back to work ... so long as that didn't mean being separated from Sofia; she wasn't ready for that. Not yet. So Wescott had arranged for her to work from home. She jogged down the stairs, thoughts already filling with her latest project: creating a modern wing for a Victorian hospital.

As she opened the door, Carrie was trying to remember whether you were supposed to tip couriers. So when she saw who was on the other side, she froze with surprise.

Josh Skelter stood before her wearing a brown leather jacket and a sideways smile.

'Good morning. I hope you don't mind my dropping by unannounced.' He held up a pink bag with string handles. 'I bought a little gift for Sofia, but the police wouldn't let me have your phone number, so I couldn't call ahead.' The wind picked up, rifling through his hair. 'I know it's a bit early, but five-year-olds aren't known for their luxury lie-ins, so I thought I'd take a chance.' The side-smile spread so that the two sides balanced out.

Carrie blinked, thrown off stride by this unexpected social situation. What was the correct response? Was she supposed to invite him in? Or just take the bag, thank him and send him on his way? Fortunately, his next words provided the answer.

'Is it OK to pop in for a minute? I'd really like to say hi to Sofia and give her the gift myself. But only if it's not too much bother.'

She blinked for a moment, then opened the door all the way, standing aside to let him pass.

'You rescued my daughter, treated her kindly and have been ruled out as a suspect in her abduction. You are therefore welcome to visit my home at any time without advance notice, even if social convention dictates otherwise.'

He chuckled right after she said this and Carrie wondered why.

Josh had been in her house for less than half an hour when he asked the question: the one Carrie had been hiding from since Sofia's return, refusing to let inside her head. Because she was afraid that, once it got in she'd never get it out.

The two of them were drinking coffee on the sofa, his ankle propped on a knee, foot jiggling. He had taken her through a blow-by-blow account of the rescue from the shed and his 'debrief' with the police. He'd asked how Sofia was, and Carrie

77

had told him about the hospital test results (no lasting damage from the chloroform, no signs she'd been hurt or abused while unconscious).

A long pause had followed, during which Carrie had sipped coffee, ears straining for sounds of movement upstairs.

That's when he'd said it, the words sliding into her head like a dark snake, burrowing downward to coil around her chest.

'Are you afraid Sofia's abductor might come for her again?'

The silence upstairs suddenly took on a sinister weight. She imagined a shadowy figure moving along the bedroom hallway; a black-gloved hand pushing open a door. Brown eyes, round with fear.

She put down her mug. 'I need to go check on Sofia.'

'Oh ... God. Carrie, I'm so sorry.' His voice followed her as she rushed up the stairs. 'I didn't mean to—'

But she was already at the top, dashing down the hallway, throwing open the bedroom door.

Sofia was just as Carrie had left her: eyes closed, dark hair trailing across the pillow. She shifted in her sleep, snuggling deeper into the duvet.

Relief spread outward from Carrie's core like warm liquid, loosening every part of her. She stood for a moment, watching her daughter's face, listening to the music of her breathing. Then she went back downstairs.

'I'm so sorry,' Josh repeated, when she returned to the sofa. 'I shouldn't have brought that up. And anyway, I'm sure there's nothing to worry about. The police are bound to make an arrest soon.'

'I hope you're right.'

'Tell you what.' He retrieved his cup from the coffee table. 'How about I change the subject with a completely unrelated question?'

'Yes.' She nodded gratefully. 'Please.'

He took a sip of coffee and looked at her with one eyebrow slightly raised.

'Do you remember me?'

She blinked, perplexed. What did he mean by that? He couldn't be referring to the day he'd brought Sofia back – because that would be a ridiculous. It wasn't as if she could ever forget the man who had appeared out of nowhere with her daughter in his arms, like a genie granting her dearest wish.

Carrie's thoughts moved back in time, to the moment she'd opened the door to find Josh standing there.

And then it returned to her: that first, fleeting impression that she'd seen him somewhere before.

But where? She closed her eyes, trying to pin it down. But the memory stayed maddeningly out of reach, like a fish that slipped through her fingers as she reached for it.

She shook her head. 'I have an impression that I met you at some point before the abduction, but I can't recall when or where.'

He slung an arm across the sofa-back and smiled. What kind of smile was that, she wondered. Warm? Scornful? Disappointed? She wished she could tell.

'Innovative Design of the Year.'

Carrie tilted her head, puzzled by the sudden reference to an award she'd won ... what, two months ago now? The trophy was in her office drawer: a sloping glass rectangle mounted on a bronze cube, her name etched across the front. But how did ...

Then, at last, a bubble of memory popped to the surface. Of course. She had it now.

'You presented the award.'

'Yes. My magazine sponsors the competition.'

Osman, her boss, had nominated her design and insisted that she attend the ceremony. It was the sort of social situation of which Carrie's nightmares were made: sitting rigidly at a big table, the air filled with other people's words and laughter. She remembered the surprise of her name being called and Osman's voice whispering that she should 'say something' as she got up to collect her prize. So she had said: 'I am very pleased to have won this award.'

More must have been expected, because there was a long silence as she stood on the stage, stomach twisting, a sea of faces aimed her way. Then came one or two isolated claps before the rest of the room joined in to make proper applause.

An excruciating evening from start to finish. But every now and then, when she was alone in the office, Carrie would take the trophy out of her drawer and feel a small glow at the sight of her name there: proof that, for once, she had been chosen.

'We shook hands,' she recalled. Now that she had matched his face to the award presenter, details were rushing back. 'You congratulated me.'

'I did. I thought your work was inspired. I had hoped to talk to you about it at the post-ceremony drinks, but you disappeared before I had the chance. The way you incorporated those shop facades ... Brilliant. Simply brilliant.' He took a sip of coffee, watching her over the cup's rim. 'But, as I recall, not everyone agreed. At least, not at the beginning.'

'That's right.' She remembered the arguments she'd had –

with her boss, with the client – when she'd said she wanted to preserve the little row of Victorian shop fronts running through the middle of the leisure centre site, with their quaint signs ('Sweets and Sundries', 'Tripe House', 'Books, Typewriters, Adding Machines'). 'They wanted to knock them all down.'

'But you stood your ground.'

'Yes.' She picked up her cup and sat back, taking a drink.

'I'd love to hear about your process, how you arrived at the final design. That is ... if you don't mind talking about it?'

'No, I don't mind talking.' And for once, it was true. Carrie explained, step-by-step, how she'd integrated the shop facades into a covered courtyard so that their freshly sanded facades lined one side: the Victorian past facing into the sleek, glass-ceiling present, all of it steeped in natural light.

She hadn't realised how much time had passed until she took another sip of coffee and found that it had grown cold. She became conscious of herself again, aware of the words that had been flowing from her, without the usual jolts and stalls. It was easily the longest conversation she'd had since the breakup with Simon. And even back then, it had never been like this. With Simon, the gaps had been filled by his endless supply of chatter. With Josh, there were simply no gaps to fill.

He must have edged towards her along the sofa while they were talking, because now he was just a few inches away, entering the outer edge of her personal space. His eyes looked straight into hers and she felt something shift, as though her stomach was filled with loose shards, tumbling against each other, creating friction.

She cleared her throat. 'Would you like more coffee? I can—'

'Mummy?'

81

She turned towards her daughter's voice. Sofia was standing halfway down the stairs in her pyjamas, staring at Josh with a delighted smile.

'There she is! Just the girl I was looking for.' He picked up the pink gift bag from the floor and took out a box wrapped in silver paper, placing it on the coffee table. 'I brought you something.'

Sofia raced down the stairs and knelt on the floor beside it, fingers fidgeting against the wrapped borders.

'Mummy, can I open it now?'

Carrie got as far as 'Yes, if you …' before the gift was torn open in a flurry of silver scraps. When Sofia saw what was inside the box, her mouth made an O shape.

'This looks like … no way!' Her voice turned shrill with excitement. '*It is!*'

She lifted the purple plastic case from its box. Carrie recognised it at once: a container filled with the 'Lolly Pets' that were all the rage at Sofia's school. And not just any container: the 'Pet Vet' – a collectible case containing multiple animal figures and their accessories, outrageously overpriced at sixty pounds. But it was popular. So popular, in fact, that the Pet Vet had sold out across London. Carrie knew this because she'd tried unsuccessfully to buy one ahead of Sofia's birthday.

'Wow!'

'Say thank you,' Carrie said. Funny, how she always remembered to prompt her daughter to say the things she herself so often forgot to say – especially in situations where she couldn't understand the logic behind them ('How are you?' 'Very well, thank you.' That one baffled her. Were you giving someone else credit for your own state of health?).

Sofia looked up at Josh, face rapt.

'*Thank you!*'

'Where did you find it?' Carrie asked. 'I've been hunting for one online for the last month.'

'When I decide I want something, I don't give up until I get it.' His eyes stayed on hers as he said this.

Sofia climbed up onto the sofa between them, flinging her arms around Josh's neck.

'This is the best present ever in the universe!'

He ruffled her hair. 'Well, the two of us have shared a big adventure. And you were so brave. I thought bravery like that deserved a prize.'

There was a beeping sound from the kitchen: the oven timer.

'Bread. For our breakfast,' Carrie explained, before striding towards it.

Now Josh would be socially obligated to leave so as not to delay their meal. She was surprised by a pang of disappointment. Normally it would have made her uncomfortable, having someone she barely knew in the house. She took out the baking tin and placed it on the stove before returning to the living area, intending to escort him to the door.

'Why doesn't Josh have breakfast with us, Mummy?' asked Sofia, still nestled beside him on the sofa. She turned and looked up at him. 'You can stay, can't you? Pleeease?' She clasped her hands together as though in prayer.

He laughed. 'How could I possibly say no to an invitation like that? Unless—' His gaze moved to Carrie. 'Is that OK with you? Maybe you'd prefer some alone time with Sofia? And, of course, you probably haven't made enough food for a last-minute interloper . . .'

'No, I baked a whole loaf. And there's plenty of cheese and jam.'

He rubbed his hands together.

'Well, in that case, I would be delighted to join you. But only on the condition that you let *me* take the two of *you* out for a meal next time.' He directed his next words at Sofia. 'Have you heard of the Rainforest Café?'

Her eyes seemed to double in size.

'I've never been, but Kathy from Year Two went for a birthday party and says it's just like being in a real jungle with robot gorillas hitting their own chests and birds squawking and scary storms with thunder and lightning!'

'Not too scary for you, I hope?'

Sofia shook her head firmly. 'No way. I'm brave.'

'That is certainly true. In fact, maybe you're *too* brave for the Rainforest Café. Maybe it would be boring for you.' He gave Carrie a wink. She was fairly sure it was the conspiratorial kind, like a shared joke, so she took a chance and winked back. That must have been right, because he smiled at her.

'So what do you think, Carrie?' Josh asked, as she sat back down on the other side of her daughter. 'Are you willing to brave the Rainforest of Piccadilly?'

Sofia hugged Carrie's nearest arm with both of hers.

'Please say yes, Mummy, pleeease?'

She looked down into the pleading brown eyes. Of course she was going to say yes. She would do anything for her daughter right now, even if it meant placing herself in a complex social situation. She looked over the top of Sofia's head at Josh and was surprised by the realisation that she actually *wanted* to go. That she felt pleased to have been invited.

'Yes.'

She was about to tack on one of those phrases people used in these situations ('That would be lovely' or 'It's kind of you to ask'), but before she had the chance, Josh clapped his hands together and said: 'Excellent! It's a date.'

'Yay!' Sofia cheered. And Carrie formed her mouth into the shape of a smile, so he could see how she felt inside.

This man held his daughter captive and sliced open her skin with a knife.

Juliet had to keep reminding herself of this fact. Because she was having trouble reconciling it with the man now seated across from her, hands clasped in his lap, an untouched glass of water on the interview-room table in front of him. She had known, of course, that Sofia's father would be lucid; Clearbrook wouldn't have released him otherwise. But what she hadn't anticipated was the sheer charisma of the man. Simon Ryder was warm, likeable and articulate: everything that Carrie was not.

'Do you see why I wanted to bring this piece of information to your attention?' he was saying now. Ryder's gaze shifted from her to Alistair and back again, pausing to establish eye contact with each of them. 'Can you see why I believe it's significant?'

Juliet tilted her head as she considered Ryder's theory and the information he'd built it on. It could mean something ... or nothing at all.

'I agree that this may be very significant. On the other hand, it might just be a coincidence. But you can rest assured that we have taken it on board and will pursue every line of enquiry.'

Simon gave her a long, probing look, and she had the sense that he was searching her face for clues, trying to work out whether or not she was humouring him. He must have been satisfied with what he found, because he sagged back against the interview-room chair with a sigh, looking relieved. He'd probably been worried they wouldn't take his theory seriously, given his mental health history.

'Good.' He scrubbed his face with his palms. 'Thank you.'

Alistair leaned forwards, parking his elbows on the table, and Juliet caught a sour whiff of BO. The room's air conditioner was on full, but it was waging a losing battle against the heat-wave. June was less than a week behind them and already it was thirty-four degrees outside. It didn't feel right; Britain wasn't built for this sort of heat.

'When did you and Carrie first meet?' Alistair asked.

'I guess it would have been . . . about a year and a half before Sofia was born,' Simon said. Then he crossed his arms, frowning. 'I don't understand, though; how could my romantic history with Carrie possibly be relevant, given that the relationship ended more than two years ago?'

Alistair folded his hands on the table. 'At this point, we can't say what is and isn't relevant, so you'll just have to bear with us.' Irritation tinged the words. Unlike Juliet, he clearly hadn't warmed to Ryder. Which didn't surprise her; the DI came from a staunchly working-class background, and she'd noticed the way he soured in the face of posh accents and Oxbridge educations.

Juliet gave Ryder a smile. 'The fuller the picture we can build of past and current patterns, habits and associations, the better.'

He sighed, dragging fingers through his hair. 'OK then. My

relationship with Carrie began six months before she got pregnant with Sofia. We met at a clinic, I asked her out for a drink and we just ... clicked.'

'Clicked?' Juliet echoed. 'Really?'

He side-smiled. 'I know you may find that hard to believe. But it's true. She wasn't like anyone I'd ever met before. It's what I loved about her.' He paused, eyes becoming distant. '*Love* about her. She is caring and sensitive and passionate. The fact that those things stay hidden beneath the surface ... for me, that just made them more special. Other women seem melodramatic and self-indulgent by comparison. Exhibitionists, parading their emotions for all the world to see. Fake too: full of platitudes and meaningless bullshit. Telling everyone to "have a good day". As if someone might have been planning to have a shit day, but now that you've told them not to, they're going to change course and opt for a good one instead.' Juliet shifted self-consciously in her seat. She had said those very words on her way into the station, to a couple of PCs leaving after the nightshift. Ryder was right. The exchange was pointless and empty: a meaningless word-swap. 'I don't say stuff like that any more,' he continued. 'Because of Carrie. She is the truest person I have ever known.' He tugged the collar of his heat-damp T-shirt, letting air underneath. Juliet considered the Cambridge University logo across the front. Ryder had graduated more than a decade ago. It seemed a little odd that he was still wearing it.

Alistair picked up Ryder's file and flipped through it. 'So you and Carrie had only been together six months when she got pregnant.'

'Yes. It wasn't planned. There was a ... a condom malfunction.'

'How did you feel about the pregnancy?'

'I was happy about it ... once I'd had a chance to get used to the idea. Carrie was less sure, because of her condition. And my ... episodes. But I convinced her it could work.' His voice softened. 'And Sofia was the result.'

'Did the three of you live together?'

'Not at first, though I was at her place all the time, so we might as well have been. I gave up my flat and officially moved in after Carrie's maternity leave ended, when Sofia had just turned one. I worked in the evenings so was able to handle childcare during the day.'

'And that living arrangement went on for ...' Alistair flipped over the page in his hand, scanning the words on the back. 'Two years and three months. Would you say it was successful?'

'Yes ... Well, it was for the first year and a half or so. I was taking my meds, my relationship with Carrie was in a good place and I like to think that I'm a good dad.' His eyes dropped to his lap. '*Was*. I was a good dad.'

'You're really struggling with your tenses today, aren't you?' Alistair said, putting down the page. 'Loved – love. Am – was.' He sat back, interlacing his fingers on top of his head. 'Do you find grammar complicated?'

Simon gave him a tired smile. 'I find life complicated.'

Juliet picked up the page Alistair had discarded, eyes moving down it to the section entitled 'Employment History'.

'London Walks,' she read aloud. 'I gather that was the evening work you mentioned?'

'Yeah. I led historical tours of the city. I wore a Jack the Ripper costume and showed people round murder scenes in Whitechapel.'

Alistair lifted an eyebrow 'And this . . . serial killer tribute act paid enough to cover the bills?'

'No. I did some bartending too. Occasional research gigs – historical research – on a freelance basis.'

'Right.' Alistair made no attempt to hide his scorn. 'In other words, Carrie was the main bread winner.'

'Yeah.' A sigh passed through Simon's body like a storm swell, lifting his shoulders then dropping them back down again, leaving him lower than before. Smaller. Juliet's eyes returned to the wash-worn Cambridge T-shirt. Maybe he'd held on to it for so long because it reminded him of the last time he'd felt successful, back when his future had shimmered on the horizon, warm and beckoning,

And watching Ryder's face, seeing the defeat there, she knew, in a flash of instinct, that this was what had broken them.

Alistair opened his mouth to fire off another question, but she jumped in first.

'Why did you and Carrie split up?'

There was a long pause. Ryder seemed to suddenly notice the glass of water on the table in front of him. He picked it up.

'I was an arsehole.' He took a sip of water. Then gave Juliet a tired smile. 'I'm guessing you'll want me to elaborate, since we arseholes are an eclectic breed.'

'Elaboration would be helpful, yes.'

He took a longer sip of water then wiped his lips with the side of a finger.

'I blamed her for my lack of success: the fact that I was taking care of a baby instead of building a career. Which was a steaming pile of shite. I was the one who'd insisted on being a stay-at-home dad. We could just as easily have put Sofia in a nursery. But at that point my old uni chums were scaling a dizzying array of ladders to success while I was heading off to work dressed up in a costume like a sprog at Halloween. I felt like a loser and I needed someone to blame. So I blamed her, blindsiding her with my guilt-trips and self-pity. I'd promised to always translate my facial expressions and body language into words for her, but I stopped doing that, leaving her lost and bewildered. Until the relationship broke down completely. At the time, she assumed it was her fault. That things fell apart because of her condition.' The glass returned to the table with a loud clack. 'But it was all on me.'

The raw honesty of this assessment must have softened Alistair a little, because the edge had left his voice when he asked: 'So I take it that, given the choice, you'd still be living with the two of them?'

'Of course.' Simon threw out his palms in exasperation. 'I'd do anything to be there right now. Not just because I miss them, which I do, more than anything, but because of my theory.' The dark eyes moved to Juliet's and stayed there: a steady, measuring gaze. 'The theory which you've promised to take on board. I want to be there with them because I'm scared this isn't over. That something bad is going to happen. And I won't be around to stop it.'

The words were still hanging in the air when the door to the interview room flew open and DS Hiranand leaned through.

'Sorry to interrupt. Can I just have a quick word?'

Juliet joined him in the corridor outside the interview room. 'What is it?'

'I just had a call from the park manager's office at Granger

Park. They've found something – and I think you might want to go see it for yourself.'

The park vehicle had left tracks in the soft earth, smashed wildflowers and grass embedded in the grooves. It was parked diagonally, at the base of an oak in a small clearing, right beside a padlocked gate leading out of the park.

Juliet's eyes travelled along the tread marks, stopping when they reached the vehicle. The Granger keepers called it an 'electric cart', but it looked more like a miniature jeep – park-issue white, with just enough room for a driver and a passenger squeezed together in front and a bit of cargo space behind for hauling bags of soil, plants and gardening tools.

She heard twigs snapping behind her: Alistair, returning from the park keepers' office.

She turned to see him wading through the tangle of brambles and vines on the edge of the clearing, notebook in hand.

'Mission accomplished,' he called across to her. 'The sign-in sheet shows ... Ow! You bloody bastard!' He hopped the last few steps, pulling up his trouser leg to display the deep scratch now striping his pale shin, a bead of blood welled at one end. 'Will you look at what that bramble just did to me?'

'Yes, it's practically a knife crime. But returning to the business at hand ...' She gestured towards the cart. 'Did you confirm that this thing was last seen on the day of the abduction?'

'Yes indeed.' Alistair dragged a sleeve across his shiny forehead, looking down at his notebook. 'Signed out at 2.50 p.m. by a park keeper named Nick Laude.' He flipped the book shut, one-handed. 'He never signed it back in.'

The two of them stood looking at the cart for a moment. The noonday sun clubbed them, sending a trickle of perspiration down Juliet's spine.

'So what's your take?' Alistair asked.

Her eyes moved to the twin furrows in front of the cart. They passed beneath the now locked gate, where they became dried-out trails of mud on the strip of road beyond. A second set of tracks was superimposed over the first. It had rained heavily the night before Sofia's abduction, but there hadn't been a drop since. Luckily.

She pointed to the cart.

'Sofia is drugged, then this vehicle is used to transport her here from the children's woods.' Her finger moved to the gate. 'The abductor unlocks the gate and drives her out.' She strode up to the gate and leaned against it, gesturing towards the place where the mud trails ended abruptly. 'Sofia is transferred into another vehicle parked over there. Then the cart is reversed back through the gate and abandoned. The abductor locks the gate and drives away.' She looked up and down the narrow, silent strip of road. 'No CCTV.'

'Yeah, I noticed that too.'

The heat was making Juliet feel lightheaded and she flapped the fabric of her blouse, trying to move the air against her skin.

'There's something I don't get, though: why has this cart only now been discovered? Didn't anyone flag it up during the initial police search?'

'Yeah, well, about that.' Alistair's mouth twisted into a grimace. 'Turns out there was a bit of a ... a misunderstanding.'

Juliet's heart sank, her imagination already churning up headlines thundering with police incompetence.

'What *kind* of misunderstanding?'

Alistair pulled a square of paper from his trouser pocket, unfolding it to reveal an A3-sized map labelled 'Granger Park'. He held it by the edges, angled towards her. The first thing that struck her was the shape: the park's outline was more or less rectangular, but with a large chunk missing from the top-left corner so, it resembled a fat letter L lying on its back. The area within the park's border had been coloured green, blue and grey to denote trees, water and concrete. Everything outside it had been left white.

'Where did you get this from?'

'The park office. It's the same map that was used to divide the search area into quadrants.'

Juliet placed a fingertip on the children's woods, skimming north, past the Japanese garden, following the path that had brought them here, frowning as the trail dead-ended at the park's northern border. Weird. Had she somehow picked the wrong path?

'I'm confused. Where exactly are we?'

'That's the problem.' He tapped the missing chunk of rectangle. 'We're here. This area was never assigned a team because it doesn't appear on the map.'

Juliet stared at the white space in disbelief.

'Why the hell not?'

Before Alistair could reply, a gravelly voice spoke behind them.

'I can tell you that.'

They turned to see a white-haired man with a walrus moustache emerging from the thicket of trees they'd arrived through, wearing a pair of park-issue overalls with 'Daniel' machine-stitched on to the breast pocket.

He strode up and shook Juliet's hand, then Alistair's, using a firm grip.

'Daniel Cookson. Senior Park Keeper.'

Juliet introduced herself then gestured towards the map.

'If you're able to explain why this section of the park isn't on the map, please do.'

Daniel Cookson took a pair of reading glasses from the pocket of his overalls and slowly unfolded them, one arm at a time, before putting them on. He tapped the top left corner of the page.

'Leaving this part out was Steve's idea, when the new maps came out last year.'

'Steve?' Alistair echoed, then slapped the side of his neck. Juliet watched as he inspected the contents of his palm, pulling a face.

'Steve's the new park manager,' Daniel explained. 'He thought it would be best not to draw attention to these woods, since they're closed to the public anyway. We opened the internal gate today for your lot, but normally it's kept locked with a big "Private: Keep Out" sign. Steve was worried people might be tempted to sneak in and explore if they spotted it on the map.'

'Why is it closed off?' Alistair asked, swatting at the air right in front of him.

Daniel chuckled. '*That's* why. Mosquitos. There used to be a tadpole pond over there.' He gestured vaguely towards a trail veiled with branches. 'It was a big hit with the little ones. And it wasn't just tadpoles: all sorts of mini-beasts lived there – a thriving ecosystem. We would bring groups of children, class trips and such, to learn about the life cycle. But the whole thing dried up in a drought, oh, must be five, six years ago now. When we tried to resuscitate it the following year, all we got for our troubles was a plague of mosquitos. Strangest thing. We kept trying to get rid of them, but no matter what we did, they always came back. There were loads of complaints. An American tour group even threatened to sue.' He took a cloth handkerchief out of his overalls and blew his nose into it. 'So we locked the gate, put up the sign, and haven't used it since.'

Juliet looked around the little glade, with its wildflowers and nodding trees.

'Shame.'

'Yeah.' Daniel Cookson tucked the handkerchief back in his pocket. 'It is.'

Her eyes returned to the abandoned cart. A robin landed briefly on the roof before flitting off again. A breeze rode past, bending the wildflowers. Hard to believe they were only a short drive from central London.

'We'd like to speak to your colleague, the one who signed out this cart. Nick Laude. Is he in today?'

A nod. 'He's on the afternoon shift.' Daniel glanced at his watch. 'Should be arriving in about half an hour.' His lips tightened disapprovingly beneath the moustache. 'Actually, better make that an hour. He's not the most punctual lad.'

'Can you think of a—' Alistair began, then his head flinched back and he clapped his hands in the air – 'Oh for f— why are they only going after me?' He glared at Juliet, as though she were somehow to blame.

'Maybe they're racist,' she deadpanned.

He gave her a withering look before returning his attention to Daniel. 'Can you think of a reason for bringing a park vehicle here? Is there any work being done in this area?'

95

A firm headshake. 'No. Nothing.'

'Why wasn't the cart reported missing?' Juliet asked, eyes tracking a particularly large mosquito as it buzzed past her without interest. 'Doesn't anyone check at the end of the day to make sure they're all accounted for?'

'Yes, theoretically. But there's been so much hoo-ha lately, what with the girl disappearing, police everywhere, people being questioned. Coppers crawling around on the grass looking for God knows what. It's hardly a shock the park's been thrown off its routine. And anyway, if there's an emergency, it's not uncommon for people to take the carts at odd hours without bothering to sign for them.'

Alistair lifted an eyebrow. 'Emergency? What sort of emergencies do you get here?'

'Visitors getting hurt. Peacocks getting out. Hooligans sneaking in after hours. All sorts.'

Juliet glanced towards the gate, smiling as she pictured rogue peacocks escaping over it, tails spread into opulent fans. Then her eyes dropped to the closed padlock and her smile faded.

'Who has the key to this gate?'

'No one. It's kept with all the other keys, on a hook in the storage hut.'

'Can you take us there?'

'Sure. Follow me.' And he turned and strode back towards the trail that had brought them here.

She heard another slap and turned to see Alistair flicking away an insect corpse with a look of disgust.

'Come on,' Juliet said, carefully sidestepping a nest of blackberry thorns, which Alistair promptly trod in.

'I hate bloody nature,' he muttered.

Nine

The girl with the rainbow hairband was screaming. Sofia stared at the girl's arm, at the tooth marks that had turned her skin the same colour as the floor.

Everything was red on this level. There was a yellow level at the bottom where the ball pit was and the top level was all blue. But Sofia liked the red level best because it had long tunnels and a swinging rope ladder and a curly slide that went all the way back to the bottom. So she had gone straight up to red as soon as she'd arrived at Bundy's Indoor Play Centre. But when she went through the tunnel, the rainbow hairband girl was on the other side, shouting at a boy with blond hair.

"Look what you *did*!' she screamed, holding up her arm. 'My mummy says only *animals* bite! So you're not even a *human being*! I'm going to *tell*!' Then she pushed past and fled back through the tunnel, wailing loudly. Sofia stared at the blond boy. He was older than her. Maybe six or seven.

'What are you looking at?' There was a snarl inside his voice.

'Nothing.' Sofia sat down cross-legged on the edge of the

padded floor, out of the path of the children running in and out of the tunnel. 'Why did you bite that girl?'

He looked at her with his face moving around a lot, like he was trying to decide whether or not to tell her to mind her own beeswax. But then he sat down next to her on the floor, pulling up his knees.

'She pushed me.'

Sofia shrugged. 'So?'

Children were always pushing each other in Bundy's because it was crowded and everyone wanted to go first on the slide. It was annoying, but not *super* annoying.

'*So* . . . it made me mad.'

'I get mad sometimes too. But I don't bite. Mostly I just shout. Sometimes I kick things that are on the ground, but not people.'

He picked at a spot on the floor where the red stuff was broken and a bit of foam was poking out.

'Mrs Daniels from down the road says I'm a monster.'

'She sounds mean.'

'She said it because I chased her cat one time with a stick and scared it.'

'Why did you do that? I like cats.'

'Me too. I don't know why I did it.' He pulled out a bit of foam and threw it away, looking sad. 'Sometimes I think she's right and there's a monster inside my head that jumps out whenever I get mad and makes me do bad things.'

Sofia considered this for a moment.

'Can't you put it in a cage?'

He looked up. 'What do you mean?'

'Well, the monster must be maginary, if it lives inside your head. So can't you make a maginary cage and lock it up inside?'

He considered this for a moment, frowning. Then he smiled, a big, proper smile that changed his face.

'That's a good idea. I'm going to try it.' He gave her arm a soft punch. 'Thanks.'

Sofia smiled back, feeling a glow of pride at having helped. He was OK, this blond boy, now that he wasn't biting.

'Want to go play in the ball pit?' she suggested.

'Sure!'

He jumped up. But then the smile fell off his face. He was looking at something behind Sofia. She turned around and saw a skinny man in a Bundy's T-shirt squeezing his way through the square gap at the top of the ladder leading up from the yellow level. It looked weird, seeing a grown up in here. The spaces weren't big enough.

The man ignored Sofia, pointing a finger (which was rude) right at the boy. 'You need to come with me,' he said. 'We're going to find your parent or carer and discuss the rules about biting.' He held out a hand. 'Let's go.'

But the boy shook his head, features twisting, turning red.

'No! I won't and you can't make me! You … you …' He went from red to purple, clearly struggling to think of a word bad enough. '… bucken-head!'

The man frowned and came all the way up through the gap, moving quickly towards the boy, bent over at the waist to keep from bumping his head on the low, padded ceiling.

'*Run!*' Sophia shouted.

And the blond boy scrambled off through the red tunnel with the Bundy's man lumbering after him.

★　　★　　★

'Children and parents are reminded that Bundy's has a zero-tolerance policy on biting.' The tannoy announcement was only just audible above the background roar of children.

It was too hot outside for the park, so Bundy's was packed. Children shrieked, climbed and slid through the three levels of the soft play area, crossing rope bridges and ducking through tunnels, scaling red or blue padded walls and zipping down slides. To Carrie, seated at one of the tables in front of it, the play structure looked like a giant, three-dimensional game of snakes and ladders encased in rope webbing. She fished a teabag out of her cardboard cup as she scanned the front of the red level. But Sofia must have been further back, hidden from view.

The light in the cafe area was headache-bright, casting harsh judgement on the tired parents slouched at the litter-strewn tables around her. Bundy's was well known for its terrible atmosphere and equally terrible menu. But on days when the park was ruled out by the weather, it could be a godsend. Carrie took a sip of camomile tea, which tasted of dust. Her eyes kept returning to the three layers of darting children. It was unnerving, not being able to keep a proper eye on Sofia, and she felt her stomach twist. Irrational, of course. Security was tight here; there was only one way in and out, through a locked gate policed by staff whose job it was to ensure that each child came and went with the same adult. But Carrie was taking no chances and had selected a table near the gate, so that she could monitor the comings and goings herself. So she knew her daughter was still here, somewhere among the rush and roar of children. There was nothing to worry about, nothing at all.

Are you afraid Sofia's abductor might come for her again?

The words seeped through her mind like acid, eating through the protective layer of logic.

Carrie stood up quickly, the plastic chair squeaking against the linoleum. She had to find her daughter. Now.

'She's right there.' The voice came from just behind Carrie's left shoulder, startling her. She turned to find herself looking into a familiar face. Dark, wavy hair, pale skin and blue-green eyes. Tara: the woman from the park. She stood holding a cardboard cup in one hand and pointing at the bottom level of the play structure with the other. 'If you're looking for Sofia, she's in the ball pit.'

Carrie felt herself unclench as she spotted her daughter, hip deep in multi-coloured plastic balls, giggling with another little girl as the two of them spun in circles, then fell over backwards. The balls closed briefly over their heads before they popped back up again in fresh fits of giggles.

Carrie drew in a long breath, expelling it slowly, feeling her fear leave with it.

Tara was watching her over the rim of her cup. She must have slept badly because there were grey shadows under her eyes.

'We meet again.' She smiled. 'At least this time I was actually able to find Sofia.'

'Yes.' Carrie stood looking at Tara. It felt strange, seeing her in Bundy's, casually holding a drink. Out of context. 'Thank you.'

Tara sipped from her cup (coffee, judging by the smell). 'I've thought about you a lot since the park, wondering how you were coping.' She shook her head slowly. 'I can't even imagine what you've been through, not knowing what was going on, or whether you'd ever see your child again ... It's every parent's worst nightmare.'

Carrie didn't know what the appropriate response was, so just said: 'Yes.'

'But it all turned out OK in the end, thank God.'

As Tara's eyes returned to Sofia (now tossing coloured balls in the air), Carrie's thoughts snagged on something.

'How do you know what my daughter looks like?'

'Are you kidding? *Everyone* knows what she looks like. She's been all over the news.'

'Oh. Yes. Of course.'

Sofia and her new companion waded out of the ball pit and disappeared briefly up a ladder before re-emerging on the red level. Carrie could see her daughter whispering something to the other child, hands cupped around her ear.

She had made a new friend, just like that.

Amazing.

'Shall we sit?' Tara gestured towards Carrie's table, with its empty chairs and half-finished tea, the canvas bag of toys slouched on the floor.

'Yes.'

Tara dragged one of the chairs around so that they were seated side by side, facing the play structure. She looked inside her cup, appearing to inspect the contents.

'So what's the latest on Sofia's case? Do the police have any suspects?'

'Not yet. They're still investigating.'

'Oh well. She's home safe. That's all that matters.'

No, Carrie thought. *It's not all that matters.*

Tara finished her coffee, tilting the cup all the way up.

'Are you here with your son?' Carrie asked.

'Of course. I don't think anyone comes here to soak up the atmosphere.'

Her statement was factually correct, but Tara must have found it funny, because she laughed right after she said it. Carrie manufactured a smile. She didn't get the joke, but she liked Tara and wanted to be liked back.

'Where is he?'

'Oh, he's in there somewhere.' She waved a hand in the direction of the play area without looking. 'Stirring up trouble, no doubt.'

'What's his name?'

'Peter.'

'How old is he?'

'He just turned seven.' She pushed her hands up her cheeks, catching her chin in the base of the V they made.

'Is he—'

'Look, here comes Sofia.'

Carrie opened her arms as her daughter came barrelling towards them, skirting around a large table of women arguing energetically in Spanish.

'Mummy, can we go now? I'm hot and my new friend Maisy went home and we've been here a long time already.' Then she saw Tara and her face did one of those rapid switches that meant something had surprised her.

'Hello!'

Tara smiled. 'Hello to you too.'

'You're the balloon lady!'

Tara tipped her head to one side, forehead crinkling. 'I'm sorry, the what?'

'You saved my balloon.'

'I think you have me mixed up with someone else. I would remember meeting someone with a beautiful face like yours.'

'When you saw me before my face looked like a cat with whiskers and its tongue stuck out. It was Sally McPherson's birthday party and there was face paint with different animals but they wouldn't do a penguin. My balloon floated up and got stuck in a tree and you climbed up and got it.'

Sally McPherson's party. Carrie hadn't been happy about leaving Sofia there. But the hostess's instructions had been very clear. *It's drop and go,* she'd said with a mouth-only smile. *So enjoy the peace and quiet and I'll see you at three.* Carrie had returned to Granger Park half an hour early. And felt a bruised throb when she saw the dozen or so school mums sitting on blankets, drinking prosecco from plastic wine glasses, the hostess bending towards them with a tray of cheese and crackers.

Tara laughed, slapping the table.

'Oh wow, was that *you*? What a coincidence! I nearly fell out of that tree.' She looked at Carrie, smiling. 'I run a small catering company, specialising in food for children's parties.'

'I liked that balloon,' Sofia said.

'It was an excellent balloon, well worth the climb.' She held out her hand. 'My name is Tara.'

Sofia shook it with a sombre expression. Carrie smiled inwardly: a grown-up face for a grown-up ritual.

'My name is Sofia. I'm pleased to meet you.'

A surge of affection made Carrie pull her daughter onto her lap, wrapping her in a hug.

'Tara is here with her son, Peter.'

'Where is he?' Sofia looked around. 'Can he come to our house and play?'

'Another time, maybe,' Tara answered quickly, eyes doing another dash up the play frame. 'I'm afraid we already have plans today.'

'Oh.' Sofia's features collapsed under the weight of disappointment.

Tara placed a hand on top of the curly head. 'But on Wednesday, guess what Peter and I are doing? Baking cupcakes in a *giant* kitchen that I use for work. If you're free, maybe you could come and help us out? You could meet Max the cat. He's always hanging around the back door, angling for scraps and strokes.'

'Yes!' Sofia clapped her hands. 'I want to play with Max!'

Tara turned to Carrie with a smile.

'What do you think? Are you free next Wednesday for lunch and a chat?'

Lunch and a chat. Carrie rolled the phrase around in her head. It felt warm.

'Yes.' She lifted her mouth into a smile-shape to show she was pleased by the invitation. 'Please.'

'My work kitchen is in central London, off Regent Street. Is that OK? Because if it's too much of a slog, I'm happy to make it another day when I—'

'No, that's fine. My office is near Regent Street, so I'm used to the journey.'

'Great! See you around three o'clock?'

'Yes.' Carrie could get up early on Wednesday, do a few hours' work in her study, then visit Tara after lunch. It would be good for Sofia to have another child to play with.

Tara took out her mobile. Carrie watched her name being tapped in under 'New Contact'. Tara handed the phone across.

'Just give me your number and I'll text you the address.'

Carrie carefully keyed in the digits, adding herself to the list of people Tara chose to communicate with. *New contact.* She felt shy as she handed it back.

But Tara ignored her outstretched hand. Her eyes were fixed on the top floor of the play area, forehead crinkling.

Sofia slipped down from Carrie's lap. 'Can we go home now?' She tugged at her mother's arm. 'I'm *boiling.*'

'Yes.' Carrie placed the phone carefully on the table and picked up her canvas bag. Tara was still peering up at the wall of netting with a hand above her eyes, as though shielding herself from a glare.

'Goodbye.' Carrie said, standing and pulling the bag over her shoulder. 'We're leaving now.'

Tara's head did a little jolt, as though she'd been startled by an unexpected noise. 'What? Oh. Sorry.' She got up from her chair, turning to face them. 'I'm looking forward to seeing you both on Wednesday.' She smiled down at Sofia. 'There's a park nearby where we can go afterwards. Maybe I'll even climb a tree, for old time's sake.' Sofia giggled and Tara leaned over to give her a hug. Then she straightened and looked at Carrie. 'I'm really glad we ran into each other.'

Carrie felt a lifting sense of wonder as she and Sofia walked hand in hand towards the bus stop.

She'd made a new friend, just like that.

Amazing.

*   *   *

'That's not right,' Daniel said.

The three of them were crowded together in the tiny park keepers' hut – a windowless, oven-hot space with sets of overalls hanging from one wall and shovels propped against the other. Rolled up canvas sacks were piled at the back, along with twine and a pair of hedge clippers.

A dozen or so keys dangled from small hooks screwed directly into the left-hand wall, each with a handwritten cardboard label thumbtacked beneath it ('Main playground', 'Japanese garden', 'East gate', 'Tennis courts'). Only one hook was empty, labelled 'North gate'. Daniel frowned at it.

'The keys are supposed to be returned immediately, so they should all be here when the park's open. And anyway, the north gate stays locked, so there's no need for anyone to take it in the first place.'

Juliet considered the empty hook as a bead of sweat sneaked into one of her eyes, making it sting. The heat was like a physical presence, pressing itself against her.

'How many people have access to this hut?'

'Pretty much everyone who works in the park. We're all given a key to it. Plus there's a spare hidden under the edge of the roof.'

'So whoever took Sofia must have had one – or known about the spare.' Juliet looked around at the contents of the hut, trying to see them through the eyes of a would-be abductor. 'They came in and took the gate key, and possibly one of the canvas sacks to carry her in. It would explain how she was transported to the north end of the park without anyone noticing. Let's get this area cordoned off, ready for Forensics.'

Alistair was already on the phone to the station as the three of them stepped out into the blessed shade of the children's woods. A breeze flowed past and Juliet lifted her face to it gratefully before checking her watch.

'Nearly one o'clock. May as well head to the park office. Nick Laude should be arriving any minute.'

'*Should,*' Daniel said sourly. He mopped his forehead with a handkerchief and she wondered whether it was the same one he'd used to blow his nose. 'Don't hold your breath.'

It was 1.32 when Nick Laude came hustling into the park office, looking sweaty, scruffy and harassed. He blinked in surprise as Juliet and Alistair stood up and showed him their warrant cards.

'What's this about?' He tried to back away from them, but given the size of the space, there wasn't much scope for it. The room was small enough to feel crammed with furniture, despite containing only a desk with a wooden chair behind it and two metal ones in front, a two-drawer filing cabinet and a coat tree trailing a forgotten winter scarf. Nick's eyes went to the bulletin board on the wall opposite the door – his destination, presumably. The staff sign-in sheet was pinned there, orbited by flyers promoting various park events ('Nature's Arts and Crafts', 'Opera Under the Stars', 'Become a Granger Ranger!').

Juliet and Alistair stood in the narrow gap between the metal chairs and the wall, blocking his path to the board. Juliet noticed the way his gaze skipped over them as it flitted around the room, eventually alighting on the empty wooden chair. 'Where's Steve?'

'We asked him to give us some privacy so we could ask you a few questions.' Juliet gestured towards the seat. 'Please. Sit down.'

But he remained frozen just inside the doorway. She watched his face closely, saw something flash in his eyes: alarm, intertwined with guilt.

He knows something, she thought. *Or at least, there's something he doesn't want us to know.*

Nick had a skinny neck with a prominent Adam's apple. It bobbed as he swallowed.

'Sorry, I'm afraid I can't really talk right now. I'm already late for work.'

'That's fine,' Alistair said pleasantly, perching on the front of the desk. 'If you don't have time now, we can move this conversation to the police station as soon as your shift's over.'

Nick's gaze flicked left and right a few times, as though watching an invisible tennis match. Then he closed his eyes and sighed, shoulders sagging with defeat.

'Fine.' He dropped himself onto the chair and crossed his arms, scowling like a surly teenager. 'Go ahead and ask. But I don't know nothing.'

Juliet and Alistair sat down on the metal chairs, facing him across the desk.

'Last Sunday, you signed out electric cart number five,' Juliet said.

The park keeper shrugged. 'If you say so.' His tongue flicked across his lips.

She reached into her satchel and took out the clipboard Steve had provided, pushing it across the desk.

'*I* don't.' She tapped the top sheet. 'Your signature does.' Silence. 'Can you please explain why that cart was abandoned, and has only now been discovered in a disused corner of the park?'

Nick Laude's eyes widened in a convincing display of surprise. Now that he'd recovered from the shock of being ambushed, his acting skills were starting to kick in.

'No.' He shook his head emphatically. 'I *can't* explain that. Because I didn't leave it there.'

'I see. So where exactly *did* you leave it?'

Juliet watched his eyes, waiting to see whether they would move memory-searching right or quick-thinking left. But Nick chose that moment to drag his fingers across his lids.

'In the children's woods. Beside the hut where we keep our overalls and stuff. I had to, um . . .' The fingers migrated to his pale, greasy hair. And now Juliet had her answer. Up-left. She had just enough time to think: *his next words will be a lie*, before the park keeper said: 'I had to get some equipment I needed. Then I went and did some work not far away. And when I came back the cart was gone.'

'You left the keys in the ignition?'

His mouth twitched. 'Well, yeah, everybody does. It's not like a Mercedes or nothing. Who would want to nick one? They're not allowed on normal roads – too slow. So when I came back and it was gone, I thought one of the others must have spotted it there and seeing as I'd' – he coughed behind a balled hand – 'stepped out of sight, they brought it back to HQ.'

'HQ?'

An unconvincing chuckle.

'That's what we call this place. Makes it sound more important than a one-room office with a bog and a row of electric carts parked behind.'

Juliet stared at him for a long moment. She could almost feel the effort it was taking him to maintain eye contact.

'What equipment?'

''Scuse me?'

'You said you went into the hut to get some equipment. What kind of equipment?'

'Oh. That was ... Let's see now.' His eyes slipped up-left again as he scratched his jaw, the stubble rasping in the silence. 'Clippers, I think it was. There was some brambles leaning out on one of the trails. They needed to be cut back so people wouldn't get scratched. Little 'uns especially.' He gave her a grin which was probably supposed to be winning, but instead made him appear wolfish. 'They got sensitive skin an' that. So we don't want 'em getting hurt.'

'No. We don't.' She turned to Alistair and mouthed the word 'map'. He nodded, removing the park map from his jacket pocket, unfolding it against the desk. Juliet handed Nick Laude a pen. 'Can you please mark the exact location where you cut back the brambles last Sunday at the time when the cart was being stolen?'

She watched a flare of alarm ignite in his eyes. His gaze jumped around the page. 'Um, well now ... It's hard to be exactly sure where ...'

'Really?' Alistair said, tenting his fingers. 'Why's that? Surely you must know this park like the back of your hand after having worked here for ...' He took out his notebook and made a show of flipping through the pages. 'Four years?'

'Yes, it's just, you know, I do a lot of things every day, and it's hard not to get things jumbled up in my memory. I wouldn't want to say something to you unless I was sure –' He was nodding along with his words, the bobbing motion reminding Juliet of dashboard dogs. '– *one hundred per cent sure* that I'm not

111

getting one bunch of brambles mixed up with another bunch, because, well, you know how it is.' He stretched out a smile that neither of them returned.

'No,' Alistair said. 'How is it?'

'Just ... busy. And hard to remember.'

'But you *do* remember that you left your cart by the hut? And that it disappeared? That part you are crystal clear on?'

That dashboard bob again. 'Yep, on account of I was a bit, you know, surprised someone did that.'

'Surprised,' Juliet repeated, tilting her head. 'But you never bothered to check that the cart you were responsible for had been safely returned?'

'Well, I would of, but then all hell broke loose with everyone running around looking for that little girl. So ...' He scratched a patch of skin between his elbow and the edge of his T-shirt sleeve. 'It just didn't seem like a big deal, compared to that. I mean, how important is a misplaced cart when a sprog has gone missing?'

'That's exactly what we are trying to establish,' Alistair said.

Nick's hand moved back and forth against his arm. *Scratch-scratch-scratch.*

'Well, she's back home now, that girl. I seen it on the telly. The mum sure got emotional when she opened the door and saw that bloke standing there holding her.' Juliet watched the fingers absently raking up and down, leaving angry red trails. And within them: a swarm of raised white spots. 'I don't mind telling you: it brought tears to my eyes, watching that.' Another wolfish smile. 'So I guess all's well that end's well, right?'

'No,' Alistair said. 'Because it *hasn't* ended.'

Nick Laude's forehead scrunched. 'Huh?'

112

Alistair sighed. 'It hasn't ended until we've caught whoever was behind the abduction. It hasn't ended until that person has been locked up for a very long time.'

Bob-bob went the park keeper's head. 'Well, I hope you catch 'em, I really do. And of course I'm happy to help any way I can.'

'We appreciate your cooperation,' Juliet said. She looked pointedly at his arm, with its raised spots and scratched furrows. 'That's quite a collection of mosquito bites you've got there. Care to tell me where you got them?'

Nick yanked on his T-shirt sleeve in an unsuccessful attempt to conceal them.

'I don't remember.'

'So not by the north gate then?'

'What, you mean the old tadpole pond?' A desperate-sounding chuckle. 'Course not. I got no reason to go there. No one does.'

Juliet looked him in the eye until his gaze dropped, thinking: *liar.*

Ten

'Would you like something to drink?'

There was a flash of lightning, then a rumble of thunder. A parrot let out a harsh squawk.

Carrie's eyes went from the waiter (Scottish accent, gelled hair and a purple burst of acne) down to the book-like menu in her hands. Would it be appropriate to order a glass of wine with her burger? Or would that be odd, surrounded as they were by children?

'I'll have a still water,' she decided, then looked across the table. 'Sofia? What would you like to drink with your spaghetti?'

'Apple juice!'

'One apple juice.' Carrie snapped the Rainforest Café menu shut and handed it back to the waiter before remembering to add: 'Please.'

'And you, sir?'

Josh did a quick scan of the drinks menu.

'A glass of Merlot, please.'

'Oh,' Carrie said, regretting the water.

Josh shot her a glance as he gave the waiter his menu, then

smiled, holding up two fingers like a peace sign. 'Make that two.'

She experienced a flush of something like gratitude. Her face hadn't changed, but he had still managed to read her, just from that one 'oh'. She formed her mouth into a smile to show that she was pleased. It must have looked OK, because Josh smiled back before turning his attention to Sofia. She was gazing around her with shining eyes. They were seated in a grove of simulated trees and exotic-looking plants. A stream trickled past their table, artificial birds perched on its banks. Further along, a robot gorilla roared, beating its chest.

'So what do you think of this place?' he asked her.

'It's like a magic trip to a real rainforest with real animals.' Sofia clasped her hands together, interlacing her fingers, shaking them forwards and back. 'Thank you for bringing me here!'

He ruffled her hair. 'My pleasure.' Josh's gaze moved to Carrie. 'How about you? Do you think it's a magic trip?' His mouth tugged into that sideways smile she'd seen him use before.

Carrie considered the question. It was certainly a unique experience, dining in an imitation jungle populated by robotic animals, with fake storms at regular intervals. You couldn't really call it 'magic', though, could you? Not if you understood the mechanics behind it.

'It is an excellent simulation, providing an immersive experience of an eco-system most people will never be able to experience first-hand.' She nodded, pleased with her summary. Yes, that captured the positive aspects of the café, conveying her appreciation of having been brought here. She had thought he would agree, perhaps even thank her for this favourable assessment, but instead he burst out laughing.

'You know what, Carrie?' He placed a hand on top of hers, as though they were a couple. 'You really are one of a kind. And to be clear, I mean that in a positive way.'

Carrie felt a strange, buzzing warmth in her cheeks.

'Mummy! Your face is turning pink!'

'Is it?' Carrie placed a hand against her cheek, surprised by the heat there.

'You're *blushing*!' Sofia exclaimed. 'I never saw you do that before in my whole life!'

A peel of thunder filled the pause that followed. The waiter returned with their drinks and Josh withdrew his hand to pick up his glass of wine, raising it in a toast.

'To new experiences.'

'Yes.' And she touched the rim of her glass to his.

Then Sofia's juice cup barged in, banging against their glasses, making Carrie's wine see-saw. Josh's gaze flicked briefly sideways, forehead gathering, as though someone were pulling a string there. He gave her daughter a quick smile. Then his eyes returned to Carrie's, staying there as she put the glass to her lips and took a long sip, tipping back her head.

'Would you like something to drink?'

She held up a bottle of red wine with the label facing outward, so Josh could see what kind it was. Sofia had fallen asleep on the drive home, so he had carried her upstairs to bed.

Carrie had assumed he would leave straight afterwards, but instead he'd asked if she had time for a quick chat about the upcoming issue of his magazine, saying he wanted to 'get her take'. So now, here he was, perched on one of the stools in front of her kitchen counter while she stood behind it, showing him the label of her best bottle of wine.

'Amarone,' he said, smiling. 'Perfect. My favourite.'

'Mine too.' Carrie felt a nip of anxiety as she rummaged a corkscrew from the drawer beside the sink. What if the success of their last conversation had been a fluke, a one-off, never to be replicated? What if, without Sofia's chatter, the flow of words would stop, leaving stagnant pools of silence – the kind in which so many of her attempts at friendship had drowned?

She began unscrewing the cork.

'How important are exteriors, do you think? I mean compared to what's inside?'

His words stopped her mid-twist. What did he mean by that? Was he asking what emphasis she placed on physical attractiveness versus intelligence and personality? She turned, still holding the bottle, assessing his features from across the counter: a square jaw and straight nose, medium-brown eyes framed by rectangular glasses. A good face, though not in a way that was striking or memorable. A better face than hers. She had a slim figure and shapely legs, which counted for something. But her features were pale and undeniably plain. Was that what he wanted to discuss? Whether her looks – or the lack of them – mattered?

'Whose exterior are you talking about?'

'I. M. Pei's. Comparing it to one by OMO.'

Carrie hadn't realised her body had tensed up until she felt it relax. She returned her attention to the half-skewered cork. Resumed twisting.

'You're talking about architecture.' The cork came unstuck with a satisfying pop.

'Of course. What else would I be referring to?'

Carrie took out a pair of wine glasses, placing them on the counter.

'I. M. Pei designed one of my favourite buildings in the world,' she said. 'The Bank of China Tower in Hong Kong.'

He leaned against the counter on his forearms, watching her across it.

'Interesting. Tell me what you love about it.'

Love? Had she used that word? Unlikely. It wasn't a term Carrie tossed around the way other people did, sapping it of power ('I love your dress!' 'Don't you just love this song?'). No. She didn't *love* I. M. Pei's creation. But she did have great admiration for the skyscraper, with its sharp angles and dark, gleaming surfaces, its sleek originality. She poured his wine as she tried to shape her feelings into words. 'I appreciate its asymmetry, and the way it appears folded, almost like a piece of origami.' The Amarone gurgled as she filled her own glass. 'It's striking without being showy or garish. It transformed Hong Kong's skyline, making it instantly recognisable.'

'Precisely! Which is why it's *just* the building I'm using in my example. Contrasted with one of OMO's.

'Which one?'

'Rothschild Bank's London headquarters.'

'I've seen it.' She set down the bottle and came around the counter to join him on the neighbouring stool. 'I was disappointed. A glass box, nothing more.'

'I completely agree.' He took a sip of wine. 'But here's the thing: it's stunning inside. The people who work there couldn't be happier. Conversely, the Bank of China's interior is perfectly serviceable, but nothing to set the world alight. Which brings us to the theme of my next issue: to whom does the architect

118

owe the greater responsibility – those who actually use the building, transforming it into a living, breathing space? Or to the far greater number of people who experience the design from the *outside*, where it can shape the aesthetics of an entire city? Setting aside client demands, which should take priority?' His hand circled the air in front of her. 'Discuss.'

And she did. The hours that followed were a fast-moving debate that struck at the heart of who – or what – architecture was for. Carrie argued passionately about the power and importance of aesthetics while he played devil's advocate, drawing out her views ('But Carrie, aren't you reducing buildings to mere baubles, decorating postcard skylines?' 'No, Josh, this isn't about postcards, it's about the depressive effect that a shabby, unimaginative skyline can have on a city … versus the pride of looking out and seeing something unique, even uplifting'). They talked about striking the right balance between the two, of not getting so carried away with a concept that you forgot the people inside ('Look at London City Hall,' she argued. 'Making it open and transparent may have been clever and symbolic, but assembly members complained that it was *too* open plan for separate political parties to work in').

Carrie hadn't realised how much time had passed until she went to fetch a second bottle of wine and glanced at the clock. 11.30. They had been talking for more than two hours. *She* had been talking. And it hadn't been difficult or stressful or laboured. She had opened her mouth and the words had come. Important words, delivering passionately held opinions.

Josh smiled as she leaned across the counter to refill their glasses and Carrie felt a warmth bordering on affection. It wasn't like her, forming an emotional attachment to a man she'd known only a short time. Then again, this wasn't just *any* man. This was the man who had saved Sofia.

But what was *she* to *him*? The question slipped into her thoughts as she returned to her stool, a little unsteady from the alcohol. Why was Josh here right now? Was it out of some leftover sense of obligation to the child he'd rescued, his desire to see things through? Maybe. But if that was the case, why stick around after Sofia had gone to bed? Was it conceivable that he'd wanted to spend time alone with her because he found her physically attractive? The thought set off a spark of excitement which she quickly snuffed out. No, that was silly. Josh was here because he needed an architect's opinion and she was able to provide it. This was work research. Nothing more.

He lifted his glass towards her.

'Thank you. For sharing your insight.'

'I hope my opinions were helpful. I have strong views on this subject.'

'I like women with strong views.' Then his voice changed, the pitch becoming lower, the words less crisply outlined. 'Women of passion.'

Passion. Her heart beat faster. Passion was usually associated with sex. Was Josh hinting that he wanted to have sex with her? If she had been out at a nightclub in the short black dress she used to wear before Simon and Sofia came along, she would simply have asked. Carrie had always had a very utilitarian approach to sex. Flirting was beyond her, and her dance style wasn't remotely sexy. So she would see who made eye contact, who offered to buy her a drink (she always asked for a shot of whisky: something she could toss back quickly to avoid attempts at small talk shouted against music). And then she would say:

'Would you like to have sex with me?' Some men didn't like her directness and backed away. But at the right kind of club at the right time of night, the most common response was a laugh or a shrug and a 'sure, why not?'

But this was different. The men from the clubs had been strangers, people she had never seen before and was unlikely to see again, brought briefly into her life by an itch she couldn't reach without their help. They certainly weren't there to draw out her opinions or explore her emotional connection to design.

'Carrie.' There seemed to be more breath in his voice as he said her name. His leg brushed hers and she felt something flip in her stomach. 'Carrie, I really enjoy talking to you.' And she had just enough time to think that nobody, in all her thirty-six years, had ever said those words, before he leaned over and kissed her. The contact was soft, gentle – just a brush of the lips, really. Then he stopped and sat back, eyes moving across her face. He placed a light hand on her cheek, the contact setting off a zing of electricity. When he leaned in again, the kiss was deeper, its message clearer. She felt a hunger open up inside her that was different from the simple call for physical release – a yearning that cut right through her, making her feel wild and elated and scared, all at the same time. Josh's hand slid under the hem of her jumper, moving along her spine. The kisses rolled into one another and her thoughts blurred into incoherence. All Carrie's fears and doubts and insecurities fell away, until nothing remained but this moment, this feeling. This man.

She was the one to break the chain of kisses, slipping from her stool and taking him by the hand. Neither of them spoke as she led him upstairs, stopping briefly to check on Sofia (sound asleep) before drawing Josh into her room, where they fell onto the navy duvet, rolling across it, wrapped in each other's arms.

Carrie was lying on her back, deep inside a kiss when he suddenly pulled away, the shock of broken contact registering as pain. She opened her eyes to find his face a few inches above, staring down at her. Why had he stopped? His brows were curved in two directions, like lying down S's. What did that mean? Had he changed his mind, decided he didn't want her after all?

Dismay hit her like a gut-punch. Then he touched the top button of her blouse and said: 'May I?'

She placed a palm against his cheek as relief sluiced through her.

'Yes.'

He kept asking like that, all the way through. Even when she was naked and pressed up against him, her hands urging him to come closer, to come inside. Kept asking until desire was so thick in her throat she could hardly get the words out.

May I?

Yes.

May I?

Yes.

May I?

Yes. Yes. Please.

Eleven

The sound of breaking glass jolted Carrie awake. She sat up in bed, heart jumping. Looked around the night-dark bedroom. The time glowed red on her alarm clock. 02:47. Had she imagined the noise? Was it part of a dream? But then, from downstairs, came another sound – one that sent her heart slamming into overdrive.

Footsteps. Moving around the kitchen. A slow, heavy tread.

There's a man inside the house.

Carrie's mouth went dry. She looked across at the rumpled sheet on the other side of her bed, shaded grey by the moonlight. Josh had been lying there just a few hours earlier. If only she hadn't sent him home. But Sofia had begun waking up just before dawn, complaining of nightmares, seeking refuge in her mother's bed. Carrie didn't want her running in to find a man there – even a man she knew and liked. It would be too confusing.

So now, here she was, alone in the dark, listening to an intruder prowling around her house with fear rising inside her like an icy tide.

It's Sofia's abductor. He's come back to get her.

She groped instinctively along the bedside table for her mobile. Normally she slept with her phone there, using it as a backup alarm. But not tonight. The encounter with Josh had broken her routine and the handset now lay abandoned somewhere downstairs. Panic raced through her, pushing another dose of adrenalin into her veins. She took a deep breath, releasing it slowly. Ordered herself to calm down, think things through rationally. The man moving around her living room could just be a burglar: someone keen to get in and out as quickly as possible, rather than risk getting caught. He would take her mobile, along with the TV and perhaps the small speaker she streamed music through. And then he would go.

He would not come upstairs.

Please, God, don't let him come upstairs.

Then came the sound of crunching glass. He must have stepped on the shards of whichever window he'd broken to get inside. Carrie told herself that, as soon as he left, she would call the police, then the insurance company. There was nothing down there that couldn't be repaired or replaced. It was all going to be fine. Just fine.

A stair creaked. The sound froze her insides, locked her breath in her throat.

The intruder was coming up.

I have to protect Sofia.

Throwing aside the covers, she scanned the darkened room for something to use as a weapon. Her eyes found the bedside lamp: a stem of tapered metal ending in a square, solid base.

It would have to do. Carrie pulled off the shade and yanked the plug from its socket, winding the chord around the stem.

She tiptoed to the bedroom door, brandishing it like a club. A louder creak: the loose floorboard, three stairs from the top.

He was almost here.

Slowly, silently, she eased open the door. Saw the shadowy shape of a man rising from the staircase. She held her breath, lamp at the ready, muscles taut.

But just as she was about to swing, the footsteps stopped. She heard breathing in the pause that followed, superimposed over the drumroll of her own heart.

'Carrie?'

The sound of her name sent conflicting waves of emotion crashing into each other. On one side: relief. Because the voice belonged to someone she knew. And on the other: alarm. Because that 'someone' was Simon.

Simon, breaking into her home in the dead of night.

Simon, who might even now be seeing hordes of enemies surging up the stairs behind him, ready to strike.

What if he had a knife? She tightened her grip on the lamp. If he was armed, she would do everything in her power to stop him. This time, there would be no mistakes.

Then the light sprang on, bashing her eyes, making her squint. He stood in the doorway with his hand on the switch. When he saw her brandishing the lamp, his eyes widened.

'Jesus, Carrie. What are you doing?'

'What am *I* doing? What are *you* doing, sneaking around my house in the middle of the night?'

'I had to come over! You didn't answer my calls or texts. You *never* take this long to get back to me. I couldn't sleep. I kept imagining that something terrible was happening. And knowing that Sofia's abductor is still out there . . .' He pushed his hands

125

up the sides of his face. 'So I came to check that she was OK. That *both* of you are. I called again from the doorstep so the buzzer wouldn't wake her, but you didn't pick up.'

Carrie hesitated, blinking, as she analysed this explanation. It *was* unlike her to become separated from her mobile for such an extended period of time, especially at night. So there was a logical underpinning to his fear. And his voice sounded as it normally did: neither high nor low. No wide grins or twitches, none of the signs of psychosis she'd missed last time. But how could she trust her own judgment after having gotten things so catastrophically wrong?

Years ago, her father had told her that, hiding beneath the surface layers of her disability, lay something deep and true she could rely on.

'You have good instincts,' he'd said, between the swing and thwack of his axe splitting firewood out back; he had been a multi-tasker, her father. Never a moment wasted. Not that he'd had much choice, after cancer took her mother, leaving him with a seven-year-old daughter to raise alone. 'If you don't listen to that inner voice of yours, then you might as well be deaf as well as face-blind.' The axe swooped down, cleaving the wood neatly in two. *Thwack.* 'So stop worrying about what you *aren't* able to *see* and focus on what you *are* able to *feel.*' *Thwack.* 'Because when it matters most, you'll know who to trust. You'll know it in your bones.'

Carrie had believed him back then.

Now she knew better.

She adjusted her grip on the lamp, holding it like a baseball bat.

'You broke in,' she stated.

'No, I didn't, I used the spare key.'

She cursed herself silently for not having thought to retrieve it from its hiding place inside a hollow, plastic stone on the edge of the garden. She should have done that right after Simon's episode. But wait ... if he'd used the key, then why—

'You smashed a window.'

His brows dipped briefly towards the bridge of his nose before reversing, the inner edges rising.

'Ah. You must have heard the wine glass. I bumped into the counter in the dark and it fell off and smashed on the floor. I've never known you to leave dirty dishes out overnight. That made me worry even more.'

Carrie's lids flickered as she fed this into the mix of information already being processed. Last night she had broken patterns of behaviour that had been followed without deviation throughout their entire relationship. In the context of Sofia's disappearance, Simon's concerns did seem reasonable.

But she wasn't taking any chances.

'Do you have a knife with you, Simon?'

He cleared his throat and there was a slight pause before he said: 'No.'

Was that a lie? Was he about to whip out a blade and stab her with it, for reasons even he would later struggle to identify? Her eyes frisked his body, hunting for signs of a weapon, a suspicious bulge in his coat.

His coat.

Simon was wearing the waterproof coat he took with him on boat trips: the one with lots of pockets. Why would he put that on in this weather? The worst of the heat had faded with the sun, but the night was still sultry.

'Take off your coat and put it on the bed.'

His top lip rose, uncovering coffee-stained teeth. 'Excuse me?'

'Put your coat on the bed or I will smash your head with this lamp.'

He laughed then, a strange, hollow sound.

'Carrie will you listen to yourself? You're being ridic—'

She brought the lamp's base down hard against the bedside table, making him jump, praying the sound wouldn't wake Sofia. The last thing she wanted was for her daughter to run in and witness this terrible scene.

'I don't want to hurt you, Simon. But I will.'

He stood staring at her in the long pause that followed. Then he sighed and unzipped the coat, tossing it onto the bed. She crab-stepped sideways, one hand still gripping the lamp. Reached inside the coat pockets: first the four outer ones (a packet of tissues, some chewing gum, a lighter), then the inner ones, starting with the left (cigarettes – when had he started smoking again?). She was reaching for the right-inside pocket when Simon spoke.

'Don't!' His face was pale and his throat worked. 'OK, I admit it. I *did* bring something. In case you were in trouble and I needed to protect you. So ... be careful. I don't want you to cut yourself.'

She looked down at the pocket, then slowly, gingerly, slipped her hand inside. Came up against a wooden handle. Her fingers closed around it. As she pulled it free, the tip of the blade caught on the pocket lining, scarring the fabric. Carrie recognised the knife; it was the one he had used to gut fish during his seafood phase. Different from last time – but just as dangerous.

128

She returned the lamp to the bedside table, brandishing the knife instead.

Simon leaned a shoulder against the doorframe, running fingers through his dark, curly hair. Sofia hair.

'I swear I only brought it in case I needed to protect the two of you. It's not paranoia. It's *not*.' He threw out his palms. 'I'm just a normal parent with legitimate fears.'

Carrie moved closer, the knife held in front of her, chin lifted.

'I'm no expert on normal, but I don't believe it's normal to sneak into your child's home in the dead of night carrying a weapon.' She held out her free hand. 'I'd like my key back now.'

He rummaged in the pocket of his jeans, then handed it across. She tossed it onto the bed. Simon closed his eyes. Exhaled through his mouth.

'Look, I take your point that my behaviour tonight might come across as . . . extreme. But the things that have happened recently *are* extreme. And I hate that I can't be here to protect the two of you.'

Carrie stared at him in disbelief. '*Protect* us?' she repeated, then shook her head. 'No. You are not the person who protects Sofia. You are the person I have to protect Sofia *from*.'

Simon pushed his hands up his cheeks.

'Yeah,' he said quietly, 'I guess I deserve that. And I know the . . . the mistake I made was terrible. But I'm her father, and I love her and, at some point, you're going to have to forgive me and let me try to rebuild the trust I've lost.'

Carrie closed her eyes. All the fear and anger had drained away, leaving her hollow. She suddenly realised that she was tired. Beyond tired: exhausted.

'I want you to go now, Simon.'

'I will, but ... can I just see her first? Please? I won't even step inside her room. It would put my mind at rest to know that she's here and she's OK.'

Carrie hesitated. She didn't like the idea of letting him near Sofia after he'd come into the house this way. Then again, *she* was the one holding the knife. So what harm could it do?

'OK,' she relented. 'You can look at her from the doorway. But you're not to wake her.'

He gave her a smile that wobbled in the middle. 'Thank you.'

Sofia was lying with one arm curved above her head, projected stars scattered across the wall next to her. Penguin Pete had fallen onto the floor beside the bed and Simon watched from the doorway as Carrie tucked the toy back under the duvet.

'Are the police any nearer to an arrest?' he asked.

She stroked her daughter's forehead before turning to face him. He was staring down at the bed, arms crossed, face reshaped by complicated creases.

'The DCI in charge is due to call in the morning with an update. But given that she promised to notify me immediately if there were any major developments, I believe it's safe to conclude they haven't arrested anyone.'

He nodded. The lines in the middle of his forehead looked like letter L's laid end to end.

'I'll feel better when they catch him. It scares me to think that whoever took her is still on the loose.'

'The police have ruled out everyone on both of our lists of

people who know Sofia. So they think the more likely scenario is that she wasn't specifically targeted; she just happened to come within range of whoever did this.'

His gaze stayed on Sofia.

'I think they might be wrong about that.'

Simon's words made something turn in the pit of her stomach. She crossed the room to stand in front of him, eyes battling the darkness beyond the nightlight's reach.

'Why?'

'It's just . . .' He sighed, then made a clicking noise with his tongue. 'The abductor used a penguin.'

'Yes. So?'

'So it's her favourite animal.'

'It's a lot of children's favourite animal.'

'Yes, that's what the police said when I spoke to them about it. And I know it could just be a coincidence. But what if it's not? What if whoever did this wasn't just after *a* child? What if they were after *our* child?'

His face appeared to flicker in the storm of blinks this set off. When lucid, Simon wasn't just reasonable; he was also sharp and insightful. What if he was right about this? What if the abductor had laid a trap specifically tailored to catch Sofia – and Sofia alone?

'Outside of school hours, I am with Sofia every moment of the day. Which means I was able to identify every adult who knows her well enough to be aware of her penguin preference. Are you saying the police were wrong to rule those people out? That they've made a mistake?'

'I don't know exactly *what* I'm saying. Just that the choice of bait . . .' He dragged fingers along his jaw. 'I find it unsettling.

131

Don't you find it unsettling?' Shadows filled his eye sockets, making his face appear skull-like.

She looked back towards the bed, watching the gentle rise and fall of Sofia's chest, drawing comfort from it.

'I'm tired, Simon. You need to leave.'

Carrie kept her eyes locked on her daughter. She heard Simon sigh, then a heavy tread receding down the stairs. The front door closing. Footsteps on the pavement, fading with distance.

She lifted up the unicorn duvet and squeezed into the small bed beside Sofia, careful not to wake her. She lay on her back with her eyes wide open, staring up at the cartoon stars with Simon's question whispering inside her head.

The choice of bait . . . don't you find it unsettling?

And, chasing behind it, her unspoken answer:

Yes, Simon, I do. I find it very unsettling.

Twelve

'Someone nicked my overalls. I swear.'

Nick Laude was sweating. His gaze darted around the interview room, from his half-empty glass of water to the recording equipment beside it, across the surface of the one-way mirror, to the filthy window in its metal cage. Juliet watched his eyes do another quick lap of the room before settling longingly on the door leading out, away from all these questions. The door to freedom.

Well, he wouldn't be getting through it any time soon. Not after what Forensics had turned up.

Alistair leaned towards him across the table.

'I'll be honest with you, Nick,' he said. 'This doesn't look good for you. Because when Sofia told us what had happened, the question we kept asking ourselves was this: how could someone drug a five-year-old girl and carry her out of a busy park without attracting attention?' He shot a glance at Juliet: 'Isn't that right?' He was bringing her in, reminding Nick that this was two against one, that the odds were stacked against him.

She nodded. 'Yes, that was the big question.'

'But then the cart turned up and just like that' – he snapped his fingers – 'we had our answer. A vehicle used to haul sacks of grass and bits of . . .' – he waved a hand in the air as though trying to snatch the right word – 'tree gubbins around is found abandoned by an unused gate connected to a barely-used side street. And as luck would have it, a strand of long, dark, curly hair was discovered in the back of that cart. None of your colleagues have hair like that, do they, Nick?'

Juliet folded her hands against the table, watching the park keeper's face as Alistair forged ahead.

'That hair is being analysed right now, but I think we all know that it came from Sofia. Plus, we've got a partial foot-print from a patch of damp earth near the old pond. Forensics is looking at that too, comparing it to your work boots.' Alistair leaned back, lacing his hands across his stomach. 'Let me map out our theory of what happened. Someone – and we're not saying it's *you* at this point – but *someone* sneaked into the park after it was closed and cut a hole in the play-ground fence the night before the abduction. Someone who knew the location of the playground's two CCTV cameras and was able to avoid them. *Someone* used a stuffed animal soaked in chloroform to lure Sofia Haversen through that hole and into the bushes, where they rendered her uncon-scious, hid her inside one of the canvas sacks from the park's storage hut and then transported her out of the park in the back of an electric cart. But what sort of person could walk around Granger Park carrying a big canvas sack, load it into the back of a park vehicle, and then drive off without drawing attention?'

Nick opened and closed his mouth a few times, like a caught

fish. He grabbed the water glass as though it were a life preserver, taking a gulp.

'Only one sort of person,' Juliet interjected, looking him in the eye. 'A park keeper in uniform.'

Alistair snapped his fingers again, making Nick twitch.

'Exactly! This as yet unnamed park keeper must have done all these things while wearing a pair of Granger Park overalls. So, obviously, we wanted to look at all the overalls for forensic evidence. Traces of Sofia's DNA or chloroform.' He leaned forwards again, narrowing the distance between them. 'Trouble is, there's one set missing. So I have to ask myself—'

'I told you!' Nick exploded. 'Someone nicked 'em! They were gone when I got in on Sunday, so I borrowed someone else's.'

'Nick, Nick, Nick,' Alistair chided, like a benevolent school teacher addressing an unruly pupil. 'Didn't anyone ever teach you that it's rude to interrupt? Don't worry. You'll get your turn to speak soon enough. Now ... where was I?' He snapped his fingers again. 'Oh yeah, that's right. The abductor takes Sofia out through the north gate, transfers her into a car or van parked on the road just outside, and reverses the cart back into the park. He changes out of his overalls – they'd look odd outside the park, plus they're covered with DNA evidence – and gets bitten by nasty mozzies in the process. Then he locks the gate behind him before driving away.'

Juliet picked up the pitcher and refilled Laude's glass, studying his face.

'What do you think of our theory, Nick? Does it make sense?'

'Anyone could get into that hut if they wanted to! There's a spare key hidden under the roof. I use it all the time!

135

Everyone who works at the park knows it's there. So why pick on me?'

'That's a fair question,' Juliet said. She switched her gaze to Alistair, who was still leaning forwards on his elbows, back hunched, staring at Laude like a vulture waiting for its prey to stop struggling. 'Shall I go ahead and answer it?'

'Be my guest.'

Nick began picking at a loose piece of skin on his thumb, avoiding her gaze. She sat back, lacing fingers behind her head as she waited for him to make eye contact, allowing the seconds to stack up, using the silence as leverage. Finally, reluctantly, his gaze flicked up to meet hers. Juliet flashed him a bright smile.

'OK, Nick, let's run through the list of facts that led us to invite you here for this nice, informal chat.' She held up one finger. 'Fact number one: you are the person who signed out the cart in which a hair, believed to be Sofia Haversen's, was found.' She raised another finger, making a peace sign. 'Fact number two: your uniform is the only one that's missing.'

'But I just—'

'Please let me finish. Her ring finger joined the other two. 'Fact three: a forensics team went over all the other uniforms for skin cells or hairs, any sign that the person wearing them had come into contact with Sofia. And they're all clean. Well, not *clean*. Nobody ever seems to wash those things, which is a tad disgusting. But clean in terms of forensic evidence.' She paused while his eyes moved to the three raised fingers, no doubt wanting to see if there was anything more, whether a fourth finger would rise to join them. Juliet waited another beat before lifting her pinky. 'And last but not least, there's your alibi . . .' She let the words trail off, watching his reaction. Nick's eyes fled to the door again, staying there this time. His Adam's apple bobbed. 'I asked about the clippers you would have had to use to cut those pesky brambles. There's only one pair for the whole park, which is a shame. Cutbacks, I'm told. No money to replace the two pairs that broke. Anyway, as luck would have it, someone used that last remaining pair to cut some string two days before Sofia went missing. Not really what they're meant for, but needs must. And according to our very capable forensics team, the traces of string are still there, undisturbed. Which means those clippers haven't been used since that Friday.' There was a long silence. When his eyes finally broke away from the door, he picked up his glass again and stared down into it, as though carefully considering its contents. Juliet leaned forwards, speaking gently. 'So why don't you help us out, Nick. Why don't you help *yourself* out – by telling us what you were *really* doing the day Sofia disappeared?'

His eyes moved up-left as he considered his response. For a few long seconds, the only sound in the room was the accelerated rasp of his breathing.

Then Nick Laude straightened in his chair. He lifted his chin and pushed back his shoulders, arms clamping across his skinny chest. Juliet felt something sink inside her. Because she already knew exactly what his next words would be.

'I want to speak to a lawyer.'

'I'm so pleased to see you!'

Tara stood in the doorway of the industrial kitchen wearing a big smile and a cowl-necked dress with a flair of corduroy at the hem: the sort of dress that would have made Carrie look

137

ridiculous, but on Tara looked chic, as though she might be French.

Carrie peered past her shoulder, expecting to see a dark-haired, blue-eyed boy hiding shyly behind her. But there was no one – just a cavern of metal surfaces and hanging pots. She felt a jab of worry. Wasn't this supposed to be a playdate? Had she misunderstood somehow?

'Come in, come in!' Tara beckoned Carrie and Sofia towards a large table covered with ingredients: flour, eggs, butter, chocolate chips. The kitchen must also have been used by a cookery school, because they passed a poster advertising a pasta-making workshop taught by a visiting Italian chef.

'Where's Peter?' Sofia asked, eyes hunting for the promised playmate. Carrie looked anxiously at the shifting geography of her daughter's face, watching confusion dig a trench between her brows.

There were four stools lined up in front of the table. Tara lifted Sofia onto one of them, crouching slightly so that their eyes were level.

'Sweetie, I'm afraid I have some disappointing news. Peter's father came and took him to his house.'

'Why did he do that when Peter was supposed to be playing with *me*?'

'There was a . . . a miscommunication. I didn't realise his dad was coming today until he was already here, so it was too late.'

'Couldn't you just tell him Peter had a new friend coming over?'

'I'm afraid not. It would have made him very upset.'

Sofia's lower lip was protruding. Uh oh. A pout. Carrie knew from experience that pouts could quickly escalate into tantrums.

138

Then Tara whispered something in Sofia's ear. The effect was immediate; the lip retracted and a smile curved up to take its place.

Carrie stared at her daughter's changed face in amazement, then looked at Tara. 'What did you just say?'

'That to make up for Peter not being here, Sofia and I are going to bake magical-anything cupcakes.'

Sofia greeted this statement with a hyperactive nod. She grabbed Tara's fingers.

'Can we really put anything we want on top?'

'Yes.' Tara looked down at the small hand clutching hers with a smile that Carrie hadn't seen her use before, as though all of her features were melting. 'That's what makes them magical.'

'Anything in the whole world?'

'Sure. We could even make ...' She sucked her lips all the way in and her eyebrows plunged into a deep V. Then her features reversed; her mouth widened and the V inverted. 'Spider cupcakes!'

Sofia burst out laughing. 'Spider cupcakes! Yes, let's make those! Or knickers cupcakes.' She clapped her hands. 'Or both! Knickers on spiders!'

'Knickers on spiders?' Tara pressed a finger against her lower lip. 'Hmm. That might be tricky. Spiders are awfully small and the knickers would have to be a funny shape to fit them, what with all the legs.' She turned and gave Carrie a wink, so Carrie winked back.

Sofia was squealing with laughter now.

'I didn't mean the spiders to be *wearing* the knickers, silly! The spiders can go on *top* of the knickers, like a decoration!'

'Ah, I see. OK, then. We can make cupcakes with spiders

and knickers and ice cream with chocolate sauce.' She leaned closer to Sofia and placed an opened hand, like a wall beside her mouth, angled towards her ear. 'Just because I really like ice cream and chocolate sauce.'

'Me too! I love them!' Sofia clapped again. She was bouncing up and down on the stool now.

'Of course, there would be room for *more* ice cream and chocolate sauce if we skipped the spiders and the knickers. But it's up to you. What do you think?'

'Let's just do the ice cream and chocolate sauce! We can save the spiders and knickers for next time.'

'Deal.' And they slapped their hands together in a high five.

Carrie was blinking fast as she looked at Tara's face. She had learned over the years that not all smiles were good. There were bitter ones and sarcastic ones, sad smiles and grimaces. And, of course, the smile Simon had given her *that day*.

Carrie was pretty sure the melty smile Tara was wearing once again wasn't any of those. But she still wished she knew what it meant.

Carrie had decided against bringing the car, so she and Sofia walked hand in hand to the nearest bus stop: on Conduit Road, opposite a restaurant renowned for its displays of modern art. A statue of a faceless dog stood on the façade, carved muscles taut.

'He hasn't got a nose,' Sofia observed.

'Yes. The artist made him like that on purpose.'

'Why?'

'I don't know.'

They stared at it for a moment longer before Sofia lost interest.

'I like Max the cat,' she said. 'It's too bad he's not allowed to come inside. But I guess Tara's right about people not wanting to find any fur inside their food.'

'He seemed happy enough out back. He probably belongs to one of the shop owners nearby.'

'He did a big purr when I petted him. He's cute. I thought he'd be smaller, though. Tara said he was a kitten.'

'Did she?' Carrie searched her memory. 'I remember her mentioning him at Bundy's, but I'm pretty sure she said he was a cat.'

'Not in Bundy's. Before. At the park.'

They reached the bus stop. The electronic board informed her that the number twenty-two would arrive in three minutes.

'Oh. You mean at Sally's party.'

A white van with tinted windows was moving slowly towards them down the road. Carrie took Sofia's arm, drawing her back from the edge of the pavement. She felt her body stiffen as it drew near. Was it her imagination, or was the van pulling sideways, towards them? Her toes clenched inside her shoes as the vehicle drew level ... and then continued on its way. She released a pent-up breath.

'Mummy? *Mummy!*'

'Sorry. You were telling me about Max. What did Tara say about him?'

'She said Max was a kitten and that he had white socks made of fur on his feet and he liked to chase his own tail.' She giggled. 'But I think he's too big for a kitten.'

'He was probably much smaller when you first spoke to her. Cats grow quickly.'

'I wish I had a cat,' Sofia said. 'I've only got Penguin Pete and I love him a lot but he's not the same as a real, live pet.'

An unwelcome thought crept into the back of Carrie's mind, setting off a prickling sensation. She crouched down in front of Sofia and looked her in the eye.

'Can you tell me exactly what you told Tara in the park that day, about pets and animals?'

Sofia lifted an elbow and began picking at the edge of a plaster there.

'I told her cats were my number two favourite after penguins and she told me about Max.'

'You told her that penguins are your favourite animal?'

'Yes. She said she liked them too. We both think emperor penguins are the best.' Sofia began waving both arms over her head. 'Look, Mummy, the twenty-two is coming!'

Carrie was dimly aware of the bus heaving to a stop beside them.

A coincidence, she told herself firmly. That's all this is. It doesn't mean anything.

'Mummy, come *on*! The bus is waiting for us to get on!'

She became aware of the driver, staring down at them through the open door. Carrie grabbed Sofia's hand and hurried aboard.

'Ow, you're holding too tight!'

'Sorry.' She released her grip and followed her daughter up the steps to the top deck, waiting until they were seated before speaking again.

'So, were there any other adults at the party that you hadn't met before? I mean, besides Tara?'

She shrugged. 'Tara brought the food. It was good, especially the chocolate cake.'

'Did she have a helper with her?'

Another shrug.

'Did you talk to any other grown-ups, aside from the school mums?'

'No. Just Tara.'

'What else did the two of you talk about?'

'Nothing.' Then her face lit. 'Oh! I told her my favouritest joke about the genie and the wish. And she thought it was really funny and guess what she said?'

'What?'

Carrie watched her daughter's smile widen until it hardly seemed there was room for it on her face.

'She said if a genie gave *her* one wish, it would be to have a daughter just like me.'

Thirteen

'It's hers.'

The words pushed a shot of adrenalin through Juliet's blood. She looked instinctively at Alistair, whose desk faced hers, his files spilling across the border where the front edges met. When he saw the expression on her face, he raised his eyebrows: *What's going on?*

She mouthed: *hair is Sofia's,* and he responded with a fist pump.

'And the partial footprint?'

'A match for Nick Laude's boot.'

She experienced that satisfying feeling of facts knitting themselves together to create a net. They now had irrefutable proof that Sofia was in the back of the cart Nick Laude had signed out. That, combined with the missing uniform and the fact that he hadn't been seen in the park during the hour following the abduction, was going to make it very difficult for him to keep playing the wide-eyed innocent.

'How about the lock on the gate? Any prints?'

'Nothing, I'm afraid. It's been wiped clean.'

'That's odd,' Juliet said, half to herself. 'Why would someone careless enough to leave behind a footprint and a cart containing DNA evidence go to the trouble of wiping the lock?' She tilted back in her chair and stared at the false ceiling, with its rows of pock-marked squares. 'It seems ... inconsistent.'

'Maybe he suddenly thought of it on the way out,' the Crime Scene Manger suggested. 'Or maybe it was wiped by a more savvy accomplice.'

Juliet snapped upright. So far, there had been nothing in the evidence to suggest that more than one person was involved. But there had been nothing to prove otherwise either. In theory, one or even two or three people could have been waiting in the vehicle on the other side of the gate. Without CCTV, it was impossible to know.

'Do *you* think more than one person was involved?'

The CSM laughed. 'Nice try. But that's your department. I'm just passing along what the forensic evidence tells me.'

Juliet's hand stayed on the receiver long after she'd put it down. Her eyes went to the crime board, where Laude's picture hung alongside Sofia's, caught in a chain of hand-drawn arrows linking the girl, the hut, the gate.

'So?' Alistair was looking across at her, his face a question mark.

'So ... it looks like we have Laude. The shoe print fits too.'

'But? There's a "but" on your face.' He chuckled. 'Maybe I should rephrase that.'

She gave him a sour look.

'*But* ... what if he wasn't working alone?'

Alistair's eyebrows rose a notch.

'The CSIs found evidence of that?'

145

'No, it was just thrown out as a possibility, but ... well, it's got me thinking. Laude's not exactly the brightest bulb in the box, is he? Someone could have used him for his connection to the park. Paid him to take the girl. It would give us the one thing that's missing from our case against him: motive. Namely, money.'

Alistair propped his chin on a fist, eyes narrowing.

'So you're thinking, what, paedophile ring? Or straight-up kidnapping, with the girl rescued before the ransom demand could be made?'

Juliet weighed the two theories. They were certainly the most obvious motives for a child abduction involving more than one person. And yet ...

'You're frowning.'

'Am I?'

'Yes. We now have more than enough evidence to charge Laude. So if it turns out he *did* have accomplices, we can use what we've got as leverage to make him give them up. You should be smiling, and yet ...' His palm circled the air in front of her face. 'There sits a frown. So I have to ask: what is it about this rich bounty of evidence that displeases you?'

Juliet scrubbed her eyes with her knuckles. He was right, of course. Everything pointed to Laude. It looked as if they had their man ... or, at least, one of them. So why had her satisfaction been so short-lived?

'I promise I'll smile if he confesses.'

'Not if. *When*.'

She rolled her eyes. 'Fine. When.'

'Meanwhile, you should update the mum. Let her know we've got a suspect in custody. That should put a smile on her face.'

As Juliet reached for her phone, she was trying to form a mental image of Sofia's mother smiling. By the time Carrie Haversen's mobile began to ring, she had already given up.

Carrie tossed her phone onto the coffee table and flopped back against the sofa cushions, staring at the ceiling. Sofia was playing under the dining table, voice changing pitch as she spoke on behalf of the stuffed animals encircling her ('Please don't eat me, Mr Bear! I want to be your friend!' 'OK, why don't you come over for tea?').

Relief was sweeping through her in a warm rush, washing away the layers of fear and suspicion that had built up inside her like a dark plaque, choking off her peace of mind.

A suspect is in custody.

The once shadowy figure had been given an ordinary, human shape – had been named and fingerprinted and locked up.

One of the park workers. 'Strong evidence,' DCI Campbell had said. 'Just a few loose ends to tie up.'

So now, at last, Carrie was free. Free to lower her guard and move on with her life, to focus on her daughter and her work.

And Josh, a voice somewhere inside her added.

He'd been sneaking into her thoughts more and more over the last few days, her memory flashing out fragments of their night together as she went about her daily routine: brushing her teeth, making lunch for Sofia, working on the design for the hospital wing.

Josh's hands moving along her body.

His lips on her neck.

His voice, whispering in the dark.

'*May I?*'

Carrie's mobile buzzed against the coffee table. Her heart quickened. Maybe that was him now, calling to ask her out. She'd heard from him twice in the five days since they'd made love, but he hadn't suggested meeting up again. Perhaps this time . . .

But the thought died when she saw the screen; it was showing an unfamiliar landline number. Not Josh, then. Disappointment sank through her.

'Carrie? Are you there?'

The sound of Tara's voice pulled up the memory of their afternoon of cupcakes – and Carrie's attack of suspicion afterward. Shame throbbed inside her. How had she managed to twist an innocent chat about pets into something sinister? And how could she have thought, even for a moment, that Tara might have been involved in the abduction, when she'd been by Carrie's side less than half an hour after Sofia disappeared? It didn't make sense. She had allowed paranoia to gain the upper hand, shunting aside logic. She must never let that happen again.

'Hello, Tara.'

'Hiya. I was just calling on the off chance you're free tomorrow night? Wondering if you fancied going somewhere for a bite and some drinks?'

The invitation gave Carrie a lift of pleasure, which quickly collapsed under the realisation that she would have to say no. She glanced under the table, where Sofia was pressing a tiger and a rabbit against each other in a forced hug. She couldn't leave her alone with a babysitter; it was too soon.

'I'm not able to go out on my own just yet. I need to stay with my daughter.'

'Oh God, of course you do. Sorry, I didn't think. I got overexcited when my mother offered to give me a night off childcare. But obviously you wouldn't want to do anything to unsettle her. Or yourself, for that matter.'

'Yes, that is the situation.' Carrie cast around for a solution, not wanting to let this shiny new friendship slip away. 'You could come over here for dinner. There's red wine. And prosecco.'

Silence from the other end of the phone. Had that been an odd thing to suggest? Was Tara even now deciding that she'd made a mistake, wasting her time on a freak with no social skills?

But then: 'Sure, that sounds great. What time?'

'Sofia goes to bed at seven-thirty, so any time after that.'

'Perfect. See you then.'

'Yes. Goodbye, Tara.'

'Bye-ee.'

Tossing aside her mobile, she jumped up from the sofa, propelled to her feet by a sudden burst of energy.

Her life had turned a corner. The abductor was safely behind bars. She had an affectionate new lover. And maybe, just maybe, a new friend.

'Hey, Mummy, you're doing a real smile!'

Sofia had stuck her head out from under the table, where she was crouching on her hands and knees, watching Carrie's face with a look of delight.

'Am I? Carrie put a hand to her mouth. It was strange, when her features moved on their own like that. But good-strange. Special-strange. 'You're right, Sofia. I am.' And she felt the smile grow beneath her fingertips.

★　　★　　★

149

'What the hell is he doing?'

Juliet peered at the grainy image on the screen in front of her. It had come from a member of the public: mobile-phone footage of a toddler's birthday picnic, shot the day of the abduction. They'd received dozens of video and photo files in the wake of the public appeal, none of them helpful. This one had arrived late, and Juliet's expectations had been low, given that it was shot at the south end of the park, nowhere near the playground or tadpole pond. So she had delegated it to the nearest PC and quickly forgotten about it.

Until this morning.

'Show us again,' Alistair said. They were standing on either side of PC Levine, leaning over his shoulders for a closer look at the computer screen.

'No problem.' The constable's voice was bright with enthusiasm. He was new to the force, and clearly delighted to be presenting his discovery to senior officers. The screen blurred with speed as he scrolled backward, stopping at the tail end of the birthday picnic. Toddlers ran in circles with cake-smeared faces while mums packed dirty paper plates into a bin bag. A little girl raced at the camera trailing a balloon shaped like a number three and stuck out her tongue.

'There he is,' Constable Levine said, somewhat redundantly, given that this was their second viewing.

Nick Laude loped across the stretch of grass behind the party, a shovel propped against his shoulder like a rifle. He stopped when he reached the fringe of trees bordering the grassy area. Looked around. Stood for a while under a large oak, prodding at the earth with the shovel in an obvious attempt to appear busy. A Frisbee soared across the shot, chased by a woman with a dog.

Children wheeled in the foreground. Nobody was paying the slightest attention to the park keeper. Then, from somewhere on the other side of the trees, another man appeared: tall and lean, wearing jeans and a hoodie with a camouflage pattern. He walked up to Nick and they shook hands. Then Camouflage Man removed something from his back pocket and handed it across. Nick took it, nodded once, then turned and walked away with his fist clenched around whatever he'd just received.

'We need to know what's in his hand,' Juliet said. 'Can we zoom in on that?'

'Already done.' Constable Levine minimised the video and clicked on a thumbnail image on his desktop. 'I took a screen shot going in as tight as I could and then used Photoshop to clean it up. I'm sure Tech can do a more professional job, but at least this gives you the idea.'

Juliet reigned in her irritation at not having been given this information from the get-go; this was the PC's big moment and he was clearly determined to milk it. And, to be fair, he'd done a good job; the enlarged image was grainy, but clearer than she would have thought possible, given how tightly he'd zoomed in. It showed the unidentified man's hand, frozen just short of Laude's outstretched fingers. And now they could see what he was holding.

She whistled softly. 'Well, now. *That* changes things.'

'Yep.' Levine crossed his arms behind his head with a cat-who-got-the-cream smile. 'I thought you'd like it.'

Fourteen

'Wow,' Tara said, as Carrie sliced the cherry pie, trying not to let the pastry break apart. 'Not being able to read people's expressions ... that must be tough.'

Carrie turned the knife on its side, levering out a slice as she considered her answer.

Tara was seated sideways, facing her from the neighbouring stool, legs crossed, prosecco glass in hand. She had arrived an hour earlier, sweeping through the door in a sleeveless black dress, carrying homemade pie and trailing a bright stream of chatter. She'd been very understanding about the chicken (Carrie had put the oven on the wrong setting, so dinner was now an hour behind schedule), suggesting they be 'naughty' and eat pudding first.

A blob of cherry fell onto the counter as the pie wedge travelled from dish to plate.

'Yes, my condition does cause problems, especially with clients. The main one is that I can't work out whether they actually like my designs.'

'But ... don't they tell you that in words?'

'Most people are uncomfortable vocalising negative opinions, so they rely on facial expression and other non-verbal cues. My first few client meetings were not successful.' Carrie began cutting herself a slice. 'Fortunately, my boss came up with the idea of translating for me.'

'Translating?' Tara took a sip of prosecco, brows drawing towards each other. 'How?'

'He sits next to me in meetings with a notepad and writes down which emotions are being conveyed, along with advice on what to say or do next.

'And your clients are OK with that?'

'They don't know. Osman – my boss – holds the pad just under the table, so I can see it but they can't.

'Ah. Sneaky. But good-sneaky. Clever.'

'Yes. Unfortunately he's away on a site visit next Thursday, when my biggest client is passing through London and insists that we speak. So I'll have to go it alone.' Coils of tension tightened around her ribcage at the thought of that meeting. She took a slug of prosecco.

'Well, I'm good at reading people. Why don't I stand in for him?'

Carrie put her glass down slowly, absorbing this offer. For a moment, she allowed herself to imagine what the meeting would be like with Tara by her side, lighting her way through the dark maze of social cues.

But only for a moment.

'The client would never allow an outsider to attend. He's very secretive about the design.' She picked up her fork, sinking the edge through the pastry's skin. Red liquid oozed up through the crack.

Tara tapped a knuckle against her lip, forehead wrinkling. Then she took a bite of pie, making a 'hmmm' sound as she chewed.

'Could you arrange to meet him somewhere public?' Her eyebrows lifted unevenly, the left higher than the right. 'A café or restaurant?'

Carrie blinked. It seemed an odd question. How could adding more people – and therefore more potential social interactions – possibly make things better?

'Yes. But why would I wish to do so?' She popped the pie into her mouth. It was surprisingly tart: delicious, but not in the way she'd expected.

Tara's eyes moved left-right-left, as though watching a tennis game. Then she smiled. 'I've got an idea.' She slid down from her stool and began rummaging inside the handbag at her feet, taking out her mobile phone. She tapped at the screen. 'One sec, let me just …' A moment later, Carrie's handset pinged.

She read the new text: 'Unsure, sceptical. Explain your concept more clearly.'

'Is that the sort of message your boss writes?' Tara asked, tossing her phone back into the bag.

'Yes.'

'Great.' She climbed back onto her stool, overbalancing, so that she had to grab the counter to steady herself. 'That's that sorted, then.' She picked up her fork and began digging into the pie again. 'I think being allowed to eat dessert before dinner is one of the best things about being an adult.'

Carrie stared at her, baffled. '*What's* sorted? Can you clarify?'

She waited while Tara, who had just put a forkful of pie in her mouth, finished chewing.

'Sorry, that was a lot clearer in my head. I skipped right over the part about coming to the same café as you and your client. We'll need to choose a place that lets you reserve the exact table you want, so we can make sure we're next to each other. I'll watch his face and send you texts like that one, keeping it short so you don't need to touch the screen to open them.' She finished off her last bite of pie and wiped her palms against each other. 'You'll have to keep your phone on mute, obviously. And put it in your lap so you can pretend to be looking down at your plate when you're reading my messages.'

Carrie was blinking fast as her mind circled this idea, inspecting it from all angles, searching for flaws. And finding none. Hope unfolded itself inside her.

'But ... what about your work?'

Tara lifted a shoulder. 'I don't have much on next week. And if anything does crop up at the last minute, I can arrange for my partner to handle it. That's the joy of co-owning a business.'

Carrie took another bite of pie, chewing slowly as she searched for the right words to convey how touched she was by this act of generosity, to capture the scale of her gratitude. But all she came up with was: 'Thank you. Very much.'

Tara waved a hand in the air.

'It's really no problem. In fact, it'll be fun. I'll pretend I'm a spy.' She put down her fork and ran fingers through her hair. 'So ... How's Sofia getting on?'

'Nothing has changed since you last saw her.'

'Yes, but I mean ... how is she coping with the trauma? Is she having nightmares?' She picked up her prosecco glass, rotating the stem, sending liquid lapping up the curved walls.

'Does she remember anything? Anything that could help the police work out who took her?'

Carrie severed a chunk of pie with the side of her fork as she considered how best to respond. DCI Campbell had asked her not to tell anyone about the suspect until formal charges had been laid; she didn't want the press getting wind of it before they were ready.

But Tara was hardly going to go running off to the tabloids. And besides, Carrie found she really wanted to tell her. Lingering guilt over her baseless suspicions was tainting her relief over the arrest. Perhaps trusting Tara now would help make up for not having trusted her then.

'The police think they know who took her. They have a man in custody.'

Tara's eyebrows shot up.

'Oh my God, I can't believe you haven't told me! That's *huge*! I'm surprised I haven't heard anything on the news.'

'The police aren't releasing the information until he's been charged and they've asked me not to say anything. But I believe I can trust you to keep this news to yourself.'

'Of course you can! So . . . who is he?'

'One of the park keepers.'

'Wow,' Tara said. She drained her glass in one long sip, tipping back her head. Dabbed the corners of her lips with a fingertip. 'Do they know why he did it?'

'They aren't sure about that yet.'

Carrie picked up the bottle to refill Tara's glass and was surprised to find it empty. That was fast. She slid from her stool and went to the fridge to get another one. Tara's voice followed her.

'But they *are* sure they've got the right person?'

'It seems so.' Carrie grabbed another prosecco bottle from the fridge door. Just as well she'd stocked up. 'I'm told the evidence against him is strong.'

She returned to her stool. Foam hissed as she refilled their glasses.

'Well, this definitely calls for a toast.' Tara picked up her drink. 'To happy endings.'

'Yes. Happy endings.'

The rims of their glasses chimed against each other, then they drank in a mirror-image motion. There was a beat of silence while Tara sat watching Carrie's face, swaying slightly on her stool.

'How were you able to get through it?'

'Which part? Waiting for the abductor to be caught?'

'All of it.' Tara waved her drink in the air, sending liquid sloshing over the rim. Drops rained onto the counter. 'Sofia disappearing. Not knowing what to do. The helplessness.' She shut her eyes tight for a moment, making them wrinkle at the edges. 'Helplessness. I think that's the worst part. When my little girl—'

'Girl?' Carrie interrupted, confused. 'But ... I thought Peter was your only child?'

The prosecco glass froze just short of Tara's lips. She sat perfectly still, eyes fixed straight ahead. The kitchen clock measured the silence. Twelve ticks. Then she put down the glass and said: 'Yes, of course. I meant to say "boy", obviously.' She released a high-pitched laugh. 'How funny! It's because we were talking about Sofia, so I was thinking of her.' She slid from the stool

157

and smiled with her lips closed. 'I'm bursting. Do you mind if I use your loo?'

Sofia dreamed she'd discovered a door beside her bookcase leading into a secret room, but when she went through it, the door disappeared and she was trapped inside a big wooden box. She beat against the wall where the door had been, trying to scream, but no sound came out. Then a lady's voice said 'Shhhhhh, Don't be scared.' Maybe the lady knew where the door had gone? She banged against the wall again, but the room was beginning to lose its shape. The wood turned see-through, letting cartoon stars shine through. Then she could feel her bed beneath her and knew that it was just a dream, that she was safe in her room. Relief rose inside her, filling her all the way up. But then the dream-lady's voice spoke again, right near her ear.

'It's OK. I'm here.' A hand touched her forehead. Sofia sucked in air.

Someone was in her room, sitting on her bed!

She yanked herself all the way awake, heart speeding. Then she saw who was there and flopped back against the headboard. Yawned.

'Hi, Tara. What are you doing in here?'

'I was on my way to the toilet when I heard you whimpering. I thought you must be having a bad dream, so I came in to comfort you.'

'I had a nightmare. It was scary.' Sofia tried to remember what it had been about but the dream was already flickering out of reach. 'Are you and Mummy having a good playdate?'

158

Tara laughed softly. 'Yes, we are.'

'I'm glad you're my mummy's friend.'

Sleep was tugging at her now, dragging on her eyelids. But just when they were about to shut, Sofia saw something so surprising that she pushed them back up.

There was a tear on Tara's cheek. The only time Sofia had seen a grown-up cry was when she came back from being in the shed and Mummy did happy tears. But nothing sad or super-happy was happening now.

'Why are you crying? What's wrong?'

The light from the hallway caught the side of Tara's face, making the tear glisten. She wiped it off with her wrist.

'It's nothing, just my hay fever acting up.'

She smiled, but it was one of those wobbly ones that happen when you're trying to smile but there's sad underneath.

Then Sofia heard Mummy's voice calling from downstairs and Tara jumped up and ran out of the room like she'd been caught doing something bad.

Carrie was about to go upstairs – Tara had been gone a long time; maybe all the prosecco had made her ill? – when her guest suddenly reappeared, thudding down the stairs two at a time. She began wheeling across the living room floor as soon as she reached the bottom, throwing her arms out sideways.

'Let's dance!'

'You mean ... here?' Carrie blinked, caught out by the sudden gearshift, the burst of manic energy.

'Sure, why not?' Her head was bobbing, as though moving to a beat only she could hear. Her eyes looked pink, fuelling

Carrie's suspicion that she'd just been sick. 'You *do* have music, don't you?'

'Yes.' She pulled up her music streaming app and chose a list entitled 'Classic Dance Mix', sending the first track through the speakers on her bookshelf. Tara sang along, arms lifted, body swaying. Carrie recognised the song: 'Dark Horse' by Katy Perry.

Carrie turned up the volume until the air throbbed with the beat. She enjoyed dancing. She wasn't very good at it, but she liked the way it drove everything else out of her head, laying down a pattern of sound for her body to follow.

Tara was belting out the lyrics with her head thrown back. Carrie gave herself to the music, socks pivoting against wood, limbs loosened by alcohol. She had never danced like this before, with another woman, and watching Tara gyrate across the floor, she felt something inside her unbuckle, freeing her from self-consciousness, from the fear of doing or saying the wrong thing. She added her voice to Tara's, both of them loud and off-key, singing about dark passions with their hands in the air.

Five songs later, they collapsed, panting, onto the sofa.

'God, I miss dancing,' Tara said, using the hem of her dress to dab sweat from her forehead. 'I must have spent half my waking hours on the dance floor when I lived in Hong Kong.'

Carrie turned down the music.

'I didn't know you'd lived in Asia.'

'Yeah, my dad worked there when I was a teenager. My older sister never left. She's an editor at the *South China Morning Post*.'

'Oh.' Carrie tried to think how to move the conversation forwards. Should she ask more questions about Hong Kong? Or go back to talking about dancing?

'Did you stop going dancing after you left Hong Kong?'

'God, no. I used to hit Soho with my friends pretty much every weekend before I had Peter. Back when I had a social life.'

'But . . . don't your friends have children too now?' Carrie asked, puzzled. The mothers at Sofia's school seemed to socialise endlessly. She would overhear them chatting and planning, organising group picnics and 'mums' nights out'. Carrie had long since given up hope of being asked along. But Tara . . . she would have been invited. She was confident and fun: someone who knew what to say and laughed in all the right places.

'Yeah, most of my friends have kids, but . . .' Tara stopped the sentence before it was finished, head tipping back against the sofa. She stared up at the ceiling. 'Motherhood changes you, doesn't it? You lose things, lose people. You just have to find a way to move on.'

Carrie blinked as she considered this statement, unsure how to respond. She didn't really understand what it meant; she hadn't lost anything by having Sofia. She had only gained.

So she just said: 'I'll go see how the chicken's doing.'

In the kitchen, she peered into the oven (almost done . . . finally), then carried their half-empty prosecco bottle to the sofa. Tara was sitting hunched over with her forehead on her palms. She snapped upright when Carrie joined her, refilling their glasses.

They sipped their drinks without speaking. Carrie knew

that many people were uncomfortable with long silences, but Tara must not have been one of them because she didn't say another word until they were halfway through their next glass.

'Carrie, there's something I need to tell you.'

'OK.'

Tara's face performed a series of manoeuvres: first contracting (forehead bunching, lips tightening) then expanding (brows lifting, mouth opening). She looked down into her glass. Took a deep breath.

Brrrrr-rrrrrr.

Tara's body jolted, as though the door buzzer had administered an electric shock.

'Oh! That's ... are you expecting someone?'

'No.' Carrie rose, glancing towards the clock. Twenty to ten. Who would show up on her doorstep at this hour without calling first?

Brrrrr-brrrrr.

What if it was Simon, carrying a knife and riding a fresh wave of paranoia? The thought hit her like an icy slap, knocking away the warm cocoon of alcohol, sobering her instantly. If Simon was on the other side of that door, she would call the police. And if he tried to smash his way in through a window ...

She glanced towards the block of knives on the kitchen counter.

Well, hopefully it wouldn't come to that.

Squaring her shoulders, Carrie headed towards the door. But she had gone only a few paces when there was another sound: a beeping. She stopped, confused. Had the doorbell changed somehow?

'The oven,' Tara said. Oh. Of course. 'I'll get the chicken,

162

you get the door. And Carrie …' Her fingers fluttered in front of her mouth. 'Check who it is first. Just in case.'

In case *what*? Tara didn't know Simon's history and Sofia's abductor was safely locked away. So who did she think might be out there?

The doorbell buzzed again, longer this time. More insistent.

Fifteen

Juliet slid the screen shot across the interview-room table and tapped the figure in camouflage.

'Who is this man?'

Nick Laude looked at the image and flinched, before quickly recovering.

'Dunno.' He shrugged. 'Some bloke.'

'Some bloke?' Alistair repeated, leaning forwards, propping his forearms on the table next to Juliet. 'Are you saying he's a stranger?'

'Yeah. I get talking to all sorts in the park. You can't expect me to remember everyone.' He turned to the lawyer seated next to him. 'Can she?'

Juliet had crossed paths with Nick Laude's newly appointed lawyer many times over the years. Kevin Smythe: worn out, washed out, middle-aged. A greasy comb-over and an even greasier smile. Sick to the back teeth of working for legal aid. He sighed now, shaking his head.

'No, she can't. That would be unreasonable.'

'Thank you for your professional insight, Mr Smythe,' Juliet said, drawing a sharp look from the solicitor.

Alistair yawned. It sounded real, but Juliet was pretty sure it was forced, designed to convey how very bored he was with all these unimaginative, unconvincing lies.

'Here's the problem, Nick.' Alistair's tone matched his yawn: unimpressed, heard-it-all-before. 'You didn't just *talk* to this man. We also have footage of him handing you something. Which I would think makes him a bit more ... memorable.'

Nick's eyes rebounded off the walls a few times before suddenly lighting up.

Oh goody, Juliet thought sourly, *he's thought of a good lie.*

'Yeah, now I remember.' He nodded vigorously. 'He gave me a fag. I smoke, bad habit, been meaning to quit.' He flashed Alistair a nervous smile. 'But, you know how it is.' He frowned. 'I mean, you'll know if you've ever smoked.' He waited, apparently expecting Alistair to share his tobacco history. The smile dissolved in the silence that followed. 'Anyway, we're not supposed to be seen smoking in the park – promoting a healthy outdoor lifestyle and all that. But I seen this bloke having a fag and asked him for one. So that's what he handed me.'

Alistair glanced sideways at Juliet, their eyes exchanging a silent message: *Got him.*

'So you're saying that the man in this photo was handing you a cigarette,' Alistair said, folding his arms over his stomach. 'Is that correct?' Nick pulled a finger across the sweat-sheened skin above his lip. He nodded. 'Out loud, please. For the recording.'

'Yes, that's right.'

Juliet suppressed a smile of triumph as Alistair slid the file sideways, towards her. Another glance, another unspoken message: *Your turn.*

She flipped open the cover.

'In that case, perhaps you could explain *this* to me.' She reached inside and took out the blown-up image slowly, letting the suspense build before placing it on the table and pushing it across. 'Because, I have to say, that cigarette looks an awful lot like a roll of bank notes.'

Nick Laude's Adam's apple rose and fell.

'Oh.' He chewed on a dirt-rimmed thumbnail. 'Well, that . . . the thing is . . .'

'Yes?' She leaned back in her chair, crossing her legs. 'Please continue. What is *the thing*?'

His gaze squirmed beneath hers. John Smythe whispered something in Nick's ear, his face scribbled with irritation. Juliet suspected most of it was directed at his idiot client. Nick's eyes flickered between Juliet and Alistair.

'I wanna talk to my lawyer.'

Juliet spread her hands. 'Be my guest.'

'I need a moment to speak with my client *privately*.' Smythe gave her one of his oily smiles.

'Fine,' Alistair said. 'I could use a coffee anyway.'

Juliet paused the recording and they left the room. A moment later, the two of them were watching their suspect and his lawyer from the other side of the one-way mirror. Laude was ducking his head and grimacing while Smythe waved the bank-note picture in front of him.

'Now *that*,' Alistair said, aiming a finger at the cringing park keeper, 'is the face of a guilty man.'

'It is,' Juliet agreed, then surprised herself by adding: 'Guilty of *what* though?'

Alistair threw her a startled look.

'What do you mean? We have a theory we both agree on.

Everything fits: the footprint, the mosquito bites, the missing uniform, the cart, the strand of Sofia's hair.' He jerked his chin towards the scene unfolding on the other side of the glass, where Smythe was shaking the photo in front of his client's nose. 'The money.'

He was right, of course. Everything fit perfectly. Nick Laude's reaction to the video stills couldn't have been more satisfying, from an interviewer perspective. It was only as Juliet had stood here, watching through the glass, that doubt had come sneaking in through some hidden trapdoor, whispering that something wasn't right.

The door to the room opened and a constable popped his head in.

'DI Larkin, the guv wants a word.'

'Not right now. I'm in the middle of interviewing our prime suspect.'

'He's aware of that. But something's just come up in the Sanchez trial. The defence is trying to get your search tossed. He needs to talk to you ASAP.' The constable glanced towards the glass, which showed Nick Laude scratching his arm and talking to Smythe, whose face had gone a reddish-purple hue. 'He says DCI Campbell can fly solo from here.'

Alistair stamped a foot against the floor, toddler-style.

'Oh, for fuck's sake.'

There was a knock against the glass. Smythe now stood facing the one-way mirror, trying to make eye contact (guessing their position behind it a couple of feet too far to the left). He rotated his hand in a 'come here' gesture.

'It's fine,' Juliet said. 'You go. I'll finish this off.'

★   ★   ★

Juliet looked across the interview-room table, keeping her gaze carefully neutral.

'So, Nick, is there something you'd like to tell me?'

'Not so fast.' Smythe held up a hand. 'My client can explain everything in that video and is fully prepared to do so.'

'Good, then why don't we—'

'Right after you promise not to prosecute him.'

She blinked in surprise. 'Excuse me?'

'My client is willing to tell you exactly what the money was for, but only if you can guarantee that you won't charge him.'

Juliet looked at Nick Laude, who was hunched over, avoiding her eye.

'So are you asking for an immunity deal, in exchange for his testimony?' Her mood, dragged down by doubt, lifted again. It looked as though Nick *had* played a role in the abduction – and was now prepared to testify against the man who had hired him.

But Smythe shook his head.

'My client's actions were completely unrelated to this case, so his testimony would be of no value to you.'

Juliet watched Laude pick at a chip in the table's surface, flicking away a splinter with a dirty fingernail. Distaste filled her throat.

'OK, tell me what he was doing, then.'

Smythe lifted a manicured hand.

'Before he says anything I'd like a written—'

Juliet rolled her eyes. 'I'm sure we all have better things to do with this day than spend it trapped in a tiny room waiting for the wheels of justice to grind painstakingly through a bunch of pointless paperwork. Pointless because I can tell you right now that I have *zero* interest in pursuing minor offences unrelated to this one. So unless we're talking about a major crime or violent offence, I promise not to charge him. You have my word on that.'

The park keeper gave his lawyer a twitchy look. Smythe let out a sigh of resignation.

'Go ahead. Tell her.'

Juliet sat back and crossed her arms.

'OK, Nick, let's hear it.'

When Carrie looked through the peephole, her stomach did a summersault.

Josh was standing on the doorstep, features stretched by the lens. What was he doing here? Was it possible they'd made plans she'd somehow overlooked? But she quickly discounted the thought. She had read all her emails and texts. There was nothing from Josh about a visit. He had simply ... appeared. She opened the door and stood facing him, heart beating fast.

'Hello there.' He gave her that sideways smile.

'Hello.'

A sultry breeze rode in, carrying the faint smell of BBQ smoke.

'May I come inside?'

'Oh. Yes. Of course.'

Carrie felt a ripple of nerves as she led him into the living room, unsure what you were supposed to do if one guest showed up while another was already there. It wasn't a situation she'd ever expected to encounter; she had so few visitors, the possibility of two of them crossing paths had never even entered her mind.

Tara was in the kitchen, parking the roasting tin of chicken and potatoes on top of the stove, the smell of herbs and freshly cooked meat already filling the house. She smiled at him over her shoulder. Carrie assumed that smile was the just-being-polite kind, since she could see no reason to be happy about the arrival of a complete stranger.

'Tara, this is Josh. Josh, this is Tara.'

Tara put down the tea towel she'd used to take the pan out of the oven and crossed the living area to shake his hand, forehead crinkling above the smile.

'Have we met? You look familiar.'

'You've probably seen my photo in the papers, because of Sofia. And the TV news keeps re-running that clip of me carrying her to the door.'

'No.' The crinkles deepened. 'It's not that. I'm really good with faces and I could swear I've seen you somewhere before.'

'If you have, I'm afraid I don't remember. I've got one of those boring faces people always think they recognise.' He turned to Carrie. 'I'm sorry, I didn't know you had plans. I should have called first.'

'It's fine.' Carrie glanced towards Tara as she said this, hoping it was true, that she didn't mind the interruption. 'There's plenty of chicken. You can eat with us.'

'Oh no, I don't want to intrude . . .'

'You're not intruding,' Tara said. 'The more the merrier. Let me get you a drink.' As she headed towards the kitchen, she slipped on the kilim rug and nearly lost her footing, arms pinwheeling for a moment before she recovered her balance. She giggled. 'As you can see, I'm pretty merry already.'

Josh seemed to stare at Tara for a long time. Carrie looked at her too, trying to see her through his eyes: Tara, with her

170

stylish outfits and tropical eyes, giggling in a way that Carrie never had and never would.

He's probably noticing how pretty she is, a voice inside her head whispered. *Much prettier than you.*

But then Josh's eyes came back to hers and stayed there.

'Thanks for the offer, but I think I'll pass. I know a girls' night when I see one. And anyway, I only really came by to drop this off.' She hadn't noticed the briefcase in his hand until he snapped it open and took something out, handing it across. A magazine. *His* magazine.

'The latest edition of *London Architects' Monthly*, out tomorrow. This one's a bit special for me.'

Carrie stared down at the cover, which showed a wedge-shaped building whose roof sloped upward from the rear, so that the front was a floor higher than the back. Carrie's gaze swept back and forth across the structure, with its clever geometry, trying to work out why she didn't like it more. The design was original and innovative, there was no denying that. But something about it felt ... her eyes travelled along the picture once more, searching for the right word. *Cold.*

Then she registered the caption: 'A Good Year for The Vineyard: Ava Skelter's Iconic House Restored to its Former Glory.'

Carrie blinked as she absorbed the significance of the name.

'This is your mother's house?'

'Yes. Well. Mine now, technically. It's taken three years and cost more than I care to think about, but it's all been worth it. The place now looks almost exactly as it did when she first created it.' He moved closer, looking at the magazine over her shoulder. His body brushed hers and her pulse quickened. 'Wasn't she brilliant?'

Carrie looked at the photo, considering how best to answer. Josh's mother had designed the building and he had expressed pride in it, so he must want to hear a favourable assessment. She sifted through her thoughts and opinions for something positive.

'This is an original, unconventional and technically challenging piece of work.'

That answer must have pleased him, because he smiled.

'I knew someone like you would be able to appreciate it.' He glanced towards Tara. 'Anyway, I only dropped by to give you a copy. There's a whole spread on it inside. It's called 'The Vineyard' because the original structure was built on one: some aristocrat's folly. I lived there until I was seventeen. This was my bedroom.' He touched one of the windows lining the upper floor, above the plate-glass wall fronting the main level. 'I'd love to bring you there some time, if you don't mind roughing it. There's no water or electricity yet. Lots of kerosene lamps, though, which create a certain' – he touched the small of her back – 'ambiance.'

Carrie's stomach flipped as her imagination sent up images of the two of them having sex in flickering lamplight.

'Yes,' she said, feeling shy and excited. 'I would like to go there with you.'

'Good.' He cleared his throat. 'Anyway, I'll head off and leave you two ladies to your ... evening.' He nodded towards Tara, who had begun setting the table, laying out placemats. 'Lovely to meet you, Tara.'

'Likewise.'

He gave Carrie a firm kiss on the mouth before leaving, the door banging shut behind him. She stood beside the sofa holding the magazine, feeling the imprint of his kiss on her lips, thoughts tumbling.

'Well, well, well.' Tara ambled out of the kitchen with her hands full of cutlery. 'So *that's* the famous Josh.' She began placing knives and forks onto placemats.

'Yes, that's Josh.'

Carrie crossed to the kitchen, putting the magazine on the counter before selecting a carving knife and setting to work on the chicken.

'And *this* is his magazine.' Tara went over to the counter, leaning against it. She began flipping through the copy of *London Architects' Monthly*.

'Yes.'

Slices of chicken folded sideways as Carrie cut. On the edge of her vision, she could see magazine pages fanning past. When they suddenly stopped, curiosity got the better of her. Putting down the knife, she went to peer over Tara's shoulder. The magazine was open to a double-page spread of a huge living space, its floor-to-ceiling windows looking out over a stretch of grass bordered by woods. The room's back wall was made of oak, interrupted by an archway at one end and a small, ancient-looking door at the other. In the middle was a fireplace framed by slate.

Carrie inspected the room's contents with interest. The furniture reminded her of the house itself – clever but unwelcoming: chairs fashioned from leather straps bound to metal skeletons. White lacquered shelves and boxy end-tables made of glass, like giant ice cubes. A steel-framed dining table. The only homey touch was a wooden screen that divided the living and dining areas. It looked as if it might have come from India: three hinged

173

panels with a fringe of latticework along the top. It stood in the foreground in a wide 'Z', contrasting sharply with the cool, Nordic styles surrounding it.

'So this is his mother's house in' – Tara squinted at the text – '"an isolated corner of south-east Surrey".' She flipped to the next page. 'Ah, there's a map. Hmm. Magazines don't usually include those, because of security. But it's his place, so I guess it's his decision.' *Flip-flip.* 'And check it out: before and after blueprints going all the way back to its vineyard days.' When she reached the end, she put down the magazine and sat on one of the stools in front of the counter, picking up her drink. Carrie resumed carving the chicken. 'Josh must be really proud of her work, to give it so much space in his magazine.'

'Yes.'

'Quite a coincidence, that you're an architect and he runs an architecture magazine.'

'Yes,' Carrie said again, then realised it was her second one-word answer in a row, so thought she'd better expand it. 'The coincidence is a good one, since it gives us a shared interest to discuss.' She forked chicken slices onto their plates, adding potatoes and the tomato salad from the fridge.

Tara picked up the now empty prosecco bottle on the counter, holding it aloft.

'Another dead soldier.'

'There's one more. Shall I open it?'

'Abso-fucking-lutely.'

It was only as Carrie began twisting the cork out of the bottle's throat that she suddenly remembered something.

'What was it you needed to tell me?'

'Sorry?'

The cork popped free, sending foam surging upward. She held it over the sink to keep it from spilling.

'Just before Josh arrived, you said you had something to tell me.'

'Oh. Did I? I don't remember. I guess it couldn't have been very important.' Tara did a two-syllable laugh, then held out her glass for a refill. 'Tell you what, why don't we drink a toast to something that *is* important? *Crucially* important, in fact.'

'OK.' She placed the plates of food on the counter then settled onto the stool next to Tara's. 'What?'

'Our friendship.'

Our friendship. Carrie held the words tight, feeling shy and tipsy and elated, all at the same time.

'Yes,' she said. 'To . . . our friendship.'

And she raised her glass. Inside it, prosecco bubbles were racing up from the depths, popping across the surface like tiny fireworks.

Sixteen

'Fuck,' Alistair said, dragging a hand along his jaw. 'What kind of drugs?'

'Weed. Ecstasy. A bit of coke. Not huge amounts, just small orders for the rich kids in the neighbourhood. The park is a handy pick-up point, given its lack of CCTV.'

The two of them were seated at the only window table of Ella's Place, a traditional English café whose staunchly unimaginative menu centred around sandwiches and baked potatoes. It was almost closing time, and their only companions were three workers in paint-spattered overalls eating sausage rolls and crisps at the back. Juliet had chosen Ella's for their 'debrief' because of its late hours and handy location, directly across from the police station. Alistair had been tied up with the Sanchez case all evening, so was only now finding out what had happened in the interview room after he'd left. The scale of the setback.

'But what about the cart with Sofia's hair in it? The secret trip to a closed-off area of the park?'

Juliet gazed out of the window for a moment, at the night-dark clouds slung low in the sky, heavy with unshed rain. She took a sip of coffee (black, five sugars), which was predictably terrible. Ella's coffee always tasted terrible, but for some reason she kept ordering it.

'Laude leaves the cart parked by the hut with the keys in it every Sunday at around the same time before heading to the tadpole pond to pick up the drugs. He has a casual sexual relationship with the woman who brings them. They smoke a spliff together and fool around by the old pond. Hence the footprint. Hence the mosquito bites. Then he heads off to the picnic area on the south side to rendezvous with clients, pausing very occasionally to do bits of his actual job.'

Alistair rubbed his eyes with his knuckles. He suddenly looked paler, making his freckles stand out.

'So, if this checks out . . . Laude's just an unwitting pawn. The abductor knew his routine: when and where the cart would be left and how long Nick would be out of the way.'

'Not to mention where the spare key to the hut was hidden, which uniform to steal, and where the canvas sacks and gate keys were kept.' Juliet tipped her head towards her left shoulder, then her right, trying to release some of the tension that had lodged itself in her neck. 'Whoever took Sofia did their homework.'

Alistair puffed out a sigh. 'Shit.'

'Yes. Shit indeed.'

The clouds suddenly broke apart, releasing their burden. Slashes of rain cut across the glass. A man in a suit ran by, holding a soggy newspaper over his head like a shield.

'So not only have we got the wrong person, but it would appear that the *right* person is a more organised and sophisticated criminal than we'd thought.'

'Yep, that about sums it up.' Juliet said. And she took another sip of coffee, wincing at the bitter taste.

The policewoman's call arrived like a storm out of a clear blue sky, stealing the sun, draining colour from the world. Striking when Carrie's guard was at its lowest, when she was actually *happy*.

She had spent the morning working in her study, putting the finishing touches to her design for the new hospital wing while Sofia played on the floor just behind her. Apparently the stuffed animals were having a party and deciding what food to serve. From the sounds of it, the feast would be comprised of cake, chocolate drops and Haribo. Tonight Josh was coming round with a takeaway dinner for the three of them and tomorrow Tara was dropping by for coffee.

For the first time since her break-up with Simon, Carrie felt like she belonged.

Then the phone rang.

'It's not him,' Carrie echoed, after DCI Campbell broke the news. 'Whoever took her is still free.' She felt like she'd been punched in the stomach.

'I know this is disappointing. But you can rest assured that we are on the case and determined to catch the person responsible. Meanwhile, I would advise you to take extra security precautions.'

'Why would you say that?' She looked instinctively towards Sofia, lying on her stomach on the floor just behind her, arranging the animals in a circle. Carrie cupped her hand over the receiver, lowering her voice. 'You told me you'd already ruled out everyone who knows her, making it appear unlikely that this was a targeted abduction. Are you now saying that's not the case?'

A pause. DCI Campbell cleared her throat.

'New developments have led us to reassess that theory. The abduction appears to have been more carefully planned than previously believed. Someone put a lot of thought into how and when to carry it out. So, by extension, it's possible that they also put a lot of thought into which child to take.'

Carrie could feel clammy fingers of dread squeezing at her insides as she watched her daughter bounce a pair of stuffed rabbits up and down.

'Why choose Sofia?'

'That's what we need to work out. So I'm going to ask you once again, and please think very carefully before you answer: can you recall *anyone* showing a special interest in your daughter during the weeks leading up to the abduction?'

Carrie was about to say no when a voice echoed through her memory.

We're old friends, you and me, aren't we Sofia?

Should she mention the chance encounter with Tara at the birthday picnic – if only for the sake of full disclosure? The police probably wouldn't even bother looking into her, given that she'd been in the park, leading the search so soon after the abduction.

Unless ... what if they *had* to investigate everyone whose name Carrie provided – wasting precious time on a wild goose chase?

And how was Tara going to feel when she found out that Carrie had given her name to the police, had reported her for … for *what*? Chatting with Sofia and rescuing her balloon?

No. It felt wrong. They were friends. Friends were supposed to trust each other.

'There's no one,' she said. And gave her wrist a firm pinch.

Josh paced back and forth across the kilim rug, his restless energy ratcheting up Carrie's tension levels. She wished he would sit down, join her for coffee at the table. He had been halfway to work when he'd heard about the park keeper's release on Radio 4, calling her straight away to say he was coming over.

'Maybe you should stay at a hotel for a while, until whoever did this is caught. Or you're more than welcome to stay at my place. It'd be bit of a tight squeeze, but at least you'd be safe.'

'Thank you, but that's not necessary,' Carrie said. She'd spent a long time thinking after the DCI's call. And had reached a decision: it was time to accept the possibility that Sofia's abductor might never be caught. Accept it – and find a way to live with it. Because if she didn't, fear and paranoia would become the forces that shaped her child's life. Sofia would grow up never knowing a moment's freedom, under the constant surveillance of a mother who jumped at shadows. Carrie was determined not to let that happen. So she was going to take all reasonable precautions – and then force herself to move on. 'I'm having a complete security system installed. Cameras. Keypad. Everything. And I'm getting the kitchen window fixed.'

Josh finally came to a halt behind the neighbouring chair, but remained standing, fingers gripping its curved back.

He glanced towards the kitchen. 'Why?'

'It doesn't lock properly. The latch is broken.'

He blew out a puff of air, eyebrows plunging towards the bridge of his nose.

'OK. Well . . . it's better than nothing, I guess. When are they coming?'

'Thursday.'

'Thursday. If you don't want to stay at a hotel or my place, why don't I crash in your spare room until then, as an added precaution? I can be your one-man security company – at least until the real one shows up.' He looked towards Sofia, who was sitting on the sofa with her arms around her knees watching cartoons (*Octonauts*, Carrie noted absently. The episode with the narwhal).

The coffee had finished brewing, so she pushed down on the plunger as she tried to formulate a response. It was very kind of Josh, volunteering to stay and protect them. And she could understand his concern. She'd had a similar reaction when DCI Campbell had first told her the news. But now that she'd had a chance to think, she was determined to stand her ground – to remain calm and rational.

'It's been more than two weeks since the abduction. If someone really was determined to take Sofia, wouldn't they have made a move by now?'

He shook his head, fingers tight against the chair-back.

'Not necessarily. We don't know how this person's mind works. Isn't it better to be safe than sorry?'

'A high-tech security system will be installed on Thursday. Unless something happens to show we're in imminent danger, that will have to do. Because I'm not going to let this one bad experience define the rest of our lives.' She poured coffee into cups. 'Would you like some cherry pie?'

But Josh didn't respond. He was staring straight ahead, lips pressed tight, forehead folded into deep creases. His fingers drummed the chair-back, the sound overlaying the simulated call of the narwhal.

'Josh? Did you hear me?'

He blinked and looked at her.

'Yes, I heard. You and Sofia are staying here alone unless something happens to prove you're still in danger. Correct?'

'Correct.'

He shook his head. 'To me that seems a very risky strategy. But it's your decision, at the end of the day, so there's not really anything more to say. And yes'– the creases smoothed out as he finally pulled back the chair and sat down – 'coffee with pie sounds fantastic.'

Carrie lifted the corners of her mouth as she placed a mug in front of him, to show that she appreciated how concerned he was for their safety, despite having known them only a short time. But then, it had been a very intense couple of weeks; so much had happened.

Her smile must have looked OK, because he gave her one in return.

'This looks delicious.' He transferred a slice of the leftover pie onto his plate and dug in, raising a forkful towards his mouth. 'Did you make it yourself?'

'No. Tara made it.'

'Oh.' The fork returned to the plate, still carrying the chunk of pastry.

Carrie served herself a slice. 'It's very good.'

He took off his glasses and began polishing them with the tail of his shirt.

'How long have you known Tara?'

'I met her the day Sofia went missing. She helped me.'

'Really? *How* exactly?'

'She organised a search of the park. Then she called the police.'

'Hmm. And how long did this search take, from start to finish?'

Carrie took a bite of pie, wondering where Josh was going with this.

'The search itself lasted half an hour. Some mothers were around and she asked them to help, got everyone organised and sent them to different parts of the park. She was a . . . a . . .' – she paused, hunting the right words – 'a good Samaritan.'

'Right.' He seemed to be taking a long time to wipe the lenses. How dirty could they be? 'So, all told, Tara's actions probably delayed calling the police by almost an hour, factoring in the time spent giving instructions and dispatching mums all over the park. Well. Not quite *all* over, since I gather no one was sent to the part Sofia was actually taken out through?'

'She was the one who *made* the call to the police,' Carrie said, wondering why he was focusing on the things Tara *hadn't* done, rather than the things she had. 'And the area Sofia went out through is unused and fenced off, so she probably didn't know it existed.'

'Right.' He finally put his glasses back on. 'And then, lo and behold, you just happen to bump into each other at the indoor play place.'

'Bundy's. Yes. Tara was there with her son.'

'And you don't find this chance encounter a little' – he picked up his mug – 'odd?'

'No. Why would I?'

'It just seems like a remarkable coincidence.' He took a sip of coffee, leaving the pie untouched.

'I disagree. It was too hot for the park and Bundy's is the nearest indoor play centre. I don't find it surprising that we would both decide to take our children there.'

He held up an open hand. 'OK, never mind, I take it all back.' There was a pause while he sat back in his chair, drinking coffee. 'So what's Tara's son like? Do he and Sofia get on?'

'They haven't met.'

He lifted an eyebrow (the left one). 'I don't understand. You were all at the inside play place together. How could they not have met?'

Carrie took another bite of pie. It didn't taste as good as she remembered.

'Tara's son was already inside the play structure and we left before he emerged.'

'So she didn't call to him, ask that he come out so the two children could meet?'

'No.'

Josh's jaw shifted sideways, so that his teeth didn't line up. 'You *have* actually seen him, though? In the park, the day Sofia disappeared?'

'No. She dropped him off with his father right before we met.'

'And you haven't had any playdates together?'

'No. We . . . that hasn't worked out yet.' She put down her fork, no longer hungry. For reasons she couldn't define, Josh's questions were making her uneasy. 'We will soon, though. I'll call her today and set one up.'

He sipped his coffee. 'Good idea. Let me know how that goes.'

His lips pulled sideways as he said this and she wondered what that meant.

'Carrie! Hello! How are you?'

'I'm well. I'm calling to arrange a playdate with Peter.'

She stood at the kitchen window, looking out at the back garden with the mobile pressed tight against her ear. The hose-pipe ban had taken its toll, crisping the grass to a dull brown.

'A playdate,' Tara repeated, dragging out the word. 'Right. When were you thinking?'

'This afternoon. Here. I could make an early supper.'

'Oh. That's ... very soon. Let me just take a quick look at my schedule. One sec ...'

Carrie transferred the phone to her other ear, pouring herself some tap water in the pause that followed, the liquid hissing against the glass.

'Mummy.'

She glanced over her shoulder at Sofia, who was lying on the floor beside the book shelf.

'Yes, my love?'

'Have you seen my Playmobil Stephanie?'

'I think she's in the farmhouse.'

Sofia peered inside the plastic structure, part of a miniature village that had sprouted up on the living room rug.

'Oh, there she is!'

185

A rustling sound came through the phone, then Tara said: 'Looks like this afternoon is clear. So I guess it's a date.' Her voice sounded different, rising to a high note with a slight wobble. 'What time?'

'Four-thirty,' Carrie said, feeling pleased and oddly relieved. 'I'll be done work by then.'

'OK. But I should probably warn you . . .' Her voice trailed off.

'Yes? Warn me about what?'

'Actually, never mind. I'll tell you when I see you.'

Seventeen

'Let's go back to the beginning.'

The aircon in the briefing room must have broken again, because the heat was making Juliet sweat. Her eyes moved over the faces of the seven officers slouched behind the desks in front of her. Defeat hung in the air like a noxious gas. Losing their prime suspect – let's face it, their *only* suspect – had brought scathing headlines and a bollocking from the guv, strafing morale. She needed to use this briefing to get everyone re-engaged, start the creative juices flowing again.

'So.' She turned towards the whiteboard. She had taken down all the maps and photos, stacking them on the desk beside her, wiping the board clean so they could come at the case fresh. Only the photo of Sofia remained, Blu-tacked to the middle. 'Let's review what we've learned from our investigation so far.'

'That one of south London's prettiest parks is a front for drug dealing.' DS Hiranand piped up from a desk near the back, drawing a couple of sniggers.

She looked at Alistair, who was tipped back in his chair with his heels parked on a desk at the front.

'DI Larkin, why don't you talk us through the evidence from the park?' She dabbed her damp forehead with a sleeve. 'What do we know?'

Alistair swung his feet onto the floor, the front legs of his chair thumping back onto the carpet.

'We know that someone cut through a section of fence between the playground and the children's woods the night before the abduction, using bog-standard metal cutters that you can buy at B&Q. We know that whoever took Sofia Haversen gained access to the park keepers' hut, probably using the hidden spare key, put on one of the uniforms stored there and took the key that opens the north gate leading out of the park. And that they used a park vehicle to transport Sofia through that gate, leaving a strand of her hair in the back.'

'Exactly.' She put the photo of the cut fence, the hut and the cart back on the board and picked up the marker pen. 'We no longer believe that the "someone" was this man.' She stuck Nick Laude's photo above the cart and scrawled his name beneath, adding 'park keeper/drug dealer' in brackets. 'But whoever did this must have been watching Laude long enough to know his routine.'

She could hear a trapped fly buzzing against the window in the silence that followed. She scanned the room; a couple of the officers were nodding, which was a start.

'OK,' she said. 'Let's go back over the sequence of events. The cut in the fence was discovered by park staff the morning of the abduction. There's nothing from the CCTV of the streets around the park, so the abductor probably climbed over the north gate to gain entry, then cut the fence in the blind spot between the playground's two CCTV cameras. Sofia was lured through the gap and into the bushes – specifically a large bush with a dense wall of leaves around the outside but enough hollow space inside for the attacker to render her unconscious without being seen.'

She placed the photo of the stuffed penguin on the board.

'This was the bait, soaked in chloroform.' Her gaze travelled around the room, pausing briefly on each face. 'I hope I don't need to remind you that we are withholding the information about the use of toys from the public, so there is to be no mention of that detail to anyone outside of this investigation.' She turned back to the board. 'We are still trying to trace the chloroform. No luck so far. Most likely it was bought online, possibly through the dark web.' She considered the penguin photo for a moment longer before turning to face her team again. 'DI Larkin. Talk us through what happened next.'

Alistair cleared his throat. 'Then he ... '

'Or she!' DS Dutoit called out from her seat beside the window, looking annoyed, as though women were being unfairly denied equal opportunities in child abduction.

'Right,' Alistair continued. 'He *or she* hid Sofia inside one of the canvas sacks commonly used around the park, probably throwing his' – a glance towards Dutoit – '*or her* street clothes into the bag too. Sofia is then loaded onto the cart Nick Laude left beside the hut with the keys in the ignition.'

Juliet's marker began racing across the board, adding arrows and scribbling notes, filling the white spaces with scraps of information.

This isn't so bad, she told herself. *It's not as though we're back at square one. There's a lot of information here.*

They already had the what, when, where and how. They

just needed to fill the giant, who-shaped hole in the middle of their case.

Alistair continued: 'Sofia is transported to the north gate, not far from the place where our perp knows Nick will be safely out of sight by the pond with his drug-supplier-cum-girlfriend.' Juliet stuck up photos of the gate, with its closed lock. 'He or she opens the padlock with the key taken from the hut and drives Sofia out.' She added the close-up of the mud tracks on the road.

Juliet pointed to the blank space in front of the doubled-up tyre tracks. 'The perp transfers her into a vehicle parked here.' Her fingers shifted to the tracks themselves. 'We can see by the second, identical tracks superimposed over the first that the abductor reversed back through the gate and abandoned the cart, leaving no identifying prints or DNA, either in the cart or on the padlock. Ditto the gate keeper's hut.'

There was a pause. They were all looking at the board now, examining the photos and notes, searching for new links between them.

Hiranand spoke up again.

'The park keepers often wear gardening gloves. The abductor might have used a pair of those.'

'Yes, good point.' Juliet gave him an encouraging nod.

'You say the vehicle beyond the gate was "parked",' a young PC near the back said. 'How do we know someone else wasn't waiting in the driver's seat with the engine running? Could we be talking about a two- or even three-person job?'

Juliet nodded. 'We certainly can't rule that out.' She could feel the room warming up, motivation seeping back in, like circulation returning to a blood-starved limb. She snapped the lid back on the marker. 'OK. Where are we on witness appeals?'

'*Crime Stoppers* is running our re-enactment tomorrow night,' said David Gray, a pale-haired, square-jawed DS near the front. 'And we have our three-week "anniversary" witness appeal on Sunday. In light of what's happened, should we change our approach there? Because we're looking for *two* things now. Whoever did this must have spent a lot of time hanging around the park, learning Nick Laude's routine. So we need to ask if anyone suspicious was seen hanging around the park keepers' hut in the run up to the abduction. Plus our usual question: whether anyone remembers spotting someone in a park keeper's uniform in the woods shortly after Sofia disappeared. We haven't had any joy on that the previous two Sundays. But maybe this time we'll get lucky.'

Juliet was about to respond when a gruff voice spoke from the back.

'No, we won't.' Martin Greer: salt-and-pepper hair, bushy eyebrows and a nose that had been broken at some point and healed badly. A seen-it-all attitude badly paired with a lacklustre service record. He was surveying Juliet over folded arms. 'No one will remember seeing a park keeper.'

'What makes you say that?'

'Twenty-eight years' experience.' He nodded agreement with his own words. 'Because when you've been a cop for as long as I have, you learn a few things.' Juliet gritted her teeth as she schooled her features into a neutral expression. 'And one of those things is this: there's something about a work uniform that makes people invisible. Part of the scenery. Which is why it was dead clever of our man to use one.'

191

Juliet glanced towards Dutoit, but the DS didn't react; either she hadn't caught the gender reference or didn't fancy crossing swords with Greer.

'Still,' Hiranand sounded defensive. 'I think it's worth a try.'

'Definitely worth a try,' Juliet said firmly. She waited to see whether anyone else spoke before continuing. 'OK, we also need to take a closer look at our victim. Sofia Haversen's father was keen to emphasise that penguins are her favourite animal, so a stuffed penguin would be the perfect choice of bait. If this *was* a targeted abduction, then our jobs get a lot easier. Because the offender would have to be someone who knew Sofia and her routine, which dramatically reduces the pool of potential suspects.' She turned towards the stack of photos that contained all the other people associated with the case: a depressingly short stack. Carrie's picture lay on the top. Juliet blue-tacked it above and to the left of Sofia.

'This is the victim's mother.' The pale face stared out at the briefing room with its trademark blank expression. Juliet stared back, trying to think how best to sum her up. 'Carrie Haversen is a very socially isolated woman. No friends, which is sad for her but good for us, in that it limits the number of adults who came in contact with her daughter. We have already interviewed all the parents and teachers from Sofia's school who had any sort of relationship with the girl. No former sex offenders, criminal histories or red flags of any kind. Her colleagues have been ruled out for the simple reason that none of them have ever seen or met Sofia.'

She stuck Simon's picture next to Carrie's. 'Simon Ryder: Sofia's father. He suffers from psychotic episodes and has form – he once held his daughter prisoner in a closet while she was in his

192

care.' She jotted 'history of mental illness/locked up Sofia' beneath the image. 'However, he was more than a hundred kilometres away at the time she was taken. Up until now, we haven't been looking at him very closely, since he's been ruled out as a suspect and hasn't lived with Sofia and her mother for more than two years.'

'We should check his known associates,' Martin Greer said. 'Maybe Ryder introduced the girl to some nut job friend from the loony bin who took a shine to her.'

'That is a possibility.' She pointed the tip of her marker pen back and forth between Greer and Rob Potter, a morose PC with sallow skin and sharp features. 'Why don't the two of you take charge of that? But can we please be sensitive about the language we use to describe people who suffer from mental illness?'

Greer nodded, before turning and muttering to his neighbour. The words 'bloody political correctness' were pitched just loud enough to be audible. *Dick*.

Juliet picked up the last photo and stuck it on the board, pausing to consider the blandly handsome face.

'This is Josh Skelter, the man who found Sofia and brought her home. We've established that he didn't have his mobile with him at the time. But I still find it odd that he didn't borrow someone else's to call the police – or Carrie, for that matter, since Sofia knows her number by heart – instead of just showing up on the doorstep.'

'Yeah, that *is* a bit strange,' PC Potter said. 'Are we sure about his alibi?'

She shot a side-glance at the picture, thinking back to that first interview: Skelter, with his frustratingly unreadable face.

'It checks out. His secretary swears blind he was in his third-floor office, hard at work, when Sofia was taken. The security footage from both the building's lobby and the street outside backs that up; there's no sign of him.'

DS Dutoit again: 'So who does that leave us with?'

'Right now, nobody.' Her eyes hopped along the row of photos – Carrie, Simon, Josh, Nick – spaced across the board like stepping stones leading nowhere. 'Which tells us that there's someone missing from this board. I'm going to re-interview Sofia's mother. Because if that girl *was* targeted, there's a person somewhere in their lives who's been overlooked. Someone who could still pose a danger to them.'

'I'm really sorry,' Tara said. 'Peter's a bit under the weather.'

'Oh.' Carrie was standing in front of the stove, mobile held against her ear, absently stirring the simmering pan of bolognese sauce that was even now filling the house with the aroma of meat, peppers and onions.

'I'm really sorry,' Tara repeated. 'I hope we can make it another time soon.'

'Perhaps Sofia and I could come to you? Drop off the food, say a quick hello to him and ...'

'I'm afraid he might be contagious,' Tara interrupted. 'I wouldn't want Sofia to get what he's got. Liquid coming out both ends. It's pretty grim.'

'Oh. When you said he was "a bit under the weather", I thought ...'

'I was just trying to spare you the gory details. It's actually pretty bad, so ...' Her voice trailed into silence. Was she waiting for Carrie to say something? Because there was really nothing further to add. Peter wasn't coming. That was that.

'OK,' Carrie said eventually. 'Goodbye.'

She turned off the stove and sat down at the dining table, resting her chin on a palm, disappointment squeezing her chest.

'Mummy?' She turned to find Sofia standing beside her, face pursed with concern.

'Yes, my love?'

'Was that Tara?'

'Yes.'

'She's not bringing Peter over, is she?'

'No. He's sick.'

'She's never going to bring him.'

The words set off a volley of blinks. Why would Sofia say that? Did she know something Carrie didn't?

'What do you mean?' She took hold of her daughter's small hand, noticing the frayed fingernails (she'd been chewing them since the abduction). 'Did Tara tell you something?'

A small shrug. 'No. But she goes weird when she talks about him.'

'Does she? In what way?'

'Can we eat the spaghetti now? It smells yum.'

'But what made you say—' She stopped the question with a sharp shake of her head. What was she doing, hassling a five-year-old about a throwaway comment?

Ridiculous. Carrie turned back to the stove. Everything was fine. She could freeze the extra sauce for another day. Perhaps she would thaw it out for Peter to eat, after he'd recovered.

'I'll put the pasta on now. Go and play with your animals. I'll call you as soon as dinner's ready.'

'OK. Thanks, Mummy.'

Eighteen

Sofia woke up in the middle of the night to find a monster standing beside her bed.

At first she thought it was just a dream, or her imagination making pictures out of darkness, so she forced herself to stare right at it, thinking that would make the monster disappear or go back into being a shadow or maybe some clothes hanging. But it didn't work. The monster was still there, staring down at her. It was the same shape as a human, but its head was covered in something black (fur? feathers?). All except for little bits around its eyes and mouth, where she could see normal-looking skin the same colour as hers. The monster raised a finger (also black) and put it in front of its mouth, which meant *shhhh*. But Sofia didn't *shhhh*.

Sofia screamed.

The sound must have scared the monster or maybe hurt its ears, because it turned around and walked out of her room. She could hear its feet (paws?) on the stairs as it went away. Sofia pulled the covers up over her head and lay with her breath going fast and her heart bouncing like crazy, counting in a whisper.

'One, two, three ...'

She told herself that, if she made it all the way to twenty, that meant the monster was gone for good and wasn't coming back. Or, at least, it wouldn't be able to come back before she ran to Mummy.

'. . . eighteen, nineteen, *twenty*.'

Sofia threw back the duvet and sprinted down the corridor.

Carrie was dreaming that a huge hole had been torn in the roof and water was pouring in, as if the house were a torpedoed submarine. Josh was beside her, plugging the gap with balled-up newspapers. She was trying to tell him that the paper wouldn't work, that it kept dissolving, but he couldn't hear her over the sound of Sofia screaming and the thud of footsteps on the stairs.

'Mummy! Wake up!'

Carrie's eyes opened. She shook off the last tangled fragments of her dream to find her daughter standing beside the bed, the moonlight picking out the white of her pyjama top, turning its pink butterflies grey.

'What is it, sweetie? Did you have a nightmare?'

'Not a nightmare.' Sofia crawled in under the duvet, clasping her arms around her mother's neck, holding tight. Her whole body was trembling. 'A real-life monster came inside my room. It wanted to catch me.' She buried her face in her mother's neck. 'I'm scared.'

Carrie stroked her daughter's back.

'It was just a dream, my darling. It can't hurt you.'

'No, it wasn't! It was real! I woke up and the monster was

197

standing right beside my bed looking at me. But when I screamed, it went away and I came in here.'

'What did the monster look like?'

'Like a human only with dark fur.'

'You mean like a werewolf?'

'No. The fur was really short. Except for circles around its eyes and its mouth.'

'Can you describe the circles?'

'They were like normal skin, peeking out through holes in the fur.' She nestled closer, limbs twining around her. 'Can I stay here with you? Monsters never come in your room.'

An unsettling thought twisted through Carrie's mind like dark smoke. The footsteps in her dream. Could they have been real, an intruder fleeing down the stairs? And Sofia's description of the monster . . .

'Sweetie, let's pop into your room so I can show you there's nothing there.'

'No!' Sofia clung tighter. 'What if it comes back?'

'The monster is only in your imagination, darling.'

Sofia shook her head firmly, making the duvet rustle.

'I know sometimes I make things up. But not this time.'

'If I'm wrong and there's a real monster, I'm going to kick it in the butt,' Carrie said. 'Because this is a No Monster zone. Our house, our rules.'

Normally the line – lifted from a favourite story book – would have drawn out a giggle, but Sofia only burrowed deeper under the duvet.

'Please, Mummy, can we just stay here? *Please?*'

'OK.' As Carrie caressed the dark, curly hair, she focused her senses outward, reaching into the far corners of the house. She could hear the faint hiss of distant traffic beyond the window; the tick of the water heater; her daughter's breathing, still quick with remnant fear. But that was all. No creak of a floorboard or rustle of clothes, no swish of a door opening across a carpeted floor. They were alone in the house.

Which meant Sofia was imagining things. Hardly surprising, given what she'd been through. But as Carrie rearranged the duvet to cover the two of them, her daughter's words replayed in her memory.

The fur was really short. Except for circles around its eyes and its mouth.

And she couldn't help thinking that, if you swapped 'fur' for 'cloth', it sounded exactly like a description of someone wearing a balaclava.

Sofia's arms were still looped around her neck when she woke in the morning. The sound of slow, even breathing told Carrie that her daughter was deep in sleep. Gently detaching the small hands, she slipped out of bed, stretching and yawning as she stepped out into the hallway. Right. First order of business: coffee.

But on her way past Sofia's room, Carrie paused. The door was wide open and she could see the unicorn duvet lying on the floor, where Sofia must have flung it as she'd fled.

Can you describe the circles?

They were like normal skin, peeking out through holes in the monster's fur.

It was nothing. Of course it was nothing. Sofia had had a nightmare, that was all.

She went and picked up the duvet, shaking it out across the bed. The room was flooded with morning light, illuminating the red-and-white chest of drawers, the crammed bookcase and the giant wooden box filled with stuffed animals.

Disquiet needled Carrie, making her feel jumpy. Which was silly. Because there was nothing here except a fallen blanket and an empty bed.

But just as she was turning to go, something snagged her attention: a scrap of green, lying on the oval rug. It must have been concealed by the duvet. She bent to retrieve it. A piece of leaf.

The oak trees lining the street in front and the gardens behind had begun shedding in the heatwave – nature's way of conserving moisture, according to the BBC. Green leaves speckled the roofs of cars and caught on the shoes of pedestrians. Carrie placed the broken leaf on the palm of her hand, conscious of her dry throat and quickening pulse, thinking back to the previous afternoon: the hours she'd spent cleaning the house and the sense of achievement she'd felt as she'd tucked Sofia into bed, looking around at the wiped shelves and freshly laundered bedclothes.

The vacuumed, spotless floor.

'So you're saying you believe your daughter actually saw someone standing beside her bed?'

Juliet made no effort to conceal the scepticism in her voice, because she knew Carrie wouldn't be able to detect it. Then she realised what she was doing – akin to gawking at a blind person in public – and felt a stab of shame.

'Yes,' Carrie said. 'That is what I believe.'

Juliet gazed across Alistair's empty desk (he was in Granger Park with the others, trawling for fresh witnesses).

'As I'm sure you're aware, children have very vivid imaginations. It can be difficult to separate dreams from reality.'

'But the description . . . do you not agree that it sounds like a person in a balaclava?'

Juliet wondered whether she would ever get used to Carrie Haversen's voice. The flat tone. The complete lack of emotion.

'I thought she said the monster had fur?'

'That is what it would have looked like to her in the dark, having never seen a balaclava before. And there's something else.' The noise level in the station rose suddenly as half a dozen football fans were brought in, wrapped in matching scarves and singing their team song in mutinous tones, lyrics blurry with alcohol. Juliet put a hand over her other ear.

'Yes?'

'There is physical evidence to support her claim.'

Excitement sharpened Juliet's senses, straightening her spine. She took out her notebook and pen.

'What kind of evidence?'

'A piece of leaf. I found it on the floor.'

The surge of excitement drained away. She tipped back in her chair, which creaked ominously (the station's furniture hadn't been replaced for well over a decade).

'A piece of leaf,' she repeated dully.

'Yes. An oak leaf. There are oaks along my street and in my back garden.'

'And why do you believe that this leaf was brought in by an intruder?

'Because I vacuumed the floor before Sofia went to bed. It wasn't there.'

'Perhaps you took the rubbish out and tracked it back in with you ...'

'No. I didn't.'

'It could have blown in through an open window.'

'Sofia's window was shut. I keep it closed now. As a security measure.'

'If you're taking security measures, how would an intruder have been able to gain entry to your house without breaking in?'

'The kitchen window doesn't lock. It's being repaired this afternoon when my new security system is installed. Maybe the intruder discovered the broken latch and opened the window, closing it behind them on the way back out.'

Juliet's scepticism deepened as she considered this theory. It didn't really make sense. People who planned ahead and masked up either intended to smash a window or already knew of a way in: the location of a hidden key or unlocked door. They didn't risk prowling around a house in the dead of night on the off chance one of the latches might be broken.

'I suppose it's possible,' she said slowly. 'But I wouldn't call it likely.'

'Will you investigate the incident?'

Juliet flopped back against the chair, setting off another creak. She stared up at the false ceiling, with its grid of white squares.

A leaf fragment and a five-year-old's claim to have seen a monster. It didn't seem like much: a long shot at best. But long shots seemed to be their stock-in-trade these days. She thought of the officers in the park, trying to prod the memories of park regulars, hoping someone would suddenly recall having seen a random park keeper on the day of Sofia's disappearance, or a suspicious figure lurking near the storage hut in the days leading up to it. Was this really any more of a wild goose chase?

'OK,' she relented. 'I'll check the CCTV on your street. What time did Sofia come into your room?'

'4.12 a.m.'

'That's very precise.'

'I looked at the bedside clock. The intruder would have fled during the five minutes prior to that.'

'Fine. Leave it with me. I'll get back to you when we have a result.'

'Good,' Carrie said, and the phone went dead. Juliet looked at the silent receiver for a moment, then slowly put it down. She would ask PC Potter to get hold of the CCTV when he got back. Maybe if . . .

Juliet's hand was still resting on the phone when it rang.

'DCI Campbell.'

The familiar flat voice travelled down the line

'Thank you. I forgot to say that before. Goodbye.' And the phone went dead once more.

Juliet was shaking her head and smiling as she returned the receiver to its cradle.

Nineteen

Josh was about to orgasm. Carrie could tell by the change in his breathing and the arch of his back. She held on to the headboard and moved against him, building friction. His mouth opened and his eyes squeezed shut. Then a deep thrust and a strangled cry.

After withdrawing, he rolled onto his back and pulled her against his chest, murmuring into her hair. 'You got there before me that time.'

'Yes.'

'You usually take longer.'

'Yes.' The truth was, she was able to orgasm more easily with him now. He had picked up on what she wanted, learned to navigate her body, without needing to be told what to do – reading her responses and adapting to them. And more than that: he made her feel relaxed and unselfconscious. Accepted for who and what she was.

His fingers skimmed back and forth between her shoulder blades in the pause that followed.

'I've been thinking about last night's break-in.'

Carrie drew back her head to look at his face. The streetlight coming through the open window gave him a yellowish glow.

'The police don't believe a break-in actually occurred. They checked the CCTV footage of the street and didn't find anything.'

'So? The intruder could have come through the back garden to avoid CCTV.'

'That would require crossing the rear neighbour's garden and climbing a high fence.'

'Which is doable. The fence isn't that high.'

'The police believe that scenario to be unlikely, since it would have been almost impossible to return the same way while carrying Sofia.'

'"Unlikely" isn't really good enough, though, is it, where your child's safety is concerned? Surely you must be worried?'

'I've done everything I can. All the locks are now secure and the new alarm system is up and running.'

'OK.' His arms tightened around her back. 'What did the security company say their reaction time would be if someone sets off the alarm?'

'Ten minutes or less.'

'Ten minutes,' he repeated, leaving the words hanging in the air.

She returned her head to Josh's chest, feeling the rise and fall of his breathing. It had been gradually slowing since his orgasm, but now it was picking up speed again. Did that mean he was anxious: afraid for her and Sofia?

Ten minutes . . .

More than enough time for someone to snatch Sofia and run. She had been so relieved to hear that the CCTV hadn't shown anyone on the street. Perhaps, in her determination not to let paranoia take root again, she had gone too far the other way, been too quick to dismiss Sofia's claims ... and her own suspicions. Carrie's imagination stirred to life, sending up shadowy images of a masked figure looming over her daughter.

Josh shuffled beneath her, propping himself up against the pillows.

'Would you like me to stay over tonight, just to be on the safe side? I can go sleep in the spare room.'

Carrie considered this. The sense of safety that had arrived with the new security system had gone, drained away by the thought of those ten defenceless minutes.

And having another adult in the house *would* make her feel better: less alone.

'Yes,' she said. 'You can stay here tonight.'

He smiled then: a nice big, clear one. Textbook happy.

'Good,' he said. 'And who knows? Maybe you'll like having me around so much, you won't want to let me leave.'

Carrie snuggled against his chest, hearing the beat of his heart: strong and steady.

'Maybe.'

Twenty

It was strange, seeing Carrie Haversen at work. Until now, Juliet had only ever viewed her as a crime victim, the shell-shocked mother of a missing girl, stony-faced and bewildered. But within the walls of Wescott Architects, she became a different person. There was a confidence about her, a presence. And although her face was as blank as ever, Juliet could sense the creative current humming behind those expressionless eyes.

She had arrived just after eleven, flashing her warrant card at reception, mounting the stairs and walking the wide path between desks. She'd pictured white easels tilted towards architects perched on stools. Pencils tucked behind ears. But clearly that was a hopelessly outdated image. Wide-screened computers had replaced drawing boards, making it just another office filled with rows of workers tapping keyboards. The room itself was beautifully designed – vaulted spaces, angled skylights, exposed beams – but, aside from that, this could just as easily have been an accounting firm or marketing company, and Juliet found herself feeling vaguely disappointed, as though something had been lost.

Carrie's oversized computer screen was displaying a graphic of an external walkway made of glass. Print-offs of sketches and notes were draped all over her desk, covering everything except the keyboard. Carrie must have been deeply absorbed in her work, because she didn't sense there was someone standing right behind her until Juliet tapped her shoulder.

She flinched, then spun the chair to face her.

'DCI Campbell. Hello. Why are you here? Has there been a development in the case?'

'I'm afraid not. I hope you don't mind my coming by your office like this, but I need to speak to you again about your contacts.'

Carrie's neighbour shot them a glare from behind John Lennon-style glasses, clearly displeased by the interruption to his creative flow.

'I've already gone over that list. Three times.'

'I know, but I'd like to expand it to include anyone who could have come into contact with Sofia at some point over the last two months. Not just friends and acquaintances, but doctors, dentists, librarians. Couriers or pizza delivery people. Anyone and everyone who has crossed paths with your daughter, however briefly.'

A blinking pause. 'You really think it will help?'

'It might.'

Carrie gave her a single nod.

'All right, then. But I need to leave the office at 12.45 p.m. Sofia asked to return to her school's Holiday Club today, to see her friends, and I agreed to let her attend the morning session. It ends at 1.30.'

'That's fine. This won't take long.'

Carrie stared up at her without moving. It felt awkward, looming over a woman seated in an office chair. The neighbour in John Lennon glasses was now scowling openly.

'Is there a room where we can speak privately?'

'Yes.'

Carrie rose quickly enough to send her chair rolling backwards across the carpet and strode off down the path between the desks, leaving Juliet standing next to the abruptly vacated desk, the chair rotating slowly as it coasted to a stop.

Carrie made it halfway across the room before suddenly registering that Juliet wasn't with her. She stopped and turned.

'Come with me,' she said, and walked a few more steps before turning around again. 'Please.'

Juliet was smiling to herself as she followed, lengthening her stride to catch up without running. As they passed a small kitchen, Carrie hesitated, gesturing towards it. 'Can I first offer you a beverage from the kitchen? Tea or coffee?'

Juliet nodded. 'Tea would be nice.' She couldn't resist letting a few seconds tick by before adding: 'Please.'

Whatever creative juices were flowing within the walls of Wescott Architects, none of them had been channelled into designing the staff kitchen: a windowless rectangle containing a fridge, a plug-in kettle and a sink area with coffee mugs drying upside down on a tea towel.

Carrie filled the kettle before opening one of the cupboards above the counter, taking out a pair of mugs, which showed the company logo incorporated into London's skyline. As she added teabags, Juliet read the various notices Sellotaped to the cupboard doors: an advert for volunteering days at a local home-less shelter; an angry, hand-written diatribe against dumping coffee grinds down the sink ('How many times does the kitchen have to flood before people start emptying their French presses into the bin?') and a poster promoting Wescott Architects' Bring Your Kid to Work Day ('Arts and Crafts, Games and More!'). Clearly no one was responsible for taking down expired notices, because that one was dated 12 June.

She leaned closer to the poster, which showed a cartoon toddler drawing a complex building design in blue crayon.

12 June. Sixteen days before Sofia went missing. She felt the flicker of an idea.

What if—

'Do you take sugar?' Carrie's voice cut into her thoughts.

'No, just milk, thanks.' Juliet tapped the poster. 'Did your daughter participate in this?'

'In what?' She shot a glance at the poster. 'Oh. Yes. She came for a couple of hours in the afternoon.'

'So Sofia *has* been to your office.'

'Yes.' Steam rose from the kettle. Carrie poured hot water into the waiting cups.

'Because, when I interviewed you before, you said she's never come here.'

'No. I said I had never brought her into work to cover a childcare shortfall and that Simon had never dropped her off here. Or brought her by when he wasn't feeling well.'

'I only meant those as examples . . .' She stopped herself. Carrie clearly took things very literally. Juliet would have to watch for that in future. She took out her notebook, flipping it open. 'OK. So let me get my facts straight: Sofia came here on June twelfth. Was that the only time she ever entered this building?'

'Yes.' Carrie used a teaspoon to fish out the teabags, dropping them into a bin under the sink.

'So, who would have seen her? People working on your floor and their visiting families?'

'No, there were activity zones throughout the building.'

Juliet nodded, jotting this down.

'So across all departments on all four floors?'

Carrie opened the fridge door, momentarily disappearing behind it. 'Correct.'

'Did you accompany her to these activities?'

'Yes.' She reappeared with a carton of milk.

'Did she bring a toy with her?' Juliet looked up from her notebook. 'A stuffed penguin, for example?'

'No.' Carrie added milk to both mugs. 'I told her not to bring one because she was likely to lose it.'

'Roughly how many people were in the building that day?'

'I don't know. You would have to ask the organiser, Katie Muller in HR. We had to sign up, so she should have a list of all the parents and children who participated.'

Juliet noted down the name.

'What about outsiders? Clients, couriers, that sort of thing.'

'They weren't permitted to bring their children.'

Juliet bit back a laugh.

'What I mean is, was the office running normally, or was it closed to visitors while the children were here?'

'Visitors were still permitted.' Carrie opened the drawer to take out a fresh teaspoon. 'I know this because I spoke to a client briefly while Sofia was in the soft-play area created in the AV room.'

Juliet felt a pulse of adrenalin.

'So ... you *weren't* watching her the entire time?'

There was the clink of metal against ceramic as Carrie stirred milk into a cup.

'No. But we were separated for less than fifteen minutes. The client had a question about a change I'd made, so we discussed it in Osman Baig's office.'

'Osman Baig? Is he your supervisor?'

'Yes. He ... assists me with client meetings. I told Sofia to keep playing and not to leave the AV room until I got back. And she didn't.'

'But someone could have spoken to her or approached her? Asked about her favourite toy or animal while you were down-stairs?'

Carrie picked up the two mugs of tea and turned to face her.

'Sofia didn't mention such a person.'

'Are you certain she would have told you if she had?'

'Yes, she ...' Carrie began. Then her eyes shifted right through a series of rapid blinks. 'Actually, there *has* been an instance of her meeting someone in my absence and initially failing to mention it. So the accurate response must be: no, not necessarily.'

Juliet nodded. She would question Sofia later, see if she remembered speaking to anyone.

'Is there CCTV inside this building?' She hadn't noticed any on the way in. But, then, she hadn't been looking.

'Yes. There are two cameras on each floor.'

Good. If she could get hold of the footage from 12 June,

maybe she'd get lucky and find someone showing a special interest in Sofia.

Juliet considered the woman standing in front of her, a mug of tea in each hand, wondering what toll the investigation was taking on her: the rise and dash of hope.

'How are you handling the release of the park keeper? It must have come as a shock.'

'Yes. It has forced me to make some adjustments, for the sake of security. But not all of the changes have been negative.'

And just for a moment, Juliet thought she saw something – like a glimmer of light, the idea of a smile – flicker beneath the surface of Carrie Haversen's face.

Then it was gone.

Twenty-one

Carrie stood looking at the toothbrush in her bathroom mug. Colgate brand. Blue handle. The toothbrush was there because a man was staying here now. Only temporarily, of course. A week. That's what she and Josh had agreed, following the success of his 'sleepover' in the spare room (Sofia had been thrilled to discover him in the kitchen the next morning, squeaking with delight over the 'happy face pancake' he'd made her for breakfast, with its blueberry mouth and eyes).

Just an emergency measure, though. Until things settled down.

But still . . .

The sight of the toothbrush had released a strange mix of emotions: nervousness; affection; insecurity (she had, after all, failed to make a success of living with Simon). But overriding them all — a lifting sense of wonder. Carrie's eyes rose to the mirror, to her plain, blocky features. The blue toothbrush meant that, for the first time in two years, it wasn't just her and Sofia. Josh was here to care for them. 'Protect' was the word he'd used. But didn't protecting and caring amount to the same thing? She could hear him now, moving around downstairs in the kitchen: footsteps, a cupboard door closing, the clink of crockery. Then his voice, drifting up the stairs, only just audible. 'Carrie? Would you like some coffee?'

'Yes.'

'Are you coming down, so the three of us can have breakfast together?'

'Yes.'

She stared at her reflection, letting the words roll around inside her head.

The three of us. Together.

She watched her face for a little while longer, waiting to see if it would shift on its own: whether her feelings would break to the surface.

'Carrie?'

'Yes. I'm coming.'

Switching off the light, she jogged down the stairs to join them.

'So what are your plans for today?' Josh was already smearing cream cheese on a bagel when she sat down at the table. 'Looking forward to your first full day at the office?'

'Only if you're sure about staying here with Sofia ...' She glanced at her daughter, who was licking the cream cheese off her own bagel.

'Absolutely. Princess Penguin and I are going to have a ball, aren't we?'

Sofia nodded enthusiastically, then put down the bagel, which left a blob of cream cheese on her nose.

'We're making a house out of a box,' she announced.

Carrie turned to Josh, puzzled. 'A box?'

'Yeah, I swung by my place after work yesterday and picked up a box of stuff I'll need while I'm staying here. I thought it might be fun to make the box into a house once I've unpacked. Sofia has suggested that we host a tea party inside it.'

'All the penguins are invited,' Sofia said. 'But not the bears.'

Josh wiped the cream cheese from her nose with a serviette. 'Why not the bears?' he asked.

'Because bears eat penguins.'

'Ah. Good decision.' Josh rumpled her hair then looked across at Carrie. 'So there you go. We're having a civilised party, taking all necessary measures to avoid any food chain-related carnage.' He picked up another bagel and began covering it with cream cheese. 'How about you? What's on your agenda for the day?'

'I'm meeting a client.' She decided against launching into the plan to have Tara help translate, adding instead: 'Then, after-wards, I'm having lunch with a friend.' Which was true. Hearing the words out loud triggered a small thrill of pride. Strange to think that only a month ago it had just been her and Sofia against the world. And now, here she was with a good friend and a ... a ... what was Josh to her now? Boyfriend? Partner? A shy feeling of happiness stole over her.

He finished covering the bagel and put it on Carrie's plate. 'By "friend", I assume you mean Tara?'

'Yes.'

'Mummy, I'm finished eating. Can I go play with my Lego house?'

'Yes.'

Sofia slipped from her chair.

'Lunch with Tara,' Josh said. She wondered why he felt the need to repeat the information. 'That's nice. You two are getting quite close, aren't you, spending a lot of time together?' She noticed that his smile didn't disturb the upper half of his face, as though his mouth were an island, isolated from the rest of his features.

'Yes. She has been a good friend to me.' She bit into the bagel. Sesame seed. Her favourite.

'Hmm.' He propped his ankle on a knee, jiggling the raised foot. 'I think maybe you need to be a bit careful, where Tara's concerned.'

She blinked, puzzled. 'Why?'

He picked up his own bagel, biting into it, chewing for what felt like a long time.

'Well, you don't *really* know her. And there's something about her I find a bit ... odd. First she stops you from calling the police right away when Sofia goes missing, then she keeps popping up everywhere.'

'I *do* know her. And I already told you: she was the one who actually called 999. If you spent some time with her, I know you'd see—'

'You still haven't met her son, have you?'

'No, not yet.'

'Not yet,' he repeated. 'Meanwhile, she's spending a lot of time with *your* daughter. Intimate, one-on-one time. They seem to be building quite a close relationship, since there's no other child around to draw Sofia's attention away.'

Carrie stared at him, baffled. He seemed to be implying that there was some sort of link between Tara's relationship with Sofia and the fact that their playdate plans had fallen through.

217

'Explain to me what you mean by that?' She waited for him to respond, but he remained silent, eyes fixed on a point just beyond her shoulder. 'Are you saying that Tara avoids bringing her own son over in order to strengthen her bond with Sofia?'

Josh bit into his bagel.

'Assuming she even *has* a son,' he muttered through his food, the words only just audible.

Carrie stared at him across the table. She couldn't even begin to decipher what he meant by that.

'I don't understand what you just said.' She waited while he polished off the last of his bagel before asking once again: 'Explain to me?'

Josh banged his palms against each other above the now empty plate, releasing a scatter of sesame seeds.

'You know what? Forget I said anything.'

'How can I when you've only just said it?'

He sighed. 'What I mean is: ignore what I just said about Tara. Go and have a good day at the office. Enjoy your lunch.'

'But—'

'You better hurry and finish your breakfast or you'll be late for work.'

'Oh.' She glanced down at her watch. 8.30. Shit. She'd lost track of the time. 'I better leave now.'

He rose quickly and began clearing plates from the table.

'Shall I put your bagel in a bag to take with you?'

'That's not necessary.'

'Why not? Aren't you hungry?'

'I was before.' She looked out through the front window and was surprised to find the morning sun gone, replaced by a

218

gloomy, leaden sky. A new front must have come in, dragging layers of cloud that choked off the light. 'I'm not any more.'

Carrie didn't understand what Tara was doing. She had suddenly raised her hand, like a pupil with a question, and was still holding it up. Was there something she wanted to ask? Carrie stared at the open palm, blinking. Then Tara laughed and said: 'Babe, I'm trying to high-five you.'

'Oh.' Of course. How stupid. Carrie leaned across the table and aimed a slap at Tara's hand, careful not to hit too hard.

They were in Bean There: a low-ceilinged space with black-and-white floor tiles that made the wooden tables and chairs look like giant chess pieces. Red sofas lined the walls, with arty views of London framed above them. Carrie's client had just left, so the two of them had decamped to a table near the back for a debrief over coffee and peanut-butter cheesecake.

Tara picked up her latte and crossed her legs.

'I thought that went really well in the end.'

'I agree.' Carrie took a forkful of cheesecake (they were sharing a slice). 'But only because you were here. Without your texts, I would never have guessed that his initial negativity was just frustration at not being able to interpret my drawings.'

Tara smiled, fluffing out her hair with her fingers.

'I'm just glad it worked out.'

Carrie swallowed a bite of cake, basking in their shared triumph, warmed by the knowledge she had a friend who cared about her, who was prepared to go out of her way to provide help and support.

'When can I meet Peter?' she asked, keen to cement the

bond between them, to forge this one missing link in the chain of their friendship. She wanted Peter to like her the way Sofia liked Tara, so she was going to make a real effort with him. Talk and try to smile.

Carrie looked across at Tara, waiting for a response. But there was no sound except the hiss of the coffee machine and the background babble of strangers chatting. 'Peter,' she prompted eventually. 'Your son?'

Tara released a high octave laugh.

'Yes, I know who Peter is.' She put a forkful of cheesecake in her mouth, chewing and swallowing before she spoke again. 'You can meet him whenever you like, so long as I'm not working.'

'How about later this afternoon? You can bring him to our house for a playdate. Or Sofia and I could come to you.'

She made an 'um' sound and took another bite of cheese-cake. Swallowed.

'I'm afraid this afternoon's not great. I've got some paperwork that won't wait and ...'

'Tomorrow, then: Friday.'

'Oh!' She put her fork down with a clatter. Gave Carrie a big smile. 'Friday! I knew there was something I'd forgotten to ask. What do you say to a mums' night out, now that you've got Josh as a live-in babysitter? There's a new cocktail bar in Soho I've been dying to try. Underground with lots of cool spaces and flaming drinks. We can paint the town red on Friday, then meet up for a playdate on Saturday, so our children can entertain each other while we nurse our hangovers.'

Carrie blinked as she digested this idea. A night out with Tara. What would that be like? She pictured the two of them drinking cocktails, part of the social scenery, talking and laughing. Well, *she* wouldn't be laughing. Her simulated laugh wasn't up to much – worse than her smile – so she'd given up trying. But Tara would be laughing. She was good at laughing, throwing back her head as the mirth filled her body all the way to the top. She could laugh for both of them.

Carrie picked up her flat white and took a sip.

'Yes. I would like to go out for drinks with you, if Josh agrees to babysit. And then meet for a playdate on Saturday.'

'Perfect! Text me as soon as you get the green light. I'll swing by your place and we can head out from there. Say, seven–thirty, eight o'clock?'

'Yes. Good.'

'I can't tell you how much I need—' Tara's mobile rang. Carrie glimpsed the words 'Eleonore Head' on the screen and had time to think what an odd name that was before registering that Tara's face had changed. The smile was gone and her eyebrows were pushed together, curled upward at the point where they nearly met. She drew in a swift, audible breath and said: 'Sorry, one sec: I need to get this.'

She rushed for the door, answering the call when she was outside the coffee shop. The front wall of Bean There was made of glass, so Carrie could see her pacing up and down the pavement as she talked. Tara dragged a hand across her eyes. Stopped in front of the door. Her shoulders drooped forwards for a moment, then she pushed them back. Put the mobile in her pocket and came back inside.

'Sorry,' she said, sitting down for a second, then immediately standing up again. 'Something's come up. I'm afraid I'm going to have to shoot off. Shall we get the bill?'

'Oh.' Carrie looked down at the half-eaten cake and half-drunk coffee. 'Is there a problem?'

Tara gave her a rapid-fire smile.

'No, nothing that ... I just need ...' She shook her head. 'I have to go deal with something.'

'If you're in a rush, I can pay the bill, as a small expression of gratitude for your help today.'

'Thank you, that would be great, if you're sure you don't mind?'

That question must have been rhetorical, because Tara was already pulling her handbag up over her arm.

'Yes, I'm sure.'

'OK, then. See you tomorrow night.'

And she walked quickly to the door, barging into a man carrying a toddler as she pushed past, nearly knocking him over. Through the window, Carrie could see Tara breaking into a run the moment she left the café.

Twenty-two

Sofia didn't want Mummy to go out. She had been right there, only a shout away, every night-time since the scary shed. It made Sofia feel safe.

'Why can't you and Tara just stay *here*?' she asked grumpily, through the cloth of her pyjama top, as Mummy pulled it down over her head.

'I'll only be gone for a few hours, and you'll be asleep anyway.'

'But what if the monster comes back?'

'Josh will be here to keep you safe.' Mummy held out the pyjama bottoms (the comfy ones with the smiley moons) for her to step into. Maybe, if she didn't put her PJs on, Mummy wouldn't be able to go. The pyjama bottoms moved closer. 'Put your feet in here.'

'No.'

The doorbell rang. Sofia was dimly aware that she wasn't being fair, but big emotions were crashing around inside her and she couldn't make them stop.

'Tara is here. I have to go open the door for her. I'll be back in a minute.'

Then she put the PJs on the floor and rushed out of the room.

'You care more about her than me!' Sofia shouted after her, then threw herself on top of the duvet, sobbing hot tears. She couldn't explain why she was so upset, but sorrow was churning around inside her and Mummy running out of the room had made it worse. She could hear the sound of muffled voices talking downstairs. After a while, footsteps came back up. Mummy. She would feel bad when she saw all the tears she'd made happen. *Good*.

Sofia sat up on the edge of the bed, wiping away snot with the back of her hand. But it wasn't Mummy who came in. It was Tara.

'Hello, lovely girl.' She sat down beside her, the small bed creaking with the added weight. 'What's this I'm hearing, about not wanting to put on your PJs?'

'Mummy doesn't want to look after me. She just wants to go away and leave me with only half a pyjama on. I hate her.'

'No, you don't. You love her. You're just upset right now.' Tara put an arm around her shoulders. 'But I'll tell you what.' She gave Sofia a mysterious smile, like a secret was happening. 'While your Mummy and I are out tonight, I'm going to get you a special surprise, as a reward for being good.'

'What will the surprise be?'

Tara pressed a finger on Sofia's nose, like pushing a button.

'Now, if I told you *that*, it wouldn't be a surprise, would it?'

Sofia giggled in spite of herself. She was trying to cling on to being mad but her bad mood seemed to be breaking apart and blowing away, leaving only a vague sense of injustice.

'I still don't understand why you can't stay here like last time.'

'Well, we *could*, but then I wouldn't be able to get your surprise, would I?'

Sofia considered this. She did like surprises.

'Why don't we finish getting you ready for bed, and before you know it, you'll be waking up again and your mummy will be home, and the special surprise will be waiting for you, right here.' She tapped the bedside table.

Sofia felt her mood lift at the thought of waking up next to a present. Tara picked up the pyjama bottoms and crouched in front of her, holding them at her feet, the same way Mummy had. This time Sofia put her feet through the holes and stood up to let Tara hitch the pyjamas around her waist.

'There you go, beautiful girl.' She smiled. 'We make a good team, don't we?'

Sofia looked at the door again to see if Mummy was just outside, listening to make sure everything was OK. But she wasn't there. Didn't she even care about Sofia being sad? A surge of the old hurt came back.

'I wish *you* were my mummy instead of *her*,' Sofia said, in a rush of temper. Shame followed close behind, because it wasn't nice and it wasn't true. She waited for Tara to tell her what a terrible thing that was to say, because her Mummy loved her so much. But, instead, Tara leaned really close and whispered right into Sofia's ear.

'I wish that too.'

'She's an odd one, isn't she?' Josh said, bending to pick up a pair of Playmobil figures from the floor beside the coffee table.

Carrie looked at him from her station at the bottom of the

staircase, where she was standing with one hand on the bannister, ears straining for the sound of shouting or crying from above: signals that Tara's approach wasn't working and Carrie should go up and take over.

'What do you mean?'

Josh deposited the toys in the wicker basket full of plastic figures and Lego. 'Just that it's a bit unusual for a visitor to insist on trying to calm an angry child when the mother is right there and perfectly capable of handling the situation herself.'

'She's not just a visitor. She's my friend. And I thought what she said made sense.'

Josh retrieved the Moroccan throw cover puddled behind the armchair (Sofia had been trying unsuccessfully to make it into a tent), folding it carefully. He was always tidying. She couldn't recall the house ever looking so neat.

'If you say so.' He laid the throw over the back of the sofa.

Carrie returned to her vigil at the bottom of the stairs, wondering how things were going up there. She heard footsteps, then the sound of water running in the bathroom. Muffled laughter. A good sign. Perhaps she should go join them? But Tara had seemed so sure, had spoken with such authority.

She just needs a chance to cool off. It would make sense for you to stay down here and let me handle it. I'm in a better position to turn her mood around, since the negative emotions she's experiencing right now aren't directed at me.

More footsteps. Then a long silence. Carrie crept up a few stairs, listening intently.

'For God's sake, Carrie, she's *your* child! Go up there if you want to! Don't let Tara make you feel like an outsider in your own home!'

'That's not what she's doing.'

But Carrie did feel as though she was breaking a rule of some kind as she crept up the stairs, pausing when she reached the top. The door to Sofia's room was ajar, letting Tara's voice drift out.

'I'm going to fill my hungry, empty tummy, with something yummy, yummy, yummy, yummy!'

Carrie recognised the words: Roald Dahl's *The Enormous Crocodile*. The tale of a ruthless predator who assumed pleasing shapes to prey on children. The thought brought an uneasy feeling. She had never really considered the story's plot before. She would get rid of the book in the morning.

'The Enormous Crocodile crept over to The Picnic Place. There was no one in sight. "Now for Clever Trick Number Four!" he whispered to himself.'

Tara's voice stopped. Silence in the corridor.

Carrie tiptoed down the hall to the bedroom door and peered through the gap. Sofia was fast asleep. Tara was on the edge of the bed, closing the book slowly, silently, placing it on the floor. She switched off the bedside lamp and turned on the starry-sky nightlight. Pulled the duvet up around Sofia's shoulders. Then she bent over and kissed her on the forehead.

Watching that kiss gave Carrie an odd sensation in the pit of her stomach.

When Tara turned and spotted her in the doorway, she clutched at her chest.

'You scared me,' she whispered, as Carrie stepped inside the room. 'How long have you been standing there?'

There was a moment of silence as Carrie stood looking at her, trying to move past the feeling that her new friend had just crossed an invisible border, trespassing on places meant only for her and Simon.

'Not long. I came to check that everything was OK.' Saying the words made Carrie feel oddly defensive, as though she'd been caught doing something wrong.

'Of course. Sorry, I should have popped down to let you know that I was putting her to bed, but everything was going so well, I didn't want to risk breaking the mood.' They stood and looked at each other. The nightlight scattered blue stars up one side of Tara's face. 'Shall we get going?'

'Yes.'

But before she left the room, Carrie leaned over the bed and put her lips to her daughter's forehead, placing her kiss on top of Tara's.

The Good Mix was centred around a large, circular space with an octagonal bar as its nucleus. Cave-like alcoves fed on to it, like spokes in a wheel. Lamps were set into the back of each one, splashing the walls with coloured light that slowly changed from red to blue to green every few minutes.

Carrie was halfway through her third whisky when Tara prodded her arm with a stir stick and said: 'So-oooo ... tell me all about Josh.'

She ran through a mental list of information, trying to present it in order of relevance.

'He is founder and editor of *London Architects' Monthly*. He studied at Cardiff University. He is thirty-six years old. He owns a flat in Clapham.' She was aware of Tara's eyes still on hers. Did that mean she was waiting for more? She cast around in her memory. But most of their conversations had been about architecture, and she was fairly sure that wasn't what Tara had in mind. 'He doesn't like seafood.'

Tara burst out laughing and Carrie wondered why. What could be humorous about an aversion to fish?

The light in the nook faded out of green and into red.

'OK, that's not quite what I was aiming for. What's his romantic history? Has he ever been married?'

'I don't believe so.'

'You mean you're not sure?' Tara's eyebrows went quite high as she asked this.

'He has never mentioned a wife.'

'Hmm. What about his most recent relationship? Who was she? Why did it end?'

'He hasn't said anything about that. He has spoken about his mother, though, about her work as an architect. She died in a fire when he was a teenager.'

'Ah, yes, the famous mother whose house filled half the magazine. What about other family? I'm assuming he doesn't have any children from a past relationship?'

'No.' She blinked. Was she absolutely sure about that? 'He hasn't mentioned children, so I assume he doesn't have any.' Carrie took a sip of whisky, thinking as it burned its way down her throat, warming her stomach. She hadn't noticed the gaps in her knowledge of Josh until now. With Simon, there had never been any need to ask about family members or past relationships; personal information had flowed out of him in a stream of chatter. She had spent a Christmas with his endlessly bickering family (the 'pathologically selfish' sister and the elderly parents, with their bridge games and their casual racism).

Now she found herself wondering: should she have made a greater effort to learn more about Josh? Had he been waiting for her to ask, wondering why she hadn't? She sipped her whisky as the lights slowly turned blue. 'Do you think it's a problem, that I haven't spoken to him about these things?'

'Well, yes, frankly. But one that's easily resolved. Just ask him.' She picked up her cocktail, which was decorated with a chunk of pineapple impaled on a plastic sword. 'Have you met anyone from his family?'

'No.'

She sipped the cocktail's pink liquid.

'Does he have any brothers or sisters?'

'Not that I know of.'

Tara stared at her over the cocktail glass as the lights turned her face from blue to green.

'What about friends? Has he introduced you to any?'

'No.'

'Does he talk about them much?'

'No.' Carrie felt off centre as she drank the last of her whisky (now mostly ice). How had she failed to notice the absence of friends? It was such a sharp contrast to Simon, with his pub quiz posse and his football chums, the old uni mates forever crashing on the sofa.

'Do you think it's strange, that Josh hasn't shared his social circle with me?'

Red light seeped up the walls of the alcove as Tara put the blade of the plastic sword in her mouth, sucking off the fruit.

'Let's just say I think you need to know more about him, given that he's currently staying in your house. I guess maybe you've just skipped over the fact-finding stage of the relationship because things have moved so quickly.' She placed the sword on the table. 'Do you start all your relationships on fast-forward like that?'

'No. Simon and I went out on dates for six months. Then I got pregnant. Then he moved in – when Sofia was one. Then we broke up.'

'Why did you break up?'

Carrie thought back to that time, and was surprised to discover that the memory still brought a bruised throb.

Simon: facing her across the kitchen counter, voice full of strange tones and sharp edges, face twisting into patterns she'd never seen before.

'God, you just don't get it, do you, Carrie?'

'No. Explain to me.'

'You know what? I'm tired of explaining. I'm tired of my life. Tired of being nothing.'

'Nothing? But ... you're Sofia's father. How can you be nothing when your role is so important?'

'Yeah, right. And you're her mother. But you're also a successful architect.'

'What does my being an architect have to do with ...'

'You know what, Carrie? Forget it. Just forget it.'

'Forget what? You haven't explained—'

Then the front door slamming as he walked out, the bang loud enough to wake Sofia in her cot, filling the house with the sound of crying.

Carrie flagged down a passing waiter and ordered another whisky before answering Tara's question.

'We broke up because I was unable to read situations and respond appropriately.'

Tara sipped her cocktail, crunching an ice cube. 'What do

231

you mean: "read situations"? What kind of situations are we talking about?'

'Simon told me on several occasions that he was unhappy with his life with me and Sofia.'

'What exactly was he unhappy about?'

'He wouldn't say. He thought I should be able to work that out for myself. But I couldn't.'

Tara waved a hand in front of Carrie, palm turned ceilingward. 'Of *course* you couldn't. You're an emotional agnostic.' She laughed. 'Sorry, that's clearly not the right word. Remind me what it's called?'

'Social-emotional agnosia.'

'That's the one. Telling someone with . . . your condition to "read him" is like shouting at a blind person for not being able to see. If you ask me, Simon behaved like a total dick.'

'Do you really think so?' Simon *had* told her, months after they'd split, that the breakup wasn't her fault – that his behaviour had been unfair and inexcusable. But she hadn't believed him.

'I one hundred per cent *know* so.'

Carrie felt suddenly lighter, as though a weight inside her had evaporated.

'A total dick,' she repeated, feeling naughty as she said the words out loud. 'You're right. That's exactly what he was.'

'Men!' Tara rolled her eyes. 'Just promise me you'll never let Josh treat you like that.'

The whisky arrived and she took a slug, felt its warmth spreading outward from her core.

'I promise.'

Twenty-three

Carrie's boss was a patient man. Osman Baig was tall and slim, immaculately groomed and improbably dressed in a buttoned-down shirt decorated with cats silhouetted in various poses ('What can I say?' he'd smiled, when he saw Juliet staring. 'I love cats.'). He sat beside her in Wescott Architects' tiny security office, taking her through the CCTV footage, reeling off the names of almost every person Carrie and Sofia had come into contact with on their journey from one 'activity station' to the next.

'That's Lars Eigman, with his wife and daughter. And that's Tobias – I can't remember his surname, he helps out around the office twice a week for work experience, but I can find out if you need it. The blonde is Lucy Kelmann and her son: bit of a tearaway, that one.'

He clearly had a good memory for faces and names, because he was even able to identify most of the spouses. Juliet watched the footage closely, keeping an eye out for familiar faces, or anyone paying special attention to Sofia. The girl's image moved jerkily through the activities: drawing pictures and constructing

233

buildings out of blocks, playing with the architects' models, eating ice cream. But the adults surrounding her just looked like ordinary people doing their best to entertain, or at least work around, the influx of children. Disappointingly, the AV room wasn't near a security camera, so she could only scour the nearest available footage for potential suspects. No luck so far. She scrolled through the images until Carrie and Sofia crossed the main lobby of the building and left together. She watched for a few more minutes to see whether anyone followed them out.

Nothing.

She switched off the machine and gave Osman a tired smile. 'Thanks for your help.'

'*Did* I help? Have you found what you're looking for?'

She stifled a yawn. The security office was stuffy, which, combined with the semi-darkness, was making her sleepy.

'It's hard to say at this point. But I'd like to make a copy of this footage.'

'Of course.' He spread his hands, revealing silver cufflinks shaped like cat heads. 'Whatever you need. I hope you catch the man who did this.'

'Or woman,' Juliet said immediately. Then smiled to herself. Dutoit must be getting to her.

'What?! No, of course I don't have any children,' Josh said. 'Obviously I would have mentioned them if I did.'

'That's what I thought,' Carrie said, relieved. 'I told her I was pretty sure you didn't have any.'

They were at The Moon and Spoon: a small, family-friendly restaurant whose main selling point was a children's play area in the back corner. It was busy, but they had been given the lone table tucked into a nook beside the bar.

Josh lifted an eyebrow. 'Told *who*?'

'Tara. She asked me what I knew about you and suggested I find out more.'

There was one of those pauses that felt like it meant something. Then Josh said in a quiet voice: 'Oh, she did, did she?'

'Yes. It's a good idea, isn't it? Getting to know each other better?'

A shriek of childish laughter drew her eyes towards the 'Kid Zone' behind him, where Sofia and a boy she'd just met were building a tower out of blocks. Josh turned in his chair to follow Carrie's gaze, watching the two children.

'Speaking of Tara, weren't the two of you supposed to have a playdate this afternoon?'

Carrie poked at her root salad with a fork.

'Yes, that was the original plan. But we drank a lot of alcohol last night and she's feeling sick today. So we've rescheduled.' Tara's voice had sounded hoarse and croaky on the phone that morning: genuinely unwell. So Carrie had pushed her disappointment into a corner and said: of course, no problem, next week would be fine.

'I see.' He took a mouthful of soup. 'So instead of finally introducing you to her son this weekend, she took you out, got you drunk and convinced you to interrogate me.'

The facts were essentially correct, but the wording made Carrie feel uneasy. She speared a baby carrot.

'I wouldn't say "interrogate". She simply suggested I find out more about you and your background.' She put her fork down with the carrot still on it. 'Is that a problem?'

235

'Of course not. My life is an open book.' He selected a sourdough roll from the bread basket on the table, tearing off a piece. 'Ask me anything.'

'OK.' Carrie's mind travelled back to the questions Tara had raised. 'Do you have any brothers or sisters?'

'No. My mother didn't like children.' He dipped the bread into his bowl. The soup must have been hot, because she could see steam rising from it, twisting past his face. 'She didn't want to be distracted from her work.' He took a large bite of bread, watching her as he chewed.

'But she had you.'

When he smiled, his eyes narrowed but didn't crinkle the way they usually did.

'Having me was never part of her plan.' There was a candle on the table between them and Josh extended a finger, passing it through the base of the flame: first left, then right. The candle flickered with its passage. 'I'm the by-product of faulty birth control.'

'Oh.' She supposed the same could be said of Sofia. Josh must have been like that: a wonderful accident. Serendipity. How sad for him, to have lost his mother at such a young age. 'I read an article about her death. The fire.'

'Really?' His brows drew together. 'Where?'

'Online. It came up when I Googled your name.'

'I didn't think the Abbotsbury Courier had online archives. That must be a new development.'

Carrie shook her head. 'No, this was just a few lines in the *Guardian*. It said your mother was a well-known architect who'd died in a house fire. And that you had tried to save her.'

His finger moved through the flame again.

'My mother's boyfriend got drunk and passed out on the sofa with a cigarette. I was seventeen.'

'Oh.' A pause. What was it you were supposed to say? 'I'm sorry'? Of all the social conventions she'd been taught, that one struck her as the strangest: apologising for the death of someone you'd never met, as if it were somehow your fault. So instead she asked: 'What was she like?'

A small, brief smile.

'Amazing. Talented. Passionate about her work. That's how I developed an interest in architecture. I studied it myself, did a degree in it, but . . .' The flame flickered one last time before he withdrew his finger into a tight fist. 'It appears I didn't inherit her talent. And you know what they say: "Those who can, do, those who can't, set up magazines about the things they can't do."'

Carrie blinked, puzzled.

'I thought that expression applied to teaching rather than magazines?'

One side of his mouth lifted.

'That was a joke.'

'Was it? Sorry. I have difficulty with humour.'

He took her hand and squeezed it.

'You're not missing anything. It wasn't a very good joke.'

She was grateful to him for that. She thought of the house in the magazine: the cold cleverness of it.

'Were you and your mother close?'

The question seemed simple enough, but he took a long time to answer it.

'I worshipped her.' His eyes dropped to the candle again, staring down into the flame. 'I would have done anything to make her proud. To show her I was worthy. But—'

237

'Is everything OK?' The waiter's voice made Carrie jump. She followed his gaze to the root salad, uneaten on her plate.

'Yes.' She picked up her fork and popped the baby carrot into her mouth, waiting until they were alone again before continuing. 'What were you saying? About your relationship with your mother?'

He dipped his spoon into the bowl. 'I think I've said all there is to say about that.'

'Oh. OK. What about your father?'

He shrugged, one side of his mouth pulling downward. 'What about him?'

'What's he like?'

'A loser.' He took a mouthful of soup. 'A property developer without a creative bone in his body. Not fit to lick her boots.'

'I mean ... what kind of father was he?'

Another spoonful. 'The non-existent kind. They split up when I was three. That's when she saw what a mistake she'd made, tethering herself to a talentless nobody like him.'

'Do you ever see him?'

'No. He's bitter about being rejected by her, so tries to taint her memory with lies. I avoid him.'

She considered this as she ate a piece of butternut squash.

'What kind of lies?'

He waved a dismissive hand. 'There's no point getting into that, is there, since I thought you were only interested in the truth?'

'Yes. That is correct.'

He tore off another piece of bread and dipped it into the bowl.

'So ask me something else.'

Carrie didn't know why she chose the next question. Generally speaking, she didn't give much thought to people's appearances. But when she opened her mouth, out it came.

'What did your mother look like?'

His eyes moved back and forth across her face as he finished chewing the bread.

'She was beautiful.' He leaned across the table, caressing her cheek. 'Like you.'

'But I'm *not* beautiful,' she corrected.

He laughed. 'Yes, you are. You just don't see it. It's one of the things I love about you.'

The things I love about you.

She clasped on to the words, holding them tight. Obviously it wasn't the same as saying he loved her. But it was close, wasn't it? Loving things *about* someone?

He moved the candle aside and leaned closer, staring into her eyes.

'I recognised your beauty the first moment we met. I still can't believe my luck that you're here with me now, that you're mine.'

His hand was resting on the table, and she reached out tentatively to cover it with her own.

'Am I? Yours, I mean.'

'Well. Only if you *want* to be, of course. Which I sincerely hope you do.' He looked down at her hand on his and smiled. 'We belong together, Carrie. An unbeatable team. From now on, it's the two of us against the world.'

Her eyes slid past him to the Kid Zone, where Sofia was about to add another block to the skinny tower. She moved slowly, as though the block were a bomb that might go off.

'But there are three of us,' Carrie corrected.

The tower swayed and crashed to the floor, sending the two children into fits of giggles.

Josh turned in his chair to look at them, picking up his glass of water.

'Of course. That's what I meant to say, obviously. The *three* of us.'

Then he sipped his water and sat for a while, watching Sofia play, not saying anything.

Twenty-four

Juliet wished she could see the expression on the bearded man's face. She scrolled back a few frames. Froze the image. He was definitely turning his head towards Sofia as she passed. Other children had gone by without attracting his attention. Was that look significant – or was she just desperate, picking on some poor bloke who happened to glance sideways at a passing child?

Juliet leaned back in her chair and rubbed her eyes with her palms. She was tired, worn down by all the dead ends, the briefings leading nowhere. *Yes*, some of the Granger Park regulars thought they remembered seeing a park keeper loading a sack onto a cart. But, *no*, they couldn't provide any sort of description. Couldn't narrow it down by age, race, height or even gender. All they'd seen was an anonymous figure in overalls moving through the woods. Greer was right, the arsehole: uniforms were perfect camouflage.

They'd had similar luck (or lack of it) trying to track down 'anyone suspicious' spotted loitering around the park in the weeks leading up to the abduction. Well-meaning members of the public had offered up a veritable buffet of candidates: old and young, scruffy and posh, men and women. People with dogs and people without. Men in smart suits and drunks swigging from tins. Granger Park, it turned out, was positively awash with sketchy characters. But none of the descriptions matched each other and none of the so-called 'leads' sounded even vaguely promising.

Juliet's eyes drifted back to her computer screen: the man with the beard. Might as well run him by Osman, see if he knew who this person was. She took out her mobile to call him and saw, with a slap of surprise, that she had nine missed calls. Damn it. She must have forgotten to take her phone off mute after the morning briefing. When she switched the sound back on, the phone rang in her hand. Alistair's name appeared on the screen. She frowned. Shouldn't he be home in bed? He'd been coughing and blowing his nose all through the briefing, looking deeply sorry for himself, so she'd told him to go and get some rest and not to move unless there was an absolute emergency.

And yet, here he was.

'Alistair?' There was a pause that told her he was outside somewhere; she could hear the white noise of traffic, a snatch of passing conversation, a man's voice saying, 'Stand back, please.'

'Juliet? Are you there?' His voice was clogged with mucus. 'Why haven't you been answering your phone? Everyone's trying to call you.'

'Sorry, it was on mute. What's going on?'

In the background, a woman's voice began to wail: a long, rising note of hysteria.

'I'm at Tudor Park. You need to get over here right away.'

242

The wail broke apart into a series of hacking sobs. 'There's been another one.'

Carrie peered through her windscreen, trying to see what was going on. She always took Tudor Park Avenue between the office and Sofia's school and had never once come up against a traffic snarl. Yet here she was, trapped between rows of pillared Victorian houses, her view blocked by the white van in front. There must have been an accident up ahead. The van crawled forwards a few inches, its tailpipe trailing a veil of exhaust. She closed the gap and checked the dashboard clock. 1.10. If she wasn't at the school in twenty minutes, she'd be charged for a full day's holiday club.

The traffic eased forwards again, bringing Tudor Park itself into view. Carrie experienced a chill of recognition when she saw what was blocking their path: blue-and-white tape, strung across the road just short of the main entrance. A uniformed officer was standing in front of it, redirecting traffic down a side street.

It's probably nothing, she told herself firmly. *Just a fallen tree or burst water main.*

She was about to follow the flow of vehicles when she spotted DCI Campbell standing next to that other officer who had worked on Sofia's case. Alan? Albert? Something with an A. They were inside the crime tape, speaking to a dark-haired woman wearing a yellow dress and sunglasses pushed up onto her head. As Carrie watched, the woman's face seemed to collapse in on itself. Tears poured down her cheeks.

A car horn blared, jolting her back to the here and now. The uniformed policeman was pointing down the side street with one hand, using the other to wave her towards it. She turned right, following his directions, but instead of continuing on her way, she pulled into a space by the side of the road, ignoring the 'Residents Parking Only' sign.

Layers of sirens were building around her as she got out and doubled back towards the park. She couldn't tell whether they were police, fire or ambulance – only that there were a lot of them. She rounded the corner and the two police officers came back into view. DCI Campbell was jotting down notes as the dark-haired woman spoke in a tear-choked voice that carried across the crime tape.

'I only looked away for a couple of minutes, just a couple of minutes! *Where is she?* Where could she *be?*'

The words sliced into Carrie, tearing open wounds that had only just begun to heal, dragging out painful memories.

An empty climbing frame.

A lone figure in an orange headscarf.

Tara dialling 999.

She walked along the crime tape border until she drew level with the woman in yellow. Then she leaned across, the tape pressing against her thin cotton blouse.

'Has your daughter been abducted too?'

The blotchy woman turned and stared at her.

'Abducted?' she repeated. Then she grabbed at DCI Campbell's arm, shaking it hard. 'She has, hasn't she? That's what this is! Oh God, oh *God!*' And she sank, wailing, to her knees.

DCI Campbell crouched down and put an arm around the woman's shoulders, speaking quietly. Carrie caught the words 'absolutely everything we can' but nothing else.

244

Watching the woman on her knees, Carrie was swept by a wave of empathy and wished, more than ever, that she was a different kind of person: the kind who knew which words to say to make people feel better.

The male officer approached, ducking under the tape to join her on the other side.

'You should check the shed where Sofia was found,' Carrie said to him. 'In case she's there.'

'I'll make sure that we do. Meanwhile, why don't we go for a little walk, give them some space?' His voice was clogged with mucus (had he been crying too? It seemed unlikely; police officers must spend their work days hip-deep in tragedy).

She waited until they'd turned onto the street where she'd parked before speaking again.

'Did my question upset her? I didn't mean for it to.'

'I know you didn't.'

'How old is her daughter?'

'Five.'

Another throb of pain pushed against her chest. 'I hope you find her.'

'So do I. Meanwhile, the best thing you can do is stay out of the way and let us do our jobs. OK?'

'OK.'

'Thank you. We'll be in touch if there are any developments in your daughter's case.' Then he strode back towards the park.

Carrie could still hear the mother's howls as she turned to unlock her car.

Twenty-five

Juliet watched Zoe Cookson riding the zipwire, her movements made jerky by the park's CCTV footage. She scrolled forwards, sending the children and parents rushing frantically around the playground, the roundabout spinning into a blur, seesaws pumping like pistons.

There. She stopped the tape. Went back a few frames. Watched Zoe jump off the zipwire, heading along the edge of the playground towards the swings. But halfway there, she stopped. Turned towards something just outside the CCTV's field of vision. Put a hand over her mouth. Juliet already knew that, in two seconds, the girl would walk towards whatever had attracted her attention and disappear. She froze the image. Was she covering her mouth out of fear? That's what Alistair had suggested. But, to Juliet, that didn't make sense. A five-year-old girl wouldn't stand staring at something that had scared her, then walk *towards* it. She would run *away*, towards her mother.

Juliet squinted at the image, chewing on a thumbnail. She would send this to the techies, see if they could blow it up, sharpen the focus. Meanwhile ... she spooled the footage forwards to the point where Zoe walked out of the shot. She had already scoured every frame of footage in the half-hour periods before and after the point of disappearance. She dragged a hand across the back of her neck, releasing a sigh. Might as well crack on with the next half hour. She hit rewind, sending the playground's occupants running jerkily backward as time reversed itself: five minutes before the disappearance, ten, fifteen, twenty. Then on past thirty into unexamined footage. Thirty-five minutes, forty. Juliet was speeding past forty-five when she spotted something that sent a jolt right through her. She hit pause, freezing the playground at 12.04: forty-seven minutes before Zoe vanished. She leaned towards the screen, staring at the familiar figure seated on the bench at the edge of the playground. Surely that couldn't be a coincidence?

She took out her mobile and called Alistair, eyes returning to the screen, to the figure on the bench, the head turned towards the space in front of the swings where Zoe was playing hopscotch, arms out sideways, one leg bent.

'Alistair,' she said, as soon as he answered. 'I've found a link between Zoe Cookson's abduction and the Sofia Haversen case.'

Tara Weldon had the look of a woman who'd been through something. It was in her eyes and the way she held herself, as though she was struggling beneath an unbearable weight. Or maybe Juliet was just projecting that onto her because of what she now knew: the darkness that lay in her past.

But she wasn't planning to get into any of that just yet. No, for the moment, they would be sticking to the basics, keeping things polite and matter-of-fact.

'What were you doing in Tudor Park yesterday afternoon?' Alistair asked, fingers spread against the cover of the cardboard file in the middle of the interview room table.

'Tudor Park?' She frowned. 'Is this about the girl who went missing from there yesterday? Am I here as a witness? Because I'm afraid I didn't see anything. I only know about it because I got a news flash on my phone.' Alistair and Juliet exchanged a look. Tara must have caught it, because her eyes widened. 'Oh my God … you don't … . . Do you think *I* had something to do with it? Am I a *suspect*?' She stared across the table at them, her face a portrait of shocked disbelief.

She's good, Juliet thought. *I'm almost buying this.*

'For now, we're just asking you to help us out with a few questions.' Juliet flipped open the file and took out the CCTV image of Tara on the bench, pushing it across the table. 'So can you please tell us what you were doing in the park?'

Tara looked down at the photo.

'Eating my lunch. As I do most days when it's sunny.'

'Tudor Park isn't near your home,' Alistair said.

'No. It's near my work'

'Why sit in the playground? There are plenty of quieter, more peaceful locations. The rose garden, for example.'

'I don't want quiet. I like the sound of children playing.' She looked from Alistair to Juliet and back again. 'Is there something wrong with that?'

'No,' Juliet said. 'But it is unusual, for an adult to go to a playground without a child.'

'Is it? I don't see why that should be.' Tara's tone was non-chalant, almost bored. She was adapting, finding her mental footing. Which was exactly what they didn't want.

'On 28 June, you made a 999 call about a child going missing in Granger Park playground, after leading an unofficial search for her. And now, just twenty-six days later, here you are again, at yet another London park where yet another five-year-old girl has gone missing.' Juliet leaned forwards across the table, narrowing the distance between them, staring straight into Tara Weldon's eyes. 'Quite a coincidence, don't you agree?'

'Yes. I agree. It's a very weird coincidence.' Tara lifted a shoulder. 'But that's *all* it is.'

Juliet leaned back again, crossing her legs.

'So what did you have to eat?'

Tara stared. 'Excuse me?'

'Today, in the park. You say you went there to eat your lunch. What did you have?'

'Oh. It was . . .' – she dragged a finger across closed lids – 'a mozzarella and grilled vegetable sandwich. From Paul's on the High Street.'

'Really.' Juliet pushed the CCTV picture further forwards, until it was in danger of falling off the edge of the table into Tara's lap. 'Then where is it? Because all I see is an Evian bottle.'

Tara's forehead gathered as she squinted down at the image. Then her eyebrows rose suddenly, their message as clear as a pantomime actor's: *Oh, yes, NOW I remember!*

'I went to the gym this morning, which meant I was starving by lunch time. I ate the sandwich while walking to the park, so, by the time I got there, only the water was left.'

'Well, that's easy enough to check.' Juliet watched Tara closely for any sign of alarm at this statement, but her face was blank. 'So you arrived and sat on the bench, drinking water and watching Zoe play.'

'I wasn't watching *Zoe*. I don't know Zoe. I was just looking out over the playground. At all the children.'

'So you weren't paying particular attention to Zoe?'

'No.'

Juliet tapped the CCTV still. 'The thing is, it really looks like you're watching her in this picture.'

Tara looked down at the image. She shook her head, frowning.

'I suppose it's possible that I watched her for a bit. I look at a lot of children while I'm sitting in the park.'

'Especially five-year-old girls?'

She looked up sharply. 'What do you mean?'

'I've examined all the footage from the moment you sat down. Every time a girl of about that age goes by, you turn your head to watch her pass. You don't do that with girls in different age groups. And you don't appear to watch boys at all.' She leaned against the table on her forearms. 'Why is that?'

Tara's features turned to stone. She crossed her arms over her stomach.

'I don't know what you mean.'

Juliet's voice was quiet.

'I think you do.'

'All I . . .' Tara began, then flinched as the interview-room door banged open.

Juliet turned, glaring, towards the source of the interruption. Ravi Hiranand was standing just inside the room, face blazing with news.

'DCI Campbell, may I have a word? It's urgent.'

★   ★   ★

250

'This had better be bloody important,' Juliet said, the moment the door clicked shut behind her. 'I was at a very sensitive point in that interview when you came barging in.'

'Trust me, you'll want to hear this.' DS Hiranand shot a look up and down the corridor, but they were alone aside from a ponytailed WPC on her mobile at the far end. 'There's been a 999 call from a woman in South Acton. She says she's standing beside a padlocked metal building on a construction site. And there's a girl inside, screaming to be let out.'

The sun was starting to set by the time they arrived, stretching shadows across the churned earth and shading in the spaces between the skeletons of what would eventually become multi-storey buildings. Alistair parked the Mazda beside a huge wooden sign facing the road, informing passers-by that 'South Acton Mansions is a luxurious, modern development with excellent transport links.'

The ambulance had arrived ahead of them and Juliet could see Zoe sitting in the back with a blanket wrapped around her shoulders. A female medic with a pixie-cut was crouching in front of her, holding a plastic cup to the girl's lips.

Zoe had been found inside a temporary storage unit: one of the windowless metal boxes construction companies put up at the start of long-term projects. The door was hanging from its hinges; presumably the officers who'd arrived on the scene first had broken it down. A constable was winding police tape around the stem of a loading-zone sign at the side of the road.

The humidity pressed itself against Juliet's skin like a wet flannel. She took out a tissue, using it to blot her forehead.

'Twenty quid says that's the 999 caller,' Alistair said, pointing towards the trailer that had served as South Acton Mansions' HQ before a funding dispute had halted construction. A middle-aged woman in a navy dress and sandals was perched on the stairs watching the ambulance and fanning herself with a magazine. The light was fading but the temperature stubbornly refused to budge.

Juliet nodded. 'I reckon you're right. Can you take a statement, while her memory's still fresh?'

'You got it.'

'Oh, and if you happen to bump into Greer – he should be here any moment – can you tell him to do a full assessment of the site? I want to know all possible access points and the location of every CCTV camera.'

'You got it,' Alistair said again, and strode off towards the woman in navy.

Juliet returned her attention to the ambulance, where the medic was now taking Zoe's blood pressure. A uniformed PC stepped into view from behind the vehicle, looking down at his notebook. Juliet strode towards him, catching his eye as he glanced up: tall – maybe six-three – with dark hair and a rugby build.

'Can I help you?' His tone implied she'd been caught doing something wrong. Perhaps he thought she was a reporter, or a passer-by who'd sneaked under the crime tape for kicks.

She flashed her ID. 'DCI Campbell.'

His face did a rapid shift from accusatory to sheepish.

'Oh. Right. Sorry. I didn't . . .'

'And you are?'

'PC James Callaghan. First officer on the scene. I released the girl.'

She instinctively looked towards Zoe, who was watching the blood-pressure cuff inflate around her arm. When Juliet's gaze switched back again, she caught the constable looking her up and down, and wondered briefly what that told her about PC Callaghan. Was he a racist, annoyed at having to answer to a superior with her skin colour ... or just a typical bloke, discretely checking out an attractive woman?

She tilted her head towards the notebook in his hand.

'So ... bring me up to speed.'

He flipped through a few pages, then pushed back his shoulders, like a soldier snapping to attention.

'Elsbeth Parkinson, age forty-eight, was walking towards the train station from her home in the Golden Heights development' – he gestured towards the shiny block of flats beyond the construction site – 'when she heard screams and shouts for help. There were no workers on the site. She followed the shouts to a temporary storage structure, which was locked, and, as you can observe for yourself, has no windows. She called 999. Myself and PC Wilkins attended the scene. We heard a girl crying through the door and asked her to tell us her name. She said Zoe.' He flipped the notebook shut. 'We broke open the door and freed the girl.'

'Did you question her?'

The PC looked uncomfortable. 'Not formally, obviously, since that would have required her legal guardian and ...'

Juliet rolled her eyes. 'I'm not asking you to recite the police handbook on questioning juveniles. I'm asking you to tell me what you said to her when you opened the door and what she said in response.'

She waited, breath held. The clock was ticking on how much

253

longer they could hold Tara Weldon. Right now there simply wasn't enough evidence to charge her, so unless Zoe could help, they would be forced to let her go when their twenty-four hours ran out.

The PC scratched his neck and Juliet noticed a heat rash creeping out from under the collar of his police shirt.

'I asked her how she came to be inside the metal structure and she responded that she didn't know, and that she didn't see the person who brought her here. The last thing she remembered was seeing a teddy bear just outside the playground. Then waking up here. Nothing in between.'

Another stuffed toy, another victim rendered unconscious by an unseen attacker. It had to be the same offender. She looked at the metal shed, with its broken door.

'Waking up alone in the pitch dark, poor thing.'

'She wasn't in the dark.'

'Really? That metal box has its own power supply?'

'No. The abductor left a torch lying beside her, switched on.'

Juliet ran a hand across her hair as she digested this, fingers conducting an automatic check for rogue spirals. But the humidity seemed to have trapped everything in place.

'I'll go take a look. I trust you didn't move anything?'

'God, no. I know the CSM's views on such things.' His rueful smile told her he'd come up on the wrong side of the crime scene manager before.

There were two CSIs inside the shed. One was on his (or was it her? Hard to tell in those masks and plastic suits) knees using tweezers to transfer something into an evidence bag. The other was taking photos of the inflatable mattress, the flashes stuttering like lightning against the metal walls. Juliet's eyes moved to the torch on the floor, its beam sending a cone of light across the teddy bear lying in front of it, a red bow around its neck.

Juliet turned around to leave, only to walk straight into PC Callaghan, who had appeared in the doorway, the ricochet knocking her off balance. She stumbled and he caught her arm.

'Sorry, DCI Campbell. I didn't mean to creep up on you.'

He was standing so close that she had to tilt back her head to look him in the eye, making her conscious of the difference in their heights.

'It's fine,' she said, then aimed a pointed gaze at his fingers, still on her arm. He withdrew his hand quickly, falling back a step. He stood with his legs slightly apart, arms behind his back, like a soldier awaiting orders. He'd definitely spent time in the military. 'So, PC Callaghan, what's your read on this?'

'You want my opinion?' He sounded surprised. Perhaps he'd found that DCIs didn't tend to take much interest in the thoughts of lowly uniforms.

'You were the first person on the scene, and therefore the one best placed to provide a first impression. I'd like to know what that impression is.'

She watched his forehead scrunch in thought.

'The girl was upset. And hot, obviously. But I wouldn't say she was traumatised. Whoever did this took steps to minimise the victim's distress by providing a light source and an air mattress. Even a toy. That doesn't say cold-blooded criminal to me.'

'I agree.' She glanced back into the shed. 'Anything else?'

'She wasn't gagged. Most of the owners from the first phase of the property development have moved in. Their route to the train station goes right past this site. So the chances of someone hearing Zoe scream for help were very high.'

'Hmm. Good point.' She looked from the railway station to the new development, its windows lit pink by the falling sun. Sofia's location had been a much better choice, with its abandoned houses and danger signs. Did that mean the abductor was becoming more careless ... or more desperate?

There was a peel of rubber and a crunch of gravel. A police car swung into view, bouncing across the uneven ground towards the ambulance. It was still moving when the back door flew open. Zoe Cookson's mother burst out in a run, nearly losing her footing before staggering back up, racing towards the ambulance, shouting her daughter's name.

'Mummy!' The little girl jumped down from the vehicle and ran into her mother's arms, the two figures merging into one.

Juliet could feel emotion rising inside her chest, tickling the base of her throat. She swallowed it back down and returned her attention to PC Callaghan, who was watching the reunion with a broad smile.

'*So,*' Juliet said, drawing him back, 'taking into account those first impressions, what conclusions would you draw as to motive?'

He folded his arms over his chest as he considered this.

'Not some soulless child trafficker. I guess it could be a paedophile: one who's deluded himself into thinking he has an actual relationship with the girl, but ...' His voice faded out. He shook his head.

'But?' She watched his eyes flicker back and forth, as though scanning his own thoughts.

'But … it doesn't feel right. I can't put my finger on it, it's just …'

'Instinct?' she finished.

'Yes, for want of a better word.' The ambulance's engine rumbled to life, drawing their eyes towards it. The back doors were still open, so they could see the medic speaking to Mrs Cookson, who was seated sideways on a stretcher with her daughter curled up on her lap. The PC's gaze returned to Juliet. 'Now that the mum's here, are you going to ask Zoe any questions before they take her off to hospital?'

'Yes. Just one. The rest can wait.'

The little girl's head turned as Juliet stepped up into the back of the vehicle. Dark brown eyes and dark curly hair. Like Sofia. Her face was a little puffy but the tears had dried out. She looked calm – bored, almost. Amazing, the speed with which children bounced back.

'Hello, Zoe.' She gave her a warm smile and received a shy one in return. 'My name's Juliet. I'm a police officer.'

'Hi.'

'I'd like to ask you a question, but only if that's OK with your mummy.'

She looked at Emma Cookson, who nodded, arms wrapped tight around her daughter.

'What's your favourite animal in the whole world?'

The answer was immediate. 'Bunnies are my best.'

'Bunnies? Not bears?'

'No.'

'Do you have many teddy bears at home?'

A headshake.

'But you liked the teddy bear in the park?'

'It was OK. It had a red ribbon on and I like ribbons.'

'But it's still not as good as a rabbit?'

'No way.'

Juliet resisted an urge to rumple the girl's hair. The CSM would have her head on a platter if she messed around with it before they were done combing for skin cells and particles of cloth and God only knew what else.

'Thank you, Zoe. I'd like to come and visit you in the hospital for another chat, if that's OK.'

'Why can't I go home? The hospital is only for sick people and I'm not sick.'

'We just want to make extra sure you're OK. Plus it means you get to go for a ride in an ambulance. Which is pretty cool. I'll bet your friends will be impressed when you tell them about it.'

Zoe straightened in her mother's lap, eyes lighting.

'Will the blue light on top be flashing?'

Juliet glanced at the medic, who nodded.

'It will. I better leave now so that you can get going. And get flashing.' The little girl giggled. 'Bye, Zoe.'

'Bub-bye.'

Juliet hopped down to the ground, where PC Callaghan stood waiting. The medic shooed them back a few steps as she leaned out to pull the doors shut. A moment later the ambulance was lurching across the ragged earth, lights flashing, siren mute.

'Why did you ask about her favourite animal?' the PC asked.

She shot him a side-glance. 'You're an eavesdropper.'

'An investigator,' he corrected. 'The two go hand in hand. So? Why did you?'

She smiled. 'Just making conversation.'

'Well, you must—'

'Juliet!'

She turned to find Alistair striding towards her from the site office, tucking his notebook back into his pocket. He jerked his head sideways, in the direction of the Mazda, eyebrows lifting. She responded with a nod.

'So I guess you're off, then?' PC Callaghan took off his police cap, running fingers through sweat-damp hair.

'Yes.' She offered him her hand to shake. "Thank you for your assistance.' His grip was firm, but not aggressively so.

'Happy to help in any way I can. In fact' – he cleared his throat and threw back his shoulders again – 'perhaps you'd like to discuss the case over coffee some time?'

She felt her eyebrows rise before quickly schooling her features back into neutral.

'Thank you for the offer. I'll be in touch if I need you.'

'Oh. OK. Bye, then.'

'Goodbye, PC Callaghan.'

She could feel a small smile growing across her face as she turned and walked towards the car.

So not a racist, then.

Twenty-six

Carrie picked up a forkful of the spaghetti Josh had made, then put it back down again. Her stomach was too knotted for food.

The DCI was on her way over, to 'talk through the day's developments'.

What had the police found out? Had the girl in Tudor Park been taken by the same person as Sofia? And, if so, did that mean the abductions weren't targeted after all? She looked across at her daughter, who seemed to be endlessly twirling her fork against the plate. Carrie took a large slug of wine, draining her glass. Josh refilled it without a word.

He had spent the whole afternoon telling her not to jump to conclusions, to wait and hear what the police had to say. But when Sky quoted an unnamed source saying a suspect was in custody, 'believed to be female', she felt ready to jump out of her own skin.

'I'm not hungry,' Sofia said, pushing her plate all the way across the table, as though it might be radioactive.

'But spaghetti bolognese is your favourite.'

'I feel yukky.' Carrie was about to check her forehead when the doorbell buzzed.

Josh's head snapped towards the sound.

'That must be the police,' he said. 'Shall I go—'

But Carrie was already rushing towards the door.

The buzzer sounded again as she peered through the peep-hole, which offered a funhouse view of DCI Campbell and her Irish colleague. She threw open the door and stood facing them across the threshold, breath coming fast.

'Who is it?' she asked immediately. 'Who is the suspect?'

'It's too early to use the word "suspect" at this—' the police-woman began, then her head suddenly rocked back as though she'd been struck. She was staring into the house, eyes wide, lips parted. 'Why is Josh Skelter in your house?'

Carrie glanced over her shoulder at Josh, who was clearing the table, Sofia's uneaten plate of spaghetti in his hand.

'He is staying with us temporarily as an extra security measure.'

Juliet's eyebrows slid into a V-shape.

'So the two of you are ... what exactly? Friends?'

'We are in a sexual relationship.'

'Really? How ...'

'That's not important,' Carrie interrupted, as jagged nerves tore through her last scrap of patience. 'Can you just tell me who is in custody? Do you believe it to be the same person who took Sofia?'

Juliet cast one last look at Josh (now scraping food into the bin) before shifting her attention to Carrie's question.

'We haven't formally arrested anyone. We are currently

261

speaking to a person of interest, but at this stage we don't have enough evidence to lay charges.'

'Who is the person of interest?'

There was a high-pitched shriek from the direction of the street.

The three of them turned to see a pair of young women struggling out of a taxi. One of them must have been drunk, because she had lost her footing and was clinging to her friend's arm with both hands, nearly pulling her over. DCI Campbell sighed and returned her attention to Carrie.

'Can we discuss this inside, please? I need to ask you a couple of questions.'

'What do you know about Tara Weldon?'

Carrie stared across the dining table, eyes shuttling back and forth between the two officers. Sofia was lying on the sofa wearing headphones attached to her iPad, so the only sound was the clatter of cutlery as Josh loaded the dishwasher. He had retreated into the kitchen when DCI Campbell said she needed to speak to Carrie alone.

'What do you mean?'

The policewoman's notepad was in her hand, pen suspended above it.

'Had you ever crossed paths with her prior to the day Sofia went missing? Perhaps at the park?'

'No. We met for the first time that day.' She stared across at the DCI, confused, blinking. 'I don't understand this. Why are we still discussing my friends and contacts? Hasn't the investigation moved on from this stage?'

'Friends?' DCI Campbell repeated, lifting one eyebrow. 'Are you ... have you and Tara Weldon been in contact since Sofia's abduction?'

'Yes.'

The policewoman ran a hand along the side of her hair, fingers pausing on one of the clips there.

The male officer spoke for the first time.

'Tara Weldon is a person of interest in this investigation.'

His words hit Carrie like a wave, knocking right through her, upending all her newly built hope and trust, sending it scattering.

Tara was the suspect.

She sat perfectly still, waiting for the shock to fade and become manageable. But it kept rebounding, slamming back into her. The police were in her home because they believed that Carrie's best friend – let's face it, her *only* friend – had stolen and imprisoned her daughter.

She spread her fingers against the surface of the dining table, pressing down hard, taking comfort in the solidity of it, the immutable fact of the wood.

No.

This was a mistake. The police had been wrong before – not once, but twice. First about Simon, then the park keeper. And they were wrong again now.

'Tara was with me, leading the search, right after Sofia disappeared. It is therefore impossible for her to have been involved in the abduction.'

'Not *right* after,' Juliet corrected. 'According to your statement, you conducted a solo search of the entire playground and the children's woods *before* Tara appeared on the scene.'

263

'Yes. But that wouldn't have provided her with enough time to remove Sofia from the park and then transport her all the way to Perivale, let alone return afterwards.'

But even as she said the words, Carrie knew they must be redundant, because the officers would surely know that already; anyone with the most basic geography of London could have worked it out. So why were they still pointing the finger at Tara? It didn't make sense. Unless ...

'Do you think she was working with someone else? An accomplice? Because otherwise it's ...'

'Carrie,' DCI Campbell interrupted.

'Yes?'

'It would be helpful if you could just answer *my* questions for the moment. I'm not able to provide answers to yours because I don't have them yet. Right now, experts are going through the contents of Tara's computers and mobile phone, so we hope to have more information soon.'

'But *why*? Why would she do it?'

'At this point, we're still working to establish that she *did* do it,' Juliet said. 'As things now stand, the evidence is purely circumstantial. All we can say with certainty is that Tara was in both Granger Park and Tudor Park at the time of both abductions. But that could just be a coincidence.'

Could just be a coincidence.

Carrie grabbed on to the words like a lifeline. Coincidences happened. It was a fact of life. It wasn't even that big a coincidence, when you thought about it. Because although the two parks were miles apart, they were both very popular. At this time of year, tens of thousands of people probably passed through them every day. So why shouldn't there be some overlap?

But even as she clung to it, she could feel the lifeline slipping through her fingers. Because this wasn't the *only* coincidence, was it? There had been another chance meeting, another unlikely coincidence. One that she'd kept from the police.

Josh came out of the kitchen just long enough to place a steaming French press and three mugs on the table before retreating behind the counter again.

The coffee hadn't had time to steep, but Carrie pushed down on the plunger anyway, watching it descend through the brown murk. Her throat felt tight, as though it were trying to stop her next words, trap them inside.

'Tara met Sofia before the abduction.'

The two officers exchanged glances.

'You never mentioned that before,' DCI Campbell said.

'I wasn't there and only found out about it a short time ago.'

'Can you provide more details? When, where and under what circumstances?'

'At a child's birthday party at the south end of Granger Park about two weeks before the abduction.' Carrie poured coffee into mugs. 'Tara was the caterer. She rescued Sofia's balloon from a tree. They had a brief conversation.'

DCI Campbell's pen raced across the small pad.

'What did the two of them discuss during that conversation?'

'Pets and animals.'

The two officers swapped another of those glances. Carrie didn't need to be able to read faces to know what that one meant.

'Did Sofia mention her interest in penguins?'

Carrie placed the newly filled cups in front of her guests. If they wanted milk or sugar, they could add it themselves.

'Yes. Sofia was wearing face paint that made her look like a cat. Tara mentioned having a cat. Sofia said cats were her second favourite animal after penguins. That is all I know.'

DCI Campbell crossed her legs, propping the notepad on a raised knee. Her pen zipped back and forth.

'When you first met Tara, right after Sofia went missing, what *exactly* did she say to you?'

'She introduced herself and said she would help me find my daughter. Some other mums had come over and she asked them to help. Then she organised a search party, assigning people to different parts of the park.'

'But she didn't send anyone to the closed-off section at the north end, did she?' the male officer asked.

'No.' Carrie poured milk into her cup and watched the clouds it made, churning across the surface like an arriving storm.

DCI Campbell looked up from her pad.

'Did she or anyone else suggest contacting the police immediately, prior to the search?'

Carrie took a sip of coffee. It tasted weak.

'I asked her whether we should call the police. But Tara thought we would be able to find Sofia ourselves.'

This time when DCI Campbell and her colleague made eye contact, they added on a little nod as well.

The policewoman jotted on her notebook, then added a teaspoon of sugar to her coffee. 'So it was only after the search was complete and had failed to produce Sofia that Tara agreed to call 999?'

'She was the one who suggested it. And made the call herself.'

'OK.' Another teaspoon of sugar went in, then another.

'Adding the time you spent searching on your own to the time it took to organise the search party and the half-hour search itself, would it be accurate to say that the police were alerted roughly an hour after Sofia's disappearance?'

'Yes.'

More sugar. There must be five spoonfuls in there now.

'Let's move on to your subsequent encounters with Tara. When did you meet her next?'

'We ran into each other at Bundy's indoor play centre and she invited us – Sofia and me – to visit her workplace the following Wednesday. After that she came here for dinner and drinks. On a later occasion, she assisted me with a work matter, then we had lunch near my office. And we went to a bar for drinks last Friday.'

She had hoped this information would be sufficient. No such luck.

'Can you take me through those encounters, one-by-one, telling me everything you remember about them?' DCI Campbell said. 'The things you discussed and any interaction Tara had with your daughter?'

So Carrie told the two officers about the magical-everything cupcakes and Tara's help putting Sofia to bed. About the chats over coffee, then wine, then cocktails. About dancing in the living room and relationship advice in the nook of a Soho bar.

The policewoman wrote it all down, transforming warm moments of friendship into cold pieces of evidence. And as she watched DCI Campbell's pen racing back and forth, a dark stain began to creep across the memories, corrupting them. Until none of it seemed real any more.

*　　*　　*

267

Sofia felt sick. Hot and sick. Also her head hurt. She'd tried to tell Mummy about it, but then the police people came. They were gone now, but Mummy and Josh were in the kitchen, which all of a sudden seemed far away. They were talking and not paying attention to Sofia, who was lying on the sofa with the iPad beside her. She could still hear Peppa Pig in the head-phones, but she wasn't watching any more. The screen was too bright; it made her eyes hurt, and her brain kept floating away from the story. She felt a ball of sick growing inside her, getting bigger and bigger until she thought she was going to puke all over the sofa. But then it shrank back down and the sick stayed stuck inside, which was worse.

Sofia had never felt so hot before. It was scary. She wanted Mummy to give her a cuddle and some medicine. Her head flopped sideways so that her cheek was lying on the sofa. She could see Mummy and Josh standing talking to each other across the kitchen counter.

'Mummy.' Her voice came out like a whisper, even though she'd tried to shout with all her best strength. Mummy didn't hear her and she couldn't see her either, because she was facing the wrong way. But Josh was facing the right way.

He nodded in her direction and said: 'Looks like she's dozing off. Why don't I pop her up to bed, then we can discuss this further.'

Good. He could tell Mummy she was sick. He came and picked her up, making a wave of sick go up and down. It filled up her throat so she couldn't talk again until they were already upstairs, going into her room.

'I'm sick. I want Mummy.'

'Your mother and I have some very important, grown-up

things we need to talk about right now. I'll send her up a bit later.'

'But I need her *now*. I'm scared.'

Josh put her into her pyjamas and tucked her in without even remembering to brush her teeth.

'There's nothing to be scared of. All you need is a nice glass of water and a good night's sleep.' He went away and came back with water, which he put up to her mouth. She heard her teeth chattering against the glass and that made her feel even more scared.

'Close your eyes and I promise you'll feel better in the morning.'

He got up and walked to the door.

'I want Mummy,' Sofia said, starting to cry.

He looked back at her from the doorway and sighed.

'Tell you what: I'll send her up in ten minutes to give you a goodnight kiss. But only if you promise to try and go to sleep until then.'

'OK.'

Sofia lay staring at the cartoon stars feeling sick and boiling hot and headachy, listening for her mother's feet on the stairs.

But Mummy never came.

Twenty-seven

'I don't believe you wanted to harm either of these girls,' Alistair said, tapping the two photos on the interview room table. 'I understand why you did it. And I sympathise.'

Tara stared straight ahead, hands in her lap, face a blank mask. Which was hardly surprising, Juliet thought. She must have built strong walls around this subject to keep herself going for the last five years.

Tara's motive lay in the file on the table between them, spelled out on two soulless, bloodless forms. In the heartbreakingly short gap between dates.

Clarissa Weldon. Date of Birth: 2 September 2014. Date of Death: 11 August 2015. Juliet lifted the file's cover to let Tara see the birth certificate, before dropping it shut again.

'She would have been turning six soon, just like Sofia,' Alistair said softly. 'And Zoe' Juliet noticed a small tightening in Tara's jaw as her mask buckled slightly under the pressure. 'You wanted her back. So you decided to take another girl. A girl the same age as Clarissa would have been.'

Tara crossed her arms tightly over her chest. Shook her head.

'No. That's not true.'

Alistair removed another photo from the file, placing it beside the two images of Sofia and Zoe. A baby's smiling face.

'She had your ex-husband's brown eyes and your dark hair,' he said. 'Both the girls who went missing had the same colouring.'

'No.'

'No, they didn't have the same colouring? Because clearly ...'

'No, I didn't take them. No, I didn't try to steal another child to replace the one I'd lost. Clarissa is irreplaceable. It's offensive to suggest I would simply exchange her for another child, like some sort of ... broken doll. Clarissa is gone for ever and no one on this Earth can change that.'

Juliet watched Tara's features closely, waiting for the feeling to come: that satisfying sensation of facts clicking into place as pieces of the puzzle slotted themselves together to create a coherent picture. It was bound to happen at some point during this interview, as her instincts confirmed what the facts had already told her: that Tara Weldon was behind both abductions. That she had enlisted the help of a petty drug dealer to get Sofia out of the park. Perhaps Nick Laude hadn't even known what he was getting into. Perhaps she'd told him there were drugs hidden inside that sack.

Alistair drummed his fingers against the edge of the table.

'When did you and your ex-husband split up?'

He and Juliet had discussed these questions beforehand. She'd wanted him to take the lead in this interview so she could focus all her attention on Tara's voice, face and body language.

'Seven months after Clarissa died.'

'And what was the reason for that?'

271

Tara fixed him with an empty stare.

'He didn't like my grief.'

Alistair's hand dipped inside the file again, like a magician reaching into a hat. He pulled out a stapled, three-page document and held it up (*ta dah!*) so that she could see what it was. Then he tossed it onto the table beside the baby photo. Tara's gaze didn't shift. She stared across the table at him with those empty eyes.

'According to your medical records' – he circled a palm above the pages – 'you suffered from serious depression between 2015 and 2016 but refused to seek treatment.'

'What treatment would you have suggested I seek? There was a real and compelling reason for me to be incredibly sad. No cocktail of chemicals was going to change that. And anyway, I didn't *want* to numb my feelings about Clari. They were all I had left of her.'

'It didn't have to be chemicals. You could have sought counselling.'

She shook her head. 'I had no desire to pour my heart out to some stranger. I only wanted to share those thoughts and feelings with my husband. But he wanted us to *move on.*' Her eyes settled on the baby photo for a moment before she tore them away again, clamping her gaze on Alistair's. 'He put all her things in storage and said there was no point dwelling on the past. That's the word he used: *dwelling.*'

'So would it be fair to say that you have been unable to get over the loss of your daughter?'

'It would be fair to say that I will never get over that loss.'

Alistair pushed his hands up the sides of his head, taking his time, pausing ahead of his next move.

'Nick Laude is in the next interview room. We will be speaking to him as soon as we're done here. The poor lad is feeling rather stressed right now. The woman he claims to have been shagging at the time of the abduction has gone AWOL. Which means he doesn't have an alibi. So it would be accurate to say that desperation is setting in. Fortunately for Nick, we will be offering him a deal in exchange for his testimony about the two of you working together.'

Tara laughed: a hollow sound without an ounce of humour in it.

'Yeah, good luck with that.'

This wasn't working. Juliet leaned across the table on her forearms, determined to provoke a reaction.

'We know you met Sofia two weeks before she was taken. You wanted her for your own, to plug the hole Clarissa's death had left in your life. She told you about her love of penguins, so you decided to use one as bait. You knew about Laude's drug dealing and enlisted his help – perhaps threatened to report him if he didn't do as you said. And when your plan fell through, you tried again. Another park, another dark-eyed, curly-haired girl.'

Tara closed her eyes and sighed.

'Have either of you stopped for a minute to try and think this theory through? Because it doesn't stand up to any kind of scrutiny. What exactly would I do with this child afterwards, given that half the world was searching for her?'

'We *have* thought it through,' Alistair said, returning Tara's medical records to the file. 'We believe you were planning to leave the country with her, to take her to Hong Kong. You have permanent residency there and went to the trouble of obtaining it for Clarissa too, when she was still a new-born,

273

perhaps because you were thinking about emigrating. You have family there, no? A sister? Clarissa's Hong Kong passport doesn't expire for another two months and the baby in the photo could easily be Sofia or Zoe. So you could have gotten either one of them out of the country. Started a new life in Asia.' He tented his fingers in front of his chin. 'Or maybe we're giving you too much credit. Maybe you weren't thinking logically at all. Maybe you were acting on instinct, driven by emotion, by grief. Anyone would understand that. Anyone would sympathise.'

Tara's expression didn't change.

'You have my computer. You have my mobile. Any sign of an attempt to book a plane ticket?'

'You're too smart for that. My guess is you were planning to buy one at the airport. No one would think twice about a mother carrying a sleeping child onto an overnight flight.'

Juliet cut in, trying to soften the mood, bring Tara's defences down a notch.

'We know you're a good mother, Tara. No one doubts that. Despite the incredibly tough challenges you've faced. And not just Clarissa. We know all about your recent issues with—'

'Is that what we've come here to discuss?' Tara snapped. 'What kind of mother I am?'

'All we're saying is that we don't believe you meant Sofia or Zoe any harm,' Alistair said. 'Quite the opposite; you were offering them love. A new family.'

'You've got my mobile phone. And have no doubt used it to track my movements. So, tell me: is there any sign of my having gone anywhere near Perivale or South Acton on the dates in question?'

'Of course not,' Alistair said. 'That would have been careless.

274

You left your phone behind. Or perhaps arranged for your accomplice to take care of that end of things. You read about that street being evacuated and saw an opportunity: a perfect location. You didn't even need to gag your victim because there was no one around to hear her scream. Or there wouldn't have been, if Josh Skelter hadn't chosen to ignore the hazard signs.'

Tara rolled her eyes and made a scoffing sound with her throat.

Juliet could hear a prickle of irritation in Alistair's voice as he continued.

'Sofia was discovered before you had the chance to collect her. So then, lo and behold, *another* child goes missing from another park you just so happened to be in. Another girl the same age as your daughter would have been if she'd lived. You weren't planning to hold her at that construction site for long, though, were you? No sandwich this time. The location wasn't isolated, like Perivale, but you still didn't gag her. Because you didn't think you *needed* to; you were planning to collect her before she regained consciousness. But then we ruined everything by bringing you in for questioning. Holding you here until the drugs wore off and Zoe woke up and started screaming.'

He gave her a triumphant, we've-got-you stare, but Tara merely waved a hand in the air and said: 'Is there a question in there?'

'Yes, as a matter of fact, there is.' Alistair slowly gathered up the photos and documents from the table, tucking them back inside the file. 'Given all the evidence stacked against you, are you sure there isn't something you'd like to tell us ... *before* we start speaking to Nick Laude?'

A rictus-smile. 'I have no idea who that is. But you go ahead and speak to him. Don't let me keep you.'

Alistair turned towards Juliet, eyebrows lifted in a silent query: *Any ideas?*

She responded with a small head shake.

'DI Alistair Larkin terminating interview at twenty-two forty-seven,' he told the tape. Tara stared emptily into the distance as Juliet and Alistair stood up.

The interview was over and the feeling hadn't come.

Twenty-eight

'You need to stay away from her,' Josh said, chopping red onions into tiny squares. 'She's dangerous.'

Carrie closed her eyes, feeling a headache brewing behind them. She'd spent the last twenty-four hours swerving between conflicting versions of the truth and had gone to bed feeling as if her mind was tied in knots. She had hoped a good night's sleep would bring clarity, but she'd woken up just as confused and disoriented as ever, caught in a tug of war between loyalty and suspicion.

'Tara's only being questioned. That doesn't mean she's done anything wrong. The DCI herself said this could just be a coincidence. If the police aren't rushing to judgement, then nor should we.'

'You seriously believe it's just a coincidence that Tara showed up in two different parks at the same time that two different children went missing?' *Chop-chop-chop.* 'I don't think so.' He shook his head, pressing his lips together. 'Well, hopefully she'll be charged and locked up, so the question of whether or not you should see her again becomes moot.'

Carrie twisted the handle of the tin opener, wishing he would change the subject. Her insides felt heavy, as though her stomach was filled with wet sand. The opener carved a circular path around the tomato tin. Josh was cooking his 'Spanish-style omelette' for breakfast, which seemed to involve tossing eggs into a pan along with whatever else happened to be in the fridge.

'Tara is my friend. I can't just turn my back on her when we don't know that she's done anything wrong.'

'She's not your friend.' The knife rose and fell, rose and fell. Did the omelette really need that much onion? 'She only *pretended* to be your friend to gain access to your child. You mustn't let her come anywhere near Sofia again. It's too big a risk.'

'That doesn't make any sense.' She spooned tomatoes into a bowl. 'Why would Tara want to steal my child? She already has a child.'

'*Does* she? How do you know that? You've never seen him.'

And, suddenly, she understood.

That's assuming she even has a son.

Josh didn't believe Peter existed.

The shock of realisation hit her like a slap of cold water, cutting through the blurry film of confusion, leaving her sharp and alert for the first time that morning. She turned slowly towards him.

'Why would Tara claim to have a son if that's not the case?'

'So she could connect with you, as a mother, then use your relationship to gain access to Sofia.'

'But—'

Her mobile buzzed against the counter beside Josh. He glanced down at it and his mouth pulled to one side.

278

'Speak of the devil.' He held the phone out to her. 'It's Tara. I guess the twenty-four hours ran out, so they had to let her go. For now.' Carrie stared at the mobile ringing in his hand. She felt a powerful urge to turn and walk away, to go back up the stairs and back to bed. To start this day all over again.

Josh's eyebrows rose. 'Aren't you going to answer?'

Carrie took the phone. Pressed 'Accept'.

'Hello, Tara.' Her bare toes curled against the wood floor as she said her friend's name.

'Hi, Carrie.' A pause. 'I guess you've probably heard. About me being questioned?'

'Yes.'

Josh turned towards the stove, tipping onions into the frying pan.

'Can you believe it? I totally get why the police wanted to talk to me. The same person being in two different parks when two children were taken. What are the chances?'

'Slim.' She shot a side-glance at Josh. 'Though by no means impossible.'

'Well, I think it's a pretty remarkable coincidence.' Carrie could hear Tara breathing in the pause that followed. 'Look, I just wanted to make sure you know I had absolutely nothing to do with what happened to that Zoe girl. And I certainly had nothing to do with Sofia's disappearance.' Another pause. 'You *do* know that, right?'

Carrie blinked, trying to work out whether this was a serious question, or one of those hypothetical ones that always threw her. Because if a real answer was required, she wasn't sure what hers would be. Until yesterday, she had viewed Tara as her friend and confidante, a trusted ally in the struggle to overcome her

279

condition. But after the double barrage of DCI Campbell's questions and Josh's warnings, could she honestly claim to be 100 per cent certain of Tara's innocence?

And then there was the other question, the one that Josh had left ricocheting around inside her head.

'Tara, why haven't I met Peter?'

'You *have*. In the park. And at Bundy's.'

'No. I didn't see him in either of those places.'

'How odd, I could have sworn I pointed him out to you at Bundy's when he was there.'

'*Was* he there? I only have your word on that.'

The silence that followed was so long she started to wonder whether the signal had dropped.

'Hang on. What exactly are you accusing me of? Making up a seven-year-old child? Because, if I was going to construct some elaborate fantasy about my life, I'd go for something a little more exciting. An affair with Idris Elba or maybe a job at MI5.' Another pause. Carrie felt as if she was supposed to say something but couldn't think what. Then Tara sighed. 'You don't trust me at all, do you?'

And in that moment, Carrie wished, more than anything, that she could tell Tara it wasn't true – that she believed in her completely. But Josh was right: so long as even a sliver of doubt remained, Sofia's safety had to come first.

'I've learned that I have to be very careful about who I trust. My judgement can be ... flawed.'

'I get that, I do. But *this* – implying that I've been lying to you all along, that I'm some sort of, of dangerous fantasist – this isn't you. Because, in spite of all your challenges and your self-doubt, I've seen how you always give people the benefit

280

of the doubt. So what you're saying now, it's ... well. It's not the Carrie *I* know.' She made a clicking noise with her tongue. 'This is Josh, isn't it? *He's* put these ideas into your head.'

Carrie's eyes flicked to the stove, where Josh was taking eggs out of the carton. She could hear shells cracking in the gap that followed.

'He has been helping me to think things through logically ...'

She hadn't said anything funny, but Tara made an odd-sounding laugh.

'The problem is, Carrie, this isn't about logic. This is about trust. About knowing something in your gut. But if you want to talk weird coincidences ... how about the fact that a man you'd already met, who admired your work and clearly fancied you from the get-go, magically turns up at the door with your missing child? I'd say that's a pretty big coincidence. And if you want to know what *I* think—'

But Carrie never found out what Tara thought, because her next words were obliterated by a scream. It came from somewhere in the background, high-pitched and harrowing: the sound of a child in extreme pain ... or terror.

'I have to go,' Tara said quickly, and severed the connection.

Carrie put the phone back on the counter, the scream still echoing in her head, like the soundtrack of a horror film.

A terrible thought hooked itself inside her. What if the police were right to suspect Tara? What if she had captured another little girl – one who was even now shrieking for her mother? She picked up her mobile again. Maybe she should call DCI Campbell? Tell her to go over there and check?

Josh began whisking eggs, the sound superimposing itself over the fading imprint of the scream.

Logic began to reassert itself, telling Carrie that her jangled nerves were getting the better of her. After all, how many times had she heard a bone-chilling shriek in a playground and spun towards it, only to find that the cause was nothing more sinister than a pestering wasp or flung water balloon?

There was a simple, obvious explanation for that sound: it must have come from Peter. He had probably hurt himself while they were on the phone, stubbed his toe or tripped and banged his head.

Josh was wrong. Tara was with her son right now, ministering to his injury. Her chest loosened as tension released its grip.

She would call Tara back in a few minutes, apologise for having doubted that her son was there. Hopefully she would understand.

Josh's voice butted into her thoughts.

'Sofia! Breakfast is almost ready!'

She turned to find him standing at the bottom of the stairs, calling up.

No sound from above.

Carrie checked her watch. Nearly nine o'clock. Late, by Sofia's standards.

It suddenly occurred to her that she hadn't spoken to her daughter since dinner the day before. Josh had become amorous after their discussion about the DCI's visit, towing her up to the bedroom. The sex had been a welcome release from the evening's stresses and she'd abandoned herself to it, plunging into sleep straight afterwards. Which meant she'd missed giving Sofia a goodnight kiss.

Brushing past Josh, she dashed up the stairs, mounting them two at a time, pausing when she reached the top, listening.

Silence. Not the faintest sound to indicate that a living, breathing person was just a short distance away. Carrie ran the last few steps, gripped by a sudden, irrational fear that she would reach Sofia's door only to discover that there was no one on the other side.

But when she crossed the threshold, her daughter was exactly where she was supposed to be: lying under her duvet with Petie beside her, hair trailing across her face, eyes closed.

Carrie released a pent-up breath. What was wrong with her today? She needed to get a grip, stop jumping at shadows.

She pulled back the curtains, letting sunlight pour in.

'Good morning, my love. Time to wake up.'

No response. She must be sleeping very deeply.

Crouching down beside the bed, she gently drew back the veil of hair covering Sofia's cheek.

And saw the red blotches corrupting her daughter's skin. The utter stillness.

'Sofia!' she shouted, as though raising her voice would make a difference. '*Wake up!*'

But Sofia didn't stir, and when Carrie touched her forehead, the heat there sent a spike of terror straight through her heart.

'Don't panic,' Josh said.

A ridiculous, infuriating thing to say. How could she not panic when her daughter was unconscious with rashes all over her body and a searing fever the doctors had yet to explain? And anyway, he had no way of knowing whether she actually *was* panicking. Because despite the howling gale of emotion tearing around inside her, Carrie's surface remained still, unruffled by

283

the storm. She stared at her own ghostly image in the glass divider separating the waiting area from the nurse's station: her reflected self, seated bolt upright on a fake-leather chair. Her features looking exactly as they always did. She might have been sad or annoyed. Bored, even.

Why hadn't she been allowed into the examination room? How long had the doctors been in there? It was impossible to know, because time seemed to have stopped, trapping Carrie in this shrunken universe, sandwiched between Josh on one side and a table of tired magazines on the other. She picked up a copy of *Hello!* (the cover showed a blonde woman holding a baby, surrounded by Edwardian furniture), flipped through it unseeingly, then tossed it back. She jumped up from her chair and paced back and forth a few times, shaking out her arms. Sat down again. Josh tried to take her hand, but she snatched it away. She didn't want to be touched. She didn't want to hear his voice. She didn't want to hear *anyone's* voice right now except the doctor's, telling her that her daughter was going to be fine. But the doctors (three of them. That couldn't be a good sign, could it, in a cash-strapped NHS hospital?) were still with Sofia in that room. They had rushed her there as soon they saw the rash, Carrie clinging to the side of the gurney as it raced through the maze of corridors, one of the wheels squeaking maddeningly against the lino, past a girl who couldn't have been more than seven tethered to a rolling IV stand. She had no hair and the skin around her eyes looked bruised. But at least she was alive. At least she had a chance. That was what Carrie had found herself thinking on that terrible journey through the hospital, holding tight to her daughter's limp hand. If Sofia had been herself, she would have complained that it was *too* tight and snatched her fingers away. Instead of just lying there, empty, her breathing so shallow it felt as though her air supply was slowly running out. As though soon there would be none left and the breaths would stop altogether.

'What can I do to make things better?' Josh asked. 'Can I get you a coffee or something to eat? A pillow to rest your head against?'

'No.' Some dim corner of her mind registered that she'd forgotten to tag on a 'thank you', but right now she didn't care. 'I'm going to try Simon again.'

'You've already left a message. What's the point of calling again and again?'

'He's her father. He needs to know what's going on.'

It had taken Carrie by surprise, how much she wanted Simon here. Because he was the one person who would truly understand how she felt – the one who would be feeling exactly the same way. Simon alone could help her shoulder this burden of terror.

But his mobile went straight to voicemail. She'd left a message telling him to call her, that it was urgent. But more than an hour had gone by and he still hadn't replied. Which wasn't like him. Maybe he'd gone back to Clearbrook? He'd said the new medication was working ... but was he taking it every day? Maybe he no longer felt there was a compelling reason to, since she'd cut him off from Sofia.

The thought brought a slither of guilt, which she pushed aside immediately. She couldn't worry about Simon. Not now.

Carrie sat perfectly still on the fake-leather chair, as if a bomb were strapped to her chest that might go off at the slightest tremor, staring through her ghost self in the glass barrier, past

285

the nurse's station, to the sleet-grey door just beyond. The room where Sofia had been taken, where her fate was being determined right now. She sat and stared at that door, not moving a muscle, until finally it opened and one of the doctors emerged in a flash of white.

Twenty-nine

'I'm going to swing by Carrie Haversen's office,' Juliet said, logging off her computer.

Alistair, who was eating a bacon sandwich and reading Clarissa Weldon's medical records, looked up in surprise.

'Really? Why?'

'I want to go back over some of the Bring Your Kid to Work footage with her boss. Get him to identify a few more people.'

'Can't you just email him?'

'I'd rather do it in person.' She reached for her corduroy jacket. 'You're welcome to come along for the ride.'

He took a large bite of sandwich, staring at her thoughtfully as he chewed. She could hear bacon crunching.

'Are we still pursuing that angle, given that the guv has instructed us, in no uncertain terms, to focus our resources on building an air-tight case against Tara Weldon?'

Juliet threaded her arms through her jacket sleeves.

'The case against Tara is purely circumstantial. No DNA and no confession.' She bent to retrieve her satchel from under the desk. 'Until that changes, I think it would be a mistake to ignore the possibility that she's innocent.'

Alistair's chair creaked as he leaned back, lacing his fingers behind his head, elbows jutting sideways.

'We've got CCTV evidence placing her in both parks at the time of the abductions. She'd had prior interaction with Sofia, during which she obtained knowledge of her interest in penguins. Plus she tracked down and befriended Sofia's mother after the abduction was thwarted.'

'"Tracked down?"' She pulled the satchel strap up over her shoulder. 'I don't think we can say that. There's nothing to disprove Tara's claim that she bumped into Carrie at the play centre and the two of them bonded.'

Alistair snorted. 'Please. Who "bonds" with Carrie Haversen? She's un-bondable.'

'Simon Ryder did,' she pointed out. 'And until we've got something more concrete, I'm going to keep an open mind.'

'As circumstantial cases go, it's pretty strong. And not just the facts of the abduction itself, but Weldon's background too: what happened to her daughter. Her history of mental health issues. It all fits.'

'I agree.'

'You agree. And yet you're running off to pursue other lines of enquiry.'

Juliet's eyes did a quick sweep of the room, not wanting to be overheard. But they were alone, apart from Ravi, who was speaking into his phone at a desk near the back. A personal call, most likely, since he didn't have his notebook out.

'Yes. I am.'

'So, are you just covering all bases as a matter of principle ... or do you genuinely believe Tara Weldon could be innocent?'

Juliet's eyes moved to the whiteboard as she thought about her answer, scanning the photos of Carrie, Simon, Nick Laude, Sofia, Zoe. And Tara – the only one with arrows linking her to both victims.

'Maybe a bit of both.'

'Why won't you let me help you?' Josh's voice had risen a few octaves. 'All I want is to be here for you.'

Carrie's gaze didn't move from her daughter's face: the closed eyes and bruise-blue lips. The terrifying rash. Three days ago, she had wanted more than anything to know what was wrong. But as her eyes travelled along the IV tethered to her daughter's arm, she wondered whether this was any better.

She could feel Josh rubbing her back as she caressed Sofia's burning cheek. She knew he was trying to be supportive, but the truth was he was getting on her nerves. He kept offering her things: cups of tea, a blanket around her shoulders, even an architecture magazine ('to take your mind off things', as if that were possible).

Bacterial meningitis, the consultant had said, those two words sending everything inside her plunging, with a high-diving-board lurch, into icy darkness.

Meningitis. Children died from meningitis. Died, or were changed for ever, their lives stunted.

'We are flooding her body with massive doses of antibiotics to fight it,' the doctor had said. 'It will be a few day before we know whether it's worked.'

'If it doesn't work, she'll die, won't she?' The doctor had taken off his glasses and given her a look that was probably meant to convey something, which of course she couldn't read. '*Tell* me the answer. In words.'

'Yes. You need to be prepared for that possibility.'

A ludicrous thing to say. Because she could never be *prepared for that possibility*. If Sofia died, she was certain her own life would end too, as her heart recognised that it had lost its reason to beat.

So, *no*, she didn't want a blanket and, *no*, she didn't want a cup of tea and she sure as bloody hell didn't want to look at pictures of other people's buildings. She took a deep breath, fortifying herself for another night of waiting. Who could have imagined that there would be more nights just as long and as terrible as those two when Sofia was missing – trapped once again in the limbo between 'before' and 'after'.

At least, last time, there'd been a happy ending. Last time, she had been lucky. Lucky that Josh liked to go walking along an unused path. Lucky that he happened to be passing at a moment when Sofia was awake and calling out. Lucky that he was a good man. All of it had been lucky. Now she found herself wondering: what if it was *too* much luck? What if luck was a resource that could run out? What if there was none left?

Carrie hadn't realised that her hands were clenched in her lap until she felt her nails bite into the soft skin of her palms. Josh placed a hand on top of hers, and she willed him to take it away, to leave her be. She felt as though she was made of spun glass, ready to shatter at the slightest touch.

He gave the back of her hand a squeeze.

'You're not alone,' he said. 'I hope knowing that, feeling another hand on yours, provides some comfort.'

'Yes,' she said. Then her free hand reached automatically for the wrist trapped beneath his, giving the underside a hard pinch.

Juliet had only just arrived at Wescott Architects when she saw it.

Osman Baig was leading her through rows of desks towards his office, talking about the way architecture was changing ('I kind of miss the days when it was more about drawing skills and less about computer skills') while she listened and nodded, trying to imagine the dynamic between Sofia's mother and this sociable, cat-loving man, when they walked past Carrie's empty desk. Juliet shot a quick glance at it and had gone another few paces before her mind processed what her eyes had just seen. She stopped short. Turned around.

Last time she'd come here, Carrie had been sitting in the now vacant chair working on a design, her desk papered over with drawings and notes. Now, in her absence, she was able to see something that had been hidden beneath them.

A framed photo of Carrie and Sofia.

It was clearly taken in the spring, because cherry blossoms were in full bloom among the trees lining the now familiar fence. A list of 'Granger Park Playground Rules' was visible on a wooden sign in the corner of the shot. Mother and daughter were standing in front of the swings together, Carrie in jeans and a grey jumper, her face wearing the now-familiar blank expression; Sofia, on the other hand, was grinning from ear to ear. But only half her smile was visible because the other half was hidden behind a large, stuffed penguin.

Juliet picked up the photo, scanning the background: it must have been taken in the afternoon, judging by the light and the length of the shadows trailing from the children running by. None of them were wearing school uniforms.

Juliet's thoughts were moving fast, clattering over the assumptions she'd made and the theories she'd constructed. Tearing them down and starting over. Because she could see now that Bring Your Kid to Work Day was irrelevant. Anyone who'd seen this photo would have had all the information they needed – about the way Sofia looked, her love of penguins and her habit of hugging soft toys right up against her face. The fact that she went to Granger Park playground on weekend afternoons.

'Officer Campbell? Is everything OK?'

Osman Baig's voice seemed to be coming from a long way off. She turned to find him standing beside her, wearing a puzzled smile.

'I'm going to need a list of everyone who works here and has access to this floor. And all your visitor sign-in sheets for the last three months.'

Thirty

Carrie must have dozed off, because she had the dream again: the one where Sofia was buried somewhere on an endless beach and she was digging, digging, screaming soundlessly, clawing at the sand.

She jolted awake, taking a moment to make sense of her surroundings: the chair beside the bed, its wooden arm digging into the side of her waist. Pastel walls. Her daughter, hooked up to machines. Tubes carrying liquid in, wires carrying data out, sending spiky waves across the monitor. Reality came slamming back. She was in hospital. Meningitis had reduced her daughter's life to numbers and scribbles on a screen. And Carrie could do nothing but sit there and hope that the two lines kept rising and falling. That they weren't suddenly replaced by the flat signature of death.

She heard a soft snore and saw that Josh had fallen asleep in the next chair, mouth ajar, head tipped back against the mint-green wall. She watched his face for a moment. Was it bad that she was relieved he wasn't awake, that she couldn't stand another minute of his relentless support? That she wished her ex was here instead?

She and Simon had come to this very hospital when Sofia was eighteen months old. A terrifying virus had struck in the night, bringing vomiting so severe and persistent it had left her small body dangerously dehydrated.

Just because she's little, that doesn't mean she's weak, Simon had said, as they journeyed side-by-side through that long, terrifying night, stationed at their daughter's bedside, eyes never leaving her. *Babies are hardy little things. Their bodies are still under warranty. It's us knackered old adults that should be worried.* She had got the joke about the warranty and taken comfort from the point behind it: about their daughter's newness and strength. By morning, the vomiting had stopped, leaving Sofia sleeping peacefully.

And as the doors of the hospital had slid apart to release their little family back into the world, there had been a moment, captured in Carrie's memory, when she'd turned and looked at Simon's profile, and felt love rising through the heavy layers of exhaustion, making her reach for his hand, holding it tight.

Carrie checked her mobile again, but there were no messages or missed calls.

She closed her eyes and inhaled through her nostrils, holding on to the breath for a moment as she fortified herself, drawing on whatever reserves remained to get her through this day.

But just as she was about to exhale, she heard something. Not quite a whisper, it was fainter than that: air in the shape of a word. The best word in the world.

'Mummy.'

Her eyes flew open as the paused breath left her lungs.

Sofia's lids had lifted just enough to reveal a sliver of dark brown eyes, now aimed her way. Carrie leaned forwards slowly, carefully, as though this moment, and the precious cargo of hope it was carrying, might break with a sudden move.

She placed a hand on her daughter's forehead. The furnace had gone out. Sofia's skin was damp and warm.

'My love,' she said softly. 'How do you feel?'

Sofia's eyes closed and, for a second, Carrie thought she had slipped away again. But then the lids lifted, a little higher this time. And her whisper was clearer, more substantial.

'Thirsty.'

Carrie knew she should summon the doctor, tell him there'd been a change, let him start poking and prodding, running tests and shining lights and taking temperatures. But she wasn't quite ready to break the spell cast by the sound of her daughter, awake and alive, asking for water. She filled a glass from the pitcher on the bedside table, then cradled Sofia's shoulders, easing her upright and tipping the glass to her lips.

Sofia took a few sips, then fell back against the pillows. She blinked a few times, eyes opening wider. Then she smiled, and it was like the sun streaming through the window of some buried prison cell. Carrie tipped her face towards it, basking.

'She's back!' Josh's voice boomed from right beside her, making her jump.

'Yes.' Carrie touched the sweat-damp curls without removing her eyes from Sofia.

'Have you called the doctor?'

'Not yet.'

'Shall I go and get him? Or at least tell the nurses what's happened?'

'Yes.'

His shoes made a squeaking sound on the hospital floor.

She was dimly aware of the sound pausing for a moment just before he left the room, as though he were waiting for her to say or do something.

But Carrie didn't turn around.

Juliet divided the stack of papers in two, tossing half onto Alistair's desk before sitting down heavily with her share. She glanced around the room, glad that the others were all off chasing leads, building the case against Tara Weldon. She didn't want anyone else to know that she was looking in a different direction.

Alistair flipped through the top few pages, pulling a face.

'Christ, this is a lot of traffic for an architects' firm. Who are all these people?'

'Clients, interns, cleaners, visiting architecture students, friends and family of staff, delivery people ... I could go on.'

His cheeks puffed into a sigh.

'I don't suppose you could give me some clue as to exactly what it is we're looking for?'

'Nope.' Juliet rapped the bottom edges of her stack against the desk until the pages lined up, then picked up the top sheet, with its list of names and signatures. 'But we'll know it when we see it.'

The doctors said Sofia had to stay in hospital for three more nights, so they could finish the course of antibiotics and monitor her progress. But anyone could see she was getting better, the rash retreating, the colour seeping back, her eyes regaining their focus.

She was sitting up in bed. She was talking. Soon she would be coming home.

Everything was going to be OK.

Simon was on his way. He'd been four days into a 'man versus nature' camping trip in the Highlands when he'd finally picked up her messages. He'd jumped on the first train back.

Josh held Carrie's hand as they sat beside the hospital bed. But she no longer found it annoying. Quite the opposite, in fact. It felt good, knowing she had someone she could depend on in a crisis, someone who cared so deeply for her and Sofia. Josh had proven his dedication time and again, in a hundred small acts of kindness.

A bag of Solly's sesame-seed bagels sat on the bedside table, half eaten. He knew they were Carrie's favourite, so had run out to buy them for her the moment her appetite returned. Josh was a thoughtful, generous man and she was lucky to have him in her life. She had been through a terrible ordeal and he had stayed by her side, holding her tight. And if at times it had seemed a bit *too* tight, she had only herself to blame; Carrie could have told him how she felt, asked him to back off and give her some room to breathe. But she hadn't. And it wasn't as if he could read it in her face.

Josh pressed the tip of Sofia's nose with a forefinger.

'You gave us quite a scare, young lady.'

Sofia yawned hugely.

'How could I do something scary without knowing? All I bermember is feeling pukey when I ate spaghetti and then waking up in the hospital.'

Carrie stroked her daughter's forehead, revelling in the temperature there: still warmer than usual . . . but only a bit.

'You were very sick,' Josh said. 'And it's scary seeing someone you love get sick.'

'Oh.' Another yawn. 'Sorry. It was the bad germ's fault.'

'That's OK,' Carrie said. 'We'll be home in a few days, and everything will go back to normal.'

'Is Josh coming too? Is he still having a sleepover at our house?' Sofia's eyes shifted to Josh, addressing her next words to him. 'Can you keep staying with us and making bagels?'

Carrie smoothed the damp curls, trying to think how best to answer. Her daughter needed to accept that the current living arrangement was only temporary, not become too attached. Because, sooner or later, the investigation would wrap up and either the danger would pass – or they'd learn to live with it. Then Josh would go back to Clapham and he and Carrie would resume the rhythms of a normal courtship.

So she was about to tell Sofia: no, Josh wouldn't be with them much longer; he had his own house and would be returning there soon.

But Josh spoke up before she had the chance.

'Of course I'll keep staying.' He gave Carrie's fingers a squeeze. 'We're family now.'

'So?'

Alistair shrugged as he looked at the sheet Juliet had just placed in front of him. She leaned over his shoulder and tapped the signature fifth from the top.

'Yes, yes, I saw the name. I'm just wondering why you think it's significant. His job must put him on sign-in sheets for pretty much every architecture firm in London. It would almost be weirder if he *hadn't* visited a high-profile firm like Wescott. And more to the point, we've already ruled him out. He has an alibi.'

'I know that.' Juliet frowned down at the cramped, square signature. 'But given the timing, I'd like to dig a little deeper into his background.'

Alistair shrugged again as he handed back the sheet. She had the distinct impression he was starting to lose patience with this little detour away from the prime suspect.

'Suit yourself. Meanwhile, I'll finish ploughing through these.' And he sighed louder than was necessary before returning his attention to the pile of sign-in sheets on his desk.

Thirty-one

It was late by the time they arrived home from hospital. Sofia had fallen asleep in the car, so Josh carried her inside.

'I've got her,' he said over his shoulder, as Carrie followed him up the stairs. 'Why don't you crack open a bottle of wine while I put her to bed? God knows we deserve it after everything we've been through.'

'No. I want to come.'

In the bedroom, she pulled aside the unicorn duvet as he gently lowered Sofia onto her mattress.

'I'll change her into pyjamas,' Carrie said, opening a drawer, eager to reinstate normality – to throw herself into routine's warm embrace. But Josh placed a restraining hand on her arm.

'Why don't we leave her be, rather than risk waking her?'

'She won't wake,' Carrie said, throwing off his hand as irritation zipped through her. She began flipping through the stack of pyjamas. 'She's a deep sleeper.'

'In that case, it won't matter to her whether she's wearing pyjamas or leggings and a T-shirt. I say we grab the chance to relax for a moment, just the two of us. Put ourselves first for a change.'

'Sofia comes first,' Carrie said, selecting a set of pyjamas covered with scenes from Peter Rabbit. 'She always has and she always will.'

He was silent after that, as she gently lifted the T-shirt up, hurrying through the part where the cloth passed over her daughter's mouth and nose. Sofia shifted and sighed in her sleep but didn't wake. Then Carrie carefully put her arms through the PJ top, pulling it down into place, exactly as she'd done a thousand times before, the simple ritual telling her that everything was as it should be. A feeling of warmth blossomed in her core, spreading outward.

When she turned to pick up the bottoms, Josh was leaning against the wall with his hands in his pockets, staring at Sofia with his eyebrows pushed together, making the skin between them buckle. When he saw her looking, his face reconfigured into a smile.

'This is clearly a one-person job, so why don't I leave you to it and go open some wine? I'll wait for you downstairs.'

Carrie gave him a brief nod before picking up the PJ bottoms and returning her attention to her daughter.

TRAGIC SON RUNS INTO FLAMING HOUSE
IN FAILED BID TO RESCUE MOTHER

A teenage boy suffered smoke inhalation and burns after risking his life trying to save his mother from a house fire at The Vineyard, just south of Abbotsbury.

Josh Skelter, 17, was found unconscious inside the front door. Celebrated architect Lena Skelter, 42, died, along with her partner, Angus Michaels, 36, after they became trapped inside the flaming building.

Detective Inspector Aaron Wilde described the fire as a 'tragic accident'.

'Michaels ingested alcohol and then fell asleep on the sofa with a lit cigarette,' Wilde said. 'The resulting fire reached an open bottle of whisky lying beside him, which acted as an accelerant.'

Lena Skelter was asleep upstairs when the fire broke out. She shouted out the window to her son, who tried to convince her to jump to safety from the first floor. But she refused to leave without her partner. The award-winning architect ran downstairs to try to save Michaels, but was quickly overcome by smoke.

'That's when the boy ran into the burning house, ignoring the risk to his own life,' Wilde said. 'Josh Skelter is a hero.'

Juliet parked her feet on her desk as she reread the clipping the Abbotsbury Courier had sent over. The front-page story was illustrated with two photos. The largest showed an oddly-shaped house being consumed by fire. Flames licked through cracks in the plate-glass windows on the main floor, obscuring the row of smaller windows running along the level above. Below was a smaller picture: a close-up of a young Josh Skelter lying in the back of an ambulance, his skin stained with soot, an oxygen mask strapped over his mouth and nose. Juliet stared at that face for a long time, seeing shock and horror there. Stunned disbelief.

She had spoken to Osman Baig, and now knew why Skelter's name had appeared on the Wescott visitors' list. One of Carrie's designs had won a prize sponsored by the magazine, so he'd gone there to research a profile piece on the company to run alongside the main award story. The original plan had been for Josh to interview Carrie as well as Osman. But she'd had to run off early that day, after the school called to say that Sofia had fallen off a swing and banged her head.

Osman had told Juliet all about it, and even showed her a copy of the *London Architects' Monthly* article.

So Alistair was right: the visit made perfect sense. But something was nagging at her, buzzing around at the back of her skull liked a trapped wasp, driving her to go on to Google Earth and locate Eva Skelter's house. To look up the number of the police station that would have dealt with the fire.

She took one last look at the face of the boy in the ambulance.

Then she picked up the phone and began to dial.

Thirty-two

'What the hell is *he* doing here?'

Simon was standing just inside the front door, looking past Carrie's shoulder to the kitchen, where Josh was making coffee. Simon hadn't taken off his rucksack, which normally meant that he wasn't planning to stay long. Aside from that, she had no clue what his intentions were, given that he had dropped by without calling first.

'Josh is staying here.'

Simon stared at her for a moment longer, apparently waiting for more. Then he sighed. 'Explain to me.'

Explain to me. She'd almost forgotten how those three words had punctuated their relationship, passed back and forth between them. She would say them while waving an open hand in front of his face, to show she needed him to translate his expression ('That's bemused affection, Carrie', 'faint surprise mixed with cynicism', and, towards the end: 'weary resignation').

Simon had used them to signal that she had failed to provide him with enough information. ('How are you Carrie?',

'Frustrated and angry', 'Explain to me'; 'I need to ask the doctor if the baby will be like me', '"Like you?"', 'Yes'. 'Explain to me'.)

Hearing them now, she weighed her response, trying to work out exactly what he wanted, how much more information was required.

'Josh offered to stay in the spare room for a few nights. I accepted his offer.'

'Because you're in a relationship?'

'No, as an added security measure.'

'But are you?'

'Am I what?'

'In a relationship with . . .' He waved his hand towards the back of the house, where Josh was pouring coffee into two mugs. '*Him*. Mr Good Samaritan.'

'His name is Josh Skelter. Yes, we are in a relationship.'

Josh carried the two mugs to the dining table. 'Shall I make some more coffee for our guest?'

'I'm not a guest,' Simon said, leaning on the 's' so that it sounded like a snake-hiss. 'I'm Sofia's *father*, checking on my daughter's recovery. If anyone's a *guest* around here, it's you, matey.'

Josh pulled back a teak chair and sat down.

'Well, Sofia is asleep. If you don't wish to join us for coffee, we can call to let you know when she wakes up, so you don't have to hang around the house waiting.' He picked up his mug and took a sip.

Simon's features contorted and reddened. Carrie circled her palm in front of his face.

'Explain to me.'

'Absolute fucking fury.' He spat out the words, as though

they were spoiled food. 'I am outraged that I wasn't notified about this change to my daughter's living arrangements. Also deep concern that you have invited a virtual stranger into her home, on the strength of the fact that he just so happened to stumble across Sofia on a deserted path.' Simon's eyes jumped to Josh, narrowing. 'Or so he claims.'

Josh put down his cup and stretched out his legs, crossing his feet at the ankles. His features appeared completely flat as he said: 'I'm sorry my presence here displeases you. I had hoped that my staying here for a bit would make everyone feel more relaxed, but it's clearly having the opposite effect where you're concerned. As for your implication that I've been duplicitous in some way . . . my account of events surrounding the abduction has already been verified by the police. Unless . . . perhaps you think the police are in on it? A conspiracy of some kind?' He smiled, which seemed odd to Carrie, given what he'd just said. 'Well, finding out about your daughter's meningitis must have come as a shock.' He shook his head. 'A terrible shock. So no one could blame you for being thrown a little . . . off balance. Especially given your history.'

Carrie looked back and forth between the two men, noticing the way Simon was clenching and unclenching his fingers, turning them from fists into empty hands and back again.

'Do *not* try and make this about me and my condition. Yes, I have experienced *occasional* episodes of psychosis. But I'm not having one right now. I am seeing things exactly as they are.' *Fists-hands-fists-hands.* 'And I have to say, I'm impressed. In the space of just one month, you've managed to install yourself in my daughter's home. Fast work.'

Josh folded his arms.

'As I've already explained: I am only here temporarily, to make everyone more comfortable while Sofia's abductor is still at large.'

'Funnily enough, discovering that a man I know almost nothing about is staying under the same roof as my child doesn't give me a great deal of comfort.'

Simon turned to Carrie, who had been following the conversation like a tennis game, head swivelling back and forth between the two men, trying to read the situation. He spoke in a low voice.

'I don't like him being here. I have a bad feeling about it.'

'I know all about your bad feelings. I have witnessed your experience of them. And taken Sofia to hospital to repair the damage.'

Simon's features scrunched together. He sucked air through clenched teeth.

'But you admit that when I'm ... myself ... I have good instincts. You've seen that, haven't you?'

'Yes.'

'So, don't you trust them?'

'No.'

Her attention must have been completely focused on Simon, because she hadn't registered that Josh had left the table until his arm brushed hers. She turned to find him standing right beside her.

'I think we're done here,' he told Simon quietly. 'Time for you to go.'

For a few seconds, the two men just looked at each other in silence. Then Josh took a step forwards, so that they were only a few inches apart. Simon gave him a mouth-only smile.

'Yeah, OK. I'll go. But just so we're clear: I'll be watching you.'

'That's good.' Josh leaned forward, until there was no distance between them. 'Because I'll be watching you too.'

Aaron Wilde was dead. He'd keeled over at work seven years earlier clutching his chest, turned blue and been carted away, never to return.

What struck Juliet was the station sergeant's complete lack of emotion as he shared these details: chair tipped back, fingers laced across his domed belly.

Ed Keane's office spoke of a lacklustre life, both on and off the force. An outdated computer shared desk space with a potted cactus and a framed photo of a Labrador puppy. The walls were bare aside from a large map of Surrey behind him. No commendations, trophy newspaper articles or photos of handshakes with grateful politicians.

Juliet had decided to take as few notes as possible – partly to promote a guard-lowering sense of casual conversation, partly to allow her to watch his face. It wasn't a particularly pleasant face to watch: thin lips and hooded eyes; a nose mapped by veins telling of too many hours at the pub; a salt-and-pepper horseshoe wrapped around a sweaty scalp.

The chair tipped forward as he shifted his weight, planting meaty hands on the desk.

'So you said on the phone you wanted to discuss a case I worked with DI Wilde. Care to tell me which one?'

It was obvious that Keane didn't fancy her in the slightest, so when his eyes did an up-down flick, she concluded that he wasn't best pleased to find himself being questioned by a younger woman of a higher rank – especially one with her skin colour.

'Before we get into that, can I ask: did you and DI Wilde work together a lot?'

'Yes.' His lip curled as he said it.

'You didn't like him, did you?'

The answer was obvious, but she was curious to see how he'd react, how candid he'd be.

'No, I didn't.' He leaned back again, the chair creaking in protest. 'He was a dick.'

She waited for him to add a caveat about not wanting to speak ill of the dead, but he just sat there, staring across at her, his head framed by the map of Surrey. It occurred to her that her ethnicity might actually work in her favour this time. Because although she could feel the resentment coming off him in waves, he hadn't told her where to stick her nosey questions, that his relationship with a dead colleague was none of her damned business. The fact was, there weren't that many senior officers who looked like her in this part of the country – certainly nowhere near as many as in London. Keane was probably worried about letting his prejudices show, or of breaking one of the new rules surrounding the treatment of women and minorities. And it was making him overcompensate, revealing more than he had to.

'In what way was he a dick?' She flicked him a smile. 'I've found there are many different kinds.'

He scratched the pouch of skin under his chin, making it wobble.

'Egotistical, stubborn, closed-minded. Not interested in anyone's opinion but his own.'

Juliet took the Abbotsbury Courier clipping out of her satchel, pushing it across the desk.

'Is that how you would characterise his approach on *this* case?'

Sergeant Keane picked up the page and squinted at the words, then held it further away. Juliet watched with vague amusement as he moved it forwards and back, trying to bring the print into focus. *He needs reading glasses*, she thought, *but he won't admit it*. Wilde clearly hadn't been the only egotistical, stubborn man working at this station.

Keane's face suddenly lit with memory.

'Yes, I remember this fire.' His eyes widened and narrowed a few more times as he struggled to see the photos. 'It was just bad luck that the mother – what was her name again?' He must have given up on deciphering the newsprint, because his small eyes drifted memory-searching right. 'Amy? Avery?' He nodded to himself. 'That was it. Avery. She wasn't supposed to be there. She came back early from some architecture conference.'

Juliet decided not to correct him about the mother's name. She suspected she'd get further by appealing to his ego.

'I'm impressed that you can recall so much about the case, given that it was dismissed as an accident twenty years ago. You must have an amazing memory.' She sighed. 'I wish mine was as good.'

Her words had the desired effect. The sergeant's chest puffed.

'It was one of my first cases. I'd only been on the job a couple of weeks. And as for it being an accident ... let's just say, I had my doubts.' The words made Juliet's spine straighten. 'But would Wilde listen to a word I said?' He scoffed, tossing the clipping back across the desk. 'No fucking chance.'

310

Juliet's heart was gaining speed, but she kept her tone light and casual.

'What made you doubt it was an accident?'

'I interviewed the neighbours. One of them said the boyfriend had quit smoking a month earlier. They used to see him having fags in the front garden all the time, but then he stopped. He told them that Avery – what was her surname?' He ran a palm over his exposed scalp, frowning.

'Skelter.'

'Yeah, that was it. A cold, demanding bitch by all accounts. Proper ballbreaker.' Then he seemed to catch himself, adding hastily: 'That's how DI Wilde described her. I don't use those terms myself.' He gave his collar a quick tug, as though it had suddenly become too tight. 'Anyway. He told them she'd complained about his breath stinking of fags. Said she wouldn't shag him again until he quit. So he did.'

Juliet frowned. 'But if he didn't smoke, whose cigarette started the fire?'

Keane spread his hands. '*Thank* you. That's *exactly* what I said. But Wilde acted like it was a stupid question. Said the boyfriend must have fallen off the wagon. Had a few drinks, sneaked a fag, passed out.'

'How much alcohol was in his system?'

'We didn't check.'

Her mouth fell open. 'What?! Why not!?'

'Wilde said it was clearly an accident, that the force was on a tight budget, and that he wasn't going to order a bunch of expensive tests when it was obvious no crime had been committed.'

'You're joking. Two people died, and he refused to even look into the *possibility* of foul play?'

311

Keane's smile was more like a sneer. She wondered if it always looked like that, or only when he was thinking about his dead colleague.

'That was Wilde for you. He told me that when I had as many years' experience on the force as he did, I'd know an accidental sofa fire when it punched me in the face.'

Juliet ran fingertips along the sides of her head, skimming ripples of tightly pulled hair.

'OK, so assuming it really *was* arson ... any theories as to who was behind it?'

He tugged the Abbotsbury Courier clipping back across the desk, so that it was lying next to the framed Labrador. Tapped a finger on Josh Skelter's face.

'Him.'

Juliet's pulse jumped. 'Really? Why?'

'The way he kept saying his mother wasn't supposed to be home, over and over again. It was weird. Made me think maybe he set the fire to get rid of the boyfriend, not knowing she was there.'

Juliet's excitement faded.

'I don't find that particularly odd. He was shocked, grieving. The realisation that his mother would have lived if she'd stuck to her schedule must have hit him hard.'

'Well he didn't give a shit about the boyfriend. Didn't ask about him once, not even a mention.'

'His mother had just died,' Juliet said reasonably. 'He probably didn't care much about a man he'd known only a short time.'

'Not that short. More than a year. Living in the same house.'

'Still. What motive would he have had?'

The sergeant frowned, sucking in his lips. Juliet got the

impression he was starting to have second thoughts about the amount of information he was sharing.

She forged ahead quickly.

'Did you actually look into possible motives? Or did you not bother, because Wilde told you to leave it – so you ignored your instincts, kept your mouth shut and did as you were told?' It was a risky strategy – one that could rile him to the point of shutting down. Colour was rising in Sergeant Keane's face, staining it with purple blotches. She gave him the hint of a smile before continuing. 'Or did you quietly keep digging, because you knew, even back then, at the very start of your career, that your instincts were already better than Wilde's would ever be?'

Her words had the desired effect. Keane's look of badly contained outrage slowly morphed into a self-satisfied smile. He made a show of inspecting his fingernails.

'I may have gone ahead and interviewed Skelter's girlfriend.'

Juliet schooled her features into an admiring gaze.

'Really? Smart! Did she tell you anything useful?"

'Oh, yes.' He locked his fingers behind his head and pumped his eyebrows up and down twice. Seconds passed. Dear God. Was he actually pausing for dramatic effect?!

'And?' Juliet prompted, fighting to keep the irritation out of her voice.

'Apparently the boy was obsessed with winning his mother's approval.'

Juliet tried not to let her disappointment show.

'That's not terribly unusual. A lot of insecure teenagers feel that way, especially when the parent in question is aloof and rejecting.'

'Yeah, but not like this. The girlfriend said Skelter was way over the top. "Creepy" was the word she used to describe it. He worshipped the woman, saw her as some sort of female Michelangelo. Needless to say, there was no love lost between Skelter and the mother's boyfriend.'

'So what are you saying? You think he set the fire to eliminate his rival for her affections?'

'That's *exactly* what I'm saying. But then she had to go and ruin everything by arriving home early,'

Juliet considered this while Keane watched her across the desk. His hands were still locked behind his head, exposing a matching pair of armpit stains.

'What was their relationship like? Were Josh and Ava ... Avery Skelter close?'

His head shook against the interlaced fingers.

'No. But not for lack of trying on his part. The girlfriend said she'd been to his house loads of times without ever seeing the mother crack a smile. Nothing Josh did seemed to impress her. Treated him like the hired help. A proper ice queen. You can tell just by looking at her.'

'Can you? I haven't seen her picture.'

'Here, I'll show you.'

He began tapping on his computer keyboard.

Juliet's eyebrows lifted. 'You still have the case file, after all these years?'

Another sneer-smile. 'No. Her picture's online. You just need to key in "architect" and Alton Plaza; that's a shopping centre she designed. I drive past it on my way to work. Here.' He turned the screen to face her.

The woman in the photo was pale-skinned and sour-faced, standing in front of a building whose roof was a series of

314

interlocking metal curves, creating the impression of waves. It glittered in the sunlight. Ava Skelter was holding an oval trophy, looking bored and vaguely annoyed. There was a familiar silver zigzag on her finger: the ring from Josh's chain. Looking at the architect's image, Juliet was struck by a powerful sense of *déjà vu*, a conviction that she'd seen this woman somewhere before. Which, of course, was impossible.

'She won a big prize for that shopping centre,' Keane was saying. 'That's what her face looked like when she was happy. I'd hate to see it when she was fucked off.'

He clicked the mouse and the picture doubled in size, filling the screen. Short, pale hair and pale brows. Strong features and blue eyes.

And, suddenly, Juliet knew why she seemed so familiar.

Ava Skelter looked like Carrie Haversen.

Not an exact match; Ava was better looking – the nose a bit narrower, the lips slightly fuller, eyes that were blue rather than grey. But the similarity was striking.

And that's when it happened.

Somewhere deep inside her, a flash went off: a hot flare that rose through her consciousness like a bonfire spark.

'Maybe we've been looking at this case through the wrong end of the telescope.' She said the words aloud to hear how they sounded, testing them for strength, dimly aware of the sergeant's baffled face on the edge of her vision. 'Maybe we've got everything back to front ... because this was never about Sofia.'

Thirty-three

'DCI Campbell. What are you doing here?' Carrie stood in the doorway of her house, face and voice as expressionless as ever.

Juliet looked past her shoulder. Saw Sofia at the dining table, eating large, messy forkfuls of something orange. But no one else.

'Is Josh here?'

'No. He's working late.'

They stood facing each other while Juliet paused automatically to give Carrie a chance to invite her in. Which, of course, she didn't.

'May I come in?'

A volley of blinks, then Carrie opened the door all the way.

'Hi, Police Lady Juliet,' Sofia called out. Her smile was wonky with mismatched teeth: bigger new arrivals crowding out the baby teeth. 'I'm having spaghetti Os and a bagel, which looks like a ginormous spaghetti O.'

Tomato sauce encircled her mouth like a clown's makeup.

'Mmmm, sounds delicious.'

Carrie led Juliet to the sofa and perched at the other end of it, hands clasping her knees.

'I just dropped by to ask you a couple of background questions,' Juliet said. 'About Josh.'

'Josh?' She tilted her head, blinking fast. 'Why?'

'Can we get to that later? It would be helpful if you could just answer my questions first.'

Blink-blink-blink. 'OK.'

'Do you remember the first time the two of you met? Not the day he returned Sofia. Before that. Osman told me he presented you with an architecture award.'

'Yes.'

'Can you tell me what he said?'

'He made a speech about the power of architecture to ...' Juliet shook her head impatiently.

'Not the speech. What he said to *you* personally. Perhaps as he was handing the prize across? Or at the drinks afterwards?'

'I didn't stay for the drinks. However, I recall he did say something—' Her eyes shifted right. Juliet could hear Sofia slurping milk in the pause that followed. 'Yes,' Carrie said, finally. 'When he handed me the award, he said that he was a big fan of my work. Or perhaps the word was "admirer"?' She shook her head. 'I'm not certain which.'

'Anything else?'

'Just, "I'd love to talk with you about it some time."'

Juliet nodded.

'And what was your response?'

'Response?'

'Yes. What did you say in response to his invitation?'

'Nothing. It wasn't a real invitation. It's just one of those

things people say, like "It was nice to meet you".' *Blink-blink.*
'Isn't it?'

Juliet brushed past the question, forging ahead.

'So the next time you met him was when he returned Sofia?'

'Yes.'

'And after that? How many days later did you see him again?'

'The morning of the third day.'

'Mummy,' Sofia called from the dining table, 'do you want one of Josh's bagels?'

Juliet lifted an eyebrow. 'He bakes his own bagels?'

'No. The shop next to his office makes them. He often brings them home.'

'They're the best!' Sofia held up a paper carrier bag bearing the logo 'Solly's Bagels,' the 'o' represented by a cartoon bagel. 'Want one, Police Lady Juliet?'

'Maybe later, thank you.'

She returned her attention to Carrie, who was giving her that blank-faced stare that still, after all this time, made her feel uncomfortable.

'Why are you asking questions about Josh? The last time we spoke, you were focusing your attention on Tara. Has she now been ruled out?'

'I hope to be able to provide you with an update on the investigation very soon. Right now I'm just … filling in a few gaps in my knowledge.'

'But why are you interested in Josh when you yourself told me that he was in his office at the time of Sofia's disappearance?'

And there it was again. The alibi that trumped everything else: Juliet's hunches and Sergeant Keane's suspicions and the eerie similarity between Carrie and Josh's mother – a solid barrier of fact that should have stopped her cold. But she pressed on regardless.

'I'm just trying to get a fuller picture of Josh and the people associated with him. What has he told you about his mother?'

'That she was a brilliant architect. That he was her only child. That she died in a house fire when he was a teenager.'

'Has he ever mentioned what she looked like?'

'He said she was beautiful.'

'Nothing else about . . . her appearance?'

'No.'

Juliet rummaged inside her satchel for the image she'd printed off of Ava Skelter and her trophy. She handed it to Carrie, who looked at it closely for a few moments before passing it back without comment.

'Notice anything?'

'No.'

'You don't think the two of you look . . . similar?'

'She is better looking than me.'

Juliet was about to deny this out of reflexive politeness, then stopped herself.

'Yes, that's true. But you can't deny that there's a strong resemblance.'

A blinking pause. 'How could my physical similarity to the deceased mother of a man who's been ruled out as a suspect have any bearing on the case?'

As ever, it was said with no inflection or change of expression, making it impossible to judge whether Carrie was annoyed or merely curious.

Juliet had just enough time to say 'I'm looking into . . .' when her mobile rang. She looked at the screen. Alistair.

319

'Excuse me for a moment.' She got up, still holding Ava Skelter's picture, and walked towards the front door, stopping just short of it with her back to Carrie.

She kept her voice low. 'Yes?'

'We've got her,' Alistair declared dramatically.

'"Her?"'

'Tara Weldon.' He sounded surprised she'd had to ask. 'We've discovered a solid piece of evidence linking her directly to the Tudor Park abduction. Plus some new background information that goes directly to motive and proves she lied to us during the interview. Do you want me to talk you through it over the phone, or shall I set up a briefing straight away?'

Juliet glanced over her shoulder at Carrie, stiff-backed on the sofa, waiting to resume their conversation about her resemblance to the mother of a man with an air-tight alibi. A man who'd been labelled 'a hero' in the past and a good Samaritan in the present. She felt a hot rush of shame. What had she been thinking, running over here with a half-baked theory and not a shred of proof? Why had she read so much into the fact that Josh Skelter was drawn to women who reminded him of his mother? Lots of men were. This was clearly one of those rare occasions when her instincts had let her down. It did happen. The trick lay in admitting it. In knowing when to let go. She drew in a deep breath, resetting herself. OK. Time to start listening to her brain instead of her gut.

'Let's do a briefing. I can be there in' – she glanced at her watch – 'twenty minutes.'

'Great. I'll set it up.'

She shoved the picture of Ava Skelter into her pocket as

she returned to the sofa, not caring whether it got crumpled. Carrie looked up at her, hands still cupped around her knees.

'Sorry, I need to head back to the station.'

'OK.'

'Thank you for your time. Have a good evening.'

As she unlocked the car door, Juliet wondered how many sentences like that she said every day. Automatic words, drained of all significance. *Thank you for your time. Have a good evening.*

Simon Ryder was right; the only reason Carrie Haversen came across as abrupt and antisocial was because she chose not to say things she didn't actually mean.

The team was already gathered in the situation room when Juliet rushed in, slinging her bag onto the nearest empty chair with enough force to send it rolling across the floor.

'So.' She faced the rows of officers, sensing the charge in the room, the buzz of victory. She picked up a marker pen and looked at the whiteboard, with its photos, arrows and scribbled notes. Sofia and Zoe were next to each other in the centre, twin suns orbited by adult faces: Carrie Haversen, Simon Ryder, Josh Skelter, Nick Laude. Tara Weldon. 'I understand there have been some developments in the case. DI Larkin informs me that our prime suspect has been caught in a lie.' She took the lid off the marker pen and looked around the room. 'Who's going to tell me about that?'

'Me,' Dutoit said. She stood up, flushing pink, clearly nervous. Juliet gave her a nod of encouragement. 'I've been working my way through Weldon's known friends and associates. It appears she used to have a very active social life. But, after her daughter's death, she sank into a pretty deep depression and lost touch with most of them.'

Juliet nodded. 'Hardly surprising, given the circumstances.'

'Yes, but here's the interesting part. Instead of trying to move on, she became so fixated on having another daughter that she tried to adopt one in 2015, a few months after her husband left. No luck, of course. Grieving single mothers don't exactly get sent to the front of the queue.'

Juliet smiled grimly. 'So much for "no other child could ever take her place".' She turned to Tara's photo, in its chain of arrows, meeting the blue-green eyes.

You lied to my face, she thought. *Why didn't I pick up on that?*

'I'm assuming you've confirmed this with the adoption authorities?'

Dutoit's head bobbed. 'Yes.'

She jotted 'unsuccessful adoption attempt 2015' under the picture.

'Nice work. This goes directly to motive and proves she's been deceiving us from the get-go.'

Dutoit flushed again, but Juliet was fairly sure that this time it was pleasure, rather than nerves.

Juliet scanned the room. 'So ... who's next?'

Hiranand raised his hand but didn't say anything. She could feel the caged excitement all around her, the sense of a celebration waiting to break out. But as she stood looking at the DS with his arm up, apparently waiting for her to call on him, all Juliet could feel was annoyance. For fuck's sake. Was this a police briefing or a primary school class?

She ran fingers over her hair. For once, everything was neatly clipped away.

'Yes, Hiranand. Go ahead.'

Unlike Dutoit, he remained seated, elbows on the table, one hand fisted around a pen. He pumped the end with his thumb as he spoke, making it click in and out of its sheath.

'I've been looking into the stuffed animals used to lure the girls.' He lifted his chin towards the right-hand side of the board, where photos of the two toys were displayed. 'As you know, lab results showed they'd been dipped in chloroform that appears to come from the same source. There's DNA on them from the girls, but no one else. The penguin was mass produced and could have been bought pretty much anywhere. But the bear is a different story.' All eyes were now fixed on Hiranand. There was no sound in the room but his voice and the pen's click. 'It came from Hamleys. Limited edition. Expensive. Ninety-nine pounds ninety-five, to be exact.' His smile was small, but she could sense the self-satisfaction behind it. 'And guess who just so happened to go to Hamleys and purchase one of these rare and extortionate bears exactly two days before Zoe was abducted?' His eyes swept the room before stopping on Juliet.

'Tara Weldon,' she said.

A triumphant double click. 'Got it in one.'

A cheer rippled around the room, but Juliet didn't join in. She frowned.

'Tara paid with a card?'

'Yep. Lucky for us.'

'That seems ... careless.'

'Well, like Dutoit says, she's got mental health issues. She's unravelling, not thinking things through.'

Juliet considered this as she wrote 'Purchased by Tara Weldon' under the picture of the bear. She forced herself to

323

think dispassionately, to focus only on the facts. And saw that Hiranand's theory fit. Both abductions had been an odd combination of calculation and carelessness: meticulous planning, let down by basic mistakes. Because, if the girls had been gagged or drugged for longer, it was entirely likely that neither of them would ever have been found. And she could see the emotional logic behind the inconsistency; a mother driven by love and loss wouldn't have wanted to harm or terrify her young victims. Tara's maternal instincts had come into play ... and become her downfall.

'Anyone got anything else?' A brief silence and a couple of headshakes. But they didn't really need anything else. Alistair was right. They had her.

'OK.' Juliet snapped the lid back onto the pen. 'I'd say that's more than enough to charge her. Nice work, ladies and gents.'

Hiranand bobbed his head in something that was halfway between a nod and a bow. Dutoit clapped, then someone else joined in and, before she knew it, they were all clapping like teenagers at a pop concert. Juliet looked at Alistair, grinning at her from his perch on the front desk, banging his palms together with the rest of them. Normally, this was the point at which something bordering on euphoria would roll through Juliet, making her want to shout out loud.

But not this time. She looked at the delighted faces in front of her and felt nothing. Because she'd been off on her own frolic, running in the wrong direction while everyone else was busy solving the case.

This simply wasn't her victory.

*　　*　　*

'So what do you think?' Alistair asked, as the other officers filed past them out of the room.

She tossed the marker pen back onto the ledge.

'I think I haven't eaten since breakfast. Fancy grabbing a bite while we wait for the warrant to come through?'

'Sure. What do you fancy? Pizza?'

'I had pizza last night. And the night before.' Juliet massaged her temples as she followed him out into the corridor, feeling the throb of a headache starting. Regret had lodged itself inside her, leaning against her ribcage, making her chest ache. People made mistakes, she told herself firmly. It was part of life. The case had been solved and that was all that really mattered.

'You pick, then,' Alistair said, as they entered the grubby stairwell leading down to the side exit. 'Burgers, Chinese ... whatever. I'm not fussed.'

'OK.' She began running a mental inventory of all the nearby restaurants and takeaways as they descended the stairs, steps echoing in the concrete space. Comfort food, that was what she needed. Something with potatoes. Maybe cake afterwards, from the bakery next to the Italian place.

And that's when it hit her.

Solly's Bagels.

The shop next to Josh's office makes them.

Carrie's words, echoing in her memory.

Except that wasn't right. Josh Skelter's office building was located between a Greek restaurant and a pharmacy. Juliet knew that because she had been up and down Newman Road on foot, had combed through its CCTV footage. And there was no Solly's Bagels. Carrie obviously didn't know that, though, since she hadn't pinched herself after saying it.

Juliet sat down on the bottom step and took out her mobile, Googling 'Solly's Bagels', cursing herself for not having thought of this sooner. She was clearly off her game. She tapped 'Maps'.

Alistair was still heading towards the exit door in a cloud of chatter, failing to register, at first, that Juliet was no longer behind him.

She heard the sound of the metal door opening, then a pause.

'Oh. What are you doing? Researching places to eat?'

But she didn't look up. Juliet sat on the grubby step, staring down at the red marker now pointing to a spot halfway down Radich Avenue: the street parallel to Newman. She zoomed in until the bagel shop and Station House filled the screen. The two buildings backed onto each other. There was no sign of a path or alleyway linking the two roads.

'Juliet?' She looked up to find Alistair standing in front of her, frowning. 'What's going on?'

'Just give me one sec . . .'

She went onto Google Earth, homing in on Josh's building. Most of the businesses on Newman Street were separated from their rear neighbours by walls. But Station House had been extended at some point, so its ground floor stuck out further. The only thing behind it was a small stretch of concrete that ended at the back of Solly's Bagels.

'Alistair, can you do something for me?'

'OK,' he said, dragging out the second syllable (*okaaaa-aay*).

'Call Solly's Bagels on Radich Avenue and ask them if they have a back door, and whether it's left unlocked.'

'I'm sorry, you *what* now?'

'I'll explain in a minute.'

She could feel him staring at her, no doubt wondering what

326

the hell was going on. But her eyes didn't leave the screen. Her mind was already jumping ahead, to the next question. Josh's office was on the top floor. So even if there *was* a back route to the neighbouring street, how could he reach it without walking past his secretary, not to mention lobby security, with its CCTV camera? She stared at the sketchy image of the building. There had to be another way out of that room, something she wasn't seeing. She switched to Google Street View, which fed her a familiar image of the building's façade. But nothing new, nothing she'd overlooked.

Frustration was gnawing at her. She could obviously head over there right now, comb the building from front to back. Of course, the rest of her team would want to know why she'd suddenly run off, just as they were poised to make an arrest. And what exactly was she going to say to them? She rubbed her eyes with her knuckles, scanning her memory of that first visit to Josh's office, with its high ceilings, linen blinds and tidy surfaces. The secretary standing in the doorway like a chatty security guard.

Isn't it beautiful? The Observer *did a big spread on the building in their design supplement.*

Maybe …

She ran 'Observer' and 'Station House' through the search engine and was rewarded with an image gallery. She scrolled quickly through the first few shots, which showed street views, hunting for something she hadn't seen already, something that might explain how …

And there it was. Juliet stared at the arty image of a metal double-helix coiling down a wall. Beneath was the caption: 'The architect chose spiral fire escapes to maintain the juxtaposition of curves and lines.'

The stairs were attached to the back of the building, curling from the top-floor window down to the space behind Solly's. A secret shortcut to the bagel shop 'next door'.

'Yes.'

The sound of Alistair's voice broke into her thoughts, startling her. She'd become so absorbed in her search that she'd forgotten about him. He was standing with one shoulder propped against the cement wall near the door, watching her intently.

'Sorry? Yes . . . what?'

'Yes, Solly's Bagels has a back door, next to the customer loos. They leave it wedged open in the summer to let the air flow through.'

And, just like that, Josh Skelter's alibi was gone.

Juliet imagined him strolling into the shop through the back door, exchanging pleasantries, buying bagels. The familiar customer whose presence barely registered. Then leaving through the front, turning onto Radich Avenue, his secretary unaware he'd ever left. Or that he'd later returned the same way.

A shot of adrenalin sent her jumping to her feet.

'I need someone to get me the CCTV from Radich Avenue for the days Sofia and Zoe went missing.'

'Radich Avenue,' Alistair repeated slowly. 'That's right by Josh Skelter's office, isn't it?' He puffed out a sigh, his face simultaneously puzzled and concerned. 'Why are you still doing this, Juliet? We've solved the case. It's Tara. There's *proof.*'

'I know that. I just need to check this one last thing.'

He scrubbed his face with his hands.

'OK. If you've somehow managed to conjure up game-changing new evidence while walking down the back stairs, then we should probably let the others know. Shall I call another briefing?'

Juliet tapped a thumb against her bottom lip, feeling some of her excitement drain away at the thought of dragging everyone back from celebrating a job well done to second-guess their victory. And for what? Metal stairs and a bagel shop. She imagined the volley of facts they would fire at her.

Fact One: Even if Josh *could* have used the fire escape to leave the building unnoticed, that didn't prove he actually *had*.

Fact Two: Tara Weldon had been placed at the scene of both abductions. Josh Skelter had not.

Fact Three: the Hamleys bear was a damning piece of evidence linking Tara directly to the second abduction.

Fact Four: Tara had lied (convincingly enough to fool Juliet) during the police interview.

Was she really prepared to stand up in front of her colleagues and instruct them to cast all these facts aside? To inform them that the abductor was driven, not by devastating, mind-warping grief, but by the desire to start dating a plain, socially awkward woman he had met only once, because she reminded him of his mother? Oh, and that a fire Surrey police had ruled accidental twenty years ago had actually been set by Josh, to take out the competition for his mother's love?

No. She couldn't say any of those things. It sounded far-fetched, preposterous.

'No need for a briefing.' She walked past Alistair, opened the door and stepped out into the exhaust-tainted heat. 'I just want to make absolutely sure we haven't overlooked anything.'

But as the door closed behind them, Alistair caught her wrist and gently drew her around to face him, eyes searching hers.

'Look, if you've decided that we're wrong about Tara, I really would like to know about it. And I'd like to know why.'

She snatched her arm away, feeling defensive. 'I haven't decided anything yet.'

And as soon as she said the words, she realised they were true. Because, right now, she honestly couldn't say which one – Tara or Josh – she believed was guilty.

Thirty-four

Carrie had just put Sofia to bed and was tidying away toys in the living room when she glanced out the window and saw someone standing under the oak tree directly across the street, silhouetted by the sun's dying rays. A figure in a thin plastic raincoat, holding a bag. The hood was raised, burying the face in shadow. Carrie's heart lurched. Should she call Josh? He was in the study, working on his Editor's Introduction. All she had to do was shout his name and he'd come running. But something stopped her from doing that. She had spent so much of the last month boxing shadows, waiting for unseen enemies to reveal themselves or be captured by police. This time, she wanted to be the one to take action, to seize control.

Carrie flung open the door, sending a fan of light spilling across the garden. The hooded figure moved closer, crossing the road to stand in front of her gate. Carrie blinked as she saw who it was.

'What are you doing here?'

Tara pushed back the plastic hood, exposing her face. The streetlight hung shadows from her eye sockets and turned her skin sallow, making her appear older. She stood at the gate, holding her handbag by its strap.

'I need to speak to you. There are some things I have to explain. Things I should have told you sooner.'

Carrie stood frozen, caught in the pull of opposing forces, running a mental risk assessment. Of course she couldn't do anything that would endanger Sofia – even if the risk seemed small. But she also didn't want to cut Tara out of her life when the DCI herself had admitted there was a good chance she'd done absolutely nothing wrong. And the fact that DCI Campbell had come by asking questions about Josh, of all people, who everyone knew had been in his office when Sofia was taken, proved that the police were still running in circles, taking shots in the dark.

Carrie arrived at a decision. She *would* listen to what Tara had to say … but not in the house, with Sofia asleep upstairs. She stepped out onto the doorstep.

'OK. Tell me.'

Tara moved closer, stopping when she reached the bottom step, eyebrows dipping together.

'Aren't we going inside?'

'No.' Carrie shut the door behind her. 'Let's take a walk.'

'Ah.' Tara smiled with one side of her mouth. 'You mean because Sofia is inside and you think … what, that I'm going to try and snatch her?'

'As long as that remains even a remote possibility, I am not prepared to take the chance.'

'Fine,' Tara said quietly. She pulled her handbag up over her shoulder as she turned towards the street. 'Let's go.'

The day's light had bled out by the time they reached the

nearest park: an empty strip of grass with a giant cherry tree at one end and a wooden bench at the other. The gate was unlocked and they walked to the bench in silence. Carrie sat down. Tara hesitated for a moment before joining her. She drew in a deep breath, closing her eyes as she released it.

'You asked me why you've never met Peter. And I want to tell you the truth.'

Carrie felt her heart beat faster without quite knowing why. 'OK.'

'Peter has ... issues. Behavioural issues. He's been excluded from Eleonore Primary – his school – seven times already. I seem to spend half my life in the head's office, pleading with her not to make the exclusions permanent. But I'm afraid it's only a matter of time.'

'What kind of behavioural issues?'

'He gets angry ... *beyond* angry. He spins out of control, won't stop screaming. And sometimes he gets violent and hurts people. Me. Other children – which, as you can imagine, puts a strain on my friendships with their mothers. They steer clear of us because they don't want their children to get frightened or bitten. I'd probably do the same in their shoes.' She kicked a pebble lying near her foot, sending it skidding into the grass. 'I just ... didn't want that to happen with us.'

Carrie tipped her face to the darkened sky. Relief was coursing through her, making her body feel lighter and cleaner somehow: all the muddy confusion sluiced away.

'Why didn't you tell me this sooner?

'I don't know. Shame, I guess. Because the way he is ... It's my fault.'

'Why?'

Tara undid the top button of her raincoat, making the plastic crackle. Heaved out a sigh.

'When Peter was two, I had another baby. A daughter. Clarissa. She was ... perfect. I adored her. I'd always wanted a girl.' She began rubbing her hands together slowly, as though washing them. 'The first time Peter bit her, I thought it was just jealousy. I hated that he did it.' The hands stopped rubbing and retracted into tight fists. 'I think I loved him less because of it.'

Carrie's view of the park flickered in the flurry of blinks set off by this extraordinary revelation. Tara had a *daughter*? Why had she never mentioned her before? Perhaps the father had won sole custody? But then, wouldn't she be entitled to some sort of visitation, maybe on alternate weekends? Questions were crowding Carrie's head, jostling for space. But, in the end, she asked only one.

'Where is Clarissa now?'

Tara pulled her knees up onto the bench and wrapped her arms around them so that she was sitting in an upright foetal position: an oddly girlish pose.

'She died before her first birthday. Anaphylactic shock. We were in the park and she was sitting near a flower bed. And the next thing I knew, she'd been stung and ...' Her eyes squeezed shut. Carrie felt an unfolding inside her chest, a powerful tug of empathy. Because that could so easily have been her, watching helplessly as meningitis stole her child's last breath. She looked at Tara, hunched over her knees, and wondered how she'd been able to keep going – to smile and hand out food at birthday parties, watching other people's daughters turn three and four and five. Knowing that hers never would.

Slowly, tentatively, Carrie placed an arm around the bowed

shoulders. Tara leaned towards her, dabbing her eyes with a fingertip before continuing.

'I had no idea she was allergic to bee stings. It all happened so fast.' She drew in a shaky breath. 'Anyway, I was a mess after that. By the time I was able to function again, my marriage was over. My husband left and I threw myself into trying to be a good mother to Peter. But the damage had already been done.'

Carrie considered the description of Peter's symptoms: the lack of impulse control and frustration with social situations. Her own childhood had been spent bouncing from one mental health expert to the next – an army of psychiatrists, psychologists and therapists, all determined to label and fix her. Then later, after they'd given up, came the group sessions, where she'd learned techniques for working around her condition, seated in rows or circles with her fellow travellers on the road less taken. The road no one wanted to take.

And Peter's symptoms sounded all too familiar.

'Has your son been tested for underlying physiological issues?'

Tara nodded against her knees. 'He has ADHD and some other stuff I hadn't heard of and won't bore you with, since the doctors seem to change their minds about it every two minutes.'

Carrie leaned sideways to take a proper look at Tara, who remained balled up with her arms around her shins.

'If that's the case, his condition isn't your fault. Any more than my condition is my parents' fault.'

'But it *is* my fault. Because instead of helping Peter learn to cope, I retreated into depression.'

'Depression was an understandable and appropriate emotional response to the sudden death of your child.'

'That's no excuse.'

335

'Yes. It is.'

Tara met her eyes for the first time since they'd sat down. There was a tear coasting down her cheek. But she smiled.

'Thank you.'

Carrie didn't know what the 'thank you' was for – she'd only stated a fact – but she was pleased to have helped somehow, so didn't say anything as Tara freed her legs, stretching them out in front of her. 'Your mobile's ringing.'

'Oh.' Carrie took the buzzing handset from her pocket and saw, with a pulse of surprise, that it was DCI Campbell.

The policewoman didn't waste time on hellos.

'Carrie. I need you to listen very carefully to what I'm about to tell you.'

Josh was so nice. Sofia had woken from a nightmare about lions that could fly and gone downstairs for a Mummy-hug. Instead, she had found Josh standing in front of the sofa looking out the window.

'Where's Mummy?'

'She's outside.'

Sofia walked over to stand beside Josh. The sky was making a sunset and she could see Mummy and Tara standing at the bottom of the front steps.

'What are they talking about?'

'I don't know.'

She watched Mummy and Tara walk down the path and turn onto the street. They were probably going to the corner shop to buy some food. Maybe they were going to make sandwiches for snacks. The thought gave her a tummy rumble.

'I'm hungry.'

'What would you like to eat?'

'A peanut butter and jam sandwich.'

'OK, let's make one.'

'Really? Even though it's night?'

'Yes. Even though it's night.'

Sofia clapped her hands in excitement. She hadn't really thought Josh would let her have peanut butter and jam after bedtime when her teeth were already brushed.

'I'm going to pretend I'm at a sleepover and this is the midnight feast!'

Josh took Sofia's hand and led her to the kitchen, where he began taking things out of the cupboard and putting them on the counter: bread, strawberry jam, peanut butter. A plate and a big knife.

Josh fetched Sofia's special chair from the dining table, placing it in front of the counter. Then he lifted her up so she was standing on the seat, making her almost as tall as Josh. They made two sandwiches together – him doing the peanut butter and her doing the jam.

When they were done, Josh held up his palm and she high-fived it as hard as she could.

'Ouch!' he said, waving his hand in the air, making a pretend hurt face.

Sofia looked back towards the door, worried Mummy and Tara would come back and make her go straight back to bed without the sandwich. Josh must have been mind-reading her, because he said: 'Why don't we sneak out the back door and eat in the car, so your Mummy doesn't catch us?'

'You mean like a picnic?'

'Yes.' Josh gave her a big smile. 'Exactly like a picnic.'

'We're on our way over to bring Josh in for questioning,' DCI Campbell's voice said. 'New evidence has come to light opening up the possibility that he was behind Sofia's abduction.'

The policewoman's words surged through the phone, slamming into Carrie with the force of a blow, momentarily knocking the world out of alignment. The cherry tree at the end of the park duplicated itself and slid sideways for a second before snapping back into place. Carrie closed her eyes. Breathed in. Breathed out. She got up and walked to the middle of the grass. Stood facing the empty road next to it, leached grey by streetlight.

No, she told herself firmly. DCI Campbell was wrong. She *had* to be wrong, because there was proof, wasn't there? Solid, irrefutable proof of Josh's innocence.

'It can't have been him. He was at work when Sofia was taken. You told me so yourself.'

'Yes, I know we told you that, but – turn right here, Alistair, the motorway's backed up.' Carrie could hear the swish of traffic, then a distant horn. The sound of the police moving inexorably nearer, closing in on her home. On Josh. Nausea rolled through her stomach. 'I'm sorry, Carrie, but we've only just discovered there's an external fire escape linking Josh's office to the neighbouring street, which means there's a chance he used it to avoid being spotted leaving the building.'

'A "chance".' Carrie grasped at the word. 'How big a chance?'

'Difficult to say at this point. We're still waiting on the CCTV

338

from that street, to see if it shows him going out and coming back around the time of Sofia's disappearance. And Zoe's. But there is also compelling new evidence pointing in a different direction. So, as things now stand, we have two viable theories, both of which are being taken very seriously. Normally I wouldn't speak to you about this until we knew one way or the other, but given your current living situation, I took the view that you should immediately be made aware of any potential risk to Sofia's safety.'

'This chance,' Carrie said, clinging tight to the word, refusing to let go. 'It would help me if you could put it in numerical terms. Are you able to do that?'

The background hiss of traffic travelled through the phone in the pause that followed. Then DCI Campbell said: 'Fifty–fifty.'

Fifty-fifty.

The flip of a coin.

Heads, she was living with a thoughtful, intelligent man who adored Carrie and Sofia and wanted to protect them.

Tails, she was harbouring the monster who had terrorised her child.

No, it just couldn't be true.

'None of this makes sense. Why would he go to all the trouble of abducting Sofia, only to return her two days later?'

'Because taking her was never his ultimate goal.' DCI Campbell said the words slowly, enunciating each one, as though English were Carrie's second language. 'It may have been *you* he wanted all along; Sofia was just a means to an end.'

'I don't understand what you mean. Explain to me?'

'I have a theory. And to be clear, right now it *is* just a theory, that Josh became fixated on you at the awards ceremony. And when he failed to get your attention through work, he decided to try something more ... extreme. Osman mentioned your devotion to Sofia during his magazine interview at Wescott. So when Josh saw the photo on your desk showing the pair of you in Granger Park together, he came up with a plan to exploit that devotion, win your gratitude and gain entry to your life.'

Carrie closed her eyes as the words crashed into her like storm waves, washing away the ground beneath her feet – ground on which her life was now built. She fought back, throwing up barricades of logic.

'The motive you're ascribing to Josh wouldn't apply to Zoe. You have already concluded that both girls were taken by the same person, using the same method. But Josh had no motive for taking Zoe.'

'Yes, he did.' Tara's voice – from right behind Carrie's shoulder – set off a jolt of surprise. Either she'd crept up silently or Carrie had been too absorbed in the call to register what was going on around her. Tara moved nearer, aiming her words at the phone. '*I* was his motive. Josh wanted to shift suspicion onto me.'

'What the ... Is that *Tara*? What the hell is *she* doing with you!?'

'She came by to tell me something.'

Carrie sidestepped along the grass, trying to put distance between them, but Tara moved with her, still talking towards the handset.

'And another thing: I don't think deflecting blame was his only reason. I think Josh wants to end my friendship with Carrie so he can have her all to himself. I could swear I saw him following me last week just before I went to Tudor Park.

I tried to go after him, but it was Regent Street, packed with tourists as usual, and he disappeared into the crowds.'

'Carrie, listen to me. Tara should not be anywhere near you or Sofia right now! She is just as much a suspect in this case as Josh is, so you need to tell her to leave immed—' The word stopped halfway, but Carrie knew the signal hadn't dropped, because she could still hear traffic in the background. Then DCI Campbell's voice returned. 'Did Tara just say she saw Josh on Regent Street?'

'Yes.'

'Can you put me on speaker phone? I need to ask her something.'

'OK.'

Carrie held the handset in front of Tara as DCI Campbell's voice emerged, made tinny by the speaker.

'Tara, were you shopping when Josh saw you?'

'Yes, but the important thing is: I went to Tudor Park for lunch afterward. So he could have followed me and seen where I like to sit.'

'Did you buy anything? On Regent Street?'

'What? Um, yeah. But I think you're missing the point. I went—'

'What did you buy?'

Tara's brows drew together, deepening the crease already carved between them.

'What did I *buy*? Does that matter?'

'It might.'

Tara lifted a shoulder. 'A stuffed bear. From Hamleys. A "Benjy Bear", if you must know. My niece has an imaginary friend named Benjy and her birthday's coming up so . . . Anyway, that's what I'd just bought when I saw him.'

341

'Do you still have it? If we went to your house right now, would it be there?'

'No, it's in the post, on the way to Hong Kong. Why?'

'Carrie, please take me off speaker phone. I need a word with you privately.'

'OK.'

She returned DCI Campbell to her left ear, conscious of Tara, rigid and alert on her right, the two of them making her feel flanked.

'Tell Tara she needs to go home now.'

'Why did you ask about the bear?' Her mind was working fast, filling in the blank spaces in the scene Tara had described: Josh watching her enter Hamleys. Following her inside. 'Do you think he went back and bought the same bear as Tara, to use in Zoe's abduction?'

A sense of unreality washed over her as she said the words; she felt disconnected – as though she wasn't really here, and all of this was happening to someone else.

'It's too early to jump to that conclusion,' DCI Campbell said. 'Because it is equally possible that Tara *did* use the bear to abduct Zoe and is now fabricating stories to implicate Josh and cover her tracks – playing along with my theory that he would stop at nothing to become the most important person in your life.'

The storm inside Carrie had reached hurricane force. Relationships she'd built, secrets she'd shared, memories she'd cherished – all were being whipped away, until finally only one true thing remained. The most fundamental truth of all, solid and immutable.

'He could never become the most important person in my life. That will always be Sofia.'

The policewoman made a 'hmm' noise.

'Yes, but Josh wouldn't necessarily realise that, given that his own mother was . . . well. She took a different view.'

'He does realise that. I told him.'

There was a pause. She could hear a snatch of music from a car passing in the background. Then DCI Campbell spoke again.

'When did you tell him that?'

'Last week, after we got back from the hospital.' She heard a male voice mumbling, but couldn't make out the words. It must be that man she often worked with, the Irish one.

'Carrie, where is Sofia right now?'

'In bed.' She turned and walked quickly out of the park, heart hammering. 'I'm going to her.'

Her legs scissored along the pavement. She hadn't thought twice about leaving her daughter alone in the house with Josh. He'd always taken such good care of her. She told herself that this phone call didn't change that. Sofia was asleep in bed and Josh was working in his study. Everything was fine. But she broke into a run as she turned onto her street, the mobile still pressed against her ear, dimly aware of Tara's footsteps echoing behind her.

'We'll be arriving shortly to question Josh,' DCI Campbell said. 'A separate car has been dispatched to bring in Tara. Meanwhile, you are to stay away from *both* of them, do you understand? Station yourself in Sofia's room. Because as things now stand, we have two equally plausible theories and two equally likely suspects. And I don't want you or Sofia anywhere near either of them.'

Carrie reached her house, dragging fingers through her hair as she approached the door, letting the nails rake her scalp. Some small part of her hoped she wouldn't feel it, because this was all just a dream. A terrible dream. Any moment now she would wake up and find herself in bed with Josh asleep beside her, solid and reassuring. The nails dug into her skin, leaving stinging furrows.

This was no dream. Either her lover had abducted Sofia, or her best friend had.

Heads, you lose. Tails, you lose.

'Carrie?' DCI Campbell's voice prodded. 'Do you understand?'

She took out her door key. 'Yes. I understand.'

'Good. We should be with you in' – another pause, another male mumble – 'eighteen minutes. If Josh approaches you, don't let on that there's anything wrong. And it goes without saying that you're not to warn him we're coming.'

'If it goes without saying, then why did you say it?'

'It's just a … Never mind. I'll see you soon.' And the line went dead.

She shoved the phone back in her pocket and was about to slot her key in the lock when she heard running footsteps closing in from behind. Tara. Carrie turned to find her dashing up the front path, pulling to a halt as she reached the steps and saw Carrie standing at the top, facing her.

'Tara, I need you to go home now.' For once Carrie's voice matched the way she felt: flat and numb, as though all the emotion had been gouged out, leaving her hollow. 'Please.'

Tara opened her mouth, as though about to speak. But then she closed it again. Nodded.

'OK,' she said quietly. 'I'll go.'

Her footsteps were loud against the silence.

★   ★   ★

344

Carrie rushed inside and had already put one foot on the bottom stair when her mind processed what her eyes had just seen.

While she'd been outside, something had changed. Sofia's chair was in the kitchen and there were dishes and containers on the counter. As she moved closer, she saw what they were: a loaf of bread and an open jar of peanut butter. A knife lay beside it, the blade red with jam. Her stomach did a slow turn.

Peanut butter and jam sandwiches. Sofia's favourite.

Somewhere deep inside her, an alarm went off. She dashed up the stairs, ears straining ahead for the sound of Josh moving around, going through his nightly ritual (glasses off, face washed, teeth brushed, next day's clothes laid out). But the silence was complete.

When she reached the corridor, she saw, with a fresh jolt of alarm, that her daughter's door was wide open. She ran across the threshold, heart banging.

The curtains were half-open and a fat slice of moonlight lay across the floor. It picked out the rope ridges of the circular rug and the bedtime book (*Don't Let the Pigeon Drive the Bus*) splayed face-down on the floor. It threw shadows across the duvet, recasting the pink unicorns in shades of grey. Carrie stood staring down at the rumpled folds of cloth, lying against the mattress like the abandoned cocoon of a butterfly. No sleeping figure reshaping it, no gentle rise and fall of a child's breathing.

Sofia was gone.

Thirty-five

'It's going straight to voicemail,' Carrie said, shoving her mobile into the back pocket of her jeans. She looked up and down the empty street, consumed by helplessness. 'Now what do we do?'

Tara had been standing on the corner, waiting for her Uber to arrive, when Carrie had come barrelling down the pavement, shouting that Sofia was gone. Tara's eyes had gone round and her mouth had stretched wide: a cartoon image of surprise that even Carrie could read.

She had cancelled the Uber immediately.

'Now we call the police,' Tara said now, turning on her heel and marching back towards Carrie's place. 'Talk to that DCI again – Campbell – tell her what's happened.'

Carrie jogged alongside her, past the house second from end: number seventy-eight, with its neatly clipped hedge. The old woman's voice whispered in her memory.

Anyone can see he's not right in the head.

'The DCI is already on her way here.' Carrie's voice sounded hollow and distant in her own ears, and she wondered dimly whether discovering Sofia gone had somehow damaged her senses: sent a shock wave through her skull that had ruptured her ear drums.

'Still, we should tell her to hurry, and to send backup.'

The front door was ajar – she had forgotten to close it – and Carrie ran through it with Tara in her wake, stopping when she reached the dining area.

'Send it *where*?' Her legs felt rubbery, so she held on to the back of a wooden chair, leaning against it. 'We don't know where he's taken her. A shed somewhere.'

'No, I don't think so.' Tara said the words slowly, hands dropping to her hips, eyes narrowing.

'What do you mean? Explain to me.'

'Think about it; the previous abductions were planned in advance. And in both cases, the aim was for the girls to be found and freed. First by Josh himself, so he could bring Sofia back and become your hero. And as for Zoe ... He would have wanted her to be discovered too, along with that bear, to throw suspicion onto me.' Her eyes moved to the kitchen. The chair pushed up against the counter. The open jars of peanut butter and jam. 'This feels more ... spur of the moment. And his motive ... well, I don't know exactly what it could be. But it's different from before.'

'I couldn't read him.' Carrie's throat felt thick and dry, as if coated in ash. 'I couldn't tell. I thought he was kind: the man who had saved Sofia, someone I could trust, maybe even love. I should have learned by now that I can't trust anyone.'

'Yes.' Tara put an arm around Carrie's shoulders and gave them a squeeze. 'You can. But blaming yourself for what's already happened won't get us anywhere. We need to work this through logically and figure out the best, most useful thing to do next.' She paused, perhaps expecting Carrie to offer a suggestion. But panic had filled her head with static; she couldn't think.

Tara, however, could.

'So . . . Before we call the police, let's try and work out where Josh would have taken her.' She was speaking in the same tone she'd used that first day in the park: the one that made Carrie think of teachers. And just as it had back then, that voice made Carrie feel calmer now – as though someone had taken control of the situation.

'Question number one.' Tara raised her index finger. 'Where does Josh live?'

'In Clapham. A terraced house off the high street.'

She shook her head.

'They won't be there, too public.' She held up a second finger. 'Next question: does he have a holiday home? A weekend retreat on the coast or in the Cotswolds?'

'No, he . . .' She stopped. Saw again the wedge-shaped building alone on a stretch of land that had once been a vineyard.

This is your mother's house?

Yes. Well, technically mine now.

'You're blinking,' Tara said. 'You've thought of something.'

'Yes.' Carrie's fingers were already scrabbling along the kitchen counter for her car keys. She wasn't going to just stand here, waiting for other people to come to Sofia's rescue. Not this time. 'I think I know where he's taking her.'

★   ★   ★

Alistair took a turn at speed, making the tyres squeal. A group of teenagers drinking beer in a bus shelter raised their tins in a mock toast as the car roared past.

Juliet's mobile buzzed and Carrie's name appeared on the screen.

'We'll be with you in ten minutes,' she said, glancing at the GPS.

But it wasn't Carrie who answered.

'She won't be there,' Tara's voice said. Juliet could hear traffic in the background and a current of alarm passed through her. One of two suspects in the case was calling from the victim's mobile, in what was clearly a moving car.

Shit.

'What's going on, Tara?'

A car horn and an angry shout travelled through the phone. She and Alistair weren't the only ones speeding.

'Josh has taken Sofia. We think he's bringing her to his mother's old place in Surrey. We're on our way there now.'

Juliet froze, mouth ajar, as though someone had hit pause. Then Alistair did another swerve, rocking her sideways, the seatbelt digging into her ribs, breaking the spell.

'Can you put Carrie on?' She needed to find out what the hell was going on – but not from Tara. Because one suspect slinging blame at another ... that wasn't something she was prepared to take at face value.

'Sorry, but she needs to focus on driving. As you can imagine, this situation is very stressful, so you can't really expect her to drive and talk on the phone at the same time. Also it's illegal. But if there's anything you'd like to say to her, I'd be happy to pass it along.' She sounded remarkably calm for a woman racing towards a potentially dangerous criminal. It made Juliet wonder whether Tara knew something they didn't. 'You can meet us there. It's called The Vineyard and it's in . . . '

'South-east Surrey,' Juliet finished, knocking Alistair with an elbow to draw his attention to her words. He must have got the message because he pulled into the left-hand lane, which fed onto the motorway that would take them there. 'I know where it is. We'll handle things from here. I want the two of you to turn back immediately and let us deal with this. Understood?'

'Carrie is very determined to go and get her daughter. And anyway, are you sure your way is best? If Carrie really is what he wants, she might be able to talk him into handing Sofia over quietly, without provoking him or making him feel cornered. He'll listen to her.'

Carrie is very determined.

Is she, though, Tara? Juliet thought. *Or are you?*

'That's not a good idea,' she said firmly, careful not to let her suspicion show through. She needed to create the impression that they were on the same team, working together to catch the bad guy. 'I know how to deal with sensitive situations like these. I have the training. If you go blundering in there without a plan, you'll only put everyone in danger.'

She wished she could see Tara's face right now, could see her eyes. What would she find in them? Concerned determination . . . or calculating duplicity?

But all she had to go on was a voice on the phone. Words she could barely make out against the hiss of traffic.

A pause. Then: 'You're right. We need a plan.'

'That's *not* what I'm saying!'

350

'I think I – Carrie, watch out!' There was a screech of tyres and an angry horn. 'Sorry, I have to go.'

'Do *not* approach Josh Skelter under any circumstances! Do you hear me? You don't know what he's capable of!'

But Tara was already gone.

Thirty-six

'Turn here,' Tara said, looking up from her iPad, which was showing the map from Josh's magazine.

Carrie swerved off the road and onto a long, pot-holed driveway, wheels spitting gravel. The bouncing headlights picked out tall weeds in the middle and bushes leaning in from both sides. Branches lashed the car. The driveway wound left, rising towards open ground. They rounded another curve, and, suddenly, there it was: Ava Skelter's wedge-shaped house, sketched grey by the moonlight.

'Is that Josh's car?' Tara pointed to a smear of deeper darkness in the shadows beside the house.

Carrie leaned closer to the windscreen, eyes probing the gloom, until she was able to make out the hulking shape of Josh's SUV, veiled by the branches of a willow. Her heart banged against the walls of her chest. He was here. Which meant Sofia was here too. Carrie stomped on the accelerator instinctively, the pitted surface making the car lurch and wallow like a ship in a storm.

'Stop!' Tara put a hand on the steering wheel. 'We don't want him to know we're here yet.'

Of course. She should have thought of that. Carrie pulled over to the edge of the driveway, branches scratching the side of the car and crowding up against the passenger window. She switched off the engine. Her breathing sounded loud in the sudden silence. Loud and fast.

The two of them sat staring up at the house. Tara leaned towards the windscreen, squinting.

'It looks like there's a light on downstairs.'

'There's no electricity. It must be a kerosene lamp.' Carrie stared at the wavering glow. The thought of her daughter in danger, somewhere in that house, was like a hook in her chest, pulling. She unclicked her seatbelt, but Tara grabbed her arm.

'Not yet. Let's go back over the plan.'

'I already know—'

'I couldn't show you the pictures when you were driving. I think you should see them. It will make things clearer.' She held the tablet in front of Carrie, flicking away the map, whisking through the pages of Josh's magazine until she reached the now familiar image of a living room with an arch at one end and an old-fashioned door at the other. Strappy leather furniture, a folding wooden screen and a steel-framed dining table. Tara swiped away from it for a moment, flicking quickly to the blueprints before returning again. 'OK. He's parked by the side door, which leads into the kitchen. So unless he locked the door behind him – and I'll be surprised if he did, since we're in the middle of nowhere and he won't be expecting company – we should be able to go in the same way. I'll sneak through the door connecting the kitchen to the main room and hide here.' She tapped the folding wooden screen that divided the living and dining areas. 'Then you come in and stand facing him from this position.' She touched a large, black-and-grey carpet patterned with interlocking cubes. 'You'll be able to see me, but Josh won't.'

'And you'll interpret for me.'

'Yes. Same as with the client. Except using my iPad, since you obviously can't go in there holding your mobile and looking at it every time he speaks.' She ran a palm up over her forehead, pushing back her fringe. 'You should be able to read the screen from there. You'll have to look to the side a bit, so try to be discreet about that, maybe hold your hand over your eyes, like you're upset.' She minimised the photo of the room and tapped on an icon of a cartoon notebook 'This app lets me write directly on the screen using my finger as a pen, so I can make the words big enough to read. I'll have to keep the brightness setting low so that he doesn't notice the light, but you should still be able to see it.'

'OK.'

Carrie could hear the tick of the engine cooling in the silence that followed. She chewed on a thumbnail, blinking fast, trying to focus, to commit the plan to memory. But it was hard to think clearly with adrenalin chasing through her veins.

'And you remember your answers to the questions we talked about?'

'I think so.' She felt the tightness in her chest ease ever so slightly. The situation was still bewildering, still terrifying. But at least Tara would be there, guiding her through the shifting maze of expressions, gestures and inflections. Shining a light into the blacked-out spaces.

Tara sucked air through gritted teeth. 'Ready?'

'Yes.

Carrie looked through the windscreen at the house, at the stain of lamplight at one end, moving behind the thin curtains. And felt a creep of doubt.

'You really think this is better than waiting for the police?'

'Yes, I do.'

'And you believe your plan will work?'

Carrie turned sideways in her seat to look at Tara. The moonlight made her face look different: cold and hard, as though it were carved out of marble.

'It will work. Trust me.'

Sofia dreamed that she was back in the shed. But this time, she didn't yell for help because there was a monster outside and she didn't want it to hear her and come in.

She woke with a gasp. Then sat up quickly, blinking with confusion. Because she wasn't in the shed – but she wasn't at home either. She was on the floor in a strange place with closed curtains and flickery light.

'Oh good, you're awake.'

Josh! He was standing right behind her, holding a metal-and-glass container with a flame inside. Sofia smiled with relief.

'Where are we?' She looked around. There were sheets covering up all the furniture, so it looked like the room was full of weird-shaped ghosts. 'I don't bermember coming here.'

'You fell asleep in the car.'

'Oh. I'm thirsty.' She pointed at a bottle of clear liquid on the ghost-sofa behind him. 'Can I have some water?'

'Some …?' He turned to see what she was pointing at.

'Ah. That isn't water. You can't drink it. Trust me, you wouldn't want to.'

'Where's Mummy? Is she coming?'

'No, she's not.' Josh did a big sigh. 'You know, Sofia, your mother loves you very much. And sometimes I think that can affect her judgement.' He sat down on the sheet-covered sofa, sending up a puff of dust. 'It can get in the way.'

Get in the way of what? Sofia wondered. But she didn't ask out loud, because something about being here with just Josh and no Mummy was making little flips happen in her tummy.

'I want to go home now.' She could hear a quiver inside her voice.

'I'm sorry, but we can't go just yet. It wasn't my plan to bring you here tonight, but after seeing Tara talking to your mother ... Well, let's just say I don't think it's safe there right now. Tara may *seem* nice, but she's actually a very dangerous person. And a convincing liar.' He shook his head. 'Everything would be so much simpler if your Mummy didn't feel the need for all these other people in her life even though she has me, ready to give her everything she needs. If only—'

But then he stopped talking, because of a sound at the other end of the room.

Footsteps.

Someone was coming.

Tara was right: Josh hadn't bothered to lock the door behind him. They entered the kitchen without a sound, tiptoeing past a large, silent fridge and an ancient-looking stove (still hooked to a gas canister), skirting around a huge kitchen island with

356

empty hooks hanging above it, the pots that had once dangled there long since packed away.

The door to the living room was open a crack, admitting a seam of watery light. When Carrie heard Sofia's voice on the other side, the relief was tidal, the force of it nearly winding her.

The plan was for Tara to make her move while Josh's back was turned. The screen had been chosen both for its strategic location (not far from the kitchen and off to one side) and because the fringe of latticework along the top would allow her to watch Josh without being seen ... assuming he was still standing at the other end of the room. And assuming the screen hadn't been moved since the photo was taken. And that Josh didn't suddenly turn around again and spot Tara before she got into position.

Assuming, assuming, assuming.

The plan that had sounded so solidly constructed just minutes ago now seemed to have been built on quicksand, ready to sink at the slightest vibration.

Carrie watched, body wired with adrenalin, as Tara slowly eased open the door until it was just wide enough for her to fit through. She gave Carrie a brief nod before slipping through the gap in a running crouch.

Carrie closed her eyes and counted slowly backward from ten, praying she wouldn't hear the sound of Josh's voice shouting at Tara to stop, to come out of there *right now*.

Nothing.

She peered through the gap and saw, with a rush of relief, that the screen was exactly where it had been in the photo. Tara was safely installed behind it.

So far so good.

The room looked bigger than it had in the picture and the strappy furnishings were concealed beneath dust covers. Josh was standing at the far end with his back to them. Sofia was on the floor at his feet, illuminated by the lamp he was holding. Carrie fought the impulse to run straight over and sweep her into a hug.

You have to watch every move you make around him, she reminded herself. *He's not the man you thought he was. Someone capable of abducting two little girls is capable of anything.*

There was no room for error. She had to stick to the plan. Take everything one slow, careful step at a time. She drew in a long breath, filling her lungs. Released it slowly. OK. Time to make her move.

Throwing open the door, she strode into the living room, making no attempt at stealth, Tara's instructions replaying in her memory ('Walk into that room like you belong there, like you've got nothing to hide.')

She stopped in the middle of the black-and-grey carpet: behind and to the left of the spot where Tara now crouched, watching Josh's reactions through the gaps in the latticework.

He swung around to face her, mouth opening.

'Carrie? What the—'

'Hello, you two,' she interrupted. 'How are you getting on?'

'What are you doing here? I thought you were with . . .'

'Mummy!' Sofia jumped up and tried to run to her, but Josh grabbed her by the elbow and pulled her backward, making her cry out.

'Stay here with me for a sec, poppet,' he said, and wrapped an arm across her chest, trapping her against him.

Carrie looked straight at him.

'I came here to join you both. I thought it would be nice if you showed us around the house, then the three of us can travel home together.'

'I want to go home *now*.' Sofia tugged at the restraining arm with both hands. 'Josh, let go!'

'I'm afraid that's not going to happen,' he said, raising the lamp higher so that the light spread outward, catching Carrie's face. She placed a hand to her forehead, screening her eyes as her gaze shifted sideways to Tara, who was writing something on the tablet with her fingertip. She turned the screen to face Carrie.

'Freaked out, thrown off stride,' it said. Then she cleared the screen before adding: 'CALMLY ask why not.'

'Why can't we go home, Josh? It's past Sofia's bedtime.'

'Because it's not safe there.'

Sofia slapped his forearm, starting to cry. 'Let me *go*! Mummy, I'm scared!'

Carrie stepped towards her instinctively, but Josh shook his head and said: 'Stay there, please.' He gave her a brief smile. 'Much as I'd love to have you run into my arms, it's probably best not to barrel into me while I'm holding this lamp. Because if I were to drop it ... well ... These dust covers are pretty flammable.'

Was that a threat, or an expression of genuine concern about health and safety? She waited a few moments, giving Tara time to write, then screened her eyes again as she looked towards the iPad. When she saw what was written there, her heart lurched.

'Volatile. DANGEROUS. Don't move. Let him speak.'

Carrie stood perfectly still, fighting to keep her gaze from shifting downwards to Sofia, now sobbing noisily as she struggled to free herself.

359

'I want you to know that you're everything to me,' Josh said suddenly. 'That I'll always be here for you. There's nothing we can't overcome ... together.'

Should she say something in response to that? Or just nod? Carrie bowed her head so he wouldn't see her eyes shift sideways again.

'Unstable, desperate,' the iPad said. 'Say you know he's there 4 you.'

'I know you're there for me.' She swallowed before adding: 'Thank you.'

He laughed softly. 'I love how you do that: the way you pause before tacking on a thank you. In so many ways, you're just like her. But in others ... you're very different. *Good* different.' He gave her a smile. What *kind* of smile, though? She cupped a hand in front of her face to look towards Tara again.

'Affection, warmth,' the iPad told her. A screen-wipe and a fresh flurry of scribbling. 'Moment of weakness. Probably won't last.' Wipe-scribble. 'Pretend you want to hug/kiss him. Then get Sofia.'

Carrie opened her arms and took a step forwards. 'Kiss me, Josh.'

She was hoping Josh would open his own arms in response, releasing Sofia. Instead, his head reared back and his eyebrows dipped together.

Tara's screen: 'Confused. Suspicious.'

Damn. She should have just gone to him without speaking. Because when it came to expressing affection, Carrie moved in silence, doing rather than saying.

'Mummy!' Sofia's face was streaming with tears now. 'Please! I want to go home!'

Carrie felt the gravitational pull of her daughter's distress, took a step forwards.

'Hey, wait a minute,' Josh said. She froze immediately, frightened by the kerosene lamp, rocking on its wire-loop handle, the flame sputtering inside its cylinder of glass. 'How did you know I was here?'

She darted a look at Tara, who stared back, motionless. They had prepared an answer for this one; it was such an obvious question to ask. But now that the moment had come, Carrie's mind was empty, wiped blank by the sound of her daughter's frightened sobs. Panic clawed at her. All Josh had to do was open his fingers and flaming liquid would plunge to the floor, inches from the hem of the dust cover. And ... oh God, oh God, was that a fresh bottle of kerosene lying on the seat of the sofa? Her daughter's life was hanging by a thread and Carrie had no idea what to say next.

But then, like a blessing, came the faint rectangle of light in the corner of her vision. She shielded her eyes again as she read the memory prompt: 'Find My Phone!'

Of course. How could she have forgotten?

'I ... I must have dropped my mobile in your car when you drove me to work this morning. Her fingers moved instinctively to the underside of her wrist, teeth gritting as she administered a hard pinch. 'When I couldn't locate it, I did a "Find my Phone" search and saw that you'd come here. So when I ... noticed Sofia wasn't in her room, I guessed that you'd decided to show her this house, because I know how special it is to you. And I thought I'd come join you, since I love the design and wanted to see it for myself.' Her wrist was stinging from the succession of pinches that had accompanied this speech.

Josh stood without moving, face aimed her way, the raised lamp casting his eyes in shadow. Then he nodded.

The tablet: 'He believes you.'

Carrie freed a pent-up breath. The 'Find My Phone' story had been Tara's idea, the lie coming to her easily, taking no time at all. Carrie would never have thought of something like that, not in a million years. When forced from the path of truth, she tended to get lost.

Josh lowered the lamp so that it was just above Sofia's head, making the light shift and flicker. Sofia was quiet now, eyes squeezed shut, cheeks sheened with tears.

'I love you, Carrie.' Josh's voice was flat, like hers.

She froze. The declaration caught her off guard. No man had ever said those words to her before, and some small, foolish part of her was thrilled. But she didn't have a clue how to respond, so was relieved to see a rectangular glow on the edge of her vision.

'Seeking reassurance,' Tara's screen told her. 'Say it back.'

'I love you too, Josh.'

And this time, she didn't pinch herself. Because it was true. Or at least, it *felt* true. Her emotions seemed to be on a time lag, not yet caught up with the information her brain was feeding them: that Josh wasn't the man she'd thought he was. That he couldn't be trusted.

He gave her a wide smile.

'It's so good to hear you say that. I can't tell you how good.'

The screen flashed again and she placed fingertips against her forehead, palm blocking her eyes, to mask the side-glance.

'Suggest u both take Sofia home because v. late,' the screen said.

'Why don't we take Sofia home now? It's way past her bedtime.'

Sofia must have been listening and picked up on the change in Josh's mood, because she looked up at him hopefully, speaking in a trembling voice.

'Please can we go? I'm tired.'

He smiled down at her.

'I'm so sorry, poppet, I really didn't mean to keep you up so late. But I think it would be best if all three of us stayed here tonight. For safety's sake.' That response must have surprised Tara, because there was no movement from behind the screen. Josh sighed and shook his head. 'Look, I have to be honest with you, Carrie. The real reason I brought Sofia here tonight . . . It's because I saw you outside talking to Tara. And that scared me. *She* scares me. There's something not right there, something . . . missing. You can't read her and she exploits that, using your condition to burrow into your life. Waiting for you to lower your guard so she can take Sofia from you . . . again. But I see her for what she is: a manipulative and dangerous liar.'

Carrie was keenly aware of Tara, standing just a few steps away, listening. But no faint rectangle of light flickered in the corner of her eye. In fact, there was no movement of any kind.

Carrie knew she had to say something. So in the absence of Tara's guidance, she fell back on her old friend, logic.

'If you were so concerned about her coming by the house, why not just call the police?'

Josh began idly stroking Sofia's hair. 'Call them and say *what*, exactly? That a woman you consider a friend dropped by and the two of you went for a walk?' Another sigh. 'The unfortunate fact of the matter is your impairment prevents you from seeing the danger. And Tara has never been more dangerous than she is now: cornered and desperate, running out of time, knowing the police are onto her. So when she appeared out of nowhere like that ...' He shook his head. 'I'm convinced she was planning to make her move tonight. And that, being under her spell, you wouldn't listen to my warning. So I did the only thing I could think of: I brought Sofia somewhere safe for the night. Somewhere Tara couldn't find her.'

Carrie blinked as she took this in. There was a certain logic to it, if he genuinely believed that Tara was a threat. It did explain some of his behaviour tonight.

But not all of it.

'Why didn't you tell me you'd taken her? You must have realised how worried I'd be, but you didn't leave a note or call the house to let me know she was safe.'

'I know, and I am so, so sorry about that. I was planning to give you a ring on the way here, but my phone battery died.'

Carrie looked across the room at him. A lie, obviously. Although ... his mobile *had* gone straight to voicemail. But that was because he'd switched it off ...

Wasn't it?

And just for a moment, the coin flipped the other way.

What if Josh really *had* brought Sofia here because he believed her abductor had returned in the night, desperate to succeed this time ... and had duped Carrie into trusting her again?

Her thoughts returned to the moment when she'd looked outside and seen Tara on the other side of the street, hood raised, standing in the shadow of the oak tree ...

Standing? Or *hiding*?

What if she hadn't come over for a talk at all? What if she'd been looking for a way into the house, into Sofia's room ... until Carrie had spotted her? But if that were so, what was she doing here now, interpreting Josh's reactions for her?

No.

Tara was her friend. And anyway, Josh was the one with his arm clamped across her daughter's chest.

'Mummy.' Sofia's voice was small and broken, twisting her heart. 'Please take me home. I want ...'

Carrie didn't hear the rest because Josh spoke over her.

'I can tell that you still don't trust me, trust my judgement – even though all I've done is try to help you and be there for you. I love you, Carrie. But it's clear to me now that there's only room in your heart for Sofia.'

Then, at last, in the corner of her eye, the iPad flashed again, moving rapidly up and down, trying to flag her attention. When she saw what was written there, her stomach plunged.

'Unpredictable, volatile!' Wipe-scribble. 'Convince him Sofia NOT a threat to your relationship!!!'

Silence fell as Carrie struggled to digest this, to translate it into her own words. But before she could, Josh spoke again.

'Come closer.'

She swallowed. In three, maybe four paces, she would lose sight of Tara and the lifeline of messages. She took two steps towards him, then stopped, hoping that would be enough.

No such luck.

'Closer. I want to be able to see your face and hear your voice more clearly.'

She took a deep breath and then moved towards him, feeling a bolt of panic as she passed beyond the wooden screen. She had lost her interpreter and her guide. She was on her own.

Sofia was silent now, staring at her from above the clamped forearm, eyes wide with fear and confusion. What good did it do Carrie, being able to read this one face, if all it did was flood her with helpless pain?

She lifted her gaze to Josh. His lower jaw was set slightly to the right, so that his teeth weren't lined up properly. There was no point trying to guess what that meant; she didn't have a clue. So instead she focused on Tara's last message.

Convince him Sofia NOT a threat to your relationship!!!

He was watching her face and Carrie knew, in a rare flash of insight, that her next words would decide whether or not he let her daughter go.

She couldn't lie about her feelings; he would see right through that. But she could dig for the truths he wanted to hear.

She moved a step closer.

'You know what I loved about you from the start, Josh?'

His eyebrows drew closer together, turning upward in the middle.

'What?'

'The way you were with Sofia. Not just the day you brought her back, but afterwards too. Your gentleness. How you made her laugh. I loved listening to your conversations with her, watching you read stories at bedtime. Seeing those things made me . . .' She struggled to find the right words, feeling the pressure of his gaze, of her daughter's frightened face. She couldn't afford to get this wrong. She took a drag of air. Started again. 'It may have seemed to you sometimes that Sofia got in the way of our relationship. But, in fact, the opposite is true. She deepened it. The feelings that I had for you at the beginning – attraction and an appreciation of shared interests – would never have evolved

366

beyond that without her. She was the magic ingredient that transformed those ordinary things into something extraordinary. Into love. Sofia is the foundation on which my love for you is built. Without *her*, there would be no *us.'*

His eyes were clamped on her face, mouth slightly ajar, one eyebrow a shade higher than the other, and she wished desperately that she had Tara's screen to light her way, to tell her what it meant.

Carrie's whole life narrowed to this one point: standing in front of Josh, waiting to find out whether she had saved her daughter . . . or condemned her.

He looked down at Sofia. Gave her a small smile. Then – slowly, carefully – withdrew his arm.

And let her go.

Carrie crouched down as Sofia raced into her arms, clinging tight, small hands locking around the back of her neck. The relief was so powerful it seemed to dissolve Carrie's bones, making her legs feel watery.

Josh watched them, smiling, the lamplight throwing down a wavering shadow of their embrace.

'Shall we—' he began. But she never found out what he was going to suggest. Because the words were cut short by a loud, clattering sound. She turned, pulse spiking, towards the source. Something was lying on the floor, just beyond the edge of the wooden screen. Carrie realised what had happened with an icy plunge of dismay.

Tara had dropped the iPad.

Thirty-seven

'Sixteen minutes,' Alistair said. They were deep in the countryside now, darkened fields surging past the windows.

'Damn, this is taking too long. They're at least twenty minutes ahead of us.' Juliet called Carrie's phone for what must have been the twentieth time. But, like Tara's, it went straight to voicemail.

She stared through the windscreen, at the black ribbon of road rushing to meet them. A bad feeling was creeping over her: a cold prickle that spread outward, until it covered her skin.

Telling her that it was already too late.

'Fifteen minutes,' Alistair said.

'Who's there?' Josh shouted. 'Come out *right now*!'

Tara bent to pick up the fallen tablet as she stepped out from behind the screen. When he saw who it was, Josh's head reared back.

'Tara! What the hell are you ... oh Jesus, did you *follow* her here?' He turned to Carrie, crouched down about halfway between the two of them with Sofia in her arms. 'What did I tell you?! She's obsessed!'

Tara put a hand on her hip. 'Don't be ridiculous. Of *course* I didn't follow her here. I came as a friend. To help.'

'Really?' His voice was quiet. He smiled at Tara with his lips closed. 'Help in what way exactly?'

Carrie looked back and forth between the two of them, trying to understand the emotional forces in play. Did a smile and a quieter voice indicate that Josh was calming down, becoming less angry? Her eyes moved to Tara, to see whether she responded with a smile of her own.

She didn't.

'I'm helping her to interpret your reactions.' Her mouth twitched to one side. 'That's good, isn't it? You *do* want Carrie to understand how you think and feel … don't you?'

Josh stood frozen, his raised lamp stretching Tara's shadow across the interlocking cubes of the rug she now stood on. Then he tilted his head.

'And how, exactly, were you able to perform this great service to our relationship while hiding behind the furniture?'

Tara pressed a knuckle against her lip. Looked down at the iPad in her hand. Then back up at Josh.

'You know what? I'll show you.' She jotted on the screen with her fingertip, showing him the resulting message ('Puzzled, confused. Tell him how you really feel').

'See? I was just offering a bit of insight to … ease the flow of communication between you two.'

'By flashing secret messages and keeping me in the dark? You'll excuse me if I don't thank you.' He spun towards Carrie, making the lamplight swing wildly.

'Seriously?! You're letting *her* tell you what my voice and expressions mean? How can you not see that she only offered to do that so she could manipulate you, feed you misinformation?' Sofia whimpered and Carrie lifted her up, holding her against one shoulder. Josh shook his head. 'Let me guess: she told you I looked mad. Or maybe "dangerous" or "unstable".' Carrie's breath caught. How could he have known that? 'And you swallowed it all. Hook. Line. Sinker.' His shoulders sagged as he sighed. 'Look, maybe bringing Sofia here was an over-reaction. And I am genuinely sorry to have worried you. But when I looked out the window and saw her with you ... getting inside your head, convincing you to let her back in ... I guess I panicked. But you have to believe that my only motive was to keep Sofia safe. And to be clear: by "safe", I mean "far away from Tara". Because I've pieced it all together, worked out exactly how she did it.' He looked at Tara, addressing his next words to her. 'It's clever. I'll give you that. Luring Sofia into the bushes, using a park vehicle to smuggle her out to your accomplice's car. Then dashing back to the woods just in time to make a show of organising the search. Playing the good Samaritan while you bought your partner-in-crime enough time to get Sofia far away from the park before the police were *finally* called. If I hadn't happened to pass that shed when I did, the poor girl would probably be in another country by—'

'Shut up!' Tara shouted. Even in the dim light, Carrie could see the spots of colour on her cheeks. The way her eyes glittered in the lamplight. 'You can save your bullshit stories for the police, since they'll be here any second.'

Carrie's arms were starting to ache from Sofia's weight. She gently transferred her to the other shoulder, checking to see whether she had dozed off. But her daughter's eyes were open wide and her arms fastened around Carrie's neck again as she resettled on the other side.

Josh laughed softly. 'Ah, Tara, you've been playing the long game, haven't you? Getting to know Sofia, winning her trust. But she's not your child and she never will be. Not while I'm here to protect her.'

Tara jutted her chin. 'I already have a child, thank you very much. I'm not in the market for another one.'

'Ah yes. The famous son. What's his name again?'

Tara's brows dipped into a deep V. 'Why? What's he got to do with this?'

'Go on. Say his name. If you can remember what it's supposed to be.'

'Peter!' Tara shouted the name at the top of her voice, making Sofia's arms tighten around Carrie's neck. 'My son's name is *Peter*!'

A small smile curved across Josh's face. 'Well done.'

Tara made a choking noise. 'You smug, lying piece of *shit*!'

Carrie ducked instinctively as something soared past her head towards Josh. The iPad. Tara must have had good aim because it hit him square on the shoulder. The impact knocked him off balance, the jolt travelling right through his arm, making his fingers fly open.

Josh dropped the lamp.

Time seemed to slow as Carrie watched it slip from his grasp, the glass-walled flame drifting lazily downward, as though it were sinking through water. When it hit the ground, there was a crack and the tinkle of glass. Fragments arced outward. Blue-and-white flames burst through the gaps, licking the surviving shards. Then the smashed lamp began to roll across the floor: a cylindrical cage of fire travelling slowly but inexorably towards the covered sofa.

Stop-stop-stop. Carrie prayed silently. *Please stop.*

But it didn't stop – not until it had bumped against the sofa's leg. The flame flared brighter as it caught the hem of the cloth, feeding greedily. The fire leapt upward, growing as it went, spreading across the seat. The smell of singed cloth filled the air as it raced sideways, towards the bottle, with its warning red diamond. Carrie didn't need to be able to read the words beneath to know what they said. 'Caution: Flammable liquid.'

For a moment, the three of them stood staring at the fire as though hypnotised, Tara's arm still extended from the throw. The iPad lay on the floor beyond the sofa, its screen cracked and glowing.

The flames were higher now, advancing more quickly. Closing in on the kerosene bottle.

'Run!'

Tara's shout broke the spell. Carrie's head whipped from side to side, searching for the nearest exit.

The front door.

She lurched towards it, staggering under Sofia's weight, praying the kerosene bottle's glass barrier could withstand the flames just long enough to let them reach the other side. The room seemed to stretch, the door retreating before her, impossibly far. Her overburdened muscles trembled in protest. She was struggling to maintain her grip on Sofia. But she was nearly there. The door was only about five steps away now. Four. Three.

That was as far as she got.

There was a sound, like the crack of a whip. A rush of

superheated air and a bright flare of orange, as though someone had switched on a blinding light.

Carrie was thrown from her feet, back lanced with pain as glass fragments tore through her clothes, embedding themselves in her flesh. She kept her arms locked protectively around Sofia, elbows slamming against the floor as she rolled across it, the pain making her cry out. By the time she'd stopped moving, the sofa was a roaring mass of flame, pushing out a wall of heat that sucked the air from her lungs. Carrie tried to get up, but a wave of dizziness rode through her, sending her sliding to the floor.

Then everything disappeared.

She was drifting in liquid dark, weightless, completely at peace. All the fear and panic had floated away, leaving only a perfect silence that wrapped itself around her like warm silk. She surrendered herself to it, sinking through deepening layers of black.

'Mummy, wake up! I'm scared!'

Sofia!

Carrie fought against the darkness, but it kept pulling at her, trying to suck her down, folding itself over her like quicksand.

'Mummy, help!'

With a burst of determination, Carrie thrashed her way upward and broke surface.

She was lying on her back with Sofia's face directly above hers, eyes round with terror.

'It's OK, sweetie. I'm right here. I'm going to get you home.' It took a Herculean effort, but somehow she managed to drag herself up onto her knees with her daughter in her arms. She waited for a wave of dizziness to pass before planting a foot on the floor, using it to propel herself upright. Then she stood swaying, Sofia clinging to her neck. The room wheeled around her a few times before slowing to a stop. Carrie's eyes were stinging from the smoke as she took stock of her surroundings. What she saw turned her insides to liquid. The fire had spread around the room, hopscotching from one furniture-shroud to the next, roaring up the filmy curtains along the front of the house to create a blazing barrier. They'd never make it out that way. They would have to leave the way they'd come: through the kitchen. But when she turned towards it, she made a terrible discovery; sparks from the curtains had colonised the cube-patterned rug, creating a rectangular island of flame that blocked their path. Smoke rolled across the ceiling.

There was no way out.

She looked down at her daughter. Sofia's eyes were closed. Was that because of the smoke? Or to shut out the terror? Carrie kissed the top of her head thinking: *Please, God, don't let her die. Whatever else happens, Sofia must live.*

Then, like an answered prayer, came the sound of Josh's voice. 'Don't worry, everything's going to be OK.'

She turned to find him standing, miraculously unharmed, at the far end of the living room. He extended an arm towards her. 'This way.'

'Where?' Carrie asked desperately. 'How will we get out?'

He pointed into the haze of smoke behind him. 'Up the stairs, then out through one of the bedroom windows. It's a bit of a jump, there might be a twisted ankle or two, but we'll be OK.' She squinted into the shifting clouds. Saw the shape of the archway. It must lead to the stairs. Getting to Josh would mean running through the gap between a burning armchair and the flaming sofa. But it was doable ... just. And it wasn't as though she had a choice; this was their only chance.

Then, from the other end of the room, came another voice. 'No, Carrie, don't!'

Eyes streaming from the smoke, Carrie blinked until she was able to make out a figure standing beside the now flaming wooden screen.

Tara.

'Don't go with him! You won't make it. The smoke is too thick and the fire has already spread upstairs. But there's another way. Follow me!'

Carrie froze, caught between Josh on her left and Tara on her right. Paralysed by indecision. Josh was still holding a hand out towards her.

'Don't listen to her, Carrie. She's leading you into a trap! She lied to you about me with her fake iPad translations and she's lying to you again now.' His voice was hoarse from the smoke wreathed around him. 'I can save you!'

She could feel the oxygen in the room disappearing, gobbled up by the fire. White spots were eating across her vision until she could hardly see. She was gasping for breath, growing weaker. Sofia started slipping from her grasp and she fought to keep hold of her. Her daughter had never felt so heavy.

She took a step towards Josh.

'Don't!' Tara shouted over the crackle of flames. Carrie hesitated. She looked back over her shoulder. Tara was yanking at the bolt of the small, timber door at the back of the room. It slid aside and she shoved the door open with her shoulder. Beyond was nothing but darkness. What was in there? A closet? Carrie's head swam. Why would Tara want to lead them into a closet? It didn't make sense. And if she really did know a way out, why hadn't she fled already? Why was she still here?

'Come *on*!' Tara's voice was raspy and she was swaying on her feet. 'If you follow Josh, you won't make it. Maybe he knows that. Maybe this is some sort of . . . suicide pact. Or maybe he wants to fix it so that the two of you are the only ones to make it out alive, so he can have you all to himself.'

Josh barked out a laugh that turned into a coughing fit halfway through.

'Don't bring your daughter within arm's reach of that crazy bitch. She'll grab Sofia and leave you behind to die.'

There was the sound of splintering glass as a window blew out. A piece of burning cloth flew past like a flaming kite. Tara was moving towards her through the smoke, past the burning screen. Stopping when they were only a few feet apart. 'Carrie, look at me. I'm your friend. Trust me.'

She looked into Tara's streaming eyes, the whites now an angry pink. But the irises were the same as always: green–blue, like a holiday sea. Just as they'd been that first day in the park.

It's OK, love. I'll help you find your daughter.

There was a deafening boom from the kitchen and the floor shook. The stove canister, Carrie thought dimly. There must have still been some gas inside it.

'Carrie!' Josh called hoarsely from the other end of the room. 'I love you! Come with me before it's too late!'

She looked at him, standing in the smoke with his arm out, memories blowing through her like leaves in a high wind.

Josh, smiling at her across the dining table.

Josh, wiping a blob of cream cheese from Sofia's nose.

Josh whispering in the dark.

'May I?'

The heat was unbearable and the air was getting harder to breathe. The room wavered. She was seconds away from collapsing. She looked from Josh to Tara and back again.

There was no time left.

She had to choose.

'Shit!'

They were five minutes away from the Vineyard when Juliet saw the flames flickering against the night sky, staining it orange.

Alistair stepped harder on the gas, sending trees blurring past. She was on the police radio, calling for an ambulance and fire trucks, as they rounded a sharp corner at speed, slamming Juliet's shoulder into the passenger door. She put away the radio and stared grimly through the windscreen at the unnaturally bright sky.

'What do you think happened?' Alistair asked, not taking his eyes from the road. 'Could it be an accident?'

'Two fires in the same house, with the same suspect?' She shook her head. 'Seems unlikely.'

'Technically, he was never a suspect,' Alistair reminded her. 'You're talking about one cop – and an inexperienced one at that – with a vague suspicion and no proof. And anyway, what would Skelter's motive be for setting his own property on fire?'

'Same as last time: to take out a rival for the affections of the person he loves most.' A chill passed through her as she said the words. She pictured Sofia, abandoned in a flaming house. Her pain and her terror.

Another wild swerve as they lurched off the road and onto

an overgrown driveway. They jolted along it, bouncing over potholes, then veered around a white car parked to one side: Carrie's hatchback. A spark streaked through the air like a tiny comet before hitting the windscreen. Then another. They were nearly there.

'It might have been Tara,' Alistair said suddenly. 'Using the fire to bump off Carrie and steal Sofia.'

'That's insane.'

Alistair swung around a particularly deep rut, face grim.

'More insane than Josh trying to bump off Sofia so he can have Carrie to himself?'

Juliet opened her mouth to argue, then closed it again. He was right. They had two possible scenarios, each as fucked up as the other.

They burst free of the drive and into the open space beyond. Alistair let out a low whistle as the burning house loomed into view. The fire had clearly started on the main level, the heat shattering the floor-to-ceiling windows along the front, freeing tongues of flame that licked up the walls to ignite the floor above.

Juliet looked from the house to the SUV parked under a tree next to it in a careless diagonal. Josh's car.

Christ, she thought. *They're all still in there.*

The Mazda slammed to a halt in a spray of gravel. Juliet and Alistair jumped out and ran towards the house, only to be blocked by an invisible barrier of impossible heat. Juliet raised an arm, shielding her stinging eyes as she backed away, blinking until she could see again, searching the building for an entry point.

And finding none. The fire had consumed the entire main

floor. Her gaze lifted to scan the level above. One of the windows was completely broken, letting smoke pour out. She could see orange flickering behind it. Could anyone still be alive up there? It seemed unlikely. She felt a tightening in her chest as her memory flashed up an image of Sofia.

Hello, Police Lady Juliet!

Dark eyes and a bright smile made of wonky teeth.

Then, above the roar of flames and the crack of breaking glass, came a new sound. A scream. Except it wasn't like any scream Juliet had ever heard before. This was a primal note of pure agony: a long, keening cry that sliced right to her core. It was impossible to say whether it was male or female, adult or child; it barely even sounded human.

'There!' Alistair grabbed her arm and pointed towards an upstairs window.

At first, she didn't know what he meant; seeing only more flames. Then her stomach gave a sickening lurch as she registered that the flames were shaped like a human body. There was the sound of glass shattering as the figure burst through the window, plunging like some terrible comet to land on the hard earth below. As Juliet and Alistair ran towards it, a blackened arm reached towards them, before dropping to the ground. They peeled off their jackets, using them to smother the flames, already knowing it was too late. They rolled the body over, both of them gagging at the burned pork smell. Too big to be a child, Juliet noted with relief. The face was shapeless, the flesh a volcanic landscape of fissures and charred flesh. But a familiar piece of jewellery had survived. A silver zigzag on a chain.

Josh.

The smoke thickened, forcing them backward, away from the house. The sound of distant sirens cut the air, the *nee-naw-nee-naw* of an ambulance competing with the one-note blare of a fire truck. She wondered fleetingly which would arrive first.

Not that it mattered. Her eyes rose to the building being consumed in front of her, exhaling smoke through gaping windows. Her heart throbbed painfully, as though bruised. No one could be alive in there. They had arrived too late.

Alistair must have been thinking the same thing because he said: 'That poor wee girl. If only—'

'Shhhhh!' Juliet grabbed his arm. 'Did you hear that?'

'Hear what?'

'A banging, like a door?' They both listened, but now all she could hear was the rush of flames and the warble of sirens. She shook her head. Just wishful thinking. 'It must have been a beam collapsing or ...'

But then the words stopped, because something was moving behind the veils of smoke draped around the house. Just a smudge at first, a darker patch within the shifting clouds. But then it came closer, solidifying, separating itself into three shapes. Human shapes. Two large and one small.

Juliet and Alistair ran forwards as Tara and Carrie lurched out into open air, faces masked with soot. Sofia was dangling between them, held by her wrists, feet dragging along the ground. As Juliet and Alistair reached them, the two women fell to their knees and began coughing violently, tears streaming from their eyes and down their cheeks, clearing trails in the layer of black.

Sofia didn't move.

'Help her,' Carrie rasped, as Juliet bent over the limp child, groping along her wrist in a desperate search for a pulse. The sirens were close now, sawing the air. And suddenly it *did* make a difference which came first – maybe the difference between life and death.

Juliet turned towards the mouth of the driveway, breath held, waiting to see what would appear there: a fire truck or an ambulance.

Please let it be an ambulance, she prayed silently. *Please-please-please.*

The sirens filled the night.

Thirty-eight

'I went back there yesterday.'

Carrie turned sideways on the bench to look directly at Tara, placing a hand above her eyes to shield them from the sun.

'Why?'

Tara took a sip of Evian, staring towards the swings.

'I don't really know. For ... closure maybe? I wanted to see what was left of it.'

'And what *was* left?'

'Not much. A charred skeleton. Hardly anything survived. Aside from the wine cellar, obviously.'

'Obviously.' Carrie fended off the memory of the tumble down the stairs into darkness, the choking air and the desperate search for the trapdoor that would take them back outside, somewhere beyond the house. The fear that maybe there was no door, that it had been bricked up or Tara had misread the blueprints. That they were going to suffocate inside a brick cage.

She reached into the paper bag on her lap, taking out a sandwich.

'Buffalo mozzarella and chargrilled vegetables. Yours.' She

passed it across before taking out her own (ham and Swiss on rye).

They chewed in silence for a while, watching the swings. Carrie had almost finished eating when Tara spoke again.

'Did it surprise you, seeing him on the CCTV?'

Carrie considered the question as she swallowed her last bite of sandwich.

'Yes,' she said, then realised that wasn't strictly true and gave herself a pinch. Because she must have known the truth, on some buried level. Otherwise she would have gone with him.

Tara must have been watching, because she said: 'Why do you pinch yourself like that? I've seen you do it before. It looks ... painful.'

Carrie tugged the sleeve of her jacket down to cover her wrist.

'When I was a teenager, I was sent to a therapist who put elastic bands around his patients' wrists for what he called "honesty conditioning".' She crumpled the sandwich wrapper into a ball and tossed it at the bin beside the bench. It ricocheted off the rim and went in. 'He would snap it every time he caught me saying something that wasn't completely true. Then he got me to wear it all day and snap it myself. I got rid of the therapist and the elastic band eventually, but ...' Her voice trailed off.

'But the habit lives on.'

'Yes.'

'Aha! So the fact that you just pinched yourself means you *weren't* surprised to see Josh walking down Radich Avenue!'

'No, it means I overstated my view. Because part of me had clung to the belief that he was innocent. And even now, knowing what I do: that he abducted Sofia ... I still can't

383

believe that he would have gone through with it . . . left her to die in that fire. Just so he could have me to himself.' Her mind journeyed back over the relationship for the thousandth time, combing her memory for missed clues: signs that she had been living with a monster. But there was nothing. 'His behaviour was always so . . . considerate.'

'Well, he abducted your daughter and locked her in a shed. Then terrorised her by sneaking into her room in a mask, just so you'd feel threatened enough to let him stay with you.' She took a swig of Evian, swiping a hand across her lips. 'Seems pretty inconsiderate to me.'

'We don't know for certain that he was the intruder. That's just DCI Campbell's theory.'

Tara raised an eyebrow. 'You have a better one?'

'No. But I'm an architect, so not qualified to construct theories of criminal behaviour.' Carrie watched the swings rise and fall, wondering who she was actually defending: Josh . . . or herself? Maybe it was time to admit the truth: that she had loved him . . . without ever knowing him at all. She drew in a deep breath, releasing it slowly. 'But his internet searches do support the theory that he wanted Sofia out of the way.'

Tara's mouth pulled to one side.

'Oh, I don't know. It could be a coincidence. Maybe he just happened to develop a sudden interest in mastering techniques for helping recently bereaved mothers overcome their grief.'

'Do you think so? It seems an unlikely coincidence.'

Tara shook her head. 'Sorry. That was a joke – and a bad one at that. I know humour's not your thing.'

They sat in silence for a while as Carrie thought about how close she'd come to following Josh through the smoke, of bringing Sofia upstairs, into a flaming death trap. But in that last, critical moment, a voice somewhere deep inside her had spoken up, telling her to follow Tara. To trust her.

She looked at her friend's profile, watching her swig water from the bottle. Tara must have sensed her gaze, because she turned and smiled.

'Let's talk about something else.' She put the cap back on her bottle before stretching out her legs. 'How did it go at the zoo?'

'It was successful.' Carrie felt a warm glow: pride, mixed with satisfaction. 'I did what you suggested. I gave Simon fifteen minutes alone with her in the reptile house – just the two of them – while I waited outside. And it was fine. I was a bit anxious. But only a bit.'

'Well done, you! That was very brave, and a big step. Simon must be so pleased.'

'Yes.' She thought of the tight hug he'd given her after emerging from the reptile house, the murmured 'thank you' as he'd kissed the top of her head. 'He was.'

A small boy ran past holding a kite, which he flung towards the sky, only to have it plummet straight back down, hitting the ground in front of the bench. The boy stamped his foot. Carrie bent down to retrieve the fallen kite, handing it back to its owner. He stalked off, lower lip protruding.

When she turned back around, Tara was staring towards the swings, a fist pressed against her mouth, nose crinkled at the top.

'Stop worrying,' Carrie said, buttoning up her jacket, wishing they'd chosen a bench in the sunshine. Now that the heatwave had passed, autumn was nipping at the air. 'Sofia's used to dealing with people who express their emotions differently. It's going well.'

'It does seem to be.' She sighed. 'I guess my guard has been stuck in the "up" position for so long it's hard to get it back down.'

'I know how that feels.' Carrie watched the swings rising and falling. It was amazing, the endless entertainment value children derived from simply moving up and down without actually going anywhere.

'He's better with girls.' Tara placed the half-empty water bottle on the bench beside her. 'I used to think that was because he missed having a sister.' Her eyes lost focus as she stared across the playground. 'Believe it or not, I actually tried to adopt a girl, right after my husband left. Not for me. Back then I found the idea of having another girl around incredibly painful. For Peter. I thought having a new sister would . . . fix him somehow. Undo the damage.' She shook her head. 'Crazy, right? But logic and I had parted company at that point so—' Then her expression did a rapid switch, brows shooting up, mouth falling open, eyes widening.

'Hey! You told me to stop worrying!'

'Yes. Because everything is fine and I see no cause for concern.'

'But don't you see?' She grabbed both of Carrie's hands in hers, giving them a squeeze. 'I didn't *tell* you I was worried! You must have read my face!'

Carrie blinked down at the hands clasping hers as she digested this surprising claim. Worry wasn't among the more obvious emotions she was sometimes able to catch. So how *had* she known? She spooled back her memory and discovered that Tara was right; she had recognised the complicated pattern her features made whenever she talked about her fears for her son's future, or when she was worried he might be having one of his 'turns'.

'I did,' Carrie said, with a warm rush of pleasure. 'I *did* read you.'

She lifted the edges of her mouth to show that she was pleased, but Tara shook a finger back and forth in front of her face, frowning.

'No, don't do that. I know you feel things. You don't have to prove it to me by copying other people's expressions. You're my friend.' She looped her arms around Carrie's shoulders, giving her a sideways hug. 'That means I love you just the way you are.'

And as she sat beside Tara, watching the swings rise and fall, Carrie felt the slow pull of a genuine smile.

'Once I bit a piece of someone's ear off.'

'Ew, that's yuck!' Sofia pulled a face as she leaned back all the way, heels pointing at the sky. She wanted to swing as high as Peter, even though he was a year older. 'Which piece?'

He took one hand off the swing's chain to point at the bottom of his ear.

'This piece.'

'That's called the "lobe",' Sofia said in a teacher-voice. She knew lots of words. Grown-ups called that 'good vocabulary'.

She threw her upper body forwards and curled her legs under the swing, then leaned back again, pumping hard, rising high enough to see the edge of the fishpond over the trees. Mummy was on her usual bench in front of the trees, chatting with Tara. It was good, seeing Mummy have chats.

'What did the ear taste like?'

387

'Salty.'

'*Super* yuck!'

Peter pulled himself up by the chains, and put his feet on the seat, so he was swinging standing up. The sun was behind him, beaming around his head like a blinding halo, going inside Sofia's eyes and making them sting. They did that a lot since the fire. And another thing was: she ran out of breath faster because of all the smoke that went inside her lungs. But it was a lot better now than before.

'Why did you bite someone's lobe?'

For a while, there was only the creak of chains. Then Peter said: 'A Year Four boy woke up my monster.'

'How?'

'He called me a weirdo. So the monster went crazy and made me attack him.'

Sofia thought about this as she rose and fell.

'Do you think the monster will make you attack *me*?'

'Nah. It goes away when you come.'

'Maybe the monster's scared of me.'

'Maybe.' Peter put his bum back on the seat and dragged the toes of his trainers against the ground until he stopped, waiting while Sofia did the same. They sat on the motionless swings, looking at each other. 'Want to go up the rocket?' he said. 'We can race to the top.'

Sofia looked over at the red-and-blue bars, arching towards the metal star. It gave her a weird feeling, like the skin on her back suddenly got tighter. She shook her head.

'No. You have to be six years old to go up there.'

'So? The police won't catch you. And, anyway, you're turning six soon.'

Sofia shook her head again, more firmly, fingers clenching the chains,

'I don't *want* to.'

He pushed himself sideways, so that the edges of their seats bumped into each other. For a moment she was worried he might get cross and the monster would come out after all.

But then he said: 'How about the zipwire?'

Her face lit. 'Yessssss! I *love* the zipwire!'

And the two of them jumped off the swings and ran across the playground, their shadows chasing beside them, the sun warm on their backs.

Acknowledgements

I would like to thank the fantastic team at Headline Publishing, but especially my editor Katie Sunley, who championed this book, then made it so much better with her invaluable feedback. Also my agent, Teresa Chris, for her guidance and her unswerving determination to see *The Good Samaritan* published.

A special shout out to the talented Ness Lyons: friend and volunteer book editor, without whom this novel would not have been the same.

Friends and generous donors of advice Lotte Pang, Eddie Batha, Peter Higgins, Roger Ewart-Smith, Connie Lee, Clare Hayes, Clare Garnett.

Joanne Smith, for not letting my police officers stray too far from the rules of procedure.

And above all my mother and my sister Claire, for their endless supply of love, support and belief.